Praise for the warmhearted wit of

Geralyn Dawson,

"one of the best authors to come along in years"
(Jill Barnett)

The Pink Magnolia Club

"A triumphant tale of the power of friendship, love and laughter. Every woman needs a Pink Magnolia Club in her life."

—Christina Dodd

"The ladies of the Pink Magnolia Club embody all the warmth, humor, tragedy and wisdom of Southern women."

—Susan Wiggs

"Truly moving. . . . [An] inspirational meditation on love, loss, friendship, and hope. . . . Dawson offers plenty of witticisms on love and life."

—Publishers Weekly

"Courageous. . . . A powerfully moving tale."

—Bookbrowser.com

The Bad Luck Wedding Night

"*The Bad Luck Wedding Night* is . . . trademark Geralyn Dawson."

—*Romantic Times*

"Nobody turns 'bad luck' to good luck like Geralyn Dawson! The lady has the gift of taking a 'stinky' situation and turning it to perfume while those about her can only wait her *next* story!"

—*Heartland Critiques*

"Wonderful! Delightful! Entertaining!"

—romrevtoday.com

"A very satisfying and entertaining story. . . . Read *The Bad Luck Wedding Night*. But don't stop there; read all of Geralyn Dawson's books."

—HeartRateReviews.com

Simmer All Night

"Delightfully spicy—perfect to warm up a cold winter's night."

—*Christina Dodd*

The Bad Luck Wedding Cake

Also by Geralyn Dawson

The Pink Magnolia Club
The Bad Luck Wedding Night
Sizzle All Day
Simmer All Night
The Kissing Stars
The Bad Luck Wedding Cake
The Wedding Ransom
The Wedding Raffle

Available from Pocket Books

My Big Old Texas Heartache

GERALYN DAWSON

POCKET STAR BOOKS

New York London Toronto Sydney Singapore

An *Original* Publication of POCKET BOOKS

 A Pocket Star Book published by
POCKET BOOKS, a division of Simon & Schuster, Inc.
1230 Avenue of the Americas, New York, NY 10020

ISBN: 0-7434-4266-0

First Pocket Books printing August 2003

10 9 8 7 6 5 4 3 2

POCKET STAR BOOKS and colophon are registered trademarks of Simon & Schuster, Inc.

Cover art by Alan Ayers

Manufactured in the United States of America

For information regarding special discounts for bulk purchases, please contact Simon & Schuster Special Sales at 1-800-456-6798 or business@simonandschuster.com

FOR MARY DICKERSON AND PAT CODY
THANK YOU, FRIENDS

My Big
Old Texas
Heartache

Chapter One

KATE HARMON OFTEN THOUGHT that living the good life was like putting on a pair of panty hose. Just when she finally wiggled her way to a comfortable fit, she'd invariably get a runner.

At least tonight's runner was literal rather than figurative. Scowling, she kicked off a heel and eyed the spot where her little toe poked through nylon. "It's Monday night. I shouldn't have to wear hose on Monday night. That should be a law. A Constitutional right. Number seven in the Women's Bill of Rights."

"What's number six?" her seventeen-year-old son asked.

"It involves underwire bras."

"I don't think a Women's Bill of Rights exists," called Adele Watkins from the kitchen. Ryan's former nanny and Kate's dearest friend in the entire world, Adele completed the family of three who lived in a new house in a North Dallas suburb.

"We don't have a Women's Bill of Rights? See, that's the problem. Ryan, maybe you should study law rather than engineering. Think how proud I would be if my son freed the women of America from Monday night panty hose."

"Quit babbling, Kate, and get ready for your date. You have no reason to be nervous."

Kate made a face toward the kitchen and Adele.

Ryan shot her a cocky grin from the sofa, where he lounged on his spine. "I'll free you now, Mom. Don't wear 'em. Show a little bare leg with that snazzy black dress and make him drool."

"Ryan Scott Harmon. What a thing to say to your mother."

He shrugged. "Face it, Mom. You're hot. All my buddies think so."

She hesitated, pleased, then preened just a bit. "Really?"

"Yeah. For an old lady."

She threw a sofa pillow at him. "Brat. Don't you have homework to do? If not, I can find you some chores."

"Can't do it." He flashed her that devilish grin that invariably reminded her of his father, then sauntered toward the stairs. "I've got a ball game in half an hour."

"You do? Oh no. I'm going to miss it. I thought your weekday baseball games were all on Thursday this season."

"They are. This is basketball. Girls nine-to-eleven church league. I'm subbing as a referee because Mark Johnson has a big chemistry test tomorrow."

"Oh, Ryan. I'm sorry I can't be there. You know how much I hate to miss—"

"Mo-om," he interrupted, pivoting around. He placed his hands on her shoulders, leaned down, and pressed a kiss to her forehead. "I'm a ref; not a player. Parents don't come to games where their kid is only refereeing. You don't need to feel guilty about this one. In fact, I'd be embarrassed if you went."

"I don't care if you're embarrassed," Kate grumbled. "I love attending your ball games. I'm a proud member of the Bleacher Butt Brigade."

She'd labored long and hard to get to this point. Single mothers who worked full-time and attended college missed out on most Little League and Pee-Wee events. Only during the last couple of years had she been able to watch his games with any regularity.

"You're almost a senior in high school, so my opportunities to play proud-mother-in-the-stands are coming to an end all too soon. When you're in college back East, I won't be able to make many intramural games in Cambridge or New Haven."

"C'mon, Mom." He looked away and shrugged. "Go change your panty hose so you're perfect for your date."

"It's not a date," she insisted. It couldn't be. "It's a business dinner."

"Uh-huh. With *Dallas Magazine's* 'Hunk Lawyer of the Year' at one of the hottest restaurants in the Metroplex."

Kate shot him a chastising look.

He grinned back at her. "I heard you talking to Adele."

"You shouldn't eavesdrop, and of course I have to wear panty hose."

"I could make a comment here about garter belts that would probably get me in trouble." He kissed her forehead and moved away. "Enjoy yourself. You don't go out nearly enough. You can come to my ball game on Thursday, and Saturday we have a doubleheader."

A doubleheader. She loved doubleheaders. As Ryan bounded up the stairs to don his official's black-and-whites, Kate's gaze once again snagged on the run in her stockings. She sighed and glanced at the clock. Nicholas Sutherland was due to arrive in half an hour, and she still hadn't decided if she had a client meeting or a hot date. Her stomach staggered at the thought.

She'd taken the call from the offices of Sutherland, Mason, and Post expecting a question about one of her accounting clients. Hearing Nicholas Sutherland's resonant voice requesting the pleasure of her company for dinner to discuss a matter of mutual importance had her all but oozing from her chair. She'd met the man briefly twice before, once at a Dallas charity 10K run, and once at a United Way leadership meeting. He'd never paid particular attention to her. Not *that* kind of particular.

Her mind a fuddle, Kate had stammered an acceptance and hung up without clarifying the reason for the invitation. Could he possibly intend to offer her a job? Kate couldn't imagine that. While she considered herself a competent—okay, a damned fine—certified public accountant, she'd handled nothing of such professional significance as to put her on his law firm's radar screen.

But what else could he want? If he hoped to fish for personal information about one of her clients, he was out of luck. Kate had learned long ago the value of discretion. She never betrayed a client's privacy.

"Ryan is right, you know." Adele marched into the family room from the kitchen. "You need to get out and enjoy yourself more. This is the first date you've had in at least six months."

A year. Over a year. And that date had been with a local golf pro, not with a chiseled-jaw, Armani-clad attorney. "This isn't a date. It's a business dinner."

"You need to have more fun," Adele continued, eyeing her strappy stiletto heels with approval. "I thought I'd see some action in your social life after you finished up your degree and passed your CPA exam. But you're set on pursuing a partnership at Markhum and Frye instead of a sex life."

"Don't start."

Adele flicked one of her dangling earrings, a pink rhinestone star. "Somebody has to start because you certainly aren't."

"I'm going out tonight, aren't I?" Kate tucked an errant strand of blonde hair behind her ear. "On a Monday night, no less. In a little black dress and panty hose."

"What color underwear?"

"Adele!"

"Probably white. Really living on the wild side there, aren't you, honey."

Knowing she wore her best black lingerie, Kate lifted her chin, and declared, "Maybe. Maybe I will. Maybe I'll just turn on the charm and seduce Nicholas Sutherland. I could do it. I have it on good authority that I'm hot. You can ask anyone on the Milam High School baseball team."

Adele chuckled. "Oh, go change your stockings. You're as likely to vamp for that man as the Rangers are to win the American League pennant this year."

"Don't count the Rangers out already. The season just started." Maybe if the Rangers got lucky this year, she would, too. Stranger things had happened.

Kate scooped up her shoes and headed upstairs to her

bedroom, exchanging see-you-laters with her son as he breezed past her, heading for the garage and his pride and joy. The rebuilt '56 Ford pickup made her shake her head in wonder every time she caught sight of it. She didn't understand the love affair between her son and his beat-up old truck. Well, except for the pride factor. That she understood all too well.

Ryan had turned down the offer of a new Mustang from his father on his sixteenth birthday, choosing instead to use his paper route money for a set of wheels—to use the term generously. Since Ryan would rather eat dirt than accept anything from Max Cooper, Kate hadn't been shocked. The surprise came six months later when, following her promotion, she offered to help Ryan upgrade his mode of transportation. He'd chosen to stay in the junker, despite its consistent breakdowns. For a teenager, Ryan was unusually considerate of a parent's purse, plus he had a good measure of her own stiff-necked pride.

"He's not taking that truck off to college when he goes," Kate murmured as she tugged an unopened package of stockings from her lingerie chest. Of course, she needn't worry. That truck couldn't make it north of the Red River, much less all the way to New Haven, Connecticut.

So why was she even thinking about it? Maybe because Ryan's collegiate future was her favorite fantasy of late—a sad comment on her sex life, true, but nobody needed to know about that. More likely, she was concentrating on old trucks to avoid thinking about sexy lawyers.

This *had* to be a business meeting. What would she do if Nicholas Sutherland offered her a job?

She tore the plastic from the package, then removed

the stockings. Stripping off the ruined hose, she sat on the side of her bed to begin the slow process of smoothing the stockings up her legs and over her hips. She wriggled, hopped, jumped, and tugged.

Breathing like she'd run a marathon, Kate slipped into her come-hither shoes, flipped off the bedroom light, and started back downstairs. The doorbell rang. *Business dinner. It's just a business dinner.*

She peeked out the window and her stomach did a flip. Nicholas Sutherland could have come straight from a photo shoot for GQ magazine. Though tall and broad-shouldered, he had that fine-boned elegance that shouted breeding and class. He wore an Armani suit, Bruno Magli shoes, and a slim Piaget watch, and when Kate opened the door, his deep blue eyes took her breath away.

Business dinner. Business dinner. Business dinner.

With Mr. Tall, Dark, and Delicious.

"Hello, Nicholas."

"Good evening, Kate. You look lovely. I'm so pleased you were able to join me this evening."

Hmm . . . a compliment. That leaned more toward the "date" side of the equation, didn't it?

She invited him in and introduced him to a very curious Adele, who covertly shot her two thumbs up on their way out the door.

Kate noticed the neighborhood kids congregated at her curb before she noted the object of their fascination. "A limo?" she asked.

Nicholas shrugged. "I hate traffic this time of night."

He'd made reservations at a cozy French bistro in the Fort Worth Cultural District, a good forty-minute drive from Kate's house. She settled into the comfortable leather seat, surreptitiously tugged her hem hoping to cover more of her thighs, and accepted a glass of wine. He put her at ease with small talk about local sports teams and their mutual interest in long-distance running. By the time they reached Fort Worth, she'd forgotten all about business.

Danged if he didn't go and bring it up.

"I know you're probably curious about why I invited you to dinner," he said.

Because you've fantasized about me since our last meeting at the United Way party? *Oh, get hold of yourself, Kate Harmon. You're acting like a teenager.*

"I have a double purpose. I've wanted to see you again since the United Way event, but business demands have kept me from having much of a personal life."

Oh, my. Kate swallowed hard.

"Also, I do have business to discuss with you."

"Business?" she repeated, an embarrassing squeak in her voice.

Nicholas topped off her wine. "I'm on a quest, and I believe you are just the person to assist me. We'll talk about it more at dinner, all right? It appears we are almost to the restaurant. I cannot recall a time when the drive to Fort Worth passed so quickly."

She could have kept going all the way to Amarillo, Kate decided as she glanced out the window to see the graceful facade of the Kimball Art Museum. Then, just as the limo pulled into the restaurant parking lot, the cell phone in Kate's purse softly chimed. Oh, no.

"Excuse me, Nicholas," she said, reaching for her bag. "I know it's rude to take a phone call under the circumstances, but I'm the mother of a teenage son with a driver's license. I dare not . . ."

"By all means."

The phone number displayed on the cell phone's screen was her home number. *Adele, this better be good.* "Hello?"

"Kate, honey," Adele said, tension in her tone. "Your brother-in-law called. There's been a car accident. In Cedar Dell."

"An accident?" Kate sat up straight, her eyes rounded in fear. Her sister? Her dad? Oh, God. "What happened?"

"Honey, you need to go home. Fast."

Chapter Two

BRIGHT RED LETTERS against a white background formed the word EMERGENCY and Kate exhaled a relieved breath. Bethania Hospital. She'd made it. Finally.

As the limo pulled into the emergency room's circular drive, she sent another thank-you mentally winging toward Nicholas Sutherland. He'd saved her two hours of travel time by insisting she continue on to Cedar Dell in the limo.

"It's better this way," he'd told her. "You're upset and I'd worry about you driving. It's no problem for me to call another car to take me back to Dallas. Unless you'd like company on the trip. I'd be happy to ride along with you."

"Oh, no. Thank you. You've helped so much already. I can't thank you enough. I hate that our evening ended this way. I wish . . ."

"Me too," he'd said gently. "Good luck, Kate. Please let me know how everything turns out."

"He's a good man," she murmured as the automobile rolled to a stop and she reached for the door release. She exited the limo and stared at the hospital's double-wide automatic doors. Panic clogged her throat. She was almost afraid to go inside. She'd never come here worrying that somebody she loved might die . . . was dying . . . was dead. Never mind that when she'd called the number he'd left for her, her brother-in-law Alan had insisted her father's injuries, though serious, weren't life-threatening. She'd definitely heard relief in his voice when he told her Sarah's premature contractions had stopped, and that the overnight stay in the hospital was a precautionary measure on her obstetrician's part.

The two-hour trip from the west side of Fort Worth to the hospital in Cedar Dell was the longest car ride of her life. In spite of everything, she truly loved her family.

She hit the hospital's front doors running and recognized the volunteer receptionist at the emergency room desk as her eighth-grade Sunday school teacher. "Mrs. Hander? My family?"

"And you are?"

"Kate Harmon."

The woman's gaze raked her up and down. "Yes, I see. Of course. I should have realized. Did you just arrive in a limousine? And that dress—" She cleared her throat and spoke in a businesslike tone. "Your father is still in ICU, but the doctor upgraded his condition two hours ago. Sarah's up in Room 238. She and the baby are doing just great."

"Baby? She had the baby?"

"No. Her contractions have stopped. Your brother said for you to come straight up when you arrived."

"Tom?" Her brother was here? From Houston?

"He got in about an hour ago."

She didn't understand. How could Tom possibly have arrived ahead of her?

None of that mattered now. Her heels tapped against

tile as she headed for the ICU first. Memory guided her down surreal hallways and through nightmare corridors until she faced a double swinging door with a metal sign on the front that blazed in red: INTENSIVE CARE UNIT. AUTHORIZED PERSONNEL ONLY. VISITOR APPROVAL REQUIRED.

Kate pushed right on through without a pause. *Daddy. Where are you?* Her gaze searched the names written on the small white eraser boards hung by hooks attached to turquoise curtains. The ICU at Bethania Hospital was different from intensive care units in Dallas and those portrayed on TV. These weren't private rooms where beds faced windows through which family could observe the patient in all his intubated glory. Here, cubicles cramped with machines and separated by curtains surrounded a nurses' station. Monitors beeped, machines whirred, wheels rattled against the tile floor as an orderly rolled an empty bed from one spot to another. A pair of male nurses spoke softly about an upcoming NASCAR race while a doctor made notes in a chart.

From behind a curtain came a long, desperate moan that focused Kate's jumbled impressions. Feeling weak at the knees, she took determined steps forward.

She found her father in the sixth cubicle on the right. Tears filled her eyes at the sight of her greatest hero and critic laid low. How could this elderly, ill man have created such havoc in her heart and life?

Jack Harmon lay still, withered and old against the sheets. He wore white bandages, dark bruises, and sensors taped to his chest and head. An IV line ran from his forearm to a bag on a pole. *Oh, Daddy.*

"Kate?" A nurse approached. Her reserved, wary face

looked familiar, but Kate couldn't place her right away. "You are Kate Harmon, right? I'm Sue Ayer. We went to school together."

"Oh. Yes, I remember. Hello . . . I . . ."

"I'm sorry, Kate." She sounded more judgmental than sorry. "You can't be in here now. We're strict about our ten-minutes-per-hour visitation rules. Tom was with your dad until just a few minutes ago."

"Okay." Sue avoided direct eye contact, and Kate felt her former classmate was counting the years since Kate's last trip home. Or else her own conscience was gigging her. "I'll go . . . I just needed . . . how is he?"

"He's doing great," Sue assured her, urging her away from her dad and back toward the ICU entrance with more determination than sympathy. "The surgery went well. Your brother spoke at length with Dr. Hardesty, so he'll be able to fill you in on the details. I can tell you, though, that Jack is a very lucky man. Not a single bone is broken. He'll be sore, and it might take a while, but barring unexpected complications, he should recover fully."

They'd reached the ICU door. Sue pushed it open and offered Kate a smile. "Your sister is upstairs. I visited with her during my break, and I'm sure she needs to see you, too. When your father wakes up, I'll tell him you were here."

Kate nodded, then stopped. "No. Better not. He won't . . . well . . . we just better not. Thank you, Sue. It was nice to see you again."

"You, too. And Kate?" Her gaze swept down and up under a raised eyebrow. "I have no reason to suspect the worst, but just in case . . . just so you know . . . you've been away from town for a while so . . ."

"What is it?"

"Don't you think that dress is a little short for a Cedar Dell funeral?"

"Why, thanks, Sue. I'll remember that." Kate pasted on a smile and held it until Sue disappeared inside the ICU. When the door quit swinging and remained shut, she leaned against the wall, closed her eyes, and fought back tears as all the old insecurities, regrets, and disappointments came roaring back.

Welcome home, Cedar Dell Slut.

She really, really didn't want to be here. But how could she be anywhere else?

What if her dad had died today? What if he died before they found a way to make peace between them? Could she live with that?

If he had died today, she'd be forced to live with that regret.

Her teeth and stomach clenched. *Of course, you've already lived with it for half your life.*

Kate and her father never had been close. Her childhood memories starred her mother—ginger cookies and bedtime stories, shared giggles and hugs, and cuddles in the rocking chair. Her mother was everything warm and loving and supportive. Her father was gruff, stern, aloof. An authority figure. A father.

Kate had always yearned for a daddy.

She did recall—and treasure—a handful of "daddy" times. They'd built the tree house at the lake together. Danced to birdsong together beneath it. He'd taught her how to repair a ball return at Harmon Lanes, and they'd played catch in the backyard once.

For the most part, however, her relationship with her father had always been one of distance. He didn't understand her. She didn't understand him. That unavoidable fact had become clear the night his stubbornness collided with her rebelliousness to destroy her most precious dream. She'd run off and done something spontaneous and stupid, and as a result, in one of those serendipitous lessons of life, from the dust of one dream another had been born. Kate had named him Ryan.

As always, the thought of her son lifted her spirits. Kate drew a bracing breath, tugged a tissue from her purse, and dabbed at the corners of her eyes, then headed upstairs to check on her sister.

Sarah. One more dysfunctional relationship in her life.

As she approached the open door to Room 238, she heard a rumble of voices. Her brother-in-law Alan. Her brother Tom. She found her sister's higher-pitched tones reassuring. At least, she did until she heard what was being said.

"What are we going to do about Dad?"

"I don't know," Tom said. "It's a problem. He simply cannot take care of himself. He can't live alone. Not until his injuries heal, and the doctor said it could take three months for his leg to be dependable. I have a vivid mental picture of his falling and lying on the floor for hours or days at a time."

Alan said, "I hate to be hardheaded about this, but I don't want Jack and Sarah in the same house, not under these circumstances."

"Alan!" Sarah protested.

"No, this time I'm having my way. Being put on total

bed rest means just that. If Jack lived with us or we moved in with him and he needed something, you'd go crazy to get it for him."

"Don't you dare suggest that I wouldn't protect my baby," Sarah scolded. "If I'm supposed to stay in bed, I'll stay in bed."

"I'm not arguing that. I'm talking about stress. Stress brought on these contractions today, honey. Imagine living with your father under these circumstances. Talk about stressful."

Kate moved closer, stopping just outside the doorway. She watched Alan pause, shudder, then level an unyielding stare on his wife. "We've wanted this child for fifteen years. I won't have you going into premature labor because your dad drops the TV remote and whines his way through *Sally Jessy Raphael* when he wanted to be watching the History Channel."

Tom cleared his throat. "I'd take him back to Houston with me, but—"

"He'd rather die than leave Cedar Dell," Sarah said.

And she would have died had she stayed in Cedar Dell, Kate thought, stepping into the room. That pretty much summed up the basic problem between her and her dad. "Hello."

Three heads jerked in her direction. Two countenances reflected surprise. Alan looked pleased to see her.

"Kate!" Sarah exclaimed. "What are you doing here?"

Kate stiffened. "I believe families usually gather when one of them has been seriously hurt in an accident."

Tom rubbed the back of his neck. "How did you find out about the wreck?"

"Obviously not from you."

Sarah gasped. "You didn't call her, Tom? We should have called her. I'm sorry, Kate. I didn't think about it."

It was only another small arrow through her heart, which should be potholed by now. "You were busy saving your baby, Sarah," she said with a smile. "Alan phoned me."

As her sister beamed a thank-you toward her husband, Alan said, "Chief Perkins told me the police notified Tom since he was listed as next of kin on a card in Jack's wallet."

Tom hadn't bothered to contact his youngest sister. *So what else is new? The apple doesn't fall far from the tree.*

Annoyed with herself, Kate dismissed her brother and took a good long look at her sister. Sarah, looking pale and exhausted, lay with her feet propped slightly higher than her head.

Kate's concern must have shown because Sarah smiled with reassurance. "I'm all right. The baby is all right."

Kate closed her eyes, said a quick prayer of thanks.

"Daddy's situation is more serious, but Dr. Hardesty assures us that it's reasonable to expect he will have a full recovery."

"I barely saw him. The nurse said something about surgery?"

Tom nodded. "He had a deep puncture wound in his thigh. Lucky he didn't sever an artery and bleed to death."

Kate's knees suddenly felt weak, and she sank onto the black vinyl chair beside her sister's bed. "What exactly happened? He turned in front of a car?"

"A truck," Sarah responded. "He was making a left turn into the Dairy Queen parking lot. A pickup hit him broadside." She continued with a seemingly unending list of muscle damage, cuts, abrasions, bruises, and bumps suffered by their father. When Sarah started talking about heart arrhythmia, blurred vision, blackouts, and delusions, Kate began massaging her forehead between her fingers. Delusions? Strong-minded Jack?

"Dr. Hardesty expects he'll be here for three to four days," Sarah concluded. "After that . . . well . . . he can't live alone anymore. At least, not for the time being."

For a few moments, a contemplative silence descended on the room. Then Tom folded his arms and frowned. "It's too bad Cedar Dell doesn't have an assisted living center. I hate to put him in Colonial Valley."

Colonial Valley was the town's only nursing home. It was a nice enough place, but people went there to die. "Dad would never forgive us."

Sarah plucked at a loose thread on her blanket and nodded her agreement. "He doesn't want to leave his home."

"He may have to leave his home." Tom lifted his hands, palms up. "What choice do we have? I spent all afternoon on the phone trying to hire home health care. This town only has a handful of full-time providers, and they're all committed."

"What about Jenny Wilson?" Alan asked. "Ben Wright passed on last week. Jenny should be free."

"I tried her. She's already accepted another position. With Alma Peters."

Sarah sighed loudly. "Alma Peters will outlive us all."

"I do have one name I haven't tried . . . Bertie Ellis."

Kate shot her brother an incredulous look. Bertie "The Narc" Ellis had gone to school with Kate. The nickname stood for narcolepsy rather than narcotics and arose from an incident during their senior year when Bertie, a second-string tight end, had nodded off during the Class 3A football playoff between Cedar Dell and Bowie High.

"Tom, we can't use Bertie," Sarah said. "I wouldn't trust him to watch my cat, much less my father."

"I thought we could hire Bertie to tend to Dad's personal needs until he's up and around, but also call upon The Widows to take up the slack."

"The Widows?" Kate sent a beseeching gaze toward the ceiling. "Oh, jeez. They'd casserole him to death."

"Well? Can you think of a better solution?"

Actually, Kate had thought of something better—actually, someone better—but the thought, the commitment, froze on her tongue.

Alan West, insightful brother-in-law that he was, pinned her with a challenging look, and casually observed, "Seems to me y'all are overlooking the obvious."

No, Alan.

"What about Kate?"

Thanks, Alan.

Sarah's eyes rounded. Tom wrinkled a puzzled brow. "Kate?" he repeated, darting a skeptical gaze toward his sister. "What? Do you know someone who could stay with Dad? Do you have connections in the health-care industry?"

"Don't be thickheaded, Tom." Sarah turned a hopeful gaze toward her sister. "Would you do it? Would you come home and nurse Dad?"

"Kate!" Tom exclaimed, gaping at Sarah. "You're kidding. Dad's going to need help for at least three months, if not permanently. She'd rather milk rattlesnakes for a living than move back to Cedar Dell, even for the summer."

Kate offered a saccharine smile. "Thank you so much, brother dear. I find it terribly taxing to speak for myself."

He had the grace to look ashamed. "I'm sorry. It's just that . . . well . . . you know Dad. With the trouble between the two of you . . . he'd hate having you care for him."

Kate wanted to blame the hospital's antiseptic smell for the nausea churning in her stomach, but she couldn't. "So in your opinion, he'd rather go into a nursing home than have me help him?"

Tom shifted and looked away. "I didn't say that."

"Oh, didn't you?"

Anxiously, Sarah said, "Please, let's not get ugly."

"What?" Kate snapped, pinning her brother with an angry gaze. "And break family tradition?"

Kate had never forgiven her brother for the way he'd treated her when their mother died. The horrible scene outside the church following her mother's funeral had haunted their every meeting since—all five of them. The whole Harmon clan didn't gather if they could avoid it.

"Hey, I'm not the one who made a scandal of our family name. I'm not the one who—"

"That's enough." Alan stepped forward. "This isn't good for any of us, particularly Sarah and the baby."

"That's right." Lying flat on her back, Sarah still managed a regal pout. "Stress is detrimental to a woman in my condition. Now, personalities and old feuds aside, this family is in a bind, and if Kate is willing to step into the breach, I, for one, think we should be graciously grateful. Can you do it, Kate? Will you do it? Will you come home and take care of Dad?"

Kate's pulse kicked up a notch on an adrenaline rush. She forced herself to think. This decision involved other people. "I have to consider Ryan."

"If you bring him to Cedar Dell, the gossips will eat him alive," Tom warned.

Maybe. Probably. That's why she'd stayed away for fifteen years. They would gnaw on her hard-won peace of mind in several ways.

"Ryan wouldn't necessarily come with me," Kate said, thinking out loud. "He has friends at home. His Select baseball team plays through July, and we've lined up an internship for him at Loring Engineering. He'd be fine at home with Adele."

Sarah's teeth tugged at her bottom lip. "I hate to separate you from your son. It's been obvious the times we've spent together at the lake house that you and Ryan are close."

"Bring him, Kate," Alan encouraged. "Bring him and Adele. She'll keep Jack stirred up, and it'll do the boy good to spend time with his grandfather."

Nodding in agreement, Sarah said, "That's right. Dad thinks a lot of Ryan. He'd want him here. He'd want you here."

Her brother's lips twisted in a doubtful grimace, but Kate barely noticed. Deep inside, a dormant seed of hope blossomed. Maybe, just maybe, some good could come from this near disaster.

"And of course, you should bring Adele," her sister

continued, "Dad's house has plenty of room, and she'll be good company for him."

"If she can refrain from telling him off," Kate muttered. Adele had strong opinions about Jack Harmon's treatment of his daughter and grandson.

Tom shuffled. "I still think Colonial Valley might be a better option."

That was just the push Kate needed. She took a deep, bracing breath. "I want to clear it with Ryan, but yes. Yes, I'll do it. I'll come home for the summer and see to Dad."

Sarah's eyes went bright with pleasure. Alan grinned. Tom scratched at his five o'clock shadow, his mouth set in a frown. "All right, then. It's settled."

They spent the next few minutes hammering out the details of the arrangement. Because Kate would continue her accounting work during the summer, she'd need an office. They agreed that before Tom returned to Houston in five days, he would have phone lines and office equipment installed in his old bedroom. Tom would also hire Bertie and talk to The Widows about covering for them the days between their father's release from the hospital and the two weeks until Ryan's school let out for the summer. Alan promised to drop by the house often to make certain The Narc didn't spend too much time sleeping on the job.

With the plans made, her brother walked to the bed and pressed a kiss against Sarah's brow. "I'm whipped. I'll see you in the morning. You get some sleep tonight, you hear?"

"I will."

He spoke a moment with Alan, then turned toward

Kate. He gave her an awkward handshake. "Uh, thanks, Kate."

She met his gaze, so much like Jack's, briefly. "Uh, sure."

Tom left the hospital room just as a nurse arrived to take Sarah's vital signs. Suddenly exhausted, Kate seized the chance to escape. Standing, she said, "I need to be going. I want to visit Dad before I head back to Dallas."

"You shouldn't drive all that way tonight," Sarah protested, as the nurse wrapped a blood pressure cuff around her upper arm. "Stay at our house or at Dad's."

"No, I have a ride waiting and I need to work tomorrow. I've lots to do in order to be ready to return to Cedar Dell in two weeks."

She felt a sudden and unexpected urge to kiss her sister's cheek good-bye, but settled for a wave and turned to leave.

Sarah's voice stopped her at the doorway. "Kate, I know it can't be easy for you, but I really appreciate what you're doing for Dad."

Kate glanced back over her shoulder. "He's my father, too."

Sarah briefly closed her eyes, then nodded. "That's some funeral dress you're wearing, by the way."

"This old thing?" She gave the skirt a flip. "It's not my funeral dress. I save my short red one for that."

Chapter Three

MAX COOPER KNEW what he was after. The soft mist of morning. The snuggled comfort of golden curls against fluffy white. The sleepy dawn of awareness in sky-blue eyes as they opened to love.

So he waited, unmoving, steeped in the quiet peace of birdsong and snuffles. Light from a rising sun beamed through the window, traveled a snail's pace across pink-dotted Swiss, and finally kissed a button nose dusted with freckles.

Max's finger hovered. Ready . . . ready . . .

Soft as an angel's kiss, lashes lifted. Ready . . . ready . . . *Love*.

His camera shutter clicked.

"Daddy." The smile stretched with sleepy delight. "Good mornin'."

She was, quite completely, his heart. "Good mornin' to you, Shanabanana. Did you sleep well?"

"Yep." Five-year-old Shannon Cooper nodded, rubbed her eyes, and sat up in bed. She held out her arms to her father. "I'm hungry."

And so their day began.

In the kitchen, Max kept a close eye on the clock as he

whipped up Shannon's second-favorite breakfast, French toast, orange juice, and bacon. Froot Loops occupied the number-one slot. After long and intense negotiation, father and daughter had settled on a twice-a-week Froot Loops limit as long as French toast made at least one appearance each week.

"Hurry up, Shan. Breakfast is almost ready. We have fifteen minutes before we need to leave for school."

"Coming, Daddy." Sneakers thundered downstairs, and his favorite whirlwind burst into the room and took her seat at the kitchen table. "We can't be late today. Mrs. Litton said if I'm late one more time, she's going to give you a D-hall."

"Oh, yeah?" Max set Shannon's plate in front of her. "I didn't know kindergarten teachers could give D-halls to parents."

"Dad-dy." Shannon rolled her eyes theatrically. "Mrs. Litton can do *anything*."

"Hmm . . ." Max couldn't put up much of an argument with that. After all, Mrs. Litton had taken a sad, silent little girl beneath her wing and coaxed this happy, healthy live-wire kindergartner into being. Because of that, Max would serve a hundred D-hall's for Mrs. Litton if she asked.

"Is your backpack ready to go?"

Shannon nodded, then turned her attention to her breakfast. She took her last bite of French toast, then her eyes went wide. "Oh, no. I forgot. It's Show-and-Tell Day. What can I take?"

Max considered the question. "How about photographs again? You could take the ones we made together of Edinburgh Castle."

"No. That's boring. I could show them my doll Matilda. I was going to show her last week, but I didn't, and she's still at school, only I'm not in the mood for Matilda today." She licked syrup from her fork, then lifted her plate to lick it, too. A stern look from Max managed to stop her. She set down her plate and flashed a happy smile. "I have an idea."

Hopping down from her chair, she skipped across the kitchen to the junk drawer, then rummaged around for half a minute. "Here it is." She pulled out an old cork and held it up like a prize.

"You want to take a cork to show-and-tell?"

"It's a stopper, Daddy, and they are so cool. You can use it for tons of things."

Max started to ask, but thought better of it. Knowing Shannon, she'd want to demonstrate, and they'd be late to school. Again.

He'd just as soon avoid getting a D-hall.

Shortly after they moved to Cedar Dell in January and Max enrolled Shannon in kindergarten, he realized morning time management presented one of his little family's biggest challenges. For four years he and Shannon had been accustomed to doing things on their own schedule. They'd enjoyed that luxury owing to his work and Shannon's beloved Nana Jean.

Nana Jean had joined their family as a baby-sitter for infant Shannon after Max's wife, Rose, died. When Max left the Air Force a short time later and turned his photography hobby into a second career, Nana Jean came with them. The widow of a retired army staff sergeant, organization had been Nana Jean's strong suit. She'd enjoyed the constant travel Max's lucrative new job required, and she

managed to make continent-hopping with a toddler an en-
joyable experience.

Nana Jean's loving support and kick-in-the-ass attitude
helped Max make it through the most difficult time of his
life, and she became the only mother Shannon had ever
known. Losing her last September to a heart attack had
crushed both Max and Shannon. Guilty, grieving, and in
search of safety and security for the family he had left, Max
moved back to his hometown, Cedar Dell, and embarked
on his third career, that of full-time dad.

He was still trying to get the hang of it.

Today, he was off to a good start, though, delivering
Shannon to school with a kiss and three minutes to spare.
He waited by the curb, watching until she disappeared inside the front door. Despite how well kindergarten was
going for Shannon, he looked forward to the summer
break. The vacation was longer in coming this year because
of the furnace failure and burst water heaters that had delayed classes for two weeks back in January. Once school let
out for summer, he wanted to drive over to Arlington and
ride that new coaster that opened at Six Flags Over Texas.
He and his wild child were both crazy about coasters.

In the meantime, he had to go to work. He flipped down
his visor and checked the day's schedule. Well, hell. It
hadn't changed. Max had fifteen minutes before he was due
at Harmon Lanes to photograph members of the Cedar
Dell Golden Ladies morning bowling league in action.

"Just enough time to drop you at Doc Murphy's." He
glanced down at the small Heinz-57 stretched out on the
seat next to him. Max had rescued the dog from a Phoenix
animal shelter back in November in an attempt to distract

Shannon from her grief in the wake of Nana Jean's death. The dog had quickly become a member of the family. Shannon adored the animal she'd christened, to Max's dismay, Muffykins. To compound the insult, the poor dog was male. Max offered him what dignity he could by refusing to call the canine by his name. Shannon scolded Max about it at least once a day, but on that, he held firm.

Max pulled into the parking lot at the vet's and stopped the car. He fastened Mutt's leash to his collar, then set him on the ground. The dog planted his paws and whined. "Don't do that," Max warned. "I've found you in Shannon's bed the past three nights. You're getting dipped whether you like it or not."

Leaving the vet's, Max checked his watch, sighed, then glanced next door at the neon sign shaped like a bowling pin. In the six months since he'd returned to Cedar Dell, Doc Murphy's office was the closest he'd come to Harmon Lanes. That was about to change.

Harmon Lanes. In all his travels, first as an Air Force pilot, then as a photographer, he'd never stumbled upon another place quite like it.

Established in 1948, Harmon Lanes had evolved into something much bigger than a simple bowling alley. The transformation began back in the sixties, when a tornado destroyed much of Cedar Dell. To help his friends and neighbors, Jack Harmon closed off half his lanes and donated the space for meetings and events like wedding receptions, baby showers, the Tuesday morning quilting circle, and the Thursday afternoon diet-and-exercise club. At the urging of the ladies in town, he remodeled a storeroom in back where Elizabeth Beck could set up her beauty shop. According to Max's next-door neighbor, she had yet to move out.

Max had spent many an hour in that building in his youth. Jack Harmon had given him his first job. He'd polished rental shoes and built Coke floats behind the soda fountain salvaged from the storm-ravaged drugstore. Max had a vivid memory of sweeping the floor of the beauty salon while holding his breath against the assault of perm solution. The Willie Mays baseball card he'd purchased in the Harmon Lanes Gift and Antique Shop was still one of his most prized possessions.

According to Max's barber, the soda fountain continued to attract a crowd, and the community room was still the nicest one in town. The president of the Fain Elementary Parent-Teacher Association had mentioned that the quilting circle still met every Tuesday night. The diet-and-exercise group apparently had evolved into a daily 7 A.M. aerobics class.

Harmon Lanes was both special and unique, and at times since his return, Max had missed mingling at the town's social center. Up until today, he had given the place a wide berth. The fewer times he had to look Jack Harmon in the eye, the better.

Max counted twelve cars in the Harmon Lanes lot. Nice crowd for a weekday morning.

He threw the gearshift in park and turned off the ignition. He sat staring, lost in bittersweet memories. Best put a lid on memory; it hurt more often than it helped. He grabbed his camera bag from the backseat and headed for the building.

The second he opened the door he was thrown back in

time by the blend of odors and aromas—Lysol, cigarette smoke, furniture polish, perspiration, popcorn, and perm solution. At that moment, Max felt eighteen all over again. Eighteen and filled with anger and brimming with dreams.

Regrets hit him like a punch to the gut, hard and fast and ugly, and he wheezed out a breath.

"Max! Max Cooper! Over here!"

His gaze swept past the shoe rental counter, where he expected to see Jack, but didn't, to lane numbers one through four. Members of the Cedar Dell Golden Ladies bowling league were hard at play. He spied three people he recognized, and he smiled. Mrs. Dunkleburg, Mrs. Coppage, and Mrs. Kramer had been members of the Christian Ladies Benevolent Society that had been so kind to him when he was a kid. One of the first things he'd done after moving back to town was to make a substantial donation to their scholarship fund.

His smile died when he realized the Widow Gault was waving and calling his name. Loudly. There had seldom been anything benevolent about Martha Gault.

"Thank goodness you're here," she said. "We want to get these pictures in tomorrow's paper. To cheer poor Jack up."

In the process of removing his camera from its bag, Max paused. "Cheer Jack up? Why does he need cheering up?"

"You haven't heard? How can you not have heard? It's the talk of the town. Besides, you work for the newspaper. You should know the news."

Max didn't feel like going into the details of his part-time work for the local biweekly paper. "What news?"

The elderly woman's eyes lit. "About the accident, of course. You don't know? I can't believe I'm scooping the press. Jack was awfully lucky. He's going to be fine. In fact, they're both going to be fine. The doctors were worried for a while that Sarah might lose the baby, but she seems to have weathered that danger well. She's going home today. Jack will be in Bethania a few days longer. He needed surgery. If the fellow who hit him hadn't used his cell phone to call for help, Jack might have bled to death."

Max wanted to be sure he had it straight. "Jack Harmon was in a car accident? Sarah Harmon, too?"

"Jack, yes. Sarah, no. She's Sarah West now. She married Alan West not long after you left town. This is their first child. A miracle baby. They've wanted children from the beginning, but apparently Sarah had female problems that prevented . . . well . . . I shouldn't go into details. I doubt she'd care to see the particulars printed up in the Cedar Dell Times and Record News."

"Mrs. Gault. I'm not a reporter. I only take pictures. Part-time. Just to help out. Now about Jack and Sarah?"

"Well, I swan." She peered at him over the top of her glasses. "I still don't want you printing anything about our Sarah. She wasn't in the accident itself, but the stress of the news presented some alarming symptoms regarding her pregnancy. She almost worried herself into premature labor. Such a dear, sweet girl. Such a contrast to that younger sister of hers. Although, Sue Ayer is a nurse at Bethania, and she said the younger girl did come visit her dad. Showed up late in the day and in a limousine, of all things. That's just like Kate, if you ask me. Doesn't care a lick about family. Her brother arrived hours earlier, and he rushed all the way from Houston. Why, her daddy could have died."

Max went still. "Kate Harmon is in town?"

"Do you know her? Yes, of course you probably do. She and Terri Gantt were the same age, and I know you dated Terri all through high school. Everyone in town expected the two of you to marry. Such a shock when she broke up with you, but she wasn't cut out to be an Air Force wife. All that traveling. Base housing." She shuddered. "Terri married a banker, did you know that? They have three children. Live in San Francisco. Her parents are so proud of her, but you probably know that since you bought the Gantt's house when they retired to Florida. Too bad poor Jack can't feel the same way about his younger girl."

Max wanted to scold the town's worst gossip. Instead, he literally bit his tongue.

"That Kate was such a disappointment to her parents. We all knew something fishy was going on with her when she left town so fast and didn't come back. I never believed that wild talk about her attending college in California. Jack and Linnie weren't talking, though, and we respected their wish for privacy."

Yeah, right. Max chose a lens from his bag, his thoughts spinning. Kate was in Cedar Dell.

"Her poor father. He already had so much to bear when Linnie died so suddenly, and then that girl just slaps him in the face by showing up at the funeral with a baby in her arms and no ring on her finger. Jack went red as picante sauce. I feared he'd have a heart attack right in First Methodist. Thank God Tom had the presence of mind to see that Kate didn't attend the graveside service."

"Now, Martha." The Widow Mallow joined them, clucking her tongue as she wiped down her hunter green bowling ball with a lace-trimmed pink handkerchief. "You're being too hard on that girl, like always. She had every right to come to her mother's funeral. She just shouldn't have brought that baby. Not after her mama worked so hard to keep Kate's disgrace a secret."

Disgrace? He smiled grimly. *Just do your job and get out of here.*

Max glanced around the room, finding a spot over by the soft drink machines with especially harsh light. He gestured in that direction. "Mrs. Gault? Mrs. Mallow? Why don't you step over into the light and let me get a couple of shots."

"Don't you want action photos? Something that shows the bowling alley? I think that's what Jack would like best. Remember, we want to cheer him up."

"Don't worry, Mrs. Mallow. I'll get what we need."

Max snapped off a few particularly unflattering shots, delighting in his petty revenge. As much as he loved small-town living, he hated small-town gossip. Nobody read the local paper for the news; they just wanted to see what version of events got published.

And yet, today he needed to take advantage of the Widows' knowledge of everyone else's business. "Is Kate staying at her father's house?"

"Oh, no." The Widow Gault shook her head. "She went back to Dallas last night. Why, I don't think she was in town much more than an hour or so. No telling what event she was coming from in the big city; Sue said she had on a slinky black dress and heels that sure weren't made for visiting the sick. That girl is not a credit to her heritage."

So Kate *wasn't* in Cedar Dell.

"Not a credit to her heritage? Oh, Martha." A woman Max didn't know motioned the two widows away from the Dr Pepper machine. She fed it quarters, pushed a button, and as the machine thumped and clattered out a can, she folded her arms over a generous bosom and snorted. "You are such a mean-spirited old biddy. Kate Harmon is not the Jezebel you make her out to be."

"Don't you call me 'old.' I'm younger than you."

"It's not your age, it's your attitude, and yours stinks."

"Well, I never." The Widow Gault put a hand to her breast.

The other woman rolled her eyes and extended her hand toward Max. "You probably don't remember me, but I'm Lorraine King. My husband owned the Dairy Queen over on Kemp Street."

Recognition dawned quickly. "I do remember you, Mrs. King. Whenever I ordered a single cone, you'd give me a double."

"And you'd grin at me. My, oh my, you were such a handsome fella, and that grin of yours . . . my lands . . . you were a charmer even at twelve."

She was a breath of fresh air. One of the good guys, so to speak. Max smiled and brought her hand to his lips for a gallant kiss.

Lorraine King gasped, then theatrically fanned her face. "Oh, my. You are potent, aren't you?" She linked her arm through his and walked him toward Lane Four. "I understand you're not married. Darling, how do you feel about older women?"

"I think age on a woman can be downright interesting."

"Are you flirting with me, Max Cooper?"

"Yes, ma'am."

"Good! Keep it up."

"Lorraine, you stop that," the Widow Mallow scolded.

Lorraine tossed a smug look over her shoulder. "I may be one of Cedar Dell's Widows, but I'm not dead yet." She squeezed Max's arm. "They're jealous of me because Tom Harmon asked me to take the first shift looking after Jack once he's dismissed from the hospital. Martha, Melody, and I will be taking turns doing for poor Jack until Kate gets all her ducks in a row and moves home."

Max pulled up short. *Kate is moving home? To Cedar Dell?*

The Widow Gault, her pinched mouth conveying her annoyance at losing control of the conversation, sidled up next to Max. "We'll need to help out for at least two weeks, maybe a little longer. I think that Harmon girl should come home right away, but, apparently, she's determined to stay in Dallas—that's where she lives—until school lets out for the summer. She's bringing her bastard with her."

Max couldn't let that one go. He wanted to tell the old biddy off, but he settled for a mildly chastising, "Mrs. Gault, I don't think name-calling is necessary. He's just a boy, after all."

She wrinkled her nose, but thankfully, didn't respond.

"Now," Max continued, "I'd better get these pictures done or they won't make the deadline. Ladies? Y'all want to start your game?" Max forced a smile on his face and joked with the women as he took the additional action shots the editor of the newspaper had requested. The entire time, his mind was otherwise occupied.

Kate Harmon was coming back to Cedar Dell.

Unless she'd changed dramatically in the past three years, Kate would not come alone. She'd bring Ryan with her.

Ryan. Max's son.

The young man who hated his guts.

Chapter Four

ON A SATURDAY AFTERNOON in late May, Kate Harmon returned to Cedar Dell. Her son Ryan quickly decided that it was the homecoming from hell.

Ordinarily a chatterer when she drove, his mom made the entire trip from Dallas clammed up tight. Ryan wanted to pull on his MP3 player headphones and listen to music, but Adele spent the time filling the dead air with stories about the cat she'd had in the 1950s, stories Ryan and his mom had heard a thousand times. His mom consistently missed her cues to respond, and if he hadn't commented now and again, Adele's feelings would have been hurt.

They whizzed past the green-and-white city limits sign and, within minutes, drove past a small park. Ryan read the sign in the north corner—Weeks Park. They were close now.

His mother slowed the car to neighborhood speed. Then she dropped it another notch to I-don't-want-to-get-there speed.

Ryan glanced at his mom, saw she had a death grip on the steering wheel, and blew out a silent sigh. He wasn't all that thrilled about this trip himself. Oh, he looked forward to spending time with his granddad, and he liked the idea of pitching in to help family. He'd always wanted to get a look at Harmon Lanes.

If only Cedar Dell didn't come with all the people. Mom had warned him about the grilling he was liable to get. She said he'd face the Small-Town Inquisition in Cedar Dell. By that, she meant they'd quiz him about his dad.

Ryan did not want to go there.

Anxious now, Ryan searched the street signs. There. Alamo Street. The car turned.

Ryan leaned forward, looking for the two-story, plantation-style house with its wraparound porch that he would recognize from pictures rather than personal experience. All their visits with the Harmon family had taken place at the lake house. He'd been little more than a baby when he'd visited Cedar Dell one Christmas, then again when his grandmother had died. He hardly remembered anything about the place.

There. Halfway down the block. He did remember the blue shutters. As the car slowed down to a crawl, he noticed two Buicks, an Olds, and a Caddy lining the curb in front of the Harmon house.

His mother muttered "shit" beneath her breath, and Ryan's eyes went wide. His mom *never* cussed. Well, hardly ever. Something had her rattled, and the minute they stepped into the house, he knew what.

The place was swarming with old ladies.

They congregated in the kitchen, where a surprising number of casserole dishes sat lined up like soldiers on the Formica counter. Interested, Ryan moved to inspect them.

Green bean casserole. Green bean casserole. Green bean casserole. Potatoes, thank God.

One of the gray-hairs folded her arms, and said, "Jack is asleep in his bedroom. He shouldn't be disturbed." Then she fired off a glare toward one of the other women, and added, "By anyone."

His mom plastered on a smile as fake as school cafeteria cheese. "Thank you, Mrs. Gault. My family appreciates your help. Now, let me introduce my son. Ryan, this is Mrs. Gault, Mrs. Mallow, and Mrs. King."

Then things got ugly.

"Oh, look at you," said Mrs. Mallow, reaching out to pinch his cheek. "Aren't you a handsome boy. I can see a lot of your grandfather in you, but the Harmons are so fair and you're dark. You must look like your father. Is that it, son? Do you look like your father?"

Ryan shot an uneasy look toward his mother. *Shit, it started this soon?*

Nobody in Cedar Dell knew that Max Cooper was the one who'd knocked up his mother. Ryan wanted it kept that way. He didn't claim Max Cooper; he didn't want Max Cooper claiming him, even if only in the minds of the citizens of Cedar Dell.

"He has my mother's nose," said Kate, darting a reassuring look toward Ryan. "How is your daughter, Mrs. Mallow? Is she still living in Houston?"

Mrs. Mallow launched into a soliloquy about her Charlene, and Ryan thought he was off the hook. He thought too soon.

Mrs. King readjusted the sweater around her shoulders

and said, "You're a tall one, aren't you? Handsome, too. If I were forty years younger . . ."

Mrs. Gault wasn't one to be left behind. "You are tall. Harmons never had much height to them. Not a lot of families in town run to tall, actually. The Randalls do. The Handers. The Harts. Your mother dated Bobby Randall for a time, didn't she?"

Nosy, cold-hearted old women. Must be why they all wore sweaters and had the air conditioner set higher than ninety, judging by the temperature in here.

"Your grandfather mentions you make excellent grades, Ryan." Mrs. Mallow peered at him over the top of her wire-rimmed glasses. "The Harmons are better known for their athletic abilities than their minds. Are you good in math? Jeff Hander was quite talented in math."

Adele snorted, then said, "Oh, of all the foolishness. Our Kate is smart as a whip, and I'm certain you all know that. You're just trying to butt your noses into business that doesn't concern you."

"Well, I never!" said Mrs. Gault.

"Which is undoubtedly part of your problem," Adele snapped back.

"Ladies. Please." Kate smiled grimly. "If you have a question about my family, please ask me directly. I'll not have my son interrogated."

You go, Mom.

"Interrogated!" Mrs. Mallow wrinkled her nose. "Why, that's an awful thing to say when we're just taking a polite interest."

"That's an awful thing to do," Adele muttered.

Kate rolled her eyes at her friend. "I'm sorry, ladies.

We're all just a little tired today. I can't thank y'all enough for helping out with Dad until I could get here. Why, we'd have been lost without you. I'd love to hear any tips you might have for me about caring for my father."

The old women yammered on about Granddad's condition, competing with each other, interrupting one another, and Ryan seized the opportunity to excuse himself to unload the car. He was happy to do it. He'd have emptied an eighteen-wheeler all alone just to get out of the kitchen.

As Ryan toted suitcases and boxes into the house, his mother ushered the women out to their cars. Adele actually cheered when the biddies fired up their V8 engines and rolled away at the speed of a funeral procession.

Ryan, Kate, and Adele walked into the house together and Ryan heard the TV come on in his grandfather's downstairs bedroom. He must be awake.

Ryan glanced at his mom. She'd halted midstep and twisted her head toward the sound. The look on her face gave Ryan an ache inside. You'd think Granddad's bedroom housed a firing squad.

She took a deep breath, lifted her chin, and faced her father's door. Adele murmured, "Good Lord, Kate. You look like a lapsed dieter on a scale."

She pasted on another one of those fake smiles and knocked on the half-open door. "Dad? May I come in?"

"Rrrrrr."

Ryan and Adele hung back, close enough to hear, but out of Granddad's notice. Glad he hadn't barged into the room, Ryan needed a moment to get over the changes in his grandfather.

He looked old. Really old. Everything about him—

except for the fading green-and-yellow bruises—looked pale. Rather than its usual crisp, snowy white, his hair appeared dull, gray, and limp. His dry, papery skin wrinkled more than ever before. Worst of all, he . . . well . . . he smelled. Like an old person. In fact, the whole house smelled like an old person.

Ryan made a mental note to stock up on air fresheners down at the grocery store.

His mom crossed the bedroom to stand beside her father's bed. "How are you feeling, Dad?"

His gaze flicked toward his daughter, then away. "So you're here. Your brother told me you were coming, but I didn't think you'd actually dare to show up. I'll be damned if I'll pay for more phone lines."

For just a moment, his mom seemed to sink in upon herself, to crumple. Ryan gaped. He'd never seen her look like that. Then she straightened, squared her shoulders, and spoke in a calm tone. "We arrived a few minutes ago. Mrs. Gault told us you were sleeping. I'll pay for the phone lines myself."

He snorted. "Are they gone? The Widows?"

"Yes."

"Damned women. Talk about kicking a man when he's down. Won't leave me alone. Can't complain about the cooking, though. Except they bring too much and get all snippy when I eat more of one person's dish than another."

Mom moved closer to the bed. "It's good to see you, Dad. I've been worried about you."

"I guess that's why you've paid me all those visits. Wearin' black, I'm told. Bit premature, don't you think?"

Hey, now, Ryan thought, stepping forward. *No fair.* His

mom had rushed down to see Granddad the day of the accident without stopping to change clothes, and she'd spent every day since then getting ready to spend the summer here. She'd called every day, too.

Ryan opened his mouth to defend his mom, but she quelled him with a look through the door. "I spoke with Dr. Hardesty this morning, and he said you're progressing very well. He thinks that in another week you'll be able to get along without Bertie's help."

"You're not toting me to the bathroom, by God," Granddad snapped.

"No, Dad." Mom visibly summoned her patience. "Bertie will be here to assist you until you are able to take care of your personal needs yourself. Dr. Hardesty believes your recovery will progress to that point by this time next week."

"So you're only here to cook and clean."

Ryan couldn't understand why his grandfather was being such a jerk. It wasn't like him. Well, not with Ryan, anyway. Come to think of it, he often sent a zinger or two winging in Mom's direction.

Deadpan, Mom said, "That's right, Dad. I'm here to cook and clean."

He saw some emotion he couldn't quite read flashing in his mother's eyes.

She continued, "The Widows have been kind enough to stock the freezer, but I'm told the upstairs needs a thorough going-over and that it should be done today. So I'd best get to work."

When she rushed past Adele, Ryan saw tears in her eyes and his stomach made a funny dip. *C'mon, Granddad.*

Scolding words hovered on his tongue, but a lifetime of lessons to respect his elders held them back.

Adele didn't have that problem. "You old coot," she said, sailing into the room. "Haven't you heard you're not supposed to bite the hand that feeds you?"

Granddad sputtered and struggled to sit up. "Who are you?"

Adele snatched the pillow from behind him, fluffed it, and rammed it back. "We've met, but since your feeble mind has obviously forgotten, I'll reintroduce myself. I'm Adele Watkins. I've taken care of Ryan since the boy was in diapers. I took care of Kate when she needed family and didn't have a blood relative willing to help. I love those two as if they were my own, and they love me right back. They consider me family. I live with them. That means I live with them during the summer, too."

He blinked once. Twice. "Here? You think you're gonna live here?"

"I'm already moved in." Adele smiled serenely. "Honey, if you don't adjust your attitude, I promise you I'll make your days with The Widows look like heaven on earth."

Granddad's face flushed red. "Out. Get out." He grabbed a yardstick lying beside him on the bed and poked it toward a spot outside of Ryan's line of vision. "Bertie?"

Snort. Snort. Cough.

"Bertie, wake up!"

Cough. Cough. "Sure, Jack. I'm awake. You need to take a piss?"

"I want my privacy. Get this Gorgon out of here."

"Gorgon. Hmm . . ." Adele touched her head as if

feeling for snakes and shot him a scary smile. "A fan of Greek mythology, are we?"

Ryan shifted his feet. He recognized that snide tone in Adele's voice, and it boded trouble for all of them. He took it as his cue to play distraction. "Hi, Granddad."

He watched closely, waiting for that flash of pleasure he always saw in his grandfather's expression whenever they first said hello. Yep, there it was. Jack Harmon was never obvious about his affection for Ryan, but he betrayed it in subtle ways. His eyes sort of crinkled at the corners just before he frowned. He always frowned and harrumphed and grumbled, but through it all, his eyes gleamed, and the corners of his mouth twitched.

Granddad nodded. "Boy."

Adele, being Adele, wasn't done. "Cerberus is more your style."

Ryan stepped closer to the bed. "Rangers are off to a good start this year. Bats are smoking. Now if their pitching will just hold up, we might see a pennant come October."

His grandfather's clutch on the sheet eased. "Pitching's a problem every year."

"Cerberus," Adele continued, "is the three-headed dog with a dragon tail that guards the entrance to the underworld. I myself have been reading up on Nemesis. He's the god who helped avenge those who have been wronged."

Ryan shot Adele an exasperated frown, then nodded hello to a bald man dressed in overalls who looked to be about his mom's age. Obviously, this was Bertie "The Narc" Ellis.

Granddad hunched a shoulder at Adele and shook his

head. "Don't know what it's gonna take for the Rangers to get some pitching."

"I'd be happy with a decent closer in the bullpen." Making a show of glancing around the room, Ryan declared, "Nice setup you have here, Granddad. I noticed the satellite dish on our way in. Do you have the sports package?"

"Yeah."

"Cool."

The old man frowned toward the television. "Rangers are off today. Seattle's on the docket tomorrow night. You can watch in here if you want."

"Great. Thanks. I'll look forward to it." Ryan beamed him a grin, then looked to Adele. "Guess I'd better get back to work now. You want to show me where to put the stuff in the green storage box?"

Adele seized upon Ryan's offer immediately, departing without either comment or backward glance. Relieved at having defused the situation, Ryan turned to follow, saying, "See you later, Granddad. Rest good this afternoon. I'm sure glad to be here. Looking forward to this summer."

"Rrrrrr."

Kate stood at the window in her old bedroom, fingering the white eyelet curtains. Yellow gingham had hung here during her childhood. Gingham ruffles. Back then the shade had a brass pull shaped like a rabbit. She'd been a Disney girl in the midst of a Thumper stage.

Someone had redecorated since her last visit home when her mother died. Kate's old bedroom had disappeared. Miniblinds replaced window shades. Pale lemon walls now sported a neutral shade of white. A full-sized bed had supplanted her twin and took up the floor space where she'd played Barbies. Kate wondered what had happened to those dolls. She wondered what had happened to that life. This was a guest room now, and she was definitely a guest.

"An unwelcome one, at that," she muttered, turning away from the window to gaze out into the backyard. Memories ebbed and flowed. Hide-and-seek on a summer's evening, her mother setting a tray on the redwood picnic table, pouring glasses of lemonade for Tom, Sarah, and Kate. Hamster funerals under the pecan tree and toad races in the back alley. Watermelon on the back steps after chasing lightning bugs through the hot summer twilight.

The barbecue grill hadn't changed. No fancy gas grill for Jack Harmon. Cedar Dell convention held that real men use nothing but charcoal with a few mesquite chips to season the smoke when they barbecue.

A misty, wistful sense of longing swept over her. She seldom thought about those days. It had been a different life. A good life. One that had ended so abruptly, so prematurely, on a warm spring afternoon when hamburgers cooked on the grill and the hinges on the mailbox squeaked as the postman delivered the letter bringing both joy and grief.

A movement in the alley below provided a welcome distraction from old memories. Golden curls bobbed as a little girl skipped up the alley. She wore a pale pink leotard, a bright green tutu, tennis shoes, and a gold paper crown from a fast-food restaurant.

Kate grinned as she watched the girl halt at the back fence of the house catty-corner from the Harmon house across the alley. The child spoke through the waist-high picket fence to the red Irish setter wagging its tail in reply, then flourished an imaginary wand and anointed the dog. Kate wondered what grand transformation had occurred in the little girl's mind.

"Kate?" Adele asked from behind her. "You all right?"

"Yes, yes, I'm fine." She hesitated slightly, then said, "No, I guess I'm not. He doesn't want me here, Adele. He hasn't wanted me here for a long, long time."

"You knew it might be this way when you agreed to come."

Kate nodded. Experience had taught her that her father's attitude didn't change. For the first year or so of her exile, she hadn't cared. She hadn't wanted to go home. Then, as Ryan grew older, as she grew up, she'd begun to wait, to hope, that her father would relent. To a degree, with her mother's help, he had come around. Linnie Harmon wanted peace in her family. She'd wanted it whole. She'd declared she wouldn't spend another Christmas without all her children at her side.

Ryan had been three years old the first time Kate returned to Cedar Dell. She'd arrived Christmas Eve and had left Christmas Day. For the most part, the visit went well, primarily because she skipped church since Ryan was fussy, and the family kept her presence in town a secret. Her mom had been thrilled. Her dad had taken a shine to Ryan. Tom had been his usual self-absorbed self, and Kate had welcomed being ignored by him. Sarah, however, had continued the deep freeze that had begun when Kate gave birth—on her sister's wedding day.

"I don't think I'm up to paying a visit to Sarah this afternoon," Kate confessed.

"It might make you feel better, honey. Your sister wants you here."

Kate grimaced. "Only because she had no other choice."

"Now, Kate."

"It's true."

"She's already called three times in the past hour."

"She's just checking up on me. Making sure I showed up. Making sure I'm treating Dad right."

Adele snorted. "Why don't you turn on the radio and add some music to this pity party?"

Though Kate shot her friend a narrow-eyed look, she couldn't keep her lips from twitching with a grin. Adele did have a way of cutting right to the heart of a matter. "I guess I just hoped that things had changed."

Adele crossed the room and gave Kate a hug. "Of course you did. Jack almost died, and an incident like that can transform a person. It's natural for you to hope that your father would quit being an ass and come to his senses."

This time, Kate gave in to the smile. Adele never failed to call it like she saw it.

Kate returned her gaze to the window. Her eyes widened with surprise. Her dad's back gate stood open, and the little blond girl made herself at home in the tree swing that had hung from the pecan tree for as long as Kate could remember. From the way the girl acted, Kate guessed this wasn't the first time she'd done it. She wondered if her dad knew he had a regular visitor.

"He used to push me in that swing," she said with a wistful smile. "He'd play catch with my brother, and when Tom missed a ball, Dad would come over and push me."

"It's wrong for parents to favor one child over another."

Kate shrugged. Over the years, Adele had formed strong opinions about the Harmon family, mostly from things Kate had told her. This wasn't the first time she'd voiced such thoughts. Nor was it the first time Kate explained, "He was a boy. The *only* boy."

"Oh, I know that's the way the world was thirty years ago, but it still doesn't make it right. If you had a girl, you'd treat her and Ryan fair and square."

Kate watched the little girl swing and wished with all her heart she had a little girl so she could test Adele's theory. "I hope so. I try to be a good mother, Adele, but I haven't been much of a daughter."

"Now, Kate. Stop. That's not true. For as long as I've known you, I've watched you try to make peace with your dad. But your father hasn't let it happen. Don't blame yourself. Maybe he'd be different if you hadn't lost your mom, but we'll never know that."

Mom. Kate's heart gave a little twist. "Have I ever told you how many times Mom saw Ryan, Adele? Seven. She saw him a total of seven times. That's all. He was three and a half years old when my mother died, and she'd seen him seven whole times. He didn't know her at all."

"But your father—"

"Didn't want me here. That's true. Up until that last Christmas before she died when Mom forced the issue, he wouldn't let me in the door. But it was different with Mom. She'd have made the drive to Dallas twice a month if I'd given her the least bit of encouragement. I didn't and she died and I've had to feel guilty about it ever since. I'm tired of feeling guilty where my parents are concerned, Adele."

"Then don't do it anymore." Adele stalked around the room, dodging fifties' furnishings. "I swear, I don't know where all this guilt comes from. You're not Catholic. You're not Jewish. It makes no sense."

While Adele continued her rousing, if nonsensical, defense of her, Kate paid scant attention. Below her, Ryan came barreling out the back door, a basketball tucked beneath his arm, and Kate assumed he was headed for the basketball goal that hung from the roof of the detached garage. He slowed at the sight of the fairy princess in the tree swing. Kate watched them exchange words.

Ryan laughed, bounced his ball on the narrow sidewalk that led to the driveway, and nodded. He walked over to the swing and gave the little girl a push. He swung her gently, and the girl's smile spread with delight.

Then, while Kate wondered where she might find her camera, the girl's cardboard crown flew off her head, sailing end over end to land at the foot of a rosebush beside the garage. Ryan loped across the yard to retrieve it.

Just as her son bent to pick up the crown, the little girl jumped from the swing, rounded her eyes, and clapped her hands over her mouth.

That's when Kate saw him. The dark-haired man in the alley. Dressed in jeans and a T-shirt, standing with legs akimbo, arms folded, and a scolding scowl on his face. Three years had passed since she'd last laid eyes on him, but she'd recognize that disapproving expression anywhere.

Max Cooper. Jet-jockey. Talented photographer. Still tall, still broad of shoulder. Still handsome.

The son of a bitch.

Max Cooper. What the hell was he doing in Cedar

Dell? In the alley behind the Harmon house? Motioning to that little . . . girl.

"Oh, my God." Kate breathed as the pieces fell into place.

That little girl, the little princess, was Ryan's sister.

Chapter Five

"BUSTED." MAX LEVELED a stern look at the fugitive who'd gone over the fence yet again. Stubborn little female. Had he not made her a tree swing of her own in their backyard? In fact, he'd made two of the damned things. So why, he wanted to know, did she persist in escaping to the one backyard in Cedar Dell, Texas, that Max preferred to avoid?

A gentle breeze brought with it the scent of freshly mown grass, and Max watched his daughter sneeze in response. *Need to give her an allergy pill*, he thought. *Need to give her a tongue-lashing.*

It made him crazy the way Shannon sometimes disappeared on him the minute his back was turned. Potential horrors and disasters ran through his mind like movie trailers. Cedar Dell might be one of the most peaceful places on earth, but bad stuff still happened here. The good thing about these expeditions of hers was that she never went farther than the Harmons' backyard.

The bad thing was that she never went farther than the Harmons' backyard.

Max knew he had to do something to stop Shannon from going over the pickets. He'd rather chew nails than punish her, though, and she knew it. Shannon had figured out early on that with her father, big, silent tears were the greatest weapon in her arsenal.

It was at times like this that he missed Nana Jean the most. Jean had known how to lay down the law with confidence and determination. Batting teary baby blues had gotten Shannon nowhere with her nana. Yet, she'd give Max three blinks and Bambi eyes, and he was a goner.

He had to be stronger. Shannon couldn't continue to run off by herself. She must learn to mind him. For that to have a prayer of happening, Max had to quit being a marshmallow.

"All right, kiddo," he murmured, bracing himself. "This means a full thirty minutes in the time-out chair and no Barbies for a week."

Shannon spied him, and he opened his mouth to call to her. That's when he caught movement from the corner of his eye. For an instant, fear and adrenaline surged. His little angel and a stranger. A young man. Max took half a step forward before it hit him.

No stranger. This was Kate's father's house. This was Ryan. His Ryan. Everything inside Max froze.

My God, how he'd grown. He was a man. Six feet tall, at least. Broad-shouldered. Lanky. He wore a black T-shirt with red lettering spelling WILDCAT BASKETBALL, long jersey shorts, and old scruffy tennis shoes.

He had Shannon's eyes.

Max dragged a hand along his jaw. Son of a bitch. He'd never noticed that before. Shannon and Ryan. Sister and brother. Together. Together for the very first time. Dammit, where the hell was his camera?

"Hi, Daddy." Shannon ran toward him. "I'm a fairy

princess, and this is my suspect. His name is Ryan and he's seventeen years old and this is his tree swing so it can be my throne."

Not suspect. Subject. He's your subject. He's your . . . brother. Oh, God. Max shoved his hands in his pants pockets, hiding the fact they'd started to shake. He cleared his throat. "Hello, Ryan."

Ryan's head turned. His eyes widened with recognition. A beat later, they narrowed with revulsion. His hand clenched the cardboard crown, crushing one of the spires. "*Shit.* You."

"Ryan," Shannon said, aghast. "That's a bad word. You can't say that. My Nana Jean would wash your mouth out with soap if she weren't already an angel in heaven."

The emotions visible in Ryan's glare sliced through Max's heart. Fury, betrayal. Hurt. "What are *you* doing in Cedar Dell?"

"Daddy and me lives here," Shannon chimed in, her little chin going up in defense. "Why are you talking that way to my daddy?"

Ryan's mouth silently formed the word "Daddy," then his eyes widened. "She's *that* Shannon. The kid you wanted me to meet before. . . ."

As Ryan allowed the sentence to trail off, Shannon filled the void. "Stop it, you mean boy. You're hurting my crown. Daddy, he's hurting my crown!"

They all stared at Ryan's right hand. With one spire ripped completely off, a second dangling, the paper crown was definitely the worse for wear. "Shit," he repeated.

Shannon sniffled. "Princesses can't go around with broken crowns."

"I'll send you a new one," Ryan said. He marched toward the fence, shoved the mangled cardboard at Max. "Just stay away from here. Stay away from me. Both of you."

He turned and walked swiftly up the sidewalk toward the house. Max searched for words to stop him when his mother exploded out the back door, Adele at her heels. Ryan altered his path and moments later, disappeared through the side gate.

"That went well," Max muttered. So much for the mellowing properties of time.

Shannon tossed her curls. "That was mean. I don't like him anymore. Let's go home, Daddy. I think Muffykins is missing me." Hinges squeaked as she flipped the latch and pushed open the gate of the waist-high, white picket fence.

"Uh-huh . . ." Max said absently as he watched Kate Harmon advance like an avenging angel.

The years looked good on her, he thought. She'd always been a pretty girl, one of those wholesome, athletic blondes who made a fellow think of volleyball and beaches. Max found her mature beauty even more alluring.

Not that his reaction to her made a damned bit of difference. Judging by her actions over the past three years, the woman hated his guts. "Hello, Kate."

"What are you doing here?" she demanded, stopping just shy of the fence.

Maternal concern, fear, and a full measure of temper stormed in her eyes. Holding the top of the fence as a shield, Max said, "I live here. My daughter and I moved to town just before Christmas."

She folded her arms. "What? And you didn't bother to share this little detail with me?"

Max scraped his palm across his jaw, summoning his patience. "When did you ever give me a chance? Ryan hangs up on me when I call. You aren't much better. Adele's the only one who'll speak to me for more than thirty seconds."

"You could have told her." He shrugged, and Kate's foot began to tap. "What if Ryan had an emergency? What if I'd needed to reach you?"

"My cell number hasn't changed. It's still the most reliable way to reach me whether I'm living in San Francisco, Chicago, Phoenix, or Cedar Dell."

"I should have an address, too."

"Why?" he snapped. "So Ryan can drop by to visit? That happens so often."

She had the grace to look away. Max felt a tug on his hand, and he bent to scoop Shannon into his arms. "Look, if I'd moved down the street from you, I'd have tried harder to get the message through, but I didn't anticipate running into you in Cedar Dell. Besides, I thought by now you'd have heard about our move through the grapevine."

Her lips tightened still more. "When have I ever been connected to the Cedar Dell grapevine? That hasn't changed in the past three years."

The past three years. A dozen different questions about Ryan danced on his tongue, but Max knew now was not the time to voice them. Not with Miss Big Ears in his arms. Still, he couldn't stop them all. "I saw the Wildcat basketball team had a great season."

A combination of curiosity and wariness sparked in Kate's eyes. "You follow the Wildcats?"

"On the 'Net." He started to ask why the baseball coach replaced Ryan at third base when Shannon interrupted.

"You're pretty. Are you Mr. Wilson's wife?"

Kate's brows winged up as Max's brow furrowed. He asked, "Mr. Wilson?"

"The nice man who lives here. He gives Muffykins bones and calls me Dennis, even though I tell him every time my name is Shannon Michelle Cooper. He lets me swing in his swing, but I'm not supposed to go too high or too fast."

"Dad?" Kate murmured, surprise evident in her expression. "No, I'm . . . um . . . his daughter. My name is Kate."

Adele, who'd been standing a short distance away during Max and Kate's confrontation, stepped forward. "Shannon Michelle Cooper. What a beautiful name you have. I'm Adele Watkins, and I'm very pleased to meet you."

"Hello." Shannon beamed a smile, then tucked her head against Max's shoulder.

Max said, "Hello, Adele. Welcome to Cedar Dell."

"Max. I must say this is certainly a surprise." Her gaze raked him up and down. "You're looking well. Much more relaxed than the last time I saw you."

Relaxed? Not hardly. But, better than three years ago when Ryan declared he never wanted to see Max again. "Circumstances aren't as . . . stressful."

"Don't bet on it," Kate said beneath her breath.

Adele looked from Max to Kate and back again. "Shannon, would you like me to push you in the swing?"

The girl made faces while she thought about it. "No, thank you."

Nosy little minx. Max set his daughter on the ground and tried something that usually worked. "Why don't you introduce Adele to Mutt, honey?"

"Muffykins, Daddy!" She looked up at Adele. "Would you like to come, ma'am? We live six houses down the alley. It's a shortcut because we live on Greenbrier Street, and it's a lot longer when you walk on the roads."

"I would love to meet your Muffykins." Adele opened the back gate and swept through with a flourish. "I like dogs. Tell me a little bit about yours before I meet her, would you please?"

"Muffykins is a him, not a her." Seldom a shy one, Shannon took Adele's hand. "You'll love him. Everybody does, even Daddy, though he never calls him by his real name."

Max watched his daughter walk away with Adele. Once they'd moved beyond earshot, Kate spoke in a voice brimming with exasperation. "I can't believe you moved to Cedar Dell. Why? Why here?"

" 'Of all the gin joints . . .' " Max quoted Bogart in the movie *Casablanca*. He folded his arms and widened his stance. Quietly, he stated, "I needed a good place to raise my daughter, Kate. Do you recall my talking about Nana Jean?"

"Your daughter's nanny?"

"More like her mother, really. The only one she's ever known. Jean . . . um . . . passed away last fall. Shannon—hell, both of us—took it hard. I decided we needed to put down some roots. We came here because Cedar Dell is the best place I know of to do that. It's my home, too, Kate."

"I know." The breeze stirred an errant lock of hair, and she impatiently tucked it behind her ear. Sympathy softened her eyes. "I'm sorry, Max. It's horribly difficult to lose a mother, and now your little girl has lost two." She paused a moment, then added some leaves to her olive branch. "She's a beautiful child. She's how old now? Five?"

Max nodded. "She's a handful. The way she keeps me on my toes at five makes me scared to death to think ahead to fifteen."

"Thirteen was especially difficult with Ryan. Of course, with all the changes. . . ." She shrugged. "I hear with girls, thirteen can be a challenge."

"Great. Two years sooner." After wincing at the thought, Max led the conversation toward their son. "How is seventeen?"

"Good and bad." She looked over his shoulder for a few long seconds before meeting his gaze head-on. "He hasn't changed his mind, Max. He still wants nothing to do with you."

"I figured that, the way he lit out of here."

She rubbed her temples with her fingertips. "Oh, this makes my head hurt. What are we going to do? This town is too small for all of us. It'll be a zoo. People have speculated about Ryan's father since we went public at my mother's funeral. The older he gets, the more he resembles you."

"You think so?" Max couldn't keep the hopeful note out of his voice.

She rolled her eyes. "You have the same shoulders. The same way of standing. He may have my facial features and hair color, but if the two of you stood next to one another, the similarity would be obvious. Some nosy busybody in this town is bound to figure it out."

Max absently watched a blue jay swoop from the branches of the pecan tree to perch at the edge of a birdbath. "Would that be so terrible a thing?"

"What are you saying?"

"I've thought about this a lot since I heard y'all were coming to town for the summer. To be honest, it's why I didn't try to warn you during these past two weeks. This trouble with Ryan . . . it's gone on too long. I want it to end. He's my son, too, Kate. I love him. I want a relationship with Ryan again."

"Forgive me if I sound harsh, Max, but I don't care what you want. Ryan's wishes are what matters to me."

Max rubbed the back of his neck. "Are you positive you know what Ryan really wants? Do you think he knows himself? He was fourteen when your husband—"

"Ex-husband."

Roger Thurman had still been her husband at the time of the debacle, but Max wasn't of a mind to split hairs at the moment.

"—when the french hit the fries. Maybe Ryan regrets cutting me out of his life. Maybe deep down he'd like to mend matters. Maybe he just doesn't know how."

She shot him a narrow-eyed glare. "If you're trying to draw some crazy parallel between your situation with Ryan and mine with my dad, you're dead wrong."

Max blinked. Wow. That came out of nowhere. Like mother like son, hmm? "All I'm trying to say is maybe it's time we made him confront the fact that whether he likes it or not, I'm still his father. I've given him time, given him space. It hasn't worked worth a damn. You're a good mother, Kate, and I know Ryan's doing fine. But that doesn't mean he doesn't need me. That doesn't mean his life wouldn't be richer with me in it. With Shannon in it. You can see that, can't you?"

"I don't want to see that. I like our life the way it is."

He didn't bother to respond to that bit of childishness, simply maintained eye contact. After a moment, she scowled and gave a reluctant nod.

"He's nursed this grudge for three years, Max. I know my son. He won't give it up easily."

"I don't expect easy. But I want him back, and I'm ready to fight for him. Using every weapon at my disposal."

Kate blew out a long breath. "Cedar Dell."

"You said they'll figure it out eventually. Let's not wait. Let's go public, Kate. Let's tell Cedar Dell that I am Ryan's father."

Closing her eyes, Kate groaned. "Talk about the french hitting the fries. Max Cooper, do you have a clue what you are asking for?"

Jack Harmon woke from his nap to a fuzzy head, a dry mouth, and the certainty something had gone wrong. Bad wrong. Linnie?

No, Linnie was dead. She'd passed a long, long time ago. Tom? Sarah? Sarah. Her baby. The accident.

Oh, hell.

That's why he hurt. The damned car wreck. Shrapnel wounds in his leg. Shrapnel from his Cougar. Christ, he'd miss that car.

He pried open his eyes. Sunlight hurt. Somebody should pull the blinds.

Bertie Ellis sat staring at the television, the only visible sign of life a rhythmic punching of buttons on Jack's remote. Jack sent up a short, fervent prayer that by tomorrow, he could get himself to the bathroom and back. Then he'd

boot Bertie from the premises. Needing a nurse to help him
wipe his ass was humiliation enough. He shouldn't have to
put up with remote theft on top of that.

Just as he opened his mouth to demand control of the
TV, Bertie settled on the station Jack wanted to watch.
Baseball, Rangers versus the Mariners, started in ten minutes. Perfect timing. "Bertie, I gotta go. Help me to the
john, would ya?"

The effort took Jack a little longer than he'd like, and
by the time he'd collapsed back into bed, the Mariners had
men on second and third with no outs. The Rangers'
pitcher was two down in the count.

Then things really got bad.

"Good evening, you old goat." Adele Watkins swept
into the room carrying a bed tray of food.

Why did women persist in battering him with beans?
Determined not to look, Jack forced his concentration to
remain on the screen. Then the tempting aroma of roasted
beef drifted past his nose and seduced him. "Is that Widow
Mallow's rump roast?"

"Nope, it's mine. And just a warning to you, sir, the day
you or anybody else uses the 'W' word in relation to me, I'll
slap you silly. Now here." She set the tray at the foot of the
bed and flipped him a cloth napkin. "Find a comfortable
spot, and I'll set up the tray. Bertie, I've a plate ready for you
on the kitchen table."

The prospect of roast beef, mashed potatoes and gravy,
and fresh green beans energized The Narc, and he bolted
from the room. "I never would have guessed the man could
stir his stumps that fast," Adele marveled.

Jack didn't reply. He was busy digging into his supper.

The lack of response didn't affect that woman one bit. She plopped her orange pants—*orange pants on a woman her age!*—down in the La-Z-Boy beside his bed and set about ruining his digestion.

"I want to talk to you about your daughter."

Jack didn't say anything, simply continued to eat. He figured that was his best defense.

"As I've previously mentioned, I've been washing the Harmon family laundry for years. I know your secrets."

Secrets? Jack's thoughts immediately went to his finances. How could she know . . . ?

She couldn't. Nobody knew. Not Tom. Not his bookkeeper at Harmon Lanes. Not even his lawyer.

Jack swallowed a bite of creamy mashed potatoes and delicious brown gravy, licked his lips, and considered the old bat. The lake house. Had they found out he'd put the lake house up for sale?

His stomach lurched at the thought, and he set down his fork, his appetite gone. "Go away, woman. Leave me in peace."

"No. The only 'piece' you're getting is a piece of my tongue. Answer a question for me, Jack Harmon. Do you love your daughter?"

Jack blinked. "What kind of fool question is that?"

"A legitimate one. I've been part of Kate's life for fifteen years, and I've seen little evidence that you care much at all. I don't like you, Jack. If it were up to me, you'd lie there at the mercy of The Narc and The Widows. However, Kate made the decision to do her daughterly duty and return to this mean-minded little burg, and in doing so, has created for herself no end of problems. I won't allow them to become worse than need be."

Good Lord, the woman reminded him of his wife. Linnie had that same snippy note in her voice when she scolded him, usually when it had something to do with the children.

"Now, I've just passed a half hour or so with a little girl who lives in the neighborhood who, for some strange reason, thinks you are a nice man. She tells me you talk to her about your grandson. Apparently, you follow Ryan's sports activities. I have to say I'm shocked at the news. It makes me wonder what else you may be hiding."

Jack didn't like being snipped at, so he allowed his mind to wander. Though he gazed at Adele Watkins, his mind took refuge in the past. He didn't get lost there. He didn't think Adele was his dead wife or anything. That had happened once with Sarah, and it had thrown them both for a loop. No, right now he focused his mind on memories. Good memories. Long-ago memories.

Linnie had been a good wife and even after all these years, Jack missed her every day. They'd had a fine life together. Linnie kept a clean house, put tasty, hot food on the table every night, and ironed his shirts just the way he liked them. She'd been respectful of his role as the provider for the family, and he'd stayed out of her way running the household.

"Now, little Shannon Cooper seems like a bright child," Adele said. "I like to think children have a sixth sense when it comes to character judgment, so it gives me hope that you might be redeemable. You have a unique opportunity here, Jack, if you'll just open those blind eyes of yours and see it."

Linnie took care of the kids. She'd assigned them their

chores and helped them with their homework and listened to their prayers at night. She'd disciplined them, too, only calling on him when they required something extra. His involvement had been the big stick she carried, and it had worked, too. He rarely intruded in day-to-day matters. He'd liked it that way, and so had Linnie.

He hadn't a clue about what the kids had thought about it. About him.

Adele continued to yammer. "You can't go back and fix all your mistakes of the past, but it is within your power to avoid making new ones. I'm not asking you to do anything totally out of character like treat your daughter as if you love her. I do want you to be kind to Kate while we're here. No more snotty remarks like you made when we arrived. Even old goats like you can be kind. Shannon Cooper thinks so, anyway. Now, finish your supper." Adele stood and smoothed the wrinkles from her bright orange britches. "I made peach cobbler for dessert."

Peach cobbler. I hate peach cobbler. Linnie knows that. Why did she make peach cobbler?

Crickets chirped, and the melodic tones of a wind chime floated in the night air as Kate made her way toward the neighborhood park. The aroma of fried chicken drifted from the open windows of the house next door and left her teased by nausea. Kate never could eat when she was nervous. Tonight she was nervous with a capital *N*.

Far above her, pulsing white lights against the sooty sky marked an airliner headed west. She halted to watch it a moment, wishing she were aboard, headed away from the coming discussion rather than toward it.

It had been one helluva day, and it wasn't over yet. She'd rather face a month of April fifteenths than have this conversation with Ryan. If she found him, that is.

He'd spent the afternoon at Harmon Lanes, coming home for supper, then lighting out again right after dessert with his basketball and a hollow look in his eyes. Seeing Max had shaken him, that much was clear. The murkier question was his reaction now that he'd had time to think about it.

Kate suspected she'd find her son at the cement pad that served as a basketball court in Weeks Park. She used childhood shortcuts through backyards and alleys, entering the park between the swing set and the teeter-totters. She paused for a moment as nostalgia caught her in its grip.

Paint peeled from the park's thirty-year-old metal playground equipment. She eyed the tall slide, recalling the many times she'd thrown herself down it, forward, backward, feetfirst, headfirst. Sometimes two people at a time. Sometimes four. Sometimes on summer days when the metal was so hot it left long red streaks of burned skin. It was a wonder the city hadn't gotten rid of this playground equipment years ago to avoid liability issues.

But heavens, she'd had a lot of fun on the slide and swings and merry-go-round.

The *thump thump rattle* of a ball against a backboard came from the far end of the park and drew Kate toward her son. In the fading light, she watched Ryan set up a shot. Her chest ached with emotion. He had Max's hands. Big hands with long narrow fingers made for clutching a basketball. Funny, for all the times she'd studied her son searching for signs of his father, she'd never before noticed the similarity of their hands. Probably because her son hadn't matured the last time she'd seen his father.

Her son. Their son. Their secret. What was best for Ryan?

She gazed around the park, confirming their privacy, before calling, "Play a game of horse?"

His shoulders stiffened. He missed the shot he took. "No, I—"

"Please?"

A long sigh. "Sure, Mom."

Their competitions never lasted long. Depending on his mood, Ryan either dealt with her swiftly, defeating her in five shots, or he played around with her, attempting impossible shots in order to extend the game. From the first shot, she could tell it was going to be an h-o-r-s-e and out night.

She tried joking with him, acting silly, but couldn't get a smile to crack the serious expression on his face. Finally, down to only an "e," she conceded defeat. She shot Ryan the ball and said, "I didn't know Max was in town."

He dribbled the ball. *Thump. Thump. Thump.*

"The little girl said they've lived here since Christmas."

"I didn't know. I don't talk to anyone from Cedar Dell. You know that. And I've pretty much dodged Max's calls for months."

Ryan shot her a sharp look.

"It's hard for me to talk to him, Ryan. All I ever do is tell him that no, you won't talk to him."

"My shrink said I don't have to talk to him."

"Oh, I know that," Kate said, disgust lacing her tone. "I wish I'd never agreed to send you to Dr. Harliss. I don't think he's done one bit of good. In fact, I think he's exacerbated the problem, and I no longer trust his advice."

"What do you mean, you agreed? My seeing a shrink was your idea."

"No, actually, it wasn't. When months went by, and you showed no signs of letting go of your anger, Max feared I was brainwashing you against him."

"That's stupid. We never talk about him."

"He didn't know that. In custody battles, parents do that sort of thing all the time."

"A custody battle?" Ryan scoffed. "Yeah, right. C'mon, Mom. The question of custody has never come up with Max the Ass."

"Stop it. I won't have you talking that way. No matter what Max has or hasn't done, he's still your father."

Though Ryan spoke beneath his breath, she still heard his words. "You're one to talk."

Kate summoned her patience. "It's called Parental Alienation Syndrome. When you gave permission for Dr. Harliss to discuss your case with your parents, he told Max—"

"Wait a minute. I didn't say he could talk to Max. I said he could talk to you."

"Read the papers you sign next time, Hot Rod. It read *parents*. Plural."

"Shit."

"Ryan . . ." she warned.

He dribbled the basketball twice, then took another shot. Kate continued, "Dr. Harliss convinced both Max and me that you'd be better off if we backed off and gave you time to deal with . . . with . . ."

"The truth," Ryan spat. "That my *father*"— he sneered the word—"lied to me about everything important."

"Now, Ryan. He didn't . . ."

"Stop it, Mom. You always defend him. I'm so *tired* of that." *Thump. Thump. Swish.*

Halogen lights flickered. Soft white light slowly illuminated the court, and Kate studied her son's expression. Anger snapped in his eyes and flattened his mouth into a thin, grim line. Frustration ate at Kate. Ryan's maturity inevitably disappeared at the first mention of his father.

Summoning a calm, rational tone, she said, "And I'm tired of you being unreasonable about Max. You make no effort at all to give him a chance."

"And he deserves one? Hah!" *Thump. Thump. Rattle.* The ball circled the rim, then fell through the net. Ryan caught it and held it, facing Kate. "Maybe I'll give him a chance like the one he gave me when he gave you money to have me aborted."

The ugly word echoed across the night.

Kate's heart thudded. She closed her eyes. If her ex-husband were here right now, she'd slug him in the gut. She wished she'd never met Roger Thurman, much less married him. *Damn you, Roger, for your jealousy and the heartache it caused.*

Thump. Thump. Thump. Thump. Thump. Thump. Thump.

"Or maybe I should give ol' Max the chance he gave me when he arranged to give me away to strangers." Ryan dribbled the ball twice, then executed a spinning layup. "Tell me something, Mom. I've always wondered. Do adoption agencies have trucks like Goodwill parked at the edge of a

Wal-Mart parking lot? You drive up, unload the castoff, get your receipt, and go shop for dinner?"

Every word pierced Kate's heart. Despite three years, hours and hours of therapy, and every ounce of love and security she could offer, Ryan's anger seethed as strong as it had at the beginning, when his stepfather had told him the truth with an ugly twist.

"Ryan, please. I thought you'd worked your way past this."

"Oh?" He shot her the basketball. Hard. "You mean the part about your role in it all? How you opened the door on my eighth birthday and let Daddy Max and his lies stroll inside?"

That made her mad. She fired the ball back to him. "That's not fair. I made mistakes, plenty of mistakes, but letting Max Cooper come into your life was not one of them. He was a good father to you until you let Roger poison you against him."

"A good father? How can you say that, Mom? The man didn't *want* me. Not before I was born. Not when I was born. Up until I turned eight, the man was a ghost."

"He didn't disappear entirely," Kate defended. "He paid child support every month."

"Big damn deal."

"Yes, it was a 'big damn deal.' " Kate braced her hands on her hips. "His college scholarship only covered tuition and fees, and he had to work to pay the rest. He signed an Air Force contract so he could send the monthly stipend to us. Without his money, you and I wouldn't have made it."

"Okay, fine. So he paid for me, but he still didn't want me. Not for years, and then only on his own terms. We had it good with Roger, and Max had to screw everything up. He caused your divorce."

"No," Kate snapped. "You're wrong, Ryan. Max did not cause my breakup with Roger. Roger and I alone are responsible for the failure of our marriage. Not Max . . ." She narrowed her eyes and watched him carefully as she added, "and certainly not you."

Sure enough, his spine went stiff. She'd hit a nerve.

Thump. Thump. Thump. Ryan spoke in a sullen tone. "You left Roger because he told me about Max."

"I left Roger because he'd proven himself to be a cruel man."

"Because he told the truth?"

"Because he cruelly betrayed a confidence in a way intended to hurt and destroy. He put an ugly spin on the facts, Ryan. You're old enough, smart enough to see that. Maybe at fourteen that was asking too much, but now you're seventeen, almost an adult. You need to start acting like it. You need to open your eyes and ears and mind."

"To what, Mom? I know what happened. No matter how he said it, Roger told the truth. I know what Max Cooper did."

"But you don't know *why* he did it."

Thump. Thump. Thump. Thump. Thump. "I don't need to know why."

Kate took a step toward him. "That's where you're dead wrong. You do need to hear the 'why' and it needs to come from him. From your father."

"*Max.*"

"Your *father.*"

Ryan shot her a furious glare. "I thought Dr. Harliss said to give me time."

"You've had time. In hindsight, probably too much time. I let things ride because I . . . well . . . we were getting along fine, you and me and Adele. But it's not just the three of us anymore. Max lives in Cedar Dell. For the next two to three months, you and I are living in Cedar Dell. You can't ignore him any longer."

"I'll go home to Dallas," Ryan said, sounding a little bit desperate. "I'll stay with friends. I don't have to stay here."

"Yes, you do. You have a little sister living in Cedar Dell whom you need to get to know."

He threw the ball hard out into the shadows of the park. "Yeah. That's right. A sister. A kid that Max Cooper wanted."

He ran out into the park after his ball, scooped it up, and kept on running. Kate groaned and lifted her hands to her head, tugging on her hair. As her son disappeared into the darkness, her gaze fell on the merry-go-round. "And I thought being a mom was hard when my son was in diapers."

Chapter Six

By HER FOURTH FULL DAY in Cedar Dell, Kate seriously fantasized about running away from home. She devised a number of different methods to carry out her plan, ranging from sneaking out in the middle of the night with nothing more than a backpack and her brother's old Vista ten-speed, to announcing her departure by way of a banner flown from the tail of a biplane as her hired, candy-apple red limo whisked her out of town. Never mind that she'd never seen a candy-apple red limo before. Surely they existed. If they didn't, they should.

Maybe that's what she should do. Forget about accounting. Forget about partnerships. Forget about fathers and sons and old lovers and old ladies. She should go into the limo business and hire out to crazed women in the midst of a middle-aged crisis. Women drivers only—no men. She would stock the bar with V-8 juice, vitamins, and vodka. And chocolate, of course.

"What sort of middle-aged crisis can a girl have without chocolate?" she muttered, refraining, just, from giving her finicky computer a swift kick. Network, shmetwork. What she wouldn't give for her nice, comfortable, functional office right now.

She'd lost a client earlier that morning because she wasn't available to solve a crisis. When her client attempted to reach her, she'd been away from her new home office delivering empty casserole dishes to The Widows on demand. The sporadic cell phone service in Cedar Dell only compounded the problem. A point she'd make to Max, by the way, the next time the address issue came up.

The phone at the house rang just fine. Her sister called three times before noon, her brother once. Max phoned at eight-fifteen on the dot, just as he had every day this week, the call apparently his first act upon his return from dropping his daughter off at school.

He wanted updates on Ryan—what he was thinking, feeling, saying. Since her son barely spoke to her at all, Kate couldn't tell Max much. During that first eight-fifteen call, rather than hanging up right away, Max asked her about her job, and they talked for almost five minutes. The next time he phoned, they discussed his work for closer to ten. The conversation about Cedar Dell lasted a good twenty.

Kate found herself looking forward to his calls. It was strange. For half her lifetime, she'd thought of Max Cooper as Ryan's father, period. Now, in the space of a few days, he'd become . . . Max.

What was up with that?

Ryan was easier to figure out. The boy was in hiding. He seldom left his room; played video games almost nonstop. He blew up digital monsters as a means of escape.

"Well, I'm about to pull his plug," she said, scowling in the general direction of his bedroom. The hiding had gone on long enough. Sure, Max's turning up in Cedar Dell had shocked him, but that was reality, and Ryan had better deal with it. Soon.

For someone so intellectually bright and physically quick, when it came to dealing with emotional issues, the boy was slow as cold molasses.

"He must be like Max in that way," Kate muttered beneath her breath. Ryan sure didn't get it from her. She preferred dealing with problems head-on, then putting them behind her as soon as possible.

For instance, had she been the one estranged from her son, no way would it have lasted three years. Never mind what the psychologist advised, she'd have trusted her instincts and acted. Confronted the problem and fixed it.

"Speaking of which," she said, sighing and scowling at the phone. She needed to return Nicholas Sutherland's call. He, too, had phoned during her dish delivery duty, and had personally left a message on her machine asking to see her again.

She hadn't spoken with Nicholas since the night of the accident. He'd called once and talked to Adele, asking about Dad and Sarah, then mentioning that he had a business trip to take but he'd contact Kate again on his return to Dallas. Adele, being Adele, didn't let him off that easy. She pried into his motives until he stated that he and Kate still had a date to finish and a business proposition to discuss.

While the first statement intrigued her, the second made her dread returning his call. Knowing her luck he'd offer her a dream job, one that required she start next week. She'd have to turn it down, then she'd spend the next fifty years wondering "what if."

Nothing new in that. Her whole life had been what-ifs and if-onlys. When did her turn come?

The question had no answer, so she scowled at the phone, looked up Nicholas Sutherland's number in her Rolodex, then pushed the appropriate buttons.

"Mr. Sutherland's office."

"This is Kate Harmon returning Mr. Sutherland's call."

Moments later, Nicholas himself came on the line. "Kate. Please tell me you're downstairs and ready to whisk me away from the drudgery of paperwork to a deserted isle where we'll dine on passion fruit and gambol naked in the surf."

"Gambol?" she repeated with a laugh as an intriguing image of a naked Nicholas Sutherland surrounded by sand and sea flashed through her head.

"Frolic is such a sissy word, and the other verb that comes to mind probably isn't appropriate at this stage of our relationship."

Danged if her mouth didn't go dry as a West Texas July.

"When can I see you again, Kate?" he continued. "How about dinner on Thursday? Say around eight?"

Kate cleared her throat. "No, I'm sorry. I can't. I'm afraid I won't be able to come into Dallas for the foreseeable future."

"That's all right. I'll come to Cedar Dell."

Okay. What in the world was going on here? While it did her ego good to think his pursuit was personal, she sensed this mysterious business proposition provided much of the motivation.

Downstairs, her father called, "Kate? You still here? Where's Bertie? I need Bertie!"

On Kate's left, the fax line rang, and the machine started grinding away. To her right, the computer mooed at her. Ryan must have changed the sounds on her instant messaging again, the pill. Outside, the neighbor's big Labrador retriever let loose with a series of deep-throated *woofs* that Kate had learned signaled he'd treed something, usually a squirrel, and a glance out the window informed her that this time, that something was someone named Shannon Cooper. The little girl began to cry. Loudly.

Woof. Woof. Woof.

"Bertie," came her father's voice, "get your ass in here."

She simply couldn't deal with any more. "Nicholas, thank you, but no. I can't. As much as I'd love to know what this is all about, I can't. I've—"

"Help me! Harold is eating my shoe!"

"—got to go see a dog about a shoe."

She hung up the phone and dashed downstairs. On her way out the door, she discovered Bertie asleep at the kitchen table. She shook him awake, then hurried outside.

Shannon sat on the ground giggling as Harold licked her face. Her shoe was history.

Kate sat on the stoop and laughed. Hysterically.

In the empty, unending hours before dawn, Max Cooper dreamed.

Her belly swollen with child, his wife lies tethered to a hospital bed by dozens of IV lines. He wears green doctor's scrubs and carries a scalpel as he enters the room. Rose sees him, begins to struggle and scream.

Light glints off the blade as it descends. Slashes through skin.

Blood fountains. Spatters warm against him. Copper in his mouth.

Somewhere, a baby cries. Then goes silent.

Max jerked upright in bed, gasping, drenched in sweat. His eyes round with horror.

"Shit." He shuddered. "Shit. Shit. Shit."

He sat on the edge of his bed, the sheet crumpled in his fists, and tried to shake off the remnants of the recurring nightmare. He thought it might take twenty or thirty years. Guilt overwhelmed him.

God help me. He'd gone months without the dream. Almost a year. He thought he was done with this crap. "Apparently not."

He pushed to his feet and crossed the room to his dresser, where he picked up the photo of Rose and their newborn little girl. A shudder racked him again as he traced the faces with a fingertip. Such a happy day. Such a happy time.

"Oh, hell, Rosie."

She found the lump early in her pregnancy. Her doctor diagnosed it as a clogged milk duct and told her not to worry. By the time Shannon was born, it had nearly doubled in size. Even in the birthing room, her doctor dismissed her concerns.

At Rose's six-week postpartum visit, the quack finally decided the lump merited a second look. Seven months later, Max's wife was dead.

Grimacing, Max dropped the photograph onto his bed. He stumbled into the bathroom, popped three ibuprofen, and turned the shower on hot. Steam rose, clung to the mirror, obscuring his reflection. Thank God. He couldn't bear looking at himself in the aftermath of the nightmare.

It haunted him to know that treatment might have saved Rosie. It tormented him to admit he'd have opted to abort the child who was now the light of his life.

"Two for two, asshole," he said as he stepped into the shower. Sharp needles of heat pounded his skin. Shannon and Ryan. On mornings like this, he knew he didn't deserve to be a father.

Luckily, God had given his children great mothers. Kate took care of Ryan. Rose had been a lioness protecting her cub from the moment the pee stick turned blue. Had her cancer been diagnosed earlier, Rose wouldn't have terminated the pregnancy. She'd have told Max to go blow. She'd told him so later when grief had him screaming what-ifs. No regrets, she'd said.

Regrets had poured from Max like poison. In the last weeks of Rose's life, he'd resented Shannon. Hated her, almost. He'd refused to hold her for a full week after Rose died.

"I was such a shit." Max stuck his head beneath the showerhead and let the water beat against his skull until he'd drained the water heater dry.

Thank God for Nana Jean. She hadn't let it go on any longer than that. She took herself off to a movie, leaving Shannon alone with her sorry excuse for a dad. When the baby woke from her nap, he let her cry. He'd stood just outside the nursery door, a band of emotion tightening his chest like a vise until finally, maybe five minutes later, he crumbled.

He'd opened the door, marched to the crib, and lifted

his daughter into his arms. He'd sat in the rocking chair, cuddling her. Crying. Long after the baby's tears had ceased.

Max stayed in the shower while the cold water punished his skin. The memories added to the nightmare made him feel as if a cement truck had run him down. He dried off slowly, dressed, and went downstairs.

As the sun climbed above the treetops, he stood staring out the back door, a steaming mug in his hand. His thoughts kept circling back to one desperate question.

Max drained his coffee, then reached for the wall phone. He punched out the number he dialed daily on the portable receiver.

"Hello?" Kate Harmon said sleepily on the other end of the line.

"Do you think I can be a good father?"

She waited a long moment before replying. "Good morning, Max. You're calling rather early today, aren't you? It's . . . jeez. It's barely after six."

"It wasn't that I didn't love them. I did. Right from the very beginning. Rose knew it. Did you, Kate?"

A pause. "Max, what are you talking about?"

He heard the click of a lamp switch, the rustle of sheets, and punches at a pillow. "What's wrong, Max?"

He pushed open the screen door and stepped into the backyard. Above him, burgeoning white clouds hung in a dawn sky shimmering in bright shades of gold and cerulean. It was, he thought, like looking at heaven.

"Never mind. I'm sorry. I had the nightmare. You're Ryan's mother. I thought maybe . . . hell."

"*The* nightmare?"

Settling into the glider, he stretched his legs out in front of him and dropped his head back. He closed his eyes and gave her a brief, but graphic, description.

"Even a dumb-shit jet-jockey like me can figure out the symbolism. I cut the cancer out, destroyed it. Sacrificed the child to save the mother. Kate, I'd have pressured Rose to take that route had we found the cancer earlier."

"What a terrible choice to face." Her voice brimmed with understanding.

Guilt clogged his throat, and he couldn't speak.

He heard Kate's lamp click off, lending an intimacy to the moment. "I regret not meeting Rose," she said. "I always enjoyed speaking with her on the phone. She was friendly and interested in Ryan." The line hummed between them. "Does Shannon look like her mother?"

The question took him back years to the sands of Waikiki Beach during his posting at Hickam. He'd never forget the first time he saw Rose, walking along the edge of the surf, carrying sexy white sandals and eating a peach. So beautiful. Eyes the color of the ocean. She'd winked at him. Later, they joked about it being lust at first sight. "Yeah, she does."

"While Ryan looks more like you every day."

Max summoned a mental picture of his son. At eight years old. Now, almost eighteen. "My regrets are immense, Kate. Gargantuan. I made so many mistakes. My children paid for them. You and Rose paid for them."

Kate finally addressed the question that prompted his call. "You're a good father to Shannon, Max. You'll work this out with Ryan and be a good father to him again, too."

Max leaned forward, propped his elbows on his knees, and stared down at the green beneath his feet. "I need you to know that I loved him, Kate. From the very beginning. I was scared and selfish and stupid, but I always loved him."

"I screwed up with Shannon, too. Maybe not on such a grand scale as with Ryan, but for a while there, I earned F's in the 'Daddy' department. Since then I've tried so hard to make it up to her. I want to make it up to Ryan, too. More than anything, I want to make it up to Ryan. I want to be his dad again. I can be a good father to him."

She waited a long moment before replying. "I know. Ryan will figure it out, too."

"God, I hope so." Max sat up straight, plucked at a loose fleck of paint on the glider, and changed the subject. "So. What's on your agenda for today?"

They spoke a few more minutes about their plans for the day. As the conversation wound down, he stood and rubbed the back of his neck. "Kate . . . um . . . I . . . thanks. Thanks for listening to me."

"Glad to help. I know what it's like to need a sympathetic ear."

Max returned to the kitchen and fixed breakfast with a lighter heart. He decided it would be a Froot Loops day for Shannon, but he'd insist she balance it out with yogurt and a piece of fruit, too.

He'd just added bacon for himself to the frying pan when he heard the toilet flush upstairs. A few minutes later, Shannon walked into the kitchen, fists rubbing her eyes, her mouth open wide in a yawn. "Good mornin', Daddy."

"Good morning, Shanabanana."

She had her mother's smile.

Gladness filled Max's heart.

The day began like the day before for Kate. Total disaster.

The Widow Mallow came calling with a coffee cake before the Folgers had finished brewing. Mrs. Gault followed almost on her heels with homemade donuts. Wearing only boxers and his favorite Texas Rangers shirt—the homemade one declaring YANKEES SUCK—Ryan stubbed his toe on the way into the kitchen and let loose with a widow-scandalizing stream of curses. Then Bertie called to say he'd be late. Kate's dad would have to wait for afternoon to take his shower, and he'd try to refuse the bedpan.

Kate blamed it all on Max Cooper for starting her day prematurely.

Her business phone rang half a dozen times by eight-thirty. She finally cleared the kitchen of widows at nine, but only after promising to provide a plate of cookies for the church bake sale on Sunday.

When Adele suggested she bring store-bought, Kate choked on her orange juice. Having a child out of wedlock struck a serious blow to Kate's reputation. But store-bought cookies at a church bake sale? The entire Harmon family would have to leave town in disgrace.

After a bit of persuasion, her father agreed that Ryan could help him get washed and dressed. Ryan did the chore cheerfully, finishing up just as The Narc put in an appearance, then disappeared back into his room. Soon, Kate heard the sound of swords clashing and guns blasting and buildings exploding.

"Stupid video games," she muttered as the power to her calculator went off. She refused to allow him to spend the summer wasting his time with digital destruction. The boy needed a summer job, one that looked good on his college applications. It wouldn't hurt him to find volunteer work to do, too. Not only was it a good use of a teenager's time, but university admissions offices viewed volunteer hours favorably when considering an application.

At that point the fax machine spat out another problem, and for the next few hours, Kate worked without a major interruption. She was in the middle of a payroll report when Adele stuck her head into the room. "Your dad is going stir-crazy today, honey. He wants to go to Dairy Queen for lunch, and then take in a matinee. That new Mel Gibson movie. Thought I'd go along, too."

Kate set down her pencil. A movie? That shouldn't be too much for Dad. "You're planning to drive, I hope? I'm not sure I trust Bertie behind the wheel."

"Actually, Ryan's coming with us."

"You're kidding."

"Nope. Said he's in the mood for onion rings. We need to take your car, anyway. We won't all fit in Bertie's truck."

Kate smiled. Having the house all to herself sounded heavenly.

She worked in peace until the rumbling in her stomach sent her downstairs in search of something to eat. She made a sandwich and sat at the table. Halfway through her meal, as she gazed around the kitchen, she noticed a cobweb hanging in the corner above the refrigerator. "So that's what Martha Gault stared at so smugly this morning."

It wouldn't do. It was one thing to be known as the Slut

of Cedar Dell, but she'd be damned if they'd talk about her housekeeping skills, too. Kate had more pride than that.

She made a quick trip upstairs and changed into a sports bra and her rattiest cut-off jean shorts. She pulled her hair into a Cindy Lou Who ponytail atop her head, turned on the radio, and went to work. An hour later, she'd conquered the dining room and the powder room downstairs. As soon as she finished the family room, she intended to tackle the kitchen.

Kate stood at the top of a ladder cleaning a ceiling fan and singing along with Jimmy Buffett when the doorbell rang. She glanced at the clock. Time for the overnight mail delivery. Good. She'd been waiting on a set of contracts. Kate drew her dust rag along the fan blade, and called, "Come on in, Mike. It's open. Leave the package on the dining room table for me, would you?"

The man who stepped inside wasn't Mike the delivery guy. The man who stepped inside wore an Armani suit. Dressed in a sports bra and cutoffs, Kate had the handle of a hot pink feather duster stuck down her pants.

Nicholas Sutherland's blue eyes gleamed. "Hello, Kate."

"I'm tired." Jack struggled to his feet in the movie theater lobby. "I want to go home. Now."

In the process of digging a Junior Mint from the box, Bertie Ellis looked up with alarm. "But the show starts in five minutes."

Adele popped a kernel of buttered popcorn into her mouth. "What's the matter with you, Jack? It was your idea to see this matinee."

Ryan looked at his grandfather, noted the determined glint in his eye. Adele wasn't going to win this one.

"I'm tired. I want to leave now. You and Bertie stay and watch the movie. Ryan can take me home. You weren't all red-hot about seeing this show anyway, were you, boy?"

"No, sir. Romantic comedies aren't my thing. I'll be happy to take you home."

"Fine." Adele glared at Jack. "We'll all go. It's Bertie's job to—"

"To do what I say," Jack snapped back, his glare even meaner than Adele's. "I don't want him lurking around watching me sleep this afternoon. You and Bertie stay and watch the movie, and Ryan will pick you up when it's over."

He turned to Ryan. "Go get the car, son. I'll meet you out front."

Ryan could tell Adele intended to put up a fuss, so he leaned over and kissed her cheek. "It's okay, Adele. I'll stay with him. I think there might be a baseball game on this afternoon."

She grumbled a moment before giving in. Ryan grabbed a handful of her popcorn, winked, then stepped outside the cool, dark theater lobby into the hot afternoon air.

He whistled his way to the parking lot. Granddad had been right. He didn't mind missing the movie, although he'd just as soon not go back to his granddad's house. Those walls were closing in on him.

Ryan liked video games as much as the next guy, but a few days of nonstop gaming left him looking for something else to occupy his time. At home in Dallas, he'd call his friends and go out. He'd stop by the rec center and join a pickup game of basketball or cruise by Corvette City to dream a little. He'd have plenty of activities to choose from in Dallas, and none of them required that he check over his shoulder every five minutes like he had today at Dairy Queen.

If Max Cooper had walked into that restaurant today, Ryan would have puked up his onion rings.

This entire situation made Ryan crazy. He didn't want to think about Max Cooper. Especially didn't want to see him. Didn't want to get to know the man's daughter, no matter what his mother said.

"Should never have left Dallas without my truck," he muttered as he fished in his pocket for his mother's keys. So what if it needed a new alternator. And hoses. And a fan. He could have hung around a few days until the shop finished the repairs. Then he wouldn't be stuck without his own wheels.

Better yet, he could go home and get the truck. And not come back. He could live by himself for the summer. He bet if he groveled, he could get that engineering internship back. That would make Mom happy. He could keep the grass cut and the flowers watered. She worried about her flowers. He was responsible. Mom could trust him.

She'd kill him if he went home without her permission.

She'd already told him no when he asked about spending the summer in Dallas by himself. Five different times. Her stance on the matter was downright unreasonable, in his opinion. He was almost eighteen years old. Almost an adult.

That argument got him nowhere when he'd used it last night. She'd told him *almost* was the operative word, and that if he wanted to be treated like an adult, he needed to quit acting like a child by hiding in his room all day.

"I'm not hiding." Ryan thumbed the keyless entry remote and unlocked his mother's car. He just hadn't wanted to stumble across Max Cooper at the Dairy Queen while looking for a fast-food fix.

This entire father business made him crazy. What was he supposed to do? Just forget and forgive? Not hardly. Why should he? He didn't need Max Cooper. He didn't need a sister. He had Mom and Adele. Granddad.

His granddad was cool. Crusty, but cool.

He settled into the driver's seat, started the car, and pulled out of the parking space, heading for the box office at the front of the theater. Bertie held the door open as Jack shuffled outside.

Ryan stopped next to the two men, then hopped out to help get his grandfather and his walker inside. As they pulled away from the curb, he told Ryan to take a right on Pecan. "That's not the way home, Granddad."

"We're not going home."

Ryan shot him a look. "We're not?"

"Keep your eyes on the road. No. We're going to the bowling alley. I got work that needs attending to."

Ryan processed that for half a block. "But you said—"

"I lied." His thin, dry lips stretched in a satisfied grin. "Slicker than snot on a doorknob, too."

Ryan considered this a moment. "Mom's gonna blow a gasket."

Jack's shrug declared his lack of concern.

Gravel crunched beneath the tires as Ryan turned into

the Harmon Lanes parking lot. He pulled the car into the handicapped parking space closest to the door, then helped his grandfather maneuver the wheeled walker inside Harmon Lanes.

The lady at the front desk looked up. A smile split her face. "Look everybody. The boss is back!"

Time paused in its march. Bowling balls stopped rolling. Vanilla Cokes quit flowing. The bell on the old brass cash register didn't ring a single sale. Ryan watched with interest as the patrons and employees of Harmon Lanes gathered their leader to their proverbial bosom.

A man whose name tag read JOE BARTON, ASSISTANT MANAGER sauntered over to Jack, and said, "Hey, boss. Ball return is broken in Lane Four again. You want me to order that gear we talked about getting or should I jury-rig it again?"

A guy about Ryan's age wiped his hands on his white apron, leaving behind a smear of chocolate. "Mr. Harmon, we're completely out of strawberry syrup. You want me to call the supplier?"

"Jack Harmon, it's about time you showed up." A woman with bright, bottle red hair scurried out of the beauty shop and shook a perm rod at him. "Do you know my hot water's been on the blink for two days? I can't give shampoos with ice-cold water."

"Oh, quit your griping," Jack responded, his voice gruff. "Y'all make it sound like this place has gone to hell in a handbasket since I've been gone. If a man can't take a few days off without everything around him falling apart, then I need to fire some folks."

Then, because this was Cedar Dell, where the English

language apparently took a little twist, the crowd around Jack broke out into smiles. The beauty shop lady said, "See to my hot water first, boss. It's most important."

With a wave, a handshake, or a kiss on the cheek, they all went back to their jobs. Jack leaned on his walker with a smile on his face.

Ryan decided he'd never seen his grandfather look so happy.

Jack disappeared into his office to work, and Ryan passed the time by bowling a couple games. Afterward, he stopped by the soda fountain, ordered a Dr Pepper, and struck up a conversation with the pretty girl working behind the counter.

Anne Tucker liked to gossip. She knew everything about everybody in town—including one detail Ryan found fascinating about the newcomer, Max Cooper. He didn't bowl. Hardly ever came into Harmon Lanes. In fact, the only time she remembered his being there was the day he took The Widows' photo for the newspaper.

Ryan paid for his drink and headed for his grandfather's office, a plan brewing in his brain.

Jack couldn't find his checkbook. It belonged in his desk, but he'd gone through every drawer and rifled through every paper and still hadn't found it. He wondered if it might have fallen beneath the furniture, but he couldn't get down and look. He'd have to ask for help.

Dammit.

Jack knew no one had swiped it. In thirty years, he'd never had anything stolen from his office at Harmon Lanes.

No, the checkbook was just misplaced, and it would turn up eventually. Problem was, he needed it now. Right now.

He had to figure out why his bank statement showed his balance at less than a hundred dollars.

"Lousy, no-good bank," he muttered. Before the national chain swallowed up the Cedar Dell State Bank, Jack could have called the bank and talked to a real live person to straighten out the problem. Those days were over. Now he had to call an eight hundred number and talk to a machine. Heaven forbid he'd need to speak to a human to get his questions answered. They charged a fee for that. Shoot, they charged a fee for everything. Going down to the bank in person wouldn't solve anything, either. They'd just tell him to pick up the phone and dial customer service. "Customer service, hell. A man's better off burying his money in the backyard."

If he had money buried in his yard, he could dig it up and go buy a new car. He was starting to worry about not having his own transportation. The kids were bound to give him hell about getting something to replace the Cougar.

He'd miss that fire engine red sports car. He'd bought it on his eightieth birthday, and it had made him the talk of the town for a month. Folks had stopped by Harmon Lanes to give him a hard time, telling him right to his face how foolish it was for an old coot like him to buy a car like that. His barber, Fred Rawlins, had told him he was forty years too late to be having a midlife crisis. Jack had conceded there might be a grain of truth in the charge, but primarily, he'd bought the car because he liked the looks of it. Liked the power of it.

As soon as the insurance money came in, he'd go buy another, by God. Damned if he'd give up his keys. Tom and Sarah had been hinting at that lately. Tom had left a YMCA Senior Transportation Service brochure on Jack's desk last time he was home, and Sarah had come right out and asked him not to drive at night anymore. So far, no one had dared suggest he give up driving altogether, but he feared that was next.

"To hell with them," he grumbled. *He* was the parent, *they* were the children. His life was still his to lead. If he wanted to drive, by God, he'd drive. Because the day someone took away his car keys would be the day he'd lose his independence.

On that black day, they might as well plant him in the ground.

"Granddad? Can I talk to you a minute?"

Jack looked up to see Ryan standing in the doorway. He waved him inside. "Do me a favor, boy. Look under my desk and see if I dropped anything."

"Sure."

With the ease and grace of youth, Ryan dropped down onto all fours and came up with a pen, a handful of change, and, thank goodness, Jack's checkbook.

"I knew you had a lot of friends, Granddad. Everybody bringing food by the house, why I've never seen so many casseroles in my life. And I don't know who invented tuna casserole, but I wish they'd found something else to do that day."

"Rrrrr." He opened the check register and began to mark off the checks that had cleared. Electric bill. Water bill. Barbershop.

Ryan took a seat in the orange plastic chair opposite Jack's desk. "I've been eavesdropping out there. Everyone's real excited to have you back. They all think you look great, except for the bruise on your cheek, that is. The guys playing chess at the soda fountain started arguing about that. Can't decide on what shade of green it is. I stirred the pot a bit when I said it's shaped like Idaho."

"What do you want, boy?" Jack frowned at his check register. That's peculiar. He hadn't recorded a description for check number 7526. That wasn't like him at all.

"I've been thinking."

"Is that unusual for you?"

"Well, it *is* summer. I try not to do much thinking this time of year. Try to save all that for school."

"Don't want to waste it."

"Exactly."

Jack looked up from his checkbook. Wasn't like the boy to hem and haw. "Get to the point, son."

"Yeah, I guess I should."

Ryan dipped his head in a bashful manner so reminiscent of Linnie's that it caused Jack's heart to catch.

"I need to get a summer job, and I'd like it to be here at Harmon Lanes. I'm a good, trustworthy worker. I'm willing to do whatever needs doing around here. I'll help at the soda fountain, work maintenance on the ball returns. Anything you want. This place is cool."

Jack frowned. "What's your mama say about this?"

Ryan grimaced at that. "I haven't talked to her, and to be perfectly honest, I don't think she'll be too hot on the idea."

"She have something against working?"

"Mom?" Ryan laughed. "Not hardly. She thinks every teenager should have a job of some sort, even if they don't need the money. She and my stepdad used to go round and round about that. Roger didn't like my weekend job interfering with things he wanted to do, but Mom always said it's never too early to learn responsibility."

Humph. Never did think much of Roger Thurman.

"The thing is," Ryan continued, "she wants me to have a summer job that will look good on college applications. I'm pretty good in math, and I like to tinker around with things, so my mom thinks I should be an engineer. Before we decided to come here for the summer, she had arranged an internship for me at a mechanical engineering firm in Dallas. It would have been an okay job, I guess, except I didn't want to be an intern. I kinda doubt I even want to be an engineer."

Jack leaned back in his chair and scratched the back of his neck. It'd be nice to have the boy around the place this summer, away from the house and the women, where he could get to know him better. However, unless business had picked way up since he'd been out, Harmon Lanes couldn't support another employee. Hell, he could barely pay the ones he already had.

With regret, he said, "I'm not gettin' between you and your mama."

"It wouldn't be like that. I'm not asking you to say anything to her at all. I'll do all the talking. I just need to know if I can have a job. I figure she's going to get around to this in a day or two, so I need to have my ducks in a row first."

"I already have a couple of high school kids on the payroll, son. Don't really need anyone else."

Ryan leaned forward, his expression pleading. "I'll work for minimum wage. Shoot, I'd work for free, but Mom would have a cow about that. She has me saving for college. She has a spreadsheet worked up with quarterly goals I'm expected to meet. It's awful, Granddad, living with an accountant."

An accountant. Jack still had a difficult time picturing his daughter as a bean counter. Not the bookkeeping side of it. Kate always did keep good track of her money, and Harmon Lanes had employed a female bookkeeper or two over the years. They did a good job. But a certified public accountant? That was a man's position.

Jack's gaze strayed to the black vinyl checkbook. *Bet she could straighten out this mess in short order.*

Yeah, well, that would never happen. The thought of her digging around his financial business gave him the shakes. Wasn't any of her business what he did with his money.

She sure as hell didn't need to know what he intended to do with the lake house.

Jack's gaze drifted toward the framed photograph of their place at Possum Kingdom Lake. It was the same photograph the Realtor used to advertise it in the newspaper and on the Internet. Kate, herself, had taken that picture just last year, and she'd gotten a good shot not just of the house, but of the tree house.

The tree house always made him think of Kate.

Nestled among the spreading boughs of a hundred-year-old live oak, the structure bore the scars of more than twenty years of weather. Dappled sunlight spilled through a fist-sized hole in a wood shingle roof missing half a dozen shakes. Pockmarked plywood walls stood as silent witness to the fury of dozens of hailstorms, and on the west side a window shutter dangled by a single rusted hinge.

In his mind's eye, Jack saw the tree house as it had been when first built. The bright blond color of fresh lumber. Window shutters painted a peaceful forest green, with shiny brass hinges. He remembered how it was the day he helped Kate hang the finishing touch—a sign that read: HARMON'S HIDEOUT. NO TRESPASSING. Wonder what happened to that old sign.

Though Jack planned the structure as a playhouse for all three of his children, he'd expected Tom to use it most. He'd been wrong. From the moment he drove the first nail through the first pine board into the sturdy branch, the tree house became Kate's. She'd fetched and carried and hammered her heart out, long after her brother and sister had abandoned the task. Jack had gotten a real kick out of it, for those two spring weekends at the lake house while Harmon's Hideout took shape, Jack had been closer to his youngest than at any time before . . . or anytime since.

He let out a heavy sigh.

"Granddad?" Ryan leaned forward in his seat. "I'll do a real good job for you. I'll be the best hire you've ever made."

Jack cleared his throat. "You'd be better off looking for something else. Best I could do for you is part-time at minimum wage. Budget simply has no more give in it."

Ryan sat thinking, drumming his fingers on his knee. "She might go for that more easily, anyway. I could find some volunteer work to fill in the rest of the time. That's important to Mom, too. She's bound to bring it up."

His mouth broke out into a wide grin. He stood and held out his hand. "When do you want me to start, Boss?"

Swallowing his reservations, Jack shook his grandson's hand and indulged in a smile of his own. "Next week's soon enough. Tell the manager to expect you for the Monday afternoon shift. If it's okay with your mama, that is."

"I'll talk her into it. This will be great. Thanks, Granddad."

"Just don't make me regret it." He picked up an ink pen. "Now skedaddle. I have work to do."

"Okay." Ryan turned to leave, then at the office doorway, he stopped. "Granddad? I'm hoping this summer you and I can get to know each other better. Family is important, you know?"

Jack thought of Linnie, of Tom and his wife and children, of Sarah and Alan. Of Kate. "Yes, I do know, son. Family is mighty important."

If only it wasn't so damned hard to get along with.

Chapter Seven

KATE'S HAND JERKED, sending a rain of dust down upon her, adding a finishing touch to her ensemble.

"Nicholas." Heat stung Kate's cheeks as she blushed for the first time in years. She scrambled down the ladder, turned off the radio, brushed the dirt from her face, yanked the feather duster from her britches, and babbled. "Welcome to my home. Actually, it's Dad's home, but he's gone to the movies and this is where I live in Cedar Dell and . . ."

"At the movies is a good sign. So he's feeling well?" Nicholas glanced down at the item in her hand, a gleam of amusement reflected in his eyes.

Oh, damn. She tossed the feather duster on the couch and tried again, doing her best to pretend she wore a suit, panty hose. A shirt. "What are you doing here?"

"I had to be in town for business, and I took a chance I'd find you here. I apologize for dropping by unannounced." He flashed a grin. "Although, I did try to phone."

Okay, maybe he'd phoned. The business line had rung half a dozen times, but she'd ignored it in favor of ammonia and a toilet bowl brush. What she found unbelievable was the fact that Nicholas Sutherland, all six feet two inches of dark-haired, broad-shouldered feminine fantasy, stood in her father's family room.

Basic manners learned in this very room dictated her response. "No need to apologize for anything, Nicholas. May I offer you something to drink? Water? Iced tea?" She took a quick mental inventory of the fridge. "Mountain Dew?"

"No, thank you. What I would like is a half hour of your time."

Mountain Dew. Of course he wouldn't drink Mountain Dew. Would James Bond drink Mountain Dew? Not hardly. That's who Nicholas reminded her of today. A young Sean Connery as James Bond.

An errant clump of dust floated slowly from the fan to land on his suit lapel. What would he do if she picked up the feather duster and got rid of it?

Good heavens, what was wrong with her? Her hormones were running amok. She cleared her throat. "I'm happy to spend some time with you, Nicholas. Please, have a seat. If you'll excuse me a moment, I'll . . . um . . . put some shoes on."

His gaze lingered on her bare feet, her toenails painted an unprofessional Louisiana Hot Sauce red. "Don't bother on my account."

Kate's toes curled.

Giving a nervous smile, she retreated to her room, then made a mad dash for the closet. Khaki slacks, a camp shirt. In her bathroom, moisturizer, a little blush. Mascara. Lip gloss. Her hair? *Oh, God, look at my hair.*

She yanked out the ponytail holder and brushed away the dust, her thoughts spinning. Lustful foot glances aside, he had business on the mind. That business proposition he'd mentioned to Adele. Kate would bet her feather duster on it. *I had to be in town for business*, he'd said. So it wasn't just about her.

Dang it.

What business could corporate attorney Nicholas James Bond Sutherland have in Cedar Dell, Texas? Somehow, she couldn't see Microsoft or Boeing moving their company headquarters to her hometown.

Finished with her hair, Kate set down her brush. She, then bolted to her closet for shoes. There. Her brown loafers. Reaching for them, she hesitated. What the heck. He'd already seen her hot-saucy toenails. Kate slipped on a pair of sandals, then quickly made her way back downstairs.

She found him perusing what Adele jokingly referred to as Jack's altar wall, his collection of autographed baseball cards. "I don't suppose these are for sale?"

"He'd come closer to selling his firstborn, and my father really likes my brother."

His laughter set her at ease. "Are you certain I can't offer you something to drink?"

A martini, shaken, not stirred?

"Actually, I have reconsidered. Iced tea would be nice."

To her surprise and discomfort, he followed her and took a seat at the kitchen table. Gazillionaires simply didn't belong in her father's breakfast room. She fixed tea for them both, set a plate of cookies between them, and sat opposite him. "How can I help you, Nicholas?"

"I'm looking for something in Cedar Dell. I'd like your help in the search."

Well. Short and to the point. Most lawyers she knew

didn't have brevity in them; the term "legal brief" was an oxymoron.

Not a job with his firm, then. Her stomach dipped with disappointment, and she realized that ever since his first call, she'd nursed a quiet hope. "The search for what?" she asked. "For whom? Who's your client? Why come to me?"

In spite of Kate's mixed feelings toward her hometown, she couldn't help but feel protective of Cedar Dell. If giving her a job didn't bring him here, something else did. Nicholas Sutherland was a powerful man, and all this charm might hide a snake. He could pose a danger to Cedar Dell. What if he wanted to acquire land to build a nuclear waste dump at the city limits?

"I'm the client. The 'what' part of your question is a rather long story."

She gave him a deadpan look. "The dust bunnies under the couch will appreciate having a little more time to put their affairs in order."

He chuckled, then leaned back in his chair and drummed his fingers on the kitchen table. His restless hands betrayed intense purpose as his tone grew serious. "I'm on a personal quest, Kate, and the path leads to your hometown."

A personal quest? Natural gas, she thought. Bet he believed the Cedar Dell hills contained natural gas, and he's after land and mineral rights. Her stomach dipped even farther. He hadn't a clue about how little local goodwill she could bring to acquisitions.

He reached into his pocket. "Have you ever seen a piece similar to this?"

He held out a figurine of a woman approximately six

inches high. Hand-carved from wood and painted in colors of silver and cream, the figure was an exquisite miniature Greek statue. Intrigued, Kate studied the lovely item, marveling at the artistry of the workmanship. The woman rose from a pillow of clouds and wore a toga-like gown fastened over her left shoulder by an inset stone that glowed a warm red. Her limbs were long and graceful, her facial features classic. "She's beautiful. Who does it depict?"

"Aphrodite."

"The goddess of beauty. Of course. I should have recognized her."

He leaned forward, as focused and alert as a wolf after prey. "You've seen something like it before? In Cedar Dell?"

"In college. An art history class."

Disappointment dropped him back in the chair. From his wallet he removed a small card, which he pushed across the table toward her. The color drawing depicted another figurine similar to the one he'd showed her, but different in subtle ways. This Aphrodite was trimmed in gold, rather than silver, and her gown fastened on the right with a green stone.

A vague memory prodded her mind. "These figurines were not mass-produced, I assume?"

"Absolutely not." The urgency in his expression belied the casual tone as he asked, "Do you recognize it, Kate?"

"I think . . . maybe . . . I don't know." She lifted the statue from the table and studied it. "You mentioned a long story . . . ?"

He nodded, sipped his tea, and began.

"My grandmother grew up as the gardener's daughter on the country estate of a leader in the French steel industry.

She married a young chauffeur, and they had two children. Girls. The Germans occupied France in 1940, and like the majority of Frenchmen, my grandmother and her husband were neither collaborators nor members of the resistance, but simple, everyday people attempting to go about the business of living in difficult times."

Kate's gaze fastened on the figurine as she wondered just where this "long story" would take them. Reverence reverberated in his voice when he spoke of his grandmother. She obviously meant something special to him.

"In 1943, the Vichy government established *Le service du travail obligatoire*, a compulsory labor service formed to provide foreign workers to Germany. When my grandfather learned he was due to be conscripted, he took his family and fled their home to join the ranks of the resistance. Their first act of defiance was to rob the steel magnate's estate of the art and treasure he'd managed to shield from the Nazis.

"The figurines?"

Nicholas nodded. "A chess set. Rumor had it that it had once graced a tabletop in the palace of Versailles."

Kate took another hard look at the chess piece. "Is Aphrodite the queen?"

"Zeus is king. The pawns are Pan." Nicholas laid the silver Aphrodite in the palm of Kate's hand. "Grandfather put a few valuables aside as insurance for his family before turning the majority of the loot over to the freedom fighters. Sadly, he was killed five months later. My grandmother and her two daughters took refuge in a convent near St. Lo and soon 'Sister Madeleine' directed daily operations of St. Cecelia's orphanage."

"She posed as a nun."

"Yes. As talk of an Allied invasion swelled, supplies grew scarce. They needed food, medicine, clothing. My grandmother was determined to see her children—all her children—survive the war. They foraged what they could, begged the rest. Stole when necessary. Mostly, she bartered for their needs, trading away one piece of the chess set at a time."

Kate fingered the bloodred brooch on Aphrodite's shoulder. "Expensive bread and cheese."

With a nod, Nicholas said, "Emotionally as well. With every chess piece, my grandmother lost another part of her beloved husband."

Kate made the logical connection. "So she bartered away the gold-and-emerald Aphrodite with a soldier from Cedar Dell?"

"No. She gave it as a reward to a Cedar Dell soldier for saving her daughter's life."

Kate leaned forward, intrigued. "What happened?"

"My mother accidentally started a fire in the attic of a half-destroyed building. She stood at an upstairs window, screaming. The soldier heard her, went into the burning building, and carried her out. When my grandmother tried to thank him, he brushed aside her gratitude saying, 'That's the way we do things in Cedar Dell, Texas.' "

How hokey. How heroic. How perfectly Cedar Dell.

"My grandmother gave him the emerald queen and told him to take it home as a souvenir to his sweetheart."

Her dad? Kate considered the idea. No. Not her father. He'd told a lot of war stories over the years, but never one like this. "It's a lovely story. I haven't heard talk of a Cedar

Dell soldier saving someone from a burning building in France, though, and that's the sort of tale that would get around town. Is this your quest, Nicholas? To find this man?"

He hesitated, lifted the chess piece from the table and twirled it between his fingers. A wry smile touched his lips. "I'd be flattering myself if I said yes. In truth, I'm searching for the emerald Aphrodite, Kate. I'm attempting to complete the chess set for my grandmother."

"You've found them all?" she asked, surprised.

"About half of them. Three years ago, my mother discovered a ruby Pan, a pawn, in an antique shop in Brussels. She never forgot the horrors of the war, the heroism of her mother, and the sacrifices of her father. She decided to restore the lost chess set in tribute to her parents. It was to be a gift for Grandmother's ninetieth birthday."

"What a sweet idea."

Nicholas gave a rueful smile. "It's as much sour as sweet, I'm afraid. Part of that long story."

Kate encouraged him with a look.

"Family always meant a lot to both my mother and grandmother. Surviving a war together brought them even closer than most mothers and daughters. My mother spoke of the deep devotion between my grandparents. She often said she believed that devotion kept Grandmother alive through the war as surely as the money from the chess pieces my grandfather left with her."

"Fairy-tale love," Kate murmured.

"It exists. I believe that. I've seen it with my own parents, and through my grandmother's stories about the special love she and my grandfather shared. It's something I aspire to, but have yet to find in a marriage myself."

Kate sneaked a look toward his ringless left hand. "I'm divorced."

She knew that from the *Dallas Magazine* article, of course. Kate flashed a quick, embarrassed smile.

Nicholas continued, with dark notes tolling in his voice. "Twenty years ago, my mother and grandmother had a falling-out. It was a terrible row. When my mother died six months ago, harsh words and hurt feelings still stood between them."

"You lost your mother? Oh, Nicholas. I'm so sorry." Kate recalled her fear in the wake of her father's accident. Much as she dreaded losing a father who'd offered her so little love, how much greater must be the grief of losing a mother Nicholas obviously adored. "What happened?"

"Cancer killed my mother. My father destroyed her relationship with her mother."

At Kate's questioning look, he elaborated. "He did something stupid, and my mother stood by him and my grandmother disapproved. It's not an unusual tale. Simply sad. My mother hoped to use the chess set to end the estrangement. For her, it represented an apology that would never be made with words. Proud women, both of them. Stubborn women. So much alike it's scary. I loved them both, and it drove me crazy to be caught in the middle."

Something about his story poked at Kate, but she didn't want to explore it. She shifted in her seat and moved on. "When is your grandmother's birthday?"

He shook his head. "Next month, but the chess set is no

longer a birthday surprise. I told her about it not long after Mother died. Grandmother's grief was killing her. She wasn't eating, took no interest in life. She went a week without leaving her bedroom. She needed to hear how much my mother cherished her."

"Did it help?" Kate asked, her gaze trailing toward the doorway leading to the living room. Leading to her father.

"Yes. Definitely. It's also giving my grandmother reason to fight. This search has rejuvenated her. Grandmother's mind is still sharp, and she is fully involved in the research." His mouth lifted in a loving smile. "She's an Internet junkie at this point. In fact, my grandmother is the one who found you."

"Really?"

"She built quite a dossier on you."

"Really." Kate didn't think she liked that, but she recognized it as a reality of living in the Information Age.

She eyed the chess piece on the table and wondered at his chances of success. "How in the world did you manage to find so many of the pieces?"

"Money. Luck. Determination. It helped tremendously that Grandmother kept a diary during the war and made notations when she gave up the pieces. They were special to her, a connection with the husband she'd loved and lost, and she noted every instance when surrendering a chess piece helped her and her daughters stay alive. Also, she told the recipients the history of the piece she relinquished. As a rule, the individual pieces of the Versailles set have been treated as treasures by those who held them."

"So what did her diary say about the Cedar Dell piece?"

"Very little. In the excitement of the fire, she forgot to

make notes. My mother was burned, and Grandmother nursed her. Months later, when she finally attempted to re-create the events, all she remembered was the soldier's comment about Cedar Dell, Texas."

He paused, frowned, and added quietly, "This is not a life-or-death matter, but it is important to me. This chess set symbolizes my grandmother's fortitude, my grandfather's sacrifice. The love my mother held inside her heart that never died. I value family, Kate, and I want to honor mine. Will you help me?"

Okay. That does it. I'm in love. She couldn't refuse a commission with a purpose this noble and loving. "What would you like me to do?"

"Talk to people. Be my assistant on this project, my emissary to the citizens of Cedar Dell. I've made a couple trips to town, but have found it difficult to establish a relationship with the people here. They're suspicious of outsiders."

Kate's mouth quirked, imagining the small-town response to his big-city dress and manner. "They probably assume you're up to no good."

"I believe they fear I intend to open a liquor store."

Wincing, Kate said, "They'd run you out of town on a rail."

"So I've been told."

Kate realized their banter made the significance of his quest bearable to discuss. "I hate to sound discouraging, but we're looking for the proverbial needle in a haystack. The Allied invasion occurred ages ago. A million things could have happened to that chess piece in the course of sixty years. In a small town, the value of a major art piece would go unrecognized. I don't mind helping you. I'll be happy to try. But I can't honestly say I'm confident of success."

"I am. You are one of them, Kate. They'll talk to you."

"You don't understand." She tried to find words to explain her unofficial status as Slut of Cedar Dell, Texas. Finally, she gave up. "Why don't you simply ask the newspaper to run a story? This is just the sort of thing a small-town paper loves."

"I could do that, and I will if need be. However, I'd prefer to avoid it if possible. Past experience has proved going public with my quest brings out the treasure hunters and troublemakers."

"Yes, you're right." Kate had a sudden vision of The Widows wearing headphones while skimming metal detectors over the ground at the park.

"I'll pay you a fair wage for your time and a significant bonus should our search prove successful."

A significant bonus. One of her favorite phrases.

The thought made her smile as she heard the front door's hinges squeak. Seconds later, Ryan shot into the kitchen. "Hey, Mom. Granddad wants to know if you have any cookies . . . oh, excuse me."

"Nicholas, I'd like you to meet my son, Ryan. Ry, this is Nicholas Sutherland."

Her son's brows winged up, and he shot her a quick, mischievous look. Knowing her son, Kate braced herself. He fooled her by acting the perfect gentleman.

Kate introduced Nicholas to her father and left the two men discussing baseball cards while she answered a business call upstairs. The call soon evolved in a conference call between her biggest client, his attorney, an IRS agent, and her. Eventually, Nicholas came upstairs and listened long enough to assess the situation. He waved good-bye, mouthed the word "later," and departed.

Kate watched from the window, as he climbed into his car and pulled away from the curb. Sighing softly, she turned her attention away from fantasy and back to the IRS.

Wildflowers painted the land in a lush carpet of oranges and golds along the edges of the farm-to-market road leading out of Cedar Dell. The late afternoon was hot and heavy, the air leaden with anticipation of the thunderhead building in the west. Max eyed the sky absently, his thoughts not on weather or the scenery or the slight pull to the right of the truck's steering. Max's thoughts, his musings, focused on his past and the pilgrimage of sorts he'd chosen to undertake on a whim.

Max was going home.

Such as it was.

The road cut through a stripped and eroded farming section where old-timers claimed a forest of oaks had once stood. Max had trouble picturing a cover of trees since the big sandstone boulders strewn across the jagged landscape gave the area a barren, almost lunar, appearance. A single stand of cedar elms, cottonwoods, and scrub oaks lined the creek bed. Against them stood another scourge upon the countryside—a dilapidated trailer house, or tornado-catcher as they were called in these parts.

He braked the truck to a stop and turned off the ignition. A quick glance to his right revealed that his daughter continued to nap. He opened the driver's side door and stepped to the ground, then quietly latched the door shut behind him.

Max studied his former home. The place never looked especially good, but now, having sat abandoned since his father died over a decade ago, the trailer appeared . . . sad. The white aluminum siding was yellowed and rusted in places. Flecks of brown paint clung to lumber, weathered and gray, on the steps that led up to the front door. A muddy hornets' nest hung at the upper left corner of the door like a swarming, buzzing porch light.

Max took a long look at the place, emotions rumbling in his gut. This place represented much of the ugliness in his life, and yet, it had fostered the independence that proved to be one of his greatest assets. If home had been a nicer place to be, if his mother hadn't left, if his father hadn't been a heavy-handed drunk, would he have worked as hard to get away from that life? Would he have achieved the success he currently enjoyed?

Financially, he'd done all right. Not rich, by any means, but comfortable. After college, he'd made a good living in the Air Force, supported his family, sent money to Kate. He'd used the time developing his skills in a hobby for which he had a passion—photography. After leaving the service, his decision to make his living by specializing in sports photography, golf in particular, had proved fortuitous. Who would have ever guessed that a photo of a particularly beautiful morning sky above a golf course in Scotland would end up as part of a major airline's logo? That one photograph made it possible for him to provide his daughter with the lifestyle he considered superior.

Shannon could grow up with small-town roots and an education broadened by travel.

Max wished it weren't too late to do the same for Ryan. He hoped he'd have the chance to do *something* for the boy. Most of all, he wanted to be his father again.

A big, blue-black grackle swooped down from the sky to perch along the trailer's roofline, calling Edgar Allan Poe's raven to Max's mind. " 'Nevermore.' "

Max shuddered, scooped a rock off the ground, and chucked it in the general direction of the bird. Wings flapped, and the grackle flew to the branches of a nearby cedar elm. Max threw another stone and chased the bird away. Chased the lingering effects of this morning's nightmare away.

Be damned if he'd let his thinking turn negative. He had an opportunity here, the best one since Kare's son of a bitch husband opened his big mouth and created this mess. He'd damn well take advantage of it. He just needed to time it right.

His timing where Ryan was concerned had been off since the git-go. It was that simple . . . and that complicated. "I've got to make him understand," he murmured. "Back then, this was all I could have given him."

Max shoved his hands into his pockets and rocked back on his heels, his gaze sweeping over the trailer house once more. "And this was awful."

He turned his back on his past and looked toward his future.

As he opened the truck's door, Shannon sat up straight and rubbed her eyes. "Daddy? Where are we?"

"That's a good question, honey. That's a real good question. But you know what? I'm fixin' to find out. Would you like to go to Kathryn's house? See if you can play there for a little bit while Daddy runs an errand?"

"Yes! She has a new playhouse in her backyard. It's so cool, Daddy. It has a real lightbulb in it and a tablecloth that's real close to being Pig Pink."

"Awesome."

Half an hour later, he knocked on the Harmons' back door. Adele answered, wiping her hands on her apron. "Why, hello, Max. I didn't expect to find—"

"Is Ryan here?" he interrupted. "I want to talk to him."

"He left a little while ago. Said he was going to the park."

"Come inside, Max." Kate walked up behind Adele. "Is Shannon with you?"

"No. I dropped her at a friend's house to play. It's time, Kate. I've thought about it all day."

"Time for what?"

"For me to talk to Ryan. He's only heard it from you and your husband and—"

"Ex-husband."

"Yeah, well, your ex-husband presented me in the poorest possible light, and I want to explain my side of it to our son. I don't want to put it off another day. We've wasted too much time. We've wasted years." Max tunneled his fingers through his hair. "I want to tell him the whys and wherefores of bad timing and good intentions. When I'm done, he can tell me to go straight to hell if he likes. But I want him to give me a good listen. I've earned that much, at least. I hope you won't fight me on—"

Kate backed away from the door, gesturing him inside. Probably preferred the neighbors didn't hear every word they said. "I won't fight. I agree with you. This situation has gone on long enough. Ryan does need to ask you a few questions, hear your answers."

Max was a little taken aback. He'd expected some show of resistance from her. Paying closer attention, he realized that Kate looked distracted and harried. He wondered if her old man was giving her a hard time. Jack was no doubt a difficult patient, and she hadn't been welcomed back with open arms by old acquaintances, he'd realized from comments overheard around town. Much as he hated to add to her burdens, their son was a priority.

Grimacing, she clasped her elbows in a self-protective gesture. "Just be aware, he's liable not to be in the most receptive of moods."

He softened his tone. "That's okay. A bad mood might be best. Might prod him to speak rather than clam up."

Adele handed him a plastic grocery sack containing two bottles of water, candy bars, and two packages of peanuts. "What's this?"

"For Ryan. Believe me, an offer of food never hurts with that boy. There's an airline-size bottle of scotch at the bottom for you in case you need it."

He turned to go. Halfway to his truck, Kate's call stopped him short. "Don't be afraid of him, Max. He may not show it, but I know my son. Deep down inside, Ryan loves you."

Please, God.

At the park, he twisted the key to turn off his engine, then sat for a moment, scanning the playground, summoning his courage. A pair of preadolescent girls played hop-scotch on the basketball court, their squares drawn on the cement in neon pink chalk. Another group of children, a mix of boys and girls, ran races between the swing set and teeter-totters. Laughter sang on the air, bringing a sense of the surreal to a situation Max considered fraught with tension.

Where was his son? The trepidation in Max's gut stretched tighter.

He wanted to do this now. He wanted . . . there . . . over in the shadows beneath that cottonwood tree. His son sat with a basketball at his side, an open notebook in his lap. Ryan worked a pencil feverishly over a page. Was he writing? Drawing something? Max couldn't tell.

Climbing down from the truck, he approached his boy. "Ryan?"

His son's head jerked up. A heartbeat later, he slammed the book shut. He glared at Max, but didn't speak.

Max fumbled for how to begin, where to begin. At a loss, he blurted the first related words that came to his mind. "My father was a drunk."

That got Ryan's attention.

"The good thing about that was that he had a personal rule against drinking on the job. He was a truck driver, and he wouldn't put other people on the road at risk. Of course, that meant he did all his drinking at home. We lived in a trailer house just west of town. Dad would get back from a trip, hit the bottle, hit me, hit the dog. First time he took a swing at my mother, she took off. Never came back. I was twelve years old. Guess she figured I could fend for myself okay."

Ryan set his notebook on the ground. "So can I. Go away."

"I made it to school every day. School bus came and got me. School saved me. I was a good student, but I excelled in sports. Not basketball as much as football and baseball. You have a better vertical jump than I did at your age. Anyway, by my junior year in high school, college scouts showed up at most every game. That was big-time happenings in little Cedar Dell."

Ryan rolled to his feet, slipped his notebook into a backpack Max hadn't noticed, and slung the strap over his shoulder. As he picked up his basketball, Max figured he was about to bolt. Great. Now what? He couldn't exactly tackle him and force him to listen.

Could he?

When Ryan took off, Max fell into step beside him. "They talked scholarships, Ryan. It was my way out of that leaking, rusting trailer. It was my way to a real future. My junior year, I quarterbacked the Cedar Dell Rattlers to the state championship. That's when the colleges started talking a pro career. Ry, one Friday night, Tom Landry came to a game."

The mention of the Dallas Cowboys' legendary head coach broke through even Ryan's stubborn defenses. "He came to watch you?"

"I don't know . . . maybe he was simply in the area and decided to catch a high school game. But it made me dream, son. Made me dream big."

Calling Ryan "son" was a mistake because he immediately closed like a clam and stepped up his pace. They approached the edge of the park, and Max knew he'd better find a way to stop him quick. He took hold of his son's arm. "Please, stop, Ryan. Let me talk to you. Just give me five minutes." Then, in a burst of insight, he added, "Out of respect for your mother, give me five minutes."

Ryan shook off his grip, but slowed down. "Leave my mother out of this."

"I can't. She's part of it. She told me where to find you. She wants you to hear what I have to say. She wants you to hear the truth."

"And I'm supposed to hear that from you? Yeah, right. Sure, dude."

"I won't lie to you."

"You have in the past."

"By omission, perhaps."

Ryan snorted with disbelief. "You be sure and explain that to Shannon when she finds out the guy who pushed her in the swing was her half brother."

"How about we go tell her right now? I'd love to be open about our relationship. In fact, I'd be happy to march into Harmon Lanes right now and announce it to the town."

"No," Ryan snapped. He shot Max a fierce, narrow-eyed glare. "Don't you dare. My mom wants it kept secret."

"Up until now, yes, she has. Do you want to know why?"

"If I do, I'll ask her. I don't need you telling me anything."

Max searched for a reply and took a risk. "Yes, you do, Ryan. You need me telling you the sorts of things a father tells his seventeen-year-old son, the stuff I wish my father had told me. I made some big mistakes when I was about your age. Big mistakes. I think I could have avoided some of them if I'd had a father who cared enough to listen and to shoot straight with me."

"Mistakes like me, you mean," Ryan said with a sneer.

"Not you," Max said quietly, insistently. "You were never a mistake."

Ryan halted abruptly, threw him a blistering glare.

Max held his ground. "When I say mistake, I'm talking about my reaction to your mother's decision to keep you. It's true that I abandoned you and your mom, Ryan. Not financially, but in every other way."

"And this is news to who?"

"I'd like to explain why. Not excuse my behavior, mind you. Explain. Maybe it won't change your mind about me, but at least you'll be working with the facts and not the exaggerations and lies that Roger Thurman told you."

Seeing the boy waver, he pressed, "See that picnic table off by itself? How about we go over there? It'll give us some privacy."

Ryan didn't move, and Max took it as a positive sign that he didn't walk off in the other direction. "Ryan? Please?"

When the scowling young man veered toward the picnic bench, Max trailed after him, victory flashing through him like a lightning strike, nervousness rolling behind it like thunder.

Ryan sat on the table, placing himself at eye level with his father. Max paced back and forth, searching for a beginning. What words would reach past Ryan's defenses and make him see Max's point of view?

"Well?" Ryan spun his basketball on the tip of his index

finger. "You asked for five minutes. What is it you have to tell me that I don't already know?"

Cocky little son of a bitch. Reminded Max of himself at that age.

"How about the truth? Bare bones, unvarnished truth."

"From you? Pull my other leg."

That's the way you want it? Okay, fine. Max looked his son dead straight in the eyes, and said, "You're right. When your mother told me she was pregnant, I knew one thing. I sure as hell didn't want to be a father."

Chapter Eight

KATE PEERED PAST the kitchen window's white eyelet curtains in the general direction of the park. She knew she couldn't see that far, but she couldn't seem to stop herself from looking. Waves of heat undulated above cement sidewalks and parked cars. Next door, the neighbor's golden Lab nuzzled pink begonias in the flower bed.

Her maternal instincts clamored. It took all her discipline not to dash to the park to observe firsthand this encounter between her son and his father.

"Honey, you're about to wear out that window glass."

Kate glanced over her shoulder to see Adele stride into the room. She'd changed her clothes and now sported hot pink capri pants and a lime green T-shirt.

"The Widows aren't out there, are they?"

She lost Kate completely. "The Widows?"

"Uh-huh. They're bound to picket against my presence in the Harmon household sooner or later. They want me gone from Cedar Dell. I threaten them."

Kate recognized the attempt for what it was—distraction—but she played along anyway."

"A threat? I never realized that about you."

"Yes. It's my roast gravy. No one can compete with my

roast gravy, and they know it." Then Adele betrayed her own anxiety by peering out the window, too. "I hope he took rope with him so he can hog-tie the boy. Ryan's liable to start running and not stop 'til he reaches Abilene."

"Something tells me that wouldn't pose too much of a problem to Max."

Adele filled a glass with tap water, leaned against the cabinets, then asked, "Are you as worried about all this as you look?"

Kate met her friend's concerned gaze. "Three years is a long time for a child to be estranged from his parent."

"Eighteen years is even longer," Adele offered, sending Kate a knowing look over the top of her eyeglasses, her tone dry as the dust on top of the fridge.

Kate's gaze shifted toward the kitchen door and the hallway that led to her father's bedroom. *A lifetime.* "Yes, I know. It's peculiar, isn't it? Max and Ryan. Dad and me. Does estrangement run in families? Is it some sort of genetic mutation, you think?"

"Oh, it's genetic, all right. The hardheaded gene. You and your daddy and your baby boy, all three have it. I'm glad to see Max working on fixing his part of the problem. I wish Jack would follow his lead."

Despair twisted Kate's heart. "I think you're dreaming there."

The phone rang, and Kate picked it up. "Hello?"

"Hello, Kate."

"Nicholas." Her stomach fluttered as she leaned against the wall, absently playing with the coiled cord. "I didn't expect to hear from you again today."

"We didn't have a chance to finish our conversation. I have something else pertinent to our business agreement I want to make clear."

"Nicholas Sutherland?" Adele quietly mouthed. She waggled her eyebrows and comically patted her hand over her heart.

"Oh? All right."

"Whatever compensation plan we develop—and we will have one—I want it understood that you are not my employee."

Kate frowned. "I don't understand."

"If you were my employee, I couldn't ask you on a date because that might be construed as harassment. That simply won't do. So, since you're not my employee, will you go out with me next Saturday night, Kate? I wish it could be sooner, but I'm leaving town on business tomorrow."

Kate's gaze flew to the window that faced the park and Ryan. And Max.

"I'm sorry, I can't. That's Fish Fry and Bingo Night. It's a big event here in Cedar Dell. I've promised my father I'd take him."

"Bingo Night in Cedar Dell?"

"And a fish fry."

"Thank you, Kate." His cultured voice sounded amused. "Yes, I'd love to join you and your father. What time shall I pick you up?"

The basketball went spinning off Ryan's finger. "What?"

"I knew I sure as hell didn't want to be a father. I was

eighteen goddamn years old. Not much older than you are now. I lived in a shit hole with a drunk for a role model. That scholarship was my ticket out of hell. Be damned if I wanted to give it up."

Ryan's breath emerged in a whoosh as if he'd been punched in the gut. What Max had said, the way he said it, shocked him to his toes.

"Was that wrong of me?" Max Cooper continued. "Let me ask you this. How would you feel in similar circumstances?"

Anger flared. "I wouldn't get myself in a similar circumstance."

"Good. I hope not. I hope you're smarter than I was at your age, and you never let your hormones get hold of your good sense. Because that's what happened to me, Ryan. I made a mistake. I made lots of mistakes where you and your mother are concerned, but you know what? I can't find it in myself to regret it too awful much. You know why? Because if things had been different, you'd be different, and I think you're just about the greatest kid in the world."

Enough. That's enough. Ryan couldn't listen to any more, couldn't hear any more, and he scooped up his ball and took off running, heading for the shelter and safety of his grandfather's house. He knew running was a childish reaction, but at that moment, he didn't care. This man scared him.

Max Cooper wanted to change things. Life was fine just as it was. He didn't need it to change. Didn't want it to change. Plus, the man was a liar. Ryan knew that. These were just more lies in a long line of them.

Approaching his grandfather's house, Ryan heard footsteps behind him. The bastard wasn't giving up. It pissed Ryan off. Made him want to shout out in anger.

"I think I told you years ago that I worked for your grandfather at Harmon Lanes when I was growing up," Max said as he jogged up beside him. "That's how I earned enough money to buy my first bike."

Bike? What the hell was he talking about now?

"Not a Harley. A Schwinn. Hated riding the school bus. I'd ride my ten-speed into town instead."

"That's a crock." Ryan stopped short, panting, certain Max Cooper was lying now and fed up with it. "Roger said you were Big-Man-on-Campus in high school. Said you drove a hot car, a 350SS Camaro and talked half the girls in the senior class out of their panties in its backseat. Guys like that don't live in trailer houses and ride ten-speeds to school."

"Okay, let's start right there." Temper singed Max's tone and gave Ryan pause. "First thing you need to understand is that Roger Thurman despised me. He was obsessively possessive when it came to your mother, and he couldn't stand that she and I had a bond—you—that wasn't going away. He told you a mixture of truth, fabrications, and out-and-out lies that had one purpose: to discredit me."

From the looks of it, Max's mood matched Ryan's. He grabbed the basketball and dribbled it on the asphalt street in front of the Harmon house. "I can show you the remains of the trailer I grew up in. I didn't own a car of any kind, much less a Camaro, until after I graduated from college, and I damn sure didn't seduce half the girls in my class. I had a steady girlfriend all through high school and I was faithful to her."

"Until you shagged my mom."

"Don't," Max snapped. He dribbled the ball hard. "Do not be disrespectful toward your mother."

Ryan lifted his chin and twisted his lips in a chastising smile which, when combined with the challenge in his gaze, spoke volumes.

Max shot the basketball at Ryan's chest. "Look, dammit. I respected your mother then, and I respect her now. The details of what happened between the two of us are private, and they'll stay that way."

Hell, *he* was the detail that happened between his mother and this man. Emotion churned inside of Ryan. He wanted to strike out. He wanted to wound. "I asked if you'd raped her."

Max Cooper actually staggered back a step. His eyes blazed, but his voice grew cold as a blue norther. "Is that what you think of me?"

A sense of power shimmered in Ryan's blood, and he twisted the knife. "I don't think of you at all. Not if I can help it."

Now Max looked as if he had a thousand pounds of torque in his jaw, and Ryan thought he might have finally driven him away. He thought too soon.

"I'm not leaving until we're done with this. Do you really want to hold this conversation in the middle of the street or shall we go inside?"

Alarm sizzled though him. "My mom's in there. We can't go in there."

"Why not? I have no secrets from your mother."

Yeah. Right.

"In fact, it might be good for the three of us to discuss this together."

Screw that. When hell freezes over, maybe, Ryan thought. Ryan started up the walk. "I'm going inside. You're not."

"Sure I am."

Jeez. The son of a bitch wouldn't give up. Ryan altered his course and walked around the house to the garage and its lopsided basketball hoop. He bounced the ball once. Twice.

He fired the basketball across the yard, turned on Max, and shouted, "I don't want to shoot hoops anymore. I don't want to talk to you anymore. I wish we'd stayed in Dallas! I wish you'd stayed . . . anywhere but here. You want to talk? Fine, we'll talk." From the depths of his heart, the soul of his dearest fantasy, came the question he'd wondered all his life. "Why the hell didn't you marry her?"

Max set his jaw. "I offered to."

"Yeah, and Mom told Roger you sounded like a charter member of Martyrs-R-Us when you said it."

"I imagine I did. That's what I've been trying to tell you, Ryan. I'm human. I screwed up, and I regret it."

Ryan wasn't about to listen, not now. "Just to get the facts straight, did you offer to marry her before or after you asked her to get an abortion?"

"I didn't ask Kate to get a goddamned abortion!"

"Oh? Was *that* a lie?" Ryan's words dripped sarcasm. "Funny, I don't recall you denying it three years ago."

He braced his hands on his hips and scowled fiercely. "I told her I'd pay for one if that was her choice."

Ryan mimicked Max's stance. "So you didn't mind the idea of her killing me."

"No, that's not what I . . . hell." Max whirled around, waved a dismissive hand. "Forget it. This isn't working."

Ryan was tired. Tired through to his bones. To his soul. He should have let it go, but he didn't. Couldn't. Some emotion he couldn't name goaded him on. He plopped down onto the lawn and called after Max. "Were you scared?"

The question brought Max up short. After a moment's hesitation, he replied, "Spitless. We both were."

Ryan stretched out his legs, gazed up at a sky and clouds now streaked with the muddy purple touches of dusk. "Why did she keep your name out of it?"

Max sat on the green grass, his knees bent. He tugged at a clump of Johnson grass between his legs. "A number of reasons. Primarily, neither one of us wanted to let down the people we loved."

"Her parents," Ryan surmised. That was a no-brainer. "Your dad would have cared?"

"Not especially, no. But it wasn't my dad I was worried about. It was the Christian Ladies Benevolent Society."

Ryan gaped in surprise as Max nodded seriously, and continued, "For the most part, excluding a Widow or two, Cedar Dell people are good-hearted. After my mom ran off, and with my dad away so much driving his truck, the Benevolent Society took me under its wing. They made sure I was fed, made sure I had clothes to wear. They gave me charity without making me feel like trailer trash. Kids my age accepted me. I loved this town, loved the people. Cedar Dell was my family, all the support and encouragement I had, and I didn't want to let my family down. Then, too, there was the college scholarship."

Ryan sat up on his elbows. He wanted to keep quiet, but curiosity won out. "You had a football scholarship to Texas A&M."

"Yes, but it only covered tuition, room, and board. I was on my own for fees and books and spending money, and the Christian Ladies Benevolent League Scholarship took care of that. Most scholarships have a few strings attached, usually maintaining a certain grade point average is one of them. This one had a morals clause."

"Oh, that's rich. Talk about screwin' up."

Max threw the Johnson grass at the cement birdbath. "I wanted to go to college. I desperately wanted to go to college. My high school coaches told me Coach Landry said as long as I stayed healthy, I could probably play pro ball."

Ryan struggled against being impressed. Coach Landry had said that about his dad? Wow.

"I loved football." Max's gaze roamed toward the lighted windows in the Harmon family room. "I hated that damned trailer. I wanted away from it more than I've ever wanted anything in my life."

Almost against his will, Ryan began to hear and understand what the man had been saying. "Marrying my mother would have kept you here."

Max looked him straight in the eyes. "We didn't want to get married. We talked it over and decided marriage wasn't right for us. We were headed in different directions in our lives. We recognized we didn't love each other enough to sustain a marriage in this town, with a child and minimum-wage jobs."

Understanding didn't mean acceptance. Didn't mean forgiveness. "Then why," he sneered, "did you have sex?"

Before Max could respond, a figure moved out from the shelter of the red-tip photinia planted at the northwestern corner of the house. His mother snapped at him. "Stop it, Ryan. Don't. That's none of your business."

Sure it was his business. It was his life they'd created by casually screwing around. He opened up his mouth to protest, but the expression on his mom's face stopped him. He knew that bulldog expression. He'd be wasting his breath. "Fine. Forget about it. I don't have time for this. I told Granddad I'd watch the ball game with him."

Leaping up, he took off, and this time, thank God, Max let him go.

The crack of a slapping screen door sounded like a gunshot interrupting the early-evening peace. Kate allowed the noise to fade away before turning to Max. He looked a little wild tonight, his dark hair mussed as if he'd repeatedly plowed his fingers through it, his blue eyes glowing with emotion. As he rolled to his feet, braced his hands on his hips and began to pace back and forth in front of her, his gaze fixed on the door through which his son had disappeared, he reminded her of a sleek, powerful mountain cat pacing a cage.

Dangerous.

Kate's blood stirred.

He'd always been sexy. Back in his glory days, he'd swaggered through the halls of Cedar Dell High melting girls' hearts with a wink and that grin of his. He'd had brains, strength, good looks, superior athletic skill, and the confidence of youth. Throw in a touch of bad boy, and he'd been hard for any teenage girl to resist.

At thirty-six, he was still smart, strong, handsome, athletic, and confident. Now, though, he'd added maturity to the mix. He'd traded in his button-front Levi's for Wranglers, his boots for scuffed and worn running shoes, and his blue chambray work shirts for form-fitting cotton T-shirts, tonight's white with a green logo that read: BUY YOUR THIN MINTS FROM DAISY GIRL SCOUTS TROOP 1241. Add the measure of doting father to the grown-up bad boy, and no woman under ninety could resist.

The teenage version of Max Cooper had turned her girlish head, but up until those life-altering moments out at the lake, her attraction to him had remained innocent. There was nothing innocent about the heat humming through her blood at the moment.

In self-defense, she brought up a topic sure to cool her down. "Interesting question our nosy son asked. Why did we have sex, Max?"

His gaze snapped toward her. A brow arched, and the tension emanating from his body eased. "From what I remember, I was eighteen and horny, and Terri Gantt was holding out for marriage."

"I didn't know that. All the kids in town thought the two of you were sleeping together."

"Nope." Max shoved his hands in the back pockets of his jeans as the neighbors' dog began to bark.

Kate sighed heavily, closed her eyes, and rubbed her temples. "I had a secret crush on you our senior year—like most every other girl at Cedar Dell High. But that night, I was striking out at my father."

Max let the truth of that drift in the evening air. Minutes passed in silence, and Kate halfway expected him to turn around and leave. Instead, out of the blue, he confessed. "It wasn't all hormones on my part, Kate."

She looked up to see him offering a smile strained with bittersweet memory. "That night, you needed me. You needed me like no one had ever needed me before. That was so . . . sexy. You made me feel powerful."

Shying away from the warmth in his expression, she didn't hold back a short, bitter laugh. "You got over needing to be needed pretty fast."

A beam of sunlight filtered through the leaves of the pecan tree and spilled across Max, adding sparkle to the glitter of emotion in his light blue eyes. "Come on, Kate. It wasn't like that. You know it."

Old feelings rose up like a tidal wave inside her. Anger and despair and fear . . . so much fear. Those first few months after Ryan's birth had been terrifying. Max had given her money, but no emotional support. When she called him to inform him of Ryan's birth and her decision to keep the baby rather than place him with the adoptive parents they'd chosen for their child, he'd gone ballistic.

Kate recalled that phone conversation with the clarity of a major disaster. He told her she'd made a stupid decision, and that it ruined Ryan's chance to have a good life with the adoptive parents. He made all the arguments Kate had made to herself before the nurse placed her newborn child in her arms.

After that, nothing else mattered.

Max didn't attend Ryan's birth. He never held him. He didn't understand the depth of her maternal love, and he'd done everything within his power to pressure her to keep her word about the adoption.

The memory of that pressure put a bite in her voice as she said, "You must have known how badly we needed you when you told me not to call you again."

"I didn't think of that at first. I was furious. Then I decided that once you realized you didn't have a safety net, you'd do the right thing—what I believed was the right thing, that is. I thought you'd see how difficult it was to care for a child all alone, and you'd give him to the Carstairses, after all."

Bitterness mingled with satisfaction that she had managed on her own, despite her father's and Max's abandonment. "That's not what happened, is it?"

"No. I underestimated you, Kate." Admiration warmed his voice. "I told you that when Ryan was eight, and I came begging to be part of his life."

She remembered that conversation, too. He'd stood on her front porch, his hat literally in his hand, sunlight gleaming off the brass on his Air Force uniform. She'd marveled that he managed to look so proud and so humble at the same time. "Yeah, but that time *I* was angry. Incensed. I couldn't believe you dared to show up out of the blue like that, asking me to forget and forgive. This huge, red rage of noise roared through my head, and I didn't hear everything you said."

"Really?" His face was dim in the twilight as he turned toward her. "You were angry? I couldn't tell."

"I almost kicked your butt off my porch and told you never to come back."

Max scratched his chin. "That's what I expected, but you seemed happy to see me."

"Not happy. I was mad and more than a little threatened, but I did my best to hide it. I decided I should be pleased for Ryan instead. He was eight years old, and he needed a dad, even a long-distance one."

"I saw him as often as the Air Force would let me."

"I know. He was so proud of you, all spit and polish in your dress blues. You were his hero." When he shook his head, grimacing, she hurried on. "He's kept the letters your wife sent during those years. Ryan read the letters to me. Rose had a gift with words. We felt like we knew your neighbors in Berlin."

Wiping his face with both hands, Max cleared his throat. "I'd like to see those letters sometime."

"I'll make sure of it."

Silence stretched between them as if to allow time to digest the heavy revelations.

Max asked, "What about now? Are you still mad?"

That was easy to answer. "A little, yeah. I'll probably always be angry about what happened then."

"Because you went through it alone."

"That, and because I was jealous of you."

"Jealous?" He looked taken aback. "Why were you jealous of me?"

"Because you got to stay out of it. Your life didn't change. You still went to college, still had a career. You never faced The Widows' probes and questions. You kept your reputation. To this day, I am still the slutty Harmon sister."

"You weren't a slut."

"Sure I was. I was a slut, whereas you—although no one knew your identity—you were just sowing wild oats."

Defensiveness bristled in his tone. "Let's be fair, here, Kate. You brought that on yourself when you changed your mind about the adoption."

"I know. And I know now that it was asking a lot of you to expect you to change your mind, too. But those first years were hard for me, Max. Really hard. And they were hard for Ryan, too. That's what's nursing his anger along now."

Max closed his eyes, let his head fall back. "God, I was so young and so stupid. Bailing out on the two of you like I did is one of the biggest regrets I have in my life."

"You didn't bail entirely. Ryan and I would never have made it without the support checks you sent."

He shook his head. "But I sent the money primarily out of guilt, and I hate knowing that about myself."

"Oh, stop it. Do you think you're the only one who has regrets? Who feels guilty? Not hardly. I still feel terrible for hurting the Carstairses. Mrs. Carstairs was so excited about the baby." She kicked at a tuft of Johnson grass. "I wonder what ever happened to them."

"The Carstairses?" Max asked. "They adopted a pair of sisters about six months after Ryan was born, an infant and a six-year-old. The older girl is in medical school at Tulane."

"You kept up with them?" Kate was incredulous.

He shrugged. "When you changed your mind, I felt bad for them. I went to see them, to apologize, and we ended up friends. In fact, it's because Karen and Jim Carstairs joined my wife to nudge me along that I got up the nerve to contact you when Ryan was eight."

Kate took a moment to digest that bit of new information. From the street came the sounds of in-line skates on asphalt and laughing children. Little had changed since her day, she thought. Back then it was roller skates and jump ropes. Sidewalk chalk. Mother-may-I and Sardines on long summer evenings. Ruining the neighbor's grass with a Slip-n-slide. Blue Popsicles that cost a dime from the Popsicle truck.

Max had it right, bringing his Shannon back here. Cedar Dell was a good place to raise children. "Do you think I should have raised Ryan here in Cedar Dell?"

Max rubbed his hand along his jaw. "He was happy growing up, wasn't he?"

"Not always. We had some difficult years."

"I never saw it. He seemed like a happy kid to me." One side of his mouth lifted. "Every time I came to visit Ryan, I expected you to meet me at the front door and say 'I told you so.' Cedar Dell is a good place, but y'all would have had your share of problems here. I don't think you should second-guess yourself. You've done an excellent job, Kate. Ryan's lucky to have you for his mother."

While Kate's heart gave a little leap at his praise, Max checked the sky, then his watch. "I need to be getting home. Shannon is due in a few minutes. Want to come have supper with us? I have stew in the Crock-Pot. We could talk some more."

The offer caught her by surprise. Kate considered for a moment and realized she'd like to take him up on it. "I'd like that, but I can't. Adele has plans later. I need to stay with Dad."

"Tomorrow, then. Come to dinner." He gave her that knee-melting grin, and added in a soft, honeyed drawl, "I haven't shared dinner with a beautiful woman in way too long."

Oh my. Max Cooper had never said anything in the least bit flirtatious to her before. Not even on the night they made a baby together. "Dinner is . . . um . . . difficult."

He reached for her hand, stroked his thumb across her knuckles. She shivered at his touch. "Then how about an after-dinner drink? Around eight? Or, if you'd rather wait until Shannon is in bed, after eight-thirty?"

"Eight is fine."

"Good." He squeezed her hand gently before releasing it. "See you then."

He gave a little salute, winked, and left. Kate stumbled into the house in a daze of confusion. What had just happened?

She made her way to the kitchen, stopping at the sink to wash her hands. Adele glanced up from her piecrust. "Okay, spill it. I've been dying to know what's going on. Ryan shot through here like summer lightning, and your sister called to say she's had three phone calls telling her Max Cooper had been seen having a *serious* discussion with Ryan in the park. I think time has run out for . . . honey, are you okay? You look white as the flour on my fingers. Did something bad happen out there?"

"I don't think so . . . I don't know. Adele, I think I just made a date with Max."

"Really? When?"

"Tomorrow night."

Adele pinched a piece of piecrust from the flour-dusted surface of the cutting board, popped it into her mouth, and grinned. "Well, what do you know. First Nicholas Sutherland, now Max. Maybe my prayers have been answered. Girl, you might finally get a sex life."

Chapter Nine

AMAZINGLY ENOUGH, the following morning passed without any major troubles or traumas. Max skipped his eight-fifteen phone call, leaving Kate with a small, but surprising sense of disappointment. Ryan left with a teammate from Dallas for a two-day baseball tournament in Weatherford, filling in for an injured former teammate who'd pulled a hamstring and couldn't play. Plans called for him to bring his truck to Cedar Dell on the return trip. Adele took herself off to a Weight Watchers meeting, and Bertie arrived on time to help Jack wash and dress before a friend stopped by for their weekly game of checkers. Kate accomplished more that morning than the rest of the week combined.

The aroma of baking cake wafted upstairs, reminding Kate that lunchtime had arrived. She sniffed the air, identified banana cream, and grinned. Adele's penchant to come home and bake after her Weight Watcher's meeting illustrated her view that calories consumed within three hours of her weekly weigh-in didn't count.

"That smells delicious," she said as she entered the kitchen.

"Tone down your taste buds, honey. You can't have any. This is my latest challenge to The Widows." Adele turned on the oven light and peeked inside. "I heard at my meeting that Mrs. Mallow has a cold, and I thought a neighborly gesture was in order."

"You're a wicked woman, Adele."

"Thank you. I do try."

Kate was halfway through a turkey sandwich when her business line rang. Realizing she'd forgotten to bring the portable downstairs with her, she made a mad dash for the stairs. Ten minutes later, she returned to her lunch with a spring in her step and a smile on her face. "Guess what, Adele. I have the best news."

"The Rangers broke their losing streak last night?"

"Don't I wish. No, that was Martin Groves. He grew up three houses down from us and was a good friend of Tom's. Sarah told me he established an engineering firm in Cedar Dell about ten years ago, so I phoned his office this morning and left a message asking him to call me."

"Oh, Kate. You asked him for a job for Ryan, didn't you?"

The chastisement in her voice put Kate on the defensive. "You have a problem with him working?"

"You know better than that. I simply don't see the harm in the boy working at a regular job this summer, one where he might meet other kids and have some fun."

"At what cost, though, Adele? His college education? An internship at Groves Engineering looks much more impressive on an admissions application than selling dip cones at the Dairy Queen or working the shoe rental counter at Harmon Lanes."

Kate couldn't stand the scent of Lysol to this day.

Adele wrinkled her nose. "You worry too much about

those college applications. He's a smart boy. He won't have trouble getting into college."

"No, but if we don't prepare, he might have trouble getting in the *right* college."

"What's the right college? One of those snooty places where they'll think less of him because he has a bit of a Southern drawl?"

"The right college is the one Ryan decides he wants to attend, his dream school. These days, you don't get into dream schools without lots of planning."

"But you're the one doing all the planning, hon. Not him. This should be Ryan's job."

Adele simply didn't understand the value of an exceptional education. To be honest, Kate doubted Ryan did, either, at this point. He was too good a kid to miss out on such an opportunity, so it was her maternal duty to oversee the process.

"If I leave it up to him, it won't get done. This is too important, Adele. It's his whole future. His life will be so much easier if we take care of business now. Believe me. I know."

Adele opened her mouth, then made a show of biting her tongue. Kate knew Adele had a lot to say on this subject. She thought Kate did too much for her son.

Kate saw Adele's point. She wanted her son to be independent, to learn to take care of his business himself, but Ryan was only seventeen. In many ways he was a mature, young adult, but in others . . . well . . . he'd rather spend time playing video games than looking ahead toward the future. If she didn't push him, prod him, he'd wake up one day wanting to study engineering at MIT or computer science at Stanford, but missed deadlines would put the kibosh on his dreams. He'd land in community college, where he'd miss the college experience.

Just like his mother.

The oven timer buzzed, and Adele turned her attention to her cake while Kate finished her sandwich. Still hungry, she rummaged in the fridge and found a bowl of leftover pasta salad. As she scooped a spoonful onto her plate, the house phone rang.

"Probably a telemarketer," she observed. "Why is it they always call during meals? Doesn't matter what time a person sits down to eat, somebody calls to sell something."

"Spy cams." Adele shook a wooden spoon at Kate. "They build them into microwave ovens these days. I read it in the *Enquirer*."

Kate snickered as she picked up the phone. "Hello?"

"May I speak with Jack Harmon, please?" a woman asked. "This is Helen Hartwick with Lake Country Realty."

"Just a moment please." Kate exited the kitchen, heard her father's voice raised in temper, and knew from experience not to hand over the phone at a moment like this. "Mr. Harmon is unavailable at the moment. May I take a message for him?"

"Yes, please. Would you tell him we've had an excellent offer on his lake house, and I'm eager to discuss details with him?"

Kate almost dropped the phone. "An offer on the lake house?"

"Yes."

"Our lake house?"

The Realtor paused. "Um . . . Mr. Harmon's house on Possum Kingdom Lake."

"There must be a mistake." Kate shook her head. "Dad would not put the lake house up for sale."

Not the one place where they'd had good times together. Nuh-uh. Kate wouldn't believe it.

The Realtor's tone grew snippy. "I assure you, miss, he listed 4743 Pike Road, Possum Kingdom Lake, Texas, with my office a few weeks ago. I have his signature on a listing agreement and an offer on the property. Please inform him he can reach me on my cell phone." She rattled off the number. "Anytime is fine."

"Wait a minute. Why would he—?"

"I'm not authorized to answer any more questions," she interrupted. "You'll need to speak with Mr. Harmon. Good-bye."

Yeah. I guess I'll just do that.

In a daze, Kate made her way toward her father's bedroom, where Jack was calling out, "Bertie? Hey, Bertie. Get your ass back here or you're fired. I don't care if today is your last day or not. I'll be hanged if I ask permission from anybody in this house to do anything I damned well feel like doing. I'm not a child to be—"

"Are you selling the lake house?" It shut him up midharangue. Kate held out the phone. "A Realtor just called. She said you have an offer on the lake house."

Her father's mouth tightened, and his gaze slid away. A familiar, painful silence stretched between them until he frowned down at his socks, and grumbled, "Where's Bertie? I need help putting on my shoes. I can manage everything else except for putting on my shoes."

Kate wasn't about to be distracted by a reminder of his infirmity. Heart pounding, she asked, "Dad, why would you sell the lake house?"

"It's not your business." His head snapped up. "It's my property, and I can do with it what I want."

His words were mean, and anger bristled in his tone, but Kate barely noticed. The sheen of moisture in his eyes held her in shock. Tears? Oh, my God. She'd never seen her father cry. Never. Not even when her mother died.

"I'm ready to go to work now," her father said. "Will you drive me, or should I have Bertie do it? He'll have to drive your car, though, because I'm not riding in his truck. Dang thing smells to high heaven since his dog got sick in it."

Kate exhaled a controlled breath. She couldn't deal with tears from her dad. Not now. She'd let the subject drop, take it up with Tom the next time he called. Or Sarah. She was due to pay Sarah a visit, anyway.

"I'll take you," Kate said, unwilling to chance The Narc's falling asleep at the wheel. She mentally reviewed the work waiting for her on her desk. "How long do you think you'll want to stay?"

"How should I know? I have work to do. In fact, you can help me with some of it. No one's done any filing for at least a couple of months."

Filing. Kate leaned wearily against the bedroom wall. The few feet of space between the doorway and the chair where her father sat suddenly seemed like a mile. A long, empty mile. She thought of the years of evening classes, the hours studying for the CPA exam. Of the baseball and basketball games she'd missed because of late-evening hours on the job. *He'll never understand. Never. I'll always be a big zero in his view. I need to get rid of any expectations of earning his love once and for all.*

"Sure, Dad." Her tone sounded as flat as her mood. "I'll do the filing."

Half an hour later, Kate stood in what had been her second home while growing up. Memories assailed her. She'd rolled hundreds of bowling balls down those lanes. This was where she'd come to think and dream about leaving Cedar Dell, of college life and career goals. Practicing her hook shot with her personal powder puff pink ball, this was where she'd planned her future.

It had proven to be a total waste of time. None of those dreams came true. Not personal goals, not career goals. No life on the West Coast, no advanced degree in environmental science. She had a job juggling numbers rather than helping to save the earth. She had no doting husband. No daughters. She'd always wanted a couple of daughters to go along with her son.

No wonder she had avoided Harmon Lanes since coming to town. More than anyplace else, these bowling lanes symbolized failure.

And now her dad expected her to file.

"To hell with that," she muttered in a burst of resentment. She had her own work to do here at Harmon Lanes, an assignment with meaning for someone who valued her abilities. Nicholas Sutherland and his chess piece. He'd slipped into her thoughts half a dozen times today. Handsome, charming, sophisticated. Powerful. Nicholas would make any woman's heart go pitter-patter. In that respect, he reminded her of Max. Funny how after such a long dry spell, she now had two men giving her hormones a charge.

Both handsome. Both charming. Yet, for the most part as different as night and day. No one would ever use the words "suave" and "debonaire" in connection with Max Cooper. The term "all-American guy" would never fit Nicholas Sutherland.

Still, Nicholas loved his family just as much as Max loved his. She wanted to find the chess piece for Nicholas. She needed to find it. She wanted him to view her as successful.

Reaching into her purse, she removed a folded slip of paper, the color copy of the ruby chess piece in Nicholas's possession. Elizabeth Beck's beauty salon was the obvious place to start.

Over the years, Elizabeth Beck's salon had grown into a thriving business. She'd expanded the storage room Jack had rented to her after the tornado destroyed her original shop. Two large plate-glass windows surrounded the street entrance door and brightened the shop with natural light. A single window beside the bowling alley entrance allowed customers to observe the action on the lanes, but cleverly placed sheer curtains provided privacy for those ladies who didn't want the world to see them in perm rods.

Kate walked into the shop and smiled. "You've changed the decor, Elizabeth. I love it."

"Hello, there, Katie-cat," Elizabeth said, using the nickname she'd given Kate when she was seven. She made a sweeping gesture with the pair of scissors in her right hand. "Collecting Scottie stuff is my newest hobby, and I ran out of room at home. First I acquired a Scottie rescue dog who runs my life, and next thing I knew, I was filling up the house with anything that was decorated with an image of that stubborn little terrier." She laughed. "I just wanted a dog, and I ended up with an illness."

Eyeing coffee mugs with a different Scottie on each, Kate saw what Elizabeth meant. "I love the paper towel holder and wastebasket. And the lamp. Wherever did you find it?"

"Marsha gave it to me for Christmas. Isn't it precious? I don't believe you've met Marsha Hopkins, have you, Kate?" She nodded toward the sinks, where a young woman with a short, stylish haircut and pretty green eyes stood above a draped client.

"I haven't had the pleasure."

Marsha's smile was bright, and her right ear sported three small gold hoops. *Triple piercing in Cedar Dell? Pretty racy.* Kate liked her immediately.

Elizabeth also introduced the two customers in the shop, women a decade older than Kate whom she vaguely remembered from school. "Marsha is my updo expert. About wore herself out the past couple weeks between prom and graduation."

Her hands covered in suds as she performed a scalp massage, Marsha said, "I wasn't as busy as Jane. She did forty-three new sets of acrylic nails the week before prom."

Elizabeth nodded. "A record. She's on a well-deserved vacation this week as a result. Has to get it in before all those new customers come back needing their fills. So, Katie-cat, are you and your boy getting settled in at your dad's house?"

"We're working on it."

"Ryan caused quite a stir here yesterday, you know."

"In what way?"

Elizabeth and Marsha shared an amused look. Marsha said, "I'm completely booked for the next month."

"Me too," Elizabeth added. "And I specialize in wet sets for the mature lady, not teenage cuts and color. Then there's the sudden surge in lane reservations. Why, up until this week, business at the bowling alley has been down for the year. Substantially down, I'm afraid. I've blamed it on the opening of the new baseball and softball fields over behind First Baptist. Between church leagues and Little League, kids stay busy most every night now. The ball games and the video games, which I think are evil."

"Now, Elizabeth," Marsha protested, before glancing at Kate. "She blames everything but the war in the Middle East on the Xbox."

"It's a fact that young people simply don't spend their time bowling like we used to do. The older set is dying off or wearing out after a game or two. But since word got out that the new boy in town—a tall, handsome, athletic fella—is coming to work at Harmon Lanes next week, we've been inundated with swarms of young ladies. And, of course, the boys will flock right along after them. Next week, I imagine this place will be a regular Love Bowl."

Kate fought not to change expression. The new boy in town? Ryan? Coming to work at Harmon Lanes?

I don't think so.

First the lake house, now this. She should never have left her office. She should have locked the door and worked nonstop. *That's what you get for being seduced by banana cream cake.*

Then, because she wanted, needed, a distraction from such disturbing thoughts, she held up the chess piece drawing for Elizabeth to see. "Do you by any chance remember anyone in town owning something similar to this?"

Elizabeth folded her arms, leaned against her station, and frowned as she studied the paper. "It's a small figurine, right? You know, I do have a vague recollection. Hmm."

"Let me see it," Marsha said.

Kate decided not to muddy the waters by explaining that the figurine was in truth a chess piece. She showed the drawing around, but drew a blank with the other women in the shop. "Why are you looking for it? It is something you lost?"

Kate offered the story she'd prepared. "It's a friend's lost family heirloom, and he's asked me to help him find it."

"*He? A Cedar Dell he?*"

Kate had no trouble reading between those lines. It was another sneak inquiry about the identity of Ryan's father. "Nicholas Sutherland is from Dallas."

"Nicholas Sutherland?" The woman with shampoo suds on her hair sat up. "I know about him. He called my neighbor's grandfather and asked questions about World War II souvenirs. Mr. Burnet wouldn't talk to him, though. He's a suspicious sort. Then my neighbor looked the guy up on the Internet and found out he's some fancy-schmancy lawyer who's worth a bundle. My neighbor tried to get his grandfather to call him back, but he wouldn't."

"Re-al-ly." Elizabeth drew the word out into very long syllables. "So you hang out with a fancy lawyer, Katie-cat?"

Kate couldn't help it. A girl never outgrew the desire to impress the hometown crowd. "Let's just say he's had iced tea at my kitchen table and leave it at that."

As the other women in the beauty shop shared a significant look, a newcomer entered the salon. The Widow Mallow took one look at the paper in Kate's hand and asked, "What are you doing with a picture of Helen Brown's figurine?"

The western sky was a symphony of vermilion and gold as the sun began its descent toward the horizon. In his house, Max was in a panic. What the hell had he done?

He'd made an after-dinner drink sound like a date, that's what. He'd followed up a perfectly innocent dinner invitation by telling her she was beautiful and asking her over for alcohol. Hell, why didn't he just say he wanted to show her his etchings?

"Daddy, not *that* pony holder." Shannon scowled at his reflection in her bedroom mirror. "I can't wear my pony holder with a doggie on it. I need my dolphins to match my pajamas."

"Where is your dolphin ponytail band?" he asked, knowing better than to waste time arguing. Some days his little girl didn't care what she wore, but on those days when she did, she cared a lot. Tonight she wanted her hair up and her bed down—she'd made an ocean out of pillows on her bedroom floor because she'd seen a TV commercial about swimming with the dolphins. How she got Mutt to wear those construction paper fins she'd tied on with ribbons, Max would never know.

"It's in the refrigerator."

Max opened his mouth, shut it without speaking, and let go of the hair he'd gathered into a ponytail. "Be quick. Miss Kate will be here any minute."

As his daughter scampered downstairs, Max sank onto

the corner of her bed. He tossed the purple plastic hair-brush end over end, catching it by the handle to toss into the air again. The dog lifted his head from one of Shannon's pillows and whined. "Don't complain to me," Max said. "Those flippers are between you and Shannon."

Mutt plopped his head back onto the pillow.

"Yeah, I know just how you feel, boy." God, had this been a strange couple of days, or what? First a nightmare trip down memory lane at his dad's place, then the battle scene with Ryan, next the twilight conversation with Kate.

And now a sort-of date. He'd never had a real date with Kate. They'd made a baby together, but they'd never shared fries at the Dairy Queen or held hands at the picture show. Did that make him look like scum, or what?

Things hadn't changed much over the years. Max couldn't remember the last time he'd had a real date. Not that he was a monk, or anything. He'd seen a few women since Rose's death. Had a semirelationship that lasted four or five months. But he hadn't gone out with a woman since moving to Cedar Dell. Come to think of it, his last date had been before Nana Jean died. That's a helluva long time for a man to go without sex. To make it even worse, he hadn't missed it all that much. Hadn't even realized it until now.

Maybe I should see a doctor.

The problems inherent in small-town dating aside, helping Shannon adjust to life without Nana Jean had used up all his energy and effort. "We've done a good job of it, too," he asserted to the pooch. "Didn't I master the French braid? Don't I have Crock-Pot cooking down pat?"

They were doing just fine without a woman around the house. Shannon wasn't sad all the time anymore. He hadn't turned any of his white underwear pink since that laundry debacle in February. Maybe he wasn't so hot baking cookies, but the slice and bake kind tasted good, too. And so what if they had a problem getting to school on time sometimes. All in all, Shannon wasn't missing out on much.

In that case, maybe he could work on getting some of what he was missing now.

"Daddy! Daddy! Daddy! The lady brought me a present. Lookit what I got! Lookie here!"

The lady. Kate. Kate was here.

Max swallowed hard, stood, and reached deep inside for a casual smile. Flying F-16s wasn't this hard.

He intended to go down to meet her, but by the time he reached the landing, Kate and Shannon were already halfway upstairs. A small basket dangled from Shannon's right hand, while her left was flung around Kate Harmon's neck in a big hug as Kate carried Shannon toward her father.

Kate wore form-hugging black slacks and a white blouse. She was grinning at Shannon and looked so beautiful he wanted to carry *her* up the stairs.

See what thinking about sex does to a man? Still, maybe a date wasn't such a bad idea after all.

"Daddy, Miz Kate brought me finger polish! Pink and red and yellow and sparkle blue. She said if it's okay with you, she'll polish me in sparkle blue now 'cause it matches my dolphins, and it'll be perfect for my ocean. She doesn't want to do Muffykins's toenails, but that's okay cause fishes don't have toenails."

"I think Mutt will understand." Max turned to his guest. "Hello, Kate. Welcome to Atlantis."

"Thank you." Kate gave Mutt a pat on the head and Max an awkward smile. The dog licked her hand, and her smile softened as she scratched Mutt behind the ears. Max answered Kate's smile with a shaky one of his own, then watched, dumbfounded and entranced, at the display of femininity that took place against the backdrop of blue sheets, a pile of pillows, and stuffed animals galore. When Shannon's giggles finally broke through his stupor, he reached for the camera he kept available on her dresser.

When Kate used a narrow brush to paint a gray dolphin on Shannon's ocean blue big toenail, Max fell a little in love.

The idea shocked him.

Max quickly put his camera down. "You girls almost finished? It's getting to be bedtime."

"But, Daddy!"

Kate laughed and snuggled Shannon, nuzzling her neck. "That's okay, honey. We'll play again soon. I found a big old box of my mother's costume jewelry that is waiting for a little girl to try on. Lots of sparkles. You'll love it."

"Can we play tomorrow?"

"Don't be pushy, Shannon," Max warned.

"Tell you what, honey. When I get home tonight, I'll check my calendar, and I'll call your daddy and make a play date for you and me. How about that?"

"Soon?"

Her smile warm, Kate tugged gently on Shannon's ponytail. "Soon. I promise."

Half an hour later, following a glass of water, two extra bedtime stories, three bathroom breaks for Shannon and one trip outdoors with Mutt, Shannon finally went down for the night.

Downstairs, Max showed Kate to the living room, where she made a sarcastic comment about his favorite, though admittedly ratty, recliner. Hiding a grin, he retreated to the kitchen, where he retrieved a pair of wineglasses from the kitchen cupboard. Pouring his favorite Napa Valley merlot, he smiled at the memory of Kate down on her hands and knees on his daughter's bedroom ocean playing fish and seagull, with Kate being the bird, Shannon the fish, and kisses the method of scoring.

As he'd watched Kate interact with his daughter, he'd been reminded of what a good mother she'd always been. He'd seen it during those too-few years when he'd been part of Ryan's life. He wondered again why she'd never had more children with Roger the Rat. He'd never asked, but he'd puzzled over it. Kate always struck him as more comfortable in the stay-at-home mom role than as a climb-the-ladder career woman.

The bits of lingering nervousness about the evening evaporated as Kate and Shannon shared giggles. Max realized he'd made too big a deal out of the whole thing. This wasn't a sport-coat-and-tie, impress-then-undress sort of date. This was a casual grown-up get-together with a five-year-old chaperone.

Besides, damned if it wasn't nice having a woman around. He'd missed it.

Maybe he should fix up a plate of cheese and crackers. Put out some fruit.

He was digging through the pantry looking for something other than animal crackers when Kate came looking for him. "Shannon is a doll, Max. I'm glad I came before you put her to bed. I haven't played girl-stuff in a long time."

Max glanced back over his shoulder. "She was in heaven. I never thought to give her nail polish."

"That's probably a good thing." Kate folded her arms and leaned casually against the doorjamb. "Some things are just better left within gender. I'll never forget what a mistake it was for me to help Ryan with a go-kart engine he was building. It's not that I couldn't use the grease gun properly. I couldn't do it in a way that suited him."

"Are you implying I wouldn't do a proper job of giving a five-year-old a pedicure?" Max asked, adopting an offended tone as he discovered a box of Ritz crackers behind the Froot Loops.

"Something like that, yes." She slipped the box of crackers from his hand, then took a plate from the glass-fronted cupboard and began to arrange the rounds in an artful circle.

"Yeah, well, I think you're probably right." Max grabbed a block of cheddar cheese from the fridge and began to slice precise squares. He'd forgotten this about women. Men ate cheese and crackers; women, canapés.

With that in mind, he grabbed a jar of olives from the refrigerator, too.

Her work with the crackers done, Kate leaned against the counter, sipped her wine, and gazed casually around the room. Max could all but see her compare it to the way Mrs. Gantt's kitchen had looked when they were growing up.

He hadn't gotten around to making many changes in here yet. The counters were still early-seventies Formica in harvest gold. The flooring was an earth-tone-patterned linoleum. An empty curtain rod hung above the window overlooking the backyard, and where the Gantts' large mahogany dining table once sat, Max's small, dented, scarred, and stained oak kitchen table took up space.

Not exactly a showplace, Max thought. "I'm taking the remodeling slow. I probably should have started with the kitchen and baths, but Shannon wanted her room done first."

"I love her built-in bookshelves and desk. I'll bet if Terri saw them, she'd be green with envy." She grinned mischievously, and added, "I still can't believe you bought Terri Gantt's house. You must have really liked that bedroom."

Max threw an olive at her. "Brat. I never saw her bedroom before I bought this house. I told you I wasn't sleeping with her. I was a virgin just like you that night."

You could have heard a soap bubble pop after that revelation. Not many guys admitted they had ever been virgins. In fact, this was Max's first time to do it.

Kate's gaze drifted to the refrigerator door, where magnets secured dozens of drawings in every color of the crayon box. Her tone turned serious. "You broke up with her right before Ryan was born. Was it because of what we did?"

Well, there goes the date.

He was surprisingly disappointed. He'd enjoyed their evening up until now, and talking about the sins of the past put a damper on a man's mood. Still, he wanted honesty between them. "Staying with Terri wouldn't have been fair. I realized I wasn't in love with her."

"Because of what happened in the tree house?"

No. Because he'd found it easier to break up with her than to confess his impending fatherhood. He dashed back a drink, treating it more like a shot of whiskey than fine wine. "She was my high school love, Kate. We grew up. We changed."

"For a long time, I felt guilty about Terri," Kate said. "Then one year at Christmastime I saw her at North Park Mall in Dallas. She just sparkled. She was six months pregnant and shopping with her husband. She told me that in him she'd found her soul mate."

She'd written something similar in her wedding gift thank-you note to Max. "I'm glad for her. Hear she has a couple of kids now."

"Three, I believe." Kate nodded toward the refrigerator and, to Max's relief, changed the subject. "You need a bigger refrigerator to hold all those drawings, Max."

He followed the path of her gaze and gave a woeful shake of his head. "I know. But every time I try to take one down, the little squirt notices. What's a dad to do?"

"You could try buying a scrapbook and asking her to make you an art book of her pictures after they 'hang' for a week. It worked with Ryan, and I treasure that scrapbook more than any valuable first edition."

"Thanks. I'll try that."

Kate sipped her wine, studied him over the top of her glass. As the seconds ticked by, Max began to feel a bit like an ant under a magnifying glass.

The woman was in a strange mood. Laughing one minute, pensive the next. Maybe she didn't want to rehash the past any more than he did. He liked the thought of that.

Max popped an olive in his mouth, then took a sip of his wine. Perhaps the evening could be salvaged after all. A nice, carefree evening sounded really good right now. He should take the plate of food into the den, then put on some music. Jazz. He'd bet Kate liked jazz. Maybe they could dance. Maybe neck a little.

His fantasy was just getting good when she interrupted it.

"When you called the other day, you wanted reassurance that you're a good father. I've thought about that quite a bit since then."

"Hold on a minute. You told me I am a good father. You can't take it back."

"I'm not taking it back. I'm elaborating." She looked into her glass, not at him. "You're a good father now, but you have to admit, that hasn't always been the case."

"But—"

She put her fingers against his lips. "Let me finish. What I'm trying to say is that your determination to heal the breach with Ryan comes at a fortuitous time." Her wistful gaze returned to the refrigerator art. "Which is a good thing because I suspect your skills are about to be tested."

His stomach sank. That didn't sound good. Max set his glass on the counter. "What's up?"

"My sister called. The Cedar Dell grapevine is on high alert. Somebody saw you speaking with Ryan at the park. They're putting two and two together and actually getting four."

All thoughts of jazz, dancing, and necking with a gorgeous woman evaporated. "They know I'm his father?"

"They've added your name to the list of suspects. It's never been there before. Your commitment to Terri kept you insulated at the time."

"I never asked her to marry me." Max grabbed his glass and the bottle of wine and sank into a seat at the kitchen table. Well. Wow. Damn. So, he'd gotten what he'd wanted. Cedar Dell would know Ryan Harmon was his.

He dragged his hand down his face. He topped off his glass, then when Kate took a seat across from him, topped hers off, too.

"Max? Are you okay with this? I thought it was what you wanted."

"I did. I do." And as he said it, he meant it. A fierce rush of gladness swept through him. "I *do*. It's great." For him, anyway. "How is Ryan going to take it?"

"That depends." She scooted closer to the table and leaned toward him. "Did he listen at all when you talked to him?"

Max reflected on the exchange and grimaced. "Not enough, probably."

"Under the very best circumstances, teenagers never listen enough, Max." Reaching across the table, Kate touched his hand. "Honestly, I think we may be in for a rough few days. Ryan is a fair kid, and he's grown up a lot in the past couple of years. I believe he'll mull over the information you gave him, and when he does, he'll find his way back to you."

"You mean it?"

"I do. He got over being mad at me, didn't he?"

Max sat back in his chair. "He was mad at you?"

"Furious. When he quit talking to you, he also quit talking to me. Didn't say a word to me for three weeks."

"Better than three years," Max grumbled.

"Much better."

She paused, and Max could tell she was working up to saying something difficult. He braced himself.

"I need to apologize to you for that, Max."

Well, now. This was a surprise.

"It was wrong of me to let this estrangement between the two of you drag on. At first I was caught up in what was happening between Roger and me, then it was easier simply to let matters stand. Easier to listen to the psychologist than my own gut feelings. I put it all out of my mind as much as possible."

Her lids covered her expressive eyes as she traced the shape of the wineglass with one finger. As much as she adored their son, the divorce must have hurt like hell, to put anything concerning him out of her mind. But Kate wasn't a whiner. Even when she could and should have been.

Now she put both hands flat on the table and looked directly at him. "That was wrong, for you and, more importantly, for Ryan. He needed a father. He needs his father. I'm glad the truth is finally coming out. I believe it will be the catalyst that brings the two of you together."

Max didn't know how to respond. He was humbled and grateful. And a part of him was angry that it had taken three years to bring them to this point. Rather than dwell on the negative, he tried to move forward. "What makes you say that?"

"Because I know your son, and I know this town. Somebody, and I'll predict right now it'll be one of The Widows, will say something that will cause Ryan to rise to your defense. Once he does that . . ." She shrugged and reached for a cracker. "He wants a reconciliation, too, Max. Deep down, he wants it, too."

"God, I hope so." The words were a prayer.

Kate took a bite of her cracker and smiled. "I'm eager to see how Ryan and Shannon get along."

"Shannon." Max winced, his gaze shifting toward the refrigerator where it froze on a drawing of him, Shannon, and the mutt in purple and orange crayon. "She doesn't know she has a brother."

"I wondered if you might have told her."

"No. Shannon doesn't know the meaning of the word 'secret,' and I didn't figure it was up to her to spill the beans." He drew a deep breath, then exhaled forcefully. "I'll have to tell her. She'll be thrilled."

"She may be a bit threatened."

Max considered it. "Possibly, but I doubt it. She's more likely to issue some threats of her own. She'll want Ryan to play with her and wear Pig Pink socks."

"Pig Pink?"

"Her most favorite color."

Kate laughed.

"She'll be a royal pain in the ass for him." Then another thought struck him. "What about your father? What will Jack say about all this?" He hesitated a second, then said, "He doesn't already know, does he? You didn't tell him after that, uh, business with Roger the Rat."

"The word is divorce, Max. After the divorce from

Roger the Rat." Kate drummed her fingers against the table. "I didn't tell him, but I don't know what my father knows or what he thinks or what he feels."

Kate popped an olive in her mouth, chewed angrily, then swallowed. She lifted her wineglass and drained it. "I do know what he's doing. He's selling the lake house."

"What? But doesn't Ryan love the lake house? He did when he was younger."

"A Realtor called. He's had an offer on it. I can't get him to talk about it with me. I don't know why he's selling it. I don't know if I can do anything to change his mind. Yes, Ryan loves it. I love it. The lake house represents the best of my childhood and the only good times we've shared with the Harmon family since my mother died. If Dad's determined to sell it, I'd like to explore the possibility of buying it myself, but I can't get him to respond to my questions with anything other than silence."

"Ryan won't like losing it."

"He'll hate it. The lake house is his favorite place in the world. It's been our vacation spot, and we made a lot of memories there. I wouldn't come home to Cedar Dell, we didn't have money to take any trips, but we used the lake house as often as I could manage. Ryan may be a basketball jock now, but his first love is fishing."

"I remember. I took him fishing a few times. All he did was talk about his trips to the lake." Max poured Kate another glass of wine. "Maybe your dad found out you made more than memories at the lake house. Maybe that's why he's selling it."

It took her a minute to make the connection, but then

she shook her head. "No. I didn't share that piece of information."

"If The Widows are doing arithmetic, he's about to learn some of it. What do you want to do about it, Kate? Shall we tell them to go to hell? We can flat out deny it if you think that's best for Ryan. Or, do we own up to it? Do you want to handle it proactively or reactively? What's best for our son?"

She thought about it for a long minute. "I think we should take control, but we may have a hard time convincing Ryan of it. I'll talk to him when he gets home tomorrow. See if he's ready to quit running. Maybe we could all go to dinner or something."

Max arched a curious brow. "Dinner?"

"I think the four of us sitting down to dinner at a public restaurant would be sufficient to 'out' us. A family outing."

Max's mouth quirked at the term—he'd never expected to be "outed" at anything. "In the most real sense of the word. That's not a bad idea. We could go to the Piccadilly after church tomorrow."

She shook her head. "That's too soon. Ryan won't be home from his tournament until late. He'll be tired, and he won't want to talk, not about this."

"Okay." After a moment's consideration, he added, "You know what would be good. We should go together to the fish fry next week. Everyone in town will be there. We'll get it over with fast."

"No. I have a date to the fish fry."

A date? She has a date. "You have a date?"

She frowned. "Yes."

"Who with?"

Annoyance sparked in her eyes. "A friend."

"What friend?"

She folded her arms. "A friend from Dallas."

"What's his name?"

"Nicholas."

"Nicholas Who?"

"Nicholas Sutherland, as if it's any of your business."

Nicholas Sutherland. The name was familiar, but Max couldn't quite place it. He shoved back his chair and carried the cheese and crackers to the sink and dumped them down the disposal. "Well, it is my business. We have issues here. Sorry that our family crisis is interfering with your social life."

She fired a look that shouted "Jerk," then said, "Let's see what Ryan wants to do. In the meantime, you might want to prepare Shannon for the circus. You know it's bound to be one."

"No, circus is too mild a word. I'm thinking along the lines of a melee."

While Kate sipped her wine, Max sulked. She shouldn't be dating some outsider. Not now. Not when their family situation was so dicey. Speaking of family situation, he'd need to tell Shannon about her brother soon. Maybe he'd tell her tomorrow over breakfast. He could make French toast and spill the beans. No, wait. He'd take her to Dairy Queen for Frito chili pie, then they could walk down to the river to throw stones in the water and he could tell her there. "What about your dad? Will you tell him?"

"About Ryan?" She considered it a minute, then grimaced. "I don't know. I'll need to think about it. It might be easier to let the news come from someone else. He'll hear it fast enough."

"True. Nothing's quite so fast as the Cedar Dell grape-vine."

He poured the last of the wine, then conversation turned toward town life, politics both local and national, and their respective careers. Kate gestured toward a photograph of an ocean sunset and asked if it was his work.

"No. I don't display my own work. Strikes me as a bit egotistical."

Kate nodded toward the candid shot that graced the buffet of Shannon examining a fuzzy green caterpillar. "What about that?"

His smile was sheepish. "Pictures of Shannon don't count. I have some of Ryan I want to bring downstairs, but until our relationship is out in the open, I figure it's best to keep them up in my office."

"Pictures of Ryan? Can I see them?"

Max took a quick mental inventory of his office and its messiness quotient. Not too bad. No more than one pair of dirty socks lying around, probably. "Sure. Follow me."

Max led her upstairs to his office. Thankfully, Kate refrained from further comment about Terri Gantt's old bedroom, and he ignored the speculative gleam in her eyes.

"Oh, Max," she said, gazing at the framed collection of photos on the wall. "These are impressive. I knew you were talented, but I . . ." Her voice trailed off as her gaze snagged on the section of family photographs.

There were two dozen photographs all together, six of Ryan, six of Shannon, two of his late wife, two of Nana Jean, and one of Kate—snapped without her knowledge when he'd sneaked into one of their son's ninth grade basketball games. The rest were landscapes, places of significance in Max's family life, like the Hawaiian beach where he'd asked Rose to marry him. The home he'd shared with Rose in Germany when Shannon was born. Nana Jean's vegetable garden at the house in Tallahassee.

"Why did you take my picture?" Kate asked. "Ryan, I understand, but why . . . hey. That's our tree house. Why do you have a . . . oh."

Her gaze shifted to one of the photos of Ryan, then back to the tree house again. A light flush stole into her cheeks. "C'mon, Max. Why not broadcast it to the world? Do you really need a reminder hanging on your wall?"

He wouldn't apologize. It was a great shot. Excellent composition. Perfect light. The tree house almost looked alive, worn and weathered, yet brimming with the memories and the energy of youth.

"Do I need a reminder?" Max repeated, his mouth quirking in a grin. "Not really. A fella never forgets his first tree house."

Ryan arrived in Cedar Dell physically exhausted and mentally refreshed. His team copped second place in the tourney, losing the championship game in an eleven-inning heartbreaker to a team from San Antonio. He'd had two hits and two RBIs, and he'd turned a nice double play to prevent a run from scoring in the sixth.

The coach had asked him to fill in again at a tourney down in Austin in two weeks, but Ryan knew better than to commit himself to that. He would be starting a new job on

Monday, and he wouldn't feel right asking for a day off so soon, not even if his boss loved baseball even more than Ryan and had demanded he call with a report following each game of the tournament. When he told his granddad his team had earned the spot in the championship game, Jack Harmon bemoaned the demise of his Cougar in the wreck. "Why, if I had my car, I'd drive down to watch the game," he'd told him during Ryan's call earlier that afternoon. "Weatherford is not that far a drive from Cedar Dell."

"Don't you know Mom would have had a cat about that," he mused as he pulled into the driveway and turned off his truck. Immediately, he was struck by the quiet of a country night.

Not that silence surrounded him. Crickets chirped and dogs barked and from the flower bed came the full-throated croak of a bullfrog. But Ryan didn't hear traffic sounds on the freeway like he did at home. He didn't hear airplanes overhead. He didn't hear . . . hurry. He heard peace and quiet and slow.

He smiled.

Light from the television flickered against the window shade in his grandfather's makeshift bedroom, and, up-stairs, lamplight shone steadily from Adele's window. His mother's bedroom and office were dark. He grabbed his gear bag from the passenger seat, slung it over his shoulder, and headed up the front walk.

The porch rocker creaked, and he stared hard into the shadows. "Mom?"

"Hi, honey. You made good time. No speeding tickets, I trust?"

He winced at the thought of a black-and-white cruiser and a few anxious minutes, but was pleased to answer honestly, "Nope. No speeding tickets."

The warning citation in his pocket didn't count.

"Whatcha doin' sittin' out here in the dark, Mom?"

"Waiting for you."

Every muscle in his body went taut. "What's wrong? Is it Granddad?"

"He's fine. Everyone's fine. I'm tired. Some of your granddad's friends came over today for a checkers tournament, so I had free time. I thought I had a lead on Mr. Sutherland's chess piece, but it turns out Helen Brown sold it in a garage sale a couple of years ago. So I took my investigation to the streets."

"You went garage sale-ing?"

"Hit every one in town today. I'd forgotten how much work it is."

"Have any luck?"

"No." She sighed. "Not anything tangible. Found a few places to look and names of people to talk with, though. Adele bought a plaster pig and a set of golf clubs." She paused a moment while he snickered, then said, "We need to talk, Ry."

Well, hell. He knew that tone. This was about Max Cooper. "I'm tired, Mom. Traffic was bad on I-20, and I got stopped by a state trooper. Scared the bejezus out of me. He clocked me going eight miles above the speed limit and let me off with just a warning, but for a little while there I had an adrenaline rush I'm still recovering from. Can't this wait until morning?"

"You must really not want to talk about your father if you'll fess up to a speeding ticket."

"A warning. Don't have to pay a fine, and it doesn't go on my record."

"Consider this your second of the night. The whispers are starting. Time is ticking away. Our secret won't last much longer in this small town."

"So?"

"They're gonna know that he's your dad."

"So?"

"That's all you have to say? So?"

"What do you want me to say? That I'm glad? Not hardly. I think the whole thing sucks if you want to know the truth. I'd like to tell those old hags to stuff it, but I won't. I know the small-town rules."

She glanced away, and had to clear her throat before she spoke. "Nevertheless, we need to deal with this. I want the four of us to go out to dinner one night next week. I'm asking for your cooperation, son. You've had time to consider, and now it's time to commit. I want you and me to join Max Cooper and his daughter Shannon for supper Wednesday night at the Cedar Dell Steak House."

"Okay. No problem."

"No problem?" She set her wineglass on the porch rail and rose from the rocking chair. "That's all? After all this trauma? Just 'no problem'?"

"Acknowledging the blood connection between me and that man will not change anything for me. This was not my secret, Mom. It was yours. Yours and his. I simply don't care one way or another what happens."

"But Ryan, people will—"

"I don't care what people will say or do or think. I spent some time thinking about it while I was away. I've figured it out, Mom. I don't care what people know or don't know. I don't care what they think. My attitude doesn't change either way."

"And what attitude are you referring to?"

"I don't like the man, respect him, or want him in my life. He's not my problem. He's your problem, and you're his problem, and I wish y'all the best dealing with it." He climbed the porch steps and continued toward the door.

"Ryan, wait. You're part of this, too."

"Not really." He stopped, looked over his shoulder. His mom's face remained in the shadows. "If you're ready to let the world in on your secret, fine. It's your secret. Not mine. If you want me to go to dinner, I'll go to dinner. But it's important you all understand one thing. Just because he's my father, it doesn't mean he's my dad."

In a hesitant, shaky voice, she asked, "Don't you want a dad, Ryan?"

He had a brief flash of memory. He and Max fishing on Lake Lewisville north of Dallas in an old fishing boat with an older Johnson outboard. They drank root beer and ate Cheetos for lunch and laughed when a swimmer put his life jacket on upside down and wore it like a diaper.

"No, Mom, I don't. Not anymore."

Chapter Ten

AS IN MANY SMALL TOWNS across the South, Sunday morning in Cedar Dell meant church and the Piccadilly Cafeteria. The order of arrival at the Piccadilly tended to run
along denominational lines. The Episcopalians ordinarily
showed up first and made a run on the pancakes, sausage,
and eggs. The Methodists and Presbyterians wandered in
next, dividing their orders evenly between the breakfast
and the brunch plate, which included a slice of roast beef,
ham, two vegetables, and a roll. The Baptists were strictly
an after noon crowd, showing a clear preference for fried
chicken and chicken-fried steak.

Green Jell-O, however, proved popular at every hour
and was considered completely nondenominational.

Kate hadn't been to the Piccadilly since the Sunday before high school graduation. She had no intention of
breaking her streak today. The idea of going to church
made her nervous enough.

For decades, the Harmon family had attended 9:00 A.M.
services at St. Stephen's Methodist Church. In Dallas, Kate
and Ryan went to mass weekly at a small, suburban Episcopal church. Showing up at St. Michael's Episcopal here in

Cedar Dell would raise almost as big a stink as having a child out of wedlock.

"Lucky thing I'm already the black sheep of the family," she muttered, second thoughts causing her reluctantly to return her most comfortable summer slacks to her closet in favor of a dress. Thank goodness she'd packed one. While she was willing to break tradition by attending St. Michael's this morning, a woman could only be so daring.

She had her dress halfway zipped when she realized that church and a dress in Cedar Dell meant panty hose and pumps rather than sandals. "Maybe I should just stay home. Maybe I could tell them I converted to Judaism, and I went to temple yesterday."

"What in the world are you mumbling about?" Adele asked from the doorway.

"Oh, nothing," Kate replied without looking up.

"Well 'oh nothing' yourself into your panty hose, would you? We're going to be late."

We? Kate glanced at her friend, and her eyes went wide. Adele wore a dress, a floral-sprigged cotton with cap sleeves, pearl buttons, and a lace collar. "Where in the world did you get that dress?"

"Awful, isn't it? I called Lenore Sundine. Nice woman. I met her at Weight Watchers. The Saturday afternoon meeting. I think I'll go to that one from now on, rather than the Thursday night meeting. More men there on Saturday. I think everything—even diet clubs—are more interesting when men are involved. I kinda have my eye on Sam Tolbin. I'm in the mood for a man again, and I just might see if there's somewhere that could go."

"Just be careful. This little old town is full of big old heartbreakers."

"Oh, I'm no dummy, darlin'. I know how to protect my heart. I've observed a champion for years now. Anyway, when I realized I need a dress, I called Lenore to borrow one. Do you know that not a single store in this entire town is open on Sunday morning? And Cedar Dell doesn't even have a Wal-Mart. Imagine that."

"Adele, excuse me. Back up. I must be misunderstanding something here. Why do you need a church dress?"

"To wear to church, dearest."

"But you don't believe in organized religion."

"But I do believe in family, and you're my family, and I'm not about to let you go by yourself. Hurry up, now."

What did family have to do with it? Kate tried to make sense of this new development. In all the years she'd known Adele, she'd never once gone to church. And she'd never, ever, worn a dress like the one she had on this morning.

"Kate! Move your butt."

"Adele, it's only eight-thirty. We have an hour. If we leave the house by ten after, we'll have plenty of time to park and take our seats before the service starts."

"Church starts at nine. We've got to hurry. Your father is already on the front porch waiting for us."

Nine? Dad? An uneasy sensation crept over her. The studied blankness in Adele's expression confirmed the suspicion that rose in her mind like a B-movie monster. "Oh, no. We're not going to St. Stephen's."

"Oh, yes we are. Your sister called while you were in the shower. She and her baby are doing so good that her obstetrician has given her permission to leave her bed for a few hours each day. She and Alan will be in church. We will attend as a family."

Kate glanced at her reflection in the mirror. She looked like she should be going to the hospital rather than church. This was good news about Sarah, great news, but Kate didn't see why that meant they'd need to make a family appearance. "We're not Methodists, Adele."

"Doesn't matter. This has nothing to do with church or religion. It's all about family. Doesn't matter whether we go to St. Stephen's or St. Michael's or St. Speedy-Service-to-Beat-the-Piccadilly-Rush. Attending services together as a family is a symbol not just to this town, but to you. You need to do this, honey."

"Why?"

"To help this family heal."

Kate sank down on the edge of her bed, staring up at her friend incredulously. The moment was surreal.

"But you don't *like* my family." Childish hurt fluttered through her. *You're supposed to be on* my *side*.

"True. I think they've treated you abominably over the years. Before this is all done, when your dad is stronger and Sarah doesn't need so much coddling, I'll tell them so. I won't waste words on your brother. I think it'll take a swift kick in the ass to catch his attention."

I'm Alice down the rabbit hole.

"In fact," Adele continued, "your brother may well be a total waste of time. Nevertheless, you . . . we . . . all of us need to try. The Harmon family needs to be healed."

"Good Lord, Adele. You sound like a television preacher, and you're dressed like his wife."

Adele fingered the lace collar on her dress. Her gaze gentled, her voice softened. "Take a good look at your father when you go downstairs, Kate. He's an old man. He won't live forever. Don't let him die with this ugliness between you. You'll regret it the rest of your life."

"I know." Kate closed her eyes. "You're right, Adele. I know it. But fixing this family? You're asking for a miracle."

"Hey, I'm going to church, aren't I?"

Kate chuckled at her friend's dry tone.

Adele crossed the room, bent over, and pressed a kiss against the crown of Kate's head. "Miracles do happen, you know. You're back home. Max Cooper and Ryan live in the same zip code and have the chance to put their relationship back on track. You had a date, even if he didn't kiss you good night."

"You were spying?"

"Of course, along with a couple of the neighbors. I must say the man let me down, leaving you at the back gate like that. He could have at least walked you to the door."

"No, he couldn't. Shannon was home alone, asleep in bed."

Adele stopped, frowned. "Oh, all right. I'll concede the point. However, he should have planned better. Not to worry, though. I'll bet Mr. Sutherland lays a big one on you next Saturday. So have a little faith, Katie, and put your panty hose on."

Kate did as she was told, her mind spinning, her stomach churning. Why she dreaded the idea of attending services at St. Stephen's so much, she couldn't say. It wasn't logical. She probably wouldn't see anyone she hadn't already run into around town. It might be nice to sit next to

Sarah at a church service again. The last time she'd done that . . . oh.

The last time the Harmon family attended church together was her mother's funeral.

No wonder the idea struck terror into her heart. That day was, by far, the worst day of her life.

As she smoothed on her hose, Kate recalled the events surrounding her mother's funeral and shuddered. Her mom, Kate's lone support in the family, suddenly gone, far too young and far too quickly. Her brother had called with the news of Linnie Harmon's aneurysm and pending services—a day and a half after their mom's death. Funeral arrangements had all been made. He and Sarah and their dad had chosen a pretty pink casket. Mom's cousins from Kansas were coming in and needed a place to stay, so, Tom had pointed out, if Kate chose to attend the services, she probably shouldn't plan on spending the night at home. It had been a cruel way to behave, even for someone as clueless as Tom.

Kate barely remembered the service itself, consumed by grief as she had been. Her one clear memory was of hugging Ryan so hard that once during the service, the three-year-old had cried out, "Stop, Mommy. You're squeeging me!"

The moments indelibly etched upon her brain, however, were those outside the church following the service, when the gossiping hoard had hovered. Somewhere in the back of her mind, Kate had known that bringing her son to his grandmother's funeral would cause a stir. After Tom's phone call, there might have been a bit of in-your-face attitude in her decision to attend with Ryan in her arms. Still, she'd never expected the situation could turn so ugly so fast at such a sad and solemn occasion.

The hens had pecked her half to death without ever speaking to her directly.

"*So she wasn't off at college in California?*" *whispered Mrs. Gault, loud enough for half of Cedar Dell to hear.*

"*Who's the father?*" *murmured another.*

"*Did her mother know about this? Poor Linnie. The scandal couldn't have been good for her heart. I wouldn't be surprised if it contributed to her death.*"

"*Who's the father?*"

"*No wonder Jack never talks about her. I knew something was peculiar about the way she disappeared back then. He always deflected questions about her.*"

Then, in a chorus, they chimed, "*Who's the father! Who's the father? Who's the father?*"

Kate hadn't been trying to cause a scene or make matters worse. She was looking for help from someone she could trust as the whispers and mutterings escalated. Like any good parishioner, she looked to her leadership for guidance. She shot a panicked glance toward the church doors and said, "*Father Winston!*"

The multitude of gasps seemed to have sucked all the air from the church steps. Martha Gault chose to clarify the point by backing away, her eyes brimming with shock. She brought her hand to cover her trembling mouth, backing slowly away from the hoard. She had everyone's attention when she unfurled her arm with a flourish and pointed. "*Father Winston is the father?*"

The funeral went to hell from there.

And so did she, as far as Jack and the town were concerned.

"Mom," Ryan shouted from downstairs, yanking her back to the present. "If you don't hurry, we won't be in time to get a good seat in the back."

Kate pulled up her hose, tucked away bad memories, and went to church with her family.

It proved to be a relatively pain-free occasion. Her brother-in-law Alan treated her warmly as usual, standing and kissing her cheek when they arrived. Sarah remained seated, a ripe Madonna, who beamed her pleasure at having her sister by her side. Even Jack seemed mellow during the service, although Kate could see lines of discomfort bracketing his face and noted he slipped an over-the-counter painkiller into his mouth during the sermon.

Upon exiting the church following the closing hymn, Jack and Sarah took seats on one of the park benches beneath the magnolia tree out front and began holding court. Adele wandered off to speak with some new acquaintances from her Weight Watchers meeting, and Kate braced herself against an onslaught. To her surprise and gratitude, it never occurred. Ryan attracted more than his share of attention, but it was the sort he welcomed, that of teenage girls. Folks were friendly to Kate, and she received three invitations to the Piccadilly. Gradually, she relaxed.

Services let out across the street at the Presbyterian church, and the milling crowd almost doubled. Kate visited with an old friend from school, Sharon Hill, now Sharon Houston, and met her husband, Lloyd, who'd established a new furniture store in town ten years ago. Before the Houstons excused themselves to pick up their children from the church nursery, Kate had secured a new client.

Pleased with herself, Kate turned to join her family just

in time to see blond curls and pink ruffles skip up to Kate's father.

"Hi, Mr. Wilson," she said, giving his wheeled walker a once over. "We just got done with church across the street and I saw you sitting here so I came over. Daddy says you had a car wreck. Did it hurt? Did you get a Big Bird Band-Aid? Did they give you a shot?"

Kate watched in awe as her gruff, grumpy father grinned and reached out to tug one of Shannon's French-braided pigtails.

"Hello, Dennis, my Menace," he replied.

"I did not get a Big Bird Band-Aid," Jack continued. "I'm sad about that. Yes, it hurt something fierce, but I'm better now."

"Good. I can give you a Pig Pink Band-Aid if you want. It doesn't have characters on it, but it is a very pretty color."

"Thank you, dear. That would be nice."

A strange combination of pleasure and injury shot through Kate. It was nice seeing him be kind to Shannon, and yet, it hurt. He'd never pulled her pigtails when she was young. He'd never teased her or given her a pet name. Not that she could remember, anyway.

What had been wrong with her that Jack Harmon couldn't love her?

"Good. Maybe you can push me on the swing again soon." Shannon frowned at his walker. "That's a funny-looking scooter. Can I play with it?"

"No, you'd better not. I need it with me. It keeps me from falling over."

"Oh. Why do you go to this church and not the one Daddy and I go to, Mr. Wilson? Our church has a prettier steeple. That's what that tall, pointy thing is on the top of it. Did you know that?"

"I do know that."

"We could have gone to your church, but I didn't want to. When we moved here, Daddy let me pick. He said he knew I'd pick this one because it had the prettiest steeple, but he was almost wrong. I almost picked the church with the pretty statue of Jesus' mother out front."

Ryan interrupted with a scoff. "You chose your religion on the basis of a church steeple?"

"Seems to be as good a reason as any," Adele observed.

Shannon frowned up at Ryan. "Are you being mean again?"

He looked at her as if she were an interesting bug. "You *are* a little princess, aren't you?"

Shannon looked at Kate. "I think he's being mean again. Make him stop it. He needs to be nice and walk me back across the street."

"I'm not being mean, and why do I need to walk you across the street?"

"Because my daddy is gonna be mad at me because I crossed by myself."

"What does that have to do with me?"

"You broke my crown."

Ryan rolled his eyes as Jack grumbled, "Oh, just walk her across the street, boy."

Shannon took Ryan's hand and started tugging him forward. Busy listening to Shannon, neither Kate nor Ryan noticed Max walking toward them. They met halfway across Main Street and as her son handed his sister over to their father, Kate was struck anew by the similarities between the two men. Same height. Same build. Same stance. "Oh, Lord."

Never mind dinner out. Somebody was bound to notice this.

All in all, it had been a lovely morning, and Kate didn't want it ruined. If somebody, like one of The Widows, made the connection and raised a ruckus on the church steps right now, she might start screaming and never stop.

As casually as possible, Kate glanced around. Well, hell. Janice Gilbert gazed right at Max, a speculative look on her face. At least the Widow Mallow wasn't looking in that direction.

"Kate, quit lollygagging around," her father said, fatigue noticeable in his voice. "I'm ready to go home."

"Sure, Dad," Kate said. Gladly. The sooner away from here the better.

Alan shot his wife a me-too look, then said, "I'll walk with you to the car, Jack. Did you see that triple play in the Astros' game last night?"

Jack allowed his son-in-law and Ryan to help him to his feet, but he shook them off as he started toward the parking lot. Kate prepared to follow, but Sarah stayed her with a hand on her arm. "How is he doing, Kate?"

The contact startled her, and Kate tried to recall the last time Sarah had touched her. She couldn't. She shrugged off the troubling thought. "Better than I expected, to be honest. He needs help getting up and sitting down, but once he's in a position he likes, he's fine." After a moment's hesitation, she added, "Sometimes he seems awfully confused. Have you noticed?"

Sarah's brow furrowed with concern. "Yes, I have. A

time or two. I don't think it's anything more than old age.
My memory certainly isn't what it used to be."

Kate suspected her father's condition might be more serious than that, and she thought it worth a call to his doctor. "I just wonder if they shouldn't do some neurological
testing."

Sarah leaned against the stone retaining wall that surrounded the old magnolia tree growing in the churchyard.
"It wouldn't hurt, I guess. Unless they want to do an MRI.
Dad has said he'll never let anyone run that test on him. He
thinks the machine is too much like a coffin."

Glancing toward the parking lot, Kate watched her father shuffle slowly toward the car. Though anxious to
leave, and not entirely comfortable with her sister, she recognized the opportunity to bring up a troublesome subject.
"Sarah, is he having financial trouble?"

"Why do you ask that?"

"It's one explanation for putting the lake house up for
sale."

"When does he plan to do that?"

"He's already done it. Someone's made an offer on it."

"Oh, dear." She pursed her lips in consideration. "Well,
he must have his reasons."

Kate gaped at her sister. That's it? He must have his reasons? Automatic acceptance? *My God, she is so much like
Mom.*

Sarah absently rubbed her back as she turned her head
to watch her husband assist her father into Kate's car. "I
don't believe he has money trouble. I know business slowed
down at Harmon Lanes for a while, but it wasn't *that* slow.

He hardly has any personal expenses. He gets his Social Security, and he has rental income from the duplex."

What duplex? Kate didn't know he owned a duplex.

"Although, come to think of it, he might have sold the duplex. I don't remember. Dad's always kept his financial matters private."

"Maybe it's time someone looked over his records," Katie said. "His health insurance has probably quadrupled in the past few years. I know mine has. Add taxes to that and utility increases—he might be having a rougher time of it than anyone knows. Also, he gets a stack of mail that I know are bills almost every day. He won't let me near them, though."

"Well, you know Dad."

No, she didn't. Not really. She never had. No matter how much she'd wanted to. "I'm just afraid something fishy is going on. It makes no sense that he'd sell the lake place without mentioning it to one of us."

It made no sense he'd cry about it, either. Not unless something was wrong.

"Maybe he told Tom," Sarah said. "Have you asked him?"

"No. I will next time he calls. He hasn't phoned Dad in the last few days."

"Oh, he does that." Sarah waved the issue away. "He'll get busy and forget to call. That's why I always try to phone a couple times a day. Dad grumbles about it, but I know he likes hearing from someone. It probably helps break up the monotony of his days."

Sarah spoke the truth, and Kate suddenly saw her sister

in a different light. How much she'd carried on her shoulders all these years, being the only family member in town. Kate knew her sister loved their father, but it could not have been easy for her. "I'll call, too, once we're back in Dallas. Even if he doesn't want to hear from me."

Sarah beamed her Madonna smile. "That's great, Kate. I hope you will. It'd be good for you both."

"In the meantime, I think I'll call Tom. See what he knows about the lake house. Something smells fishy about it to me."

"It's the bait buckets," Sarah wryly responded. "For some reason, Alan brings them up to the cabin rather than leaving them in the boathouse."

They laughed, and said their good-byes. Kate promised to call her sister if she learned anything of import from their brother. As Alan and Sarah drove off, Kate felt a tug of yearning, a longing for family ties severed since before Ryan's birth.

The drive home and her father's unending stream of complaints cured her of lingering melancholy. Upon their arrival, his refusal to grant Adele's request that they turn up the air conditioner because "the damned electric company are overcharging fascists" brought the question of her father's finances back to mind. She changed out of panty hose and pumps into shorts and sandals, and decided to poke around in his business a little bit and see what she could find.

Downstairs, she found Adele looking like herself again in bright red shorts, a blue shirt, and earrings shaped like pineapples. She had her mixing bowls out.

"I'm told The Widows are planning another assault,"

she told Kate. "Bringing pies by later today. Apple and rhubarb. Thought I'd whip up our defense."

"Lemon chess?"

"Of course."

"The war is over. Your lemon chess will whip a rhubarb pie to Dallas and back."

"Yep. Those gals don't know they're beaten yet. The pikers. Did you see that dress Martha Gault had on? It was worse than the one I wore. It's her number five."

"Five?"

"She has ten church outfits. Wears them in order no matter what the weather is. Today she wore number five."

Kate nodded sagely. "I saw you talking to Mavis Hartman, too."

Adele cracked an egg into her mixing bowl. "She told me the mayor has a little problem with gambling. You know, Kate, I might just need to go to church more often. Best source of gossip I've seen in a while."

"Visiting-on-the-church-steps as a news source in Cedar Dell comes in second only to the beauty shop." Kate handed Adele the bottle of vanilla. "Not only did I pick up a new client for myself, I learned of a great volunteer opportunity for Ryan."

"Has he talked to you about his job?" Adele said abruptly.

"What job?"

"At Harmon Lanes. He starts tomorrow."

Kate shook her head. "Actually, he begins his internship tomorrow."

"The two of you haven't talked about this yet?" Adele sighed and shook her head.

"We'll discuss it this afternoon."

"He *wants* the bowling alley job."

"He *needs* the internship. It's important for his future."

"Exactly. Think about what you said, Kate. It's Ryan's future. Not yours, and certainly not your past."

"Wait a minute. I don't—"

"This isn't about you, it's about him." She opened the flour canister and banged its pottery lid against the counter. "Have you bothered to ask the boy what he wants?"

Annoyed, Kate plopped the sugar canister down beside the flour. "He's seventeen years old. He should have a plan."

"Did you have a plan at seventeen?"

"Yes, I darn sure did, and it was a good one."

"Maybe Ryan has one, too. Maybe he has a plan that's different from the one you have for him. Maybe he's just afraid to tell you."

"Ryan can tell me anything," Kate said, bristling. "He knows that."

"Does he? I wonder."

Kate folded her arms and eyed Adele suspiciously. "Do you know something I don't? Has Ryan been talking to you?"

"Of course he has. Ryan talks to both of us." Adele twisted the dial on her mixer. Raising her voice to be heard over the whine of the beaters, she added, "The difference is, I listen."

The telephone rang right after Jack settled into his recliner with his Sunday paper, a glass of iced tea, and his television remote. He considered ignoring it, but then somebody else might pick it up, and, by God, it was his phone. His daughter had phones upstairs in her brother's old bedroom. She carried a phone around in her purse. Even the old harridan had one of those portable phones. All those phones, they should keep their grubbies off his.

"Hello?"

"Hello, Jack. Bob Reeves here."

Bob Reeves had the Fina station out on Highway 16, and he lived in a trailer out behind. Pretty piece of land, though. Bob always said the trailer was temporary until he could build, but after twenty years, it had a look of permanence about it.

Bob bowled in the Monday night league. "Y'all got a tournament scheduling problem needs fixin'?" Jack asked, deducing the reason for the call. It was that time of year.

"No. No. Everything's fine at Harmon Lanes. Finally got the ball return on number eight fixed. Was beginning to wonder if I'd have to get my tools and go at it myself."

Over my dead body, Jack thought. "What can I do for you?"

"Well . . . it's just that . . . you see . . . ah, hell. My wife wanted me to call, tell you it was sure nice to see your family in church. That grandson of yours is a handsome fella."

He paused and Jack could hear Mrs. Reeves yammer something at her husband. "Okay. Okay," Bob said to her. To Jack, he continued. "We saw him take that little Cooper girl back to her dad. My wife was struck by the . . . uh . . . well . . . she wonders . . ."

Jack braced himself. "What?"

A breath. "Oh, never mind. It's not our business any-way." He mumbled something about hoping to see Jack at the lanes soon, then disconnected.

"Damn," Jack said. He'd been afraid of this.

He no sooner returned the receiver to its cradle than the phone rang again. His stomach took a dip. *Don't an-swer it.*

Brring. Brring. Brring.

"Hey, Granddad," Ryan called on his way up the stair-case. "You want me to get that for you?"

"No," he hastened to reply. No need for the boy to run this gauntlet. Not yet, anyway. "Hello?"

"Hello, Jack," trilled the Widow Mallow. "I was so ex-cited when we came out of church at St. Michael's to see you across the street at St. Stephen's. It's wonderful you're getting out and about so soon after your accident."

Jack considered saying thanks, then hanging up, but her strawberry pie had become one of his favorites. For that, he allowed the conversation to continue. "I'm glad I could go to church this morning. Have a lot to be thankful for."

"Like that grandson of yours. Handsome fellow. Does he like strawberry pie? I have one all ready to bring over. I saw him after church with Max Cooper's little girl. She seems awfully friendly toward him. I wonder if the two of them have a . . . special connection?"

Should have let the damn phone ring.

"They're neighbors," he responded flatly. "Say, did you see Marvella Hopkins this morning? She's dyed her hair bright red. Wonder if she went to the Piccadilly to let the Baptists get a look at her." It was a perfect distraction. He'd tweaked her curiosity, and it got her off the line in seconds.

The third call came two minutes later. He eyed the phone jack with longing, but getting up to unplug it was just too danged hard. He knew better than to answer it. He knew it meant more trouble. Family trouble. Trouble he didn't want to think about.

Ring. Ring. Ring. Ring.

"Oh, hell." Jack snatched up the phone and barked, "Hello!"

"Daddy?" Sarah asked. "Is something wrong? Are you all right?"

"I'm fine," he replied, relaxing just a little. "Why are you calling? You all right? Baby okay?"

"The baby's wonderful. I'm fine. I just wanted to see how you were feeling, to make sure sitting through church wasn't too much for you."

"Sitting through that sermon was too much for everyone. The reverend gets windier every Sunday."

Jack and Sarah spoke of inconsequential matters for another few minutes before ending the call. The conversation with his daughter successfully banished thoughts of trouble from his mind, for the most part, anyway. Jack settled back in his chair with the sports section and began to read.

He was halfway through the box scores when the doorbell rang. Through the plate-glass window he spied Martha Gault, hovering over the welcome mat like a vulture, pie in hand. Jack let out a groan.

Dammit, he didn't want to deal with this.

She saw him looking at her and finger-waved. Adele entered the living room from the kitchen, frowned toward the door, then looked at him. "Want me to lock her out?"

Jack believed it was the first time the two of them had agreed on anything. "Better let her in. Longer you leave her standing on the porch, the longer she stays."

Adele muttered something about store-bought piecrust and opened the door. Martha sailed inside, ignored Adele, and declared, "Here's dessert for today's dinner."

Adele folded her arms and smirked. "Thanks for the thought, hon, but my lemon chess pie is already in the oven. Maybe you should take your pie and . . ." She paused significantly, then finished, " . . . eat it."

The Widow Gault gasped with offense, then dismissed her with a nose wrinkle. She turned to Jack. "I saw your grandson standing next to Max Cooper out in front of church. Is Max Cooper that boy's father?"

"Hey," Adele protested. "Who do you think you are, coming into our home and sticking your nose where it doesn't belong?"

Martha ignored Adele and focused her gaze on Jack. And to think he'd thought it nice to have his family with him in church today. If only he'd known. Of course, the truth was bound to come out sooner or later, but in his opinion, later was better than sooner.

Damn! He truly didn't want to deal with this.

"Well?" the Widow Gault demanded. "Is it true?"

The hell if he'd admit anything. "You're a nosy old busybody, Martha Gault, and you should be ashamed of yourself. I wouldn't tell you if Elvis Presley himself was the father of that boy."

"Don't be foolish, Jack," the Widow Mallow said, sauntering into the room from the kitchen. "Elvis died in 1977. He couldn't be Ryan's father."

"Not another one!" Adele exclaimed. "Don't you witches have anything better to do than ride your brooms to this house?"

Jack made a show of flapping his sports page, pointedly ignoring the women. Decent desserts were worth only so much.

"Max Cooper's the one, isn't he?" asked the Widow Duncan, giving Jack a start. He hadn't noticed her come in. Danged woman never bothered with knocking when she knew the rest of her coven was here.

"He worked at Harmon Lanes," she continued. "Hard-working boy, as I remember. Smart as a whip. Witty. Never caused a bit of trouble."

The Mallow woman nodded. "He had a steady girl back then. The Gantt girl. Everyone thought they'd marry. Thought he'd go on to play pro ball. Then he up and quit football and took an Air Force scholarship out of the blue. Everyone in town wondered about that at the time."

"Max Cooper. I can't believe none of us saw the resemblance before. I'll bet Linnie was beside herself. She was dear friends with the Gantt girl's mother, wasn't she? She must have been heartbroken that her daughter stole her friend's daughter's beau."

"Enough!" Jack snapped. "The three of you have a lot of nerve coming into my house and talking that way. Kate never stole anything in her life, including anyone's beau, and her mother knew it."

"So Linnie knew about the baby?"

"Of course she knew. You don't think our Kate would keep something like that from her mother."

Linnie had known about Max Cooper, too, but not because Kate had told her. Kate had refused to answer that particular question. That little detail didn't stop Linnie. His wife had reasoned it out before Ryan was ever born. After tricking Kate into revealing when and where the deed had been done, Linnie set out to discover who else might have been at the lake that day, and she'd turned up the detail that Max Cooper had been making his lawn care business rounds out at Possum Kingdom Lake.

Upon first learning the news, Jack had been ready to storm down to Texas A&M where Max was a new student and demand the boy marry his daughter. Linnie had been adamant against that action. Dear Lord, they'd had a row. His wife hadn't often put her foot down, and on the few times she did, well, a smart man listened.

She'd come to him then, cupped his face in her hands, and stared him straight in the eyes. "I'll have your promise, Jack Harmon. You'll leave that boy alone, and you'll keep your mouth shut. Promise me you'll never tell a soul that Max Cooper is the father of Kate's baby."

"I promise," he repeated now. He'd given his Linnie his promise. His word. Just because she'd passed on didn't mean he could break it all these years later.

"You promise what?" the Widow Mallow cawed. "Jack Harmon, are you drifting off again? You do that a lot."

The Widow Gault clucked her tongue as she walked over to the fireplace mantel and picked up the family photograph taken when the kids were all little. "Linnie knew? I don't believe it. She never once let on."

"It was private family business. Be careful with that picture."

Widow Mallow sniffed. "Doesn't seem so private to me. Not after that family tableau in the middle of Church Street this morning. We saw it with our own two eyes. We're right, aren't we? About Max Cooper?"

"I can't believe Linnie never let on," the Widow Duncan mused. "Of course, she was probably ashamed, her unmarried daughter turning up in a family way."

Jack glared at her. "You're dead wrong about that. Linnie wasn't ashamed of Kate. The girl made a mistake. That happens."

"Not in Cedar Dell," Widow Gault declared.

"Not that big a mistake," Widow Mallow agreed.

Enough, Jack decided. He folded his arms. "Oh yeah? Seems to me you might have made that same mistake, Clare Duncan. Seems I remember talk that you gave Joe a *warm* welcome back from the war. How much did that premature baby of yours weigh? Ten pounds, wasn't he?"

The trio gasped as one. The Widow Duncan flushed.

Kate breezed into the room. "Hello, ladies," she said, a smile pasted on her face as she took a seat in the rocking chair. "I'm sorry I couldn't meet you when you first arrived. I was upstairs on the phone with the Reverend Wilson from Cedar Dell Church of Christ. He needed help with his spreadsheet program. We have a roast in the oven and kitchen work is caught up. Now I have time to sit and visit. I understand you have a question you want to ask me?"

The Widow Gault smoothed her skirt. The Widow Mallow tugged on her sleeve. The Widow Duncan sat stiff as a board and red as a beet.

Martha Gault, always the bold one, finally said, "Yes. Yes we do. Is Max Cooper the father of your bastard son?"

Kate crossed her legs, clasped her hands, and leaned forward. Her smile widened, her eyes narrowed and glinted like sunlight off a sword. "That, ladies, is none of your business. And Martha? If you use that word in relation to my son ever again, I'll be forced to retaliate. Does the phone number 475-9386 ring a bell?"

Martha Gault's complexion bleached marshmallow white.

With The Widows shocked speechless, Adele made herself useful and ushered them out. The screen door banging shut behind them sounded even nicer than this morning's long-winded preacher's final amen.

"What's that phone number business?"

"A bail bondsman in Weatherford. Martha Gault was arrested for shoplifting in the Wal-Mart last month. Adele found out at her meeting."

"Shoplifting, hmm? Wonder why. Old harridan has more money than God. She'll want to keep that quiet as she can. Good job. She won't be lashing her tongue against our boy for a bit."

Kate sat looking shell-shocked at his defense. Jack studied his daughter and thought of her mother. *Damn, but when it came to watching out for her chick, the girl had spunk. Just like her mama.* Linnie had sat in that very same chair, her blue eyes reflecting that very same glint on the day she'd demanded he leave Max Cooper alone.

He'd wanted to force that boy to marry Kate. Linnie had talked him out of it. She said the two of them didn't love each other, that the Cooper boy would lose his scholarship and drop out of college, and they'd end up divorced in the end. She had another idea.

Jack tugged a white handkerchief from his pocket and blew his nose. Memories of Linnie washed over him, loosened his tongue. "Your mother talked me into sending you to college, you know. She had it all arranged."

Color drained from his daughter's face. "What?"

"Your mama said adopting out your baby would be the hardest thing you'd ever do, and she wanted you to have something to look forward to afterward. Kept after me about it for a month. Said you were smart as a whip, and that we'd paid Tom's way through the University of Texas. When I pointed out we hadn't paid for any college for Sarah, she reminded me of the wedding bills. I still can't believe how much money she and Sarah spent on that wedding."

"Wh—wh—" Kate's voice faltered. She cleared her throat and started again. "What arrangements?"

"She sent in applications for you. UT and Texas Tech. Maybe East Texas State. I don't recall for certain. She wanted to have news for you when the baby was born. Said you'd be drowning, and it would be just the rope to throw you."

"Let me get this straight. My giving birth to an illegitimate child somehow changed y'all's mind about letting me go off to college?"

"Yeah. It was your mama's plan. She thought going back to college would ease the hurt giving up your baby would cause you. Of course, then you decided to keep him, and that changed everything. In the end, you didn't need a rope, did you?"

Kate stood and walked to the mantel, where she picked up the photograph the Widow Mallow had studied. Her finger traced her mother's image. "Oh, I desperately needed a rope," she said softly. "But I couldn't give him up. Not once I'd seen him. Held him."

"Can't blame you. He's a pistol." Jack sneezed, then tugged a white handkerchief from his pocket to blow his nose.

Kate remained quiet a moment, but when she spoke again, she did with an edge to her voice. "I can't believe this. You were so against the idea of me going away to college."

Jack shifted in his seat. He hadn't supported his wife's plan unconditionally. After all, college was what started this whole mess. Kate had graduated high school, won a scholarship to that hippie college, but still needed traveling expenses and money for books. Jack had refused her. She'd begged and pleaded and stood there with tears rolling down her face, and he'd still told her no. That's when she'd sworn she'd find the money somewhere. Bawling and blubbering, she'd run from the house, climbed into Jack's car, and drove it—without permission—out to the lake house.

"I didn't want you so far away," he murmured, gazing at his dead wife's picture. "I was afraid for you, living in that environment."

Now Kate marched around the room propelled by anger. "You hurt me, Dad. I wanted that scholarship, that opportunity, more than anything I'd ever wanted. I'd earned it, and I was so proud. You yanked it away from me, and like a child, I went looking for comfort or revenge or maybe a mix of both. What I found wasn't childish, and it gave me Ryan."

Dreams of college had flown right out the window.

Kate had gone into labor during Sarah's wedding festivities. Torn between her daughters' needs, Linnie stayed for the wedding, hoping that, like most first babies, Kate's would take a long time coming. But the baby came fast, and Kate was all alone. Vulnerable.

She named him Ryan Scott Harmon.

"Your mama said the nurse wasn't supposed to let you see him. Said if she'd been there, it wouldn't have happened."

"I was meant to keep him," Kate declared. "Otherwise, I wouldn't have given birth on Sarah's wedding day."

"Nothing else would have kept your mama away."

"I know. I regret what happened afterward, though." Kate's decision to keep her baby had torn her and her mother apart. As hardheaded as Jack was upon occasion, Linnie had argued herself blue in the face against it with the girl.

Jack had seen right off that it was too late for Kate to give her baby up for adoption. They'd already bonded. Linnie should have seen it. Instead, out of her fear for her daughter's well-being, she'd made the situation worse. The granite-headed, two-peas-in-a-pod women spoke words in the heat of the moment that should never have seen the light of day.

Kate cut off all contact with the family and didn't begin to forgive her mother until Linnie arrived on her doorstep one December, begging her to bring Ryan home for Christmas. They were still finding their way back to one another when Linnie passed on.

After that, Jack had had his hands full just trying to make it through the day. Months passed. Years. He and Kate saw each other rarely. Almost always during visits to the lake house.

The lake house. Damn. He didn't want to think about the lake house.

He'd passed some fine times there with Ryan over the years. Fishing. Playing grease monkeys trying to keep the old motor on the boat running. Fishing. Setting off fireworks on the Fourth of July. Fishing.

He wanted to go fishing.

Maybe he'd do it. Just load up and go. He felt good today. Sharp. More like his old self. And he still owned the lake place. Hadn't accepted the offer, despite the real estate lady's whining. It was a nice offer, but not enough. He needed the full amount. Jack had a little more time yet before the deadline. The lake house was still his, and Jack could still go fishing. "By God, I'll do it. The boy can go with me."

Kate tore her gaze away from her mother's photograph. "What?"

"Fishing. I want to go fishing this afternoon. Newspaper said sandies have been running the last few days."

His change of subject appeared to throw his daughter off guard. She still wanted to talk about the past; he could see it in her eyes. But he was done with it. Linnie was gone and he was alone and that was that.

Kate sighed heavily. "Dad, the doctor gave you permission to go to Harmon Lanes for a few hours a day. To go to church once a week. He didn't say a word about going to the lake to go fishing."

"I don't need anybody's permission," he snapped. "I'm a grown man, and I'll do what I goddamned please."

Kate's mouth firmed, and her eyes gleamed disapproval. She looked so much like her mother in that moment, that a fresh wave of grief welled up and swamped Jack unawares. He missed her. Even after all these years, especially after all these years, he missed her something awful. *Oh, Linnie. Why did you have to leave me to get old all by myself?*

"Dad, I don't think—"

"Fishing's not exactly strenuous." Jack grabbed the armrests of his chair for purchase and slowly struggled to stand, glaring at Kate in warning as she approached him, attempting to help. It was the first time since the accident he'd managed to get to his feet entirely on his own. He tossed his daughter a defiant look, and added, "It'll do me good to get out in the fresh air. Do the boy good, too. He's liable to have a rough week ahead. Seein' as how Cedar Dell has figured out that Max Cooper is Ryan's father."

It was like dumping a skunk in the center of the room.

Her tone as flat as a West Texas highway, Kate said, "So you do know."

"Yeah."

"I thought you might. Did Ryan tell you?"

"No. Didn't have to. I've always known. Knew back before the boy was born."

Kate's eyes widened with shock. "Since before he was born?"

"Your mother figured it out."

"And you didn't do anything about it?" She sank down onto the sofa. "I don't believe it. I thought for sure if you knew you'd . . ."

He waited a moment after her voice trailed off, then said. "What? You thought I'd what?"

A full minute ticked by before she asked, "Why didn't you make him marry me, Daddy?"

The hurt in her tone got his back up. Gruffly, he snapped, "Is that what you wanted?"

"No." She shook her head. "No, I didn't. Not at all."

That's what her mother had said. And it had pissed him off. Did then, still did. It stabbed to the core of one of his most basic convictions.

He didn't care about the way society had changed. Modern moral views had nothing to do with him. Jack thought having children outside the holy bonds of matrimony was wrong. He believed children needed two parents. He believed Kate should have married Max Cooper and made the best of it. They should have *done the right thing.* For the boy's sake.

He didn't understand how he could have raised a child who so flagrantly rejected such basic moral teachings.

All these years later, it still angered him. It shamed him. It made him feel like she rejected everything he stood for. Those emotions put the sneer in his tone when he said, "I could have gone after Cooper, dragged him to the altar, but I figured, why should I bother? You wouldn't have listened to me. You were always dead set on doing the wrong thing."

"How did you know?" Kate pushed to her feet. "Did we ever talk about it? Did we ever talk about anything I wanted? Maybe it wasn't my decision. Did you ever consider that? Maybe Max refused to marry me."

"Is that what happened?"

She paused. "No."

"Didn't think so. The boy had honor."

"*He had honor*," she repeated, sputtering a disbelieving laugh. "I didn't get pregnant all by myself, Dad. I had help. Max ran out on me after Ryan was born. I fail to see how you can call that behavior honorable."

Jack dismissed her objection with a wave. "He was a boy. Boys are going to sow a few wild oats. That's to be expected. You should have known better. Nice girls don't do what you did. You brought your troubles on yourself. Yes, I could have gone after Max Cooper with my shotgun, but I didn't see any reason to ruin the boy's life over your mistake."

"My mistake?" Kate clenched her fists and glared her outrage. "What about *my life*, Dad? Has it ever been of any value to you at all? Am I completely without worth just because I'm a girl?"

"Oh, stop it. Now you're being melodramatic." *She sounds just like her mother.*

"Maybe so, but that's how I've felt, Dad. All my life."

In that moment, Jack felt old. Old and weary and worn-out. He simply couldn't deal with all this emotional turmoil. He couldn't deal with Kate. Not then. Not now. He'd never understood her.

Without responding, he turned and left the room.

Chapter Eleven

"WHAT'S WRONG WITH MOM?" Ryan asked Adele as he set down his fishing pole and swiped a deviled egg from the platter on the picnic table. "All she's done since we got here is sit and stare out at the water."

Adele glanced up from a copy of *Smithsonian* magazine. The gold on her pineapple earrings glinted in the sunlight. "I think she and your grandfather had a fight earlier today."

"So what else is new?" Ryan popped the egg in his mouth, then grimaced. "Did you make these eggs, Adele?"

"No. One of The Widows brought them by yesterday. I didn't try one before I stuck them in our picnic cooler. Awful, aren't they?"

"Tastes like tuna. You think she put tuna in her deviled eggs?"

"I hope that's all it is. I'm worried about cat food, myself."

"Yew." Ryan reached for a Coke and drained half the can in one long slurp. His gaze flicked from his grandfather, who sat in a lawn chair on the dock, fishing pole in hand and tackle box at his feet, to his mother. "So what did they fight about this time? Coming out here, I bet. I think it's been good for him, though. Did you see him when he caught that black bass? That's the first time I've heard him laugh in a long time."

Adele filled a plastic cup with ice, then poured a glass of tea. "Here," she said, handing it to Ryan. "Take this to your mom. Tell her I said she's brooded long enough."

Carrying the tea in one hand, his soft drink in the other, Ryan walked down toward the shady spot beneath the cottonwood beside the water where his mother sat, her hands wrapped around her knees. As he drew close, Ryan saw that she was crying.

Oh, damn.

"Mom?"

Hastily, she turned her head and wiped her eyes. When she looked back, she offered a smile too shaky to be believable. "Hi, honey."

"What's the matter, Mom?"

Her sigh bore the weight of the world. "I was just thinking about my family."

Oh. Yeah, Ryan could see how that could make her cry. Ryan loved his grandfather, but sometimes he didn't like him very much. He didn't treat his mother right, and Ryan didn't understand it. Mom was good to her dad. She tried to please him. Fixed his favorite meals, ironed his sheets. Shoot, a month ago if somebody had tried to tell him that his mom would be dividing her days between accounting, frying chicken, and ironing bedsheets, he'd have called them crazy to their face. She acted like a totally different person in Cedar Dell than she did at home. The worst part of the whole thing was, Granddad didn't seem to notice all Mom did for him. It drove Ryan crazy.

"But that's not what I want to talk to you about," his mother added.

"What is it, Mom?"

She sipped her drink and stared out at the water. "I understand you talked to your grandfather about a job at Harmon Lanes."

Oh. Ryan braced himself for the expected argument. "Yeah."

"I wish you'd talked with me first, Ryan. I've already contacted an old friend and found you an internship with Groves Engineering. It's a great opportunity for you."

"Mom, I really want to work at the bowling alley."

"This would be better for you, Ryan. You need to keep in mind—"

"Colleges. I *know*, Mom. You say it every day."

"I overdo, hmm?"

"Mom, you're a maniac about this."

"It's just so important, Ryan."

He picked a dandelion and tossed it into the water. "So is having a life, Mom. I don't have friends in this town. No baseball. At the bowling alley, I'll have the chance to meet people my age."

"There are other ways to make friends. I've worked at Harmon Lanes, Ry. It's awful. It's not a No Smoking venue. It's loud. Every single night some kid puts chewing gum in a bowling ball finger hole."

"I want to work there, Mom."

His mother folded her legs Indian-style and fiddled with the laces on her sneakers. "Working in such a public place might be difficult for you for a while."

"Why?"

"While you picked up butter at the store for Adele, The Widows came calling. They asked about you and Max."

The canned drink halfway to his mouth, Ryan froze. "What did you tell them?"

"That it's none of their business. As if that did any good," she added with a snort. "I know you think this is my problem, honey, and in many ways, you're right. I don't think you understand the attention you'll receive as a result. You'd be insulated at Groves Engineering."

Ryan drained his Coke and tossed aside the aluminum can. He stepped toward the water's edge, scooped a handful of rocks off the ground, and began skipping the flat ones. He threw the round ones, just as hard and as far as he could.

Great. Just great.

"Explain something to me, Mom. Why does anyone care? I'm seventeen years old. What does it matter to anyone who knocked you up that long ago?"

She winced. She didn't like that term, Ryan knew, but at the moment, he didn't particularly care.

"Cedar Dell is a small town. Gossip is a major industry here. Everybody knows everybody else's business, and what they don't know, they're trying to find out. That's the way it is here. Always has been and always will be, I imagine."

Ryan found a perfect skipping rock and got it to hop four times. "No skin off my nose, I guess. Everybody knowing won't change anything. I still don't want anything to do with the bastard."

"Ryan. Please. I won't have you using that kind of language. Not around me."

"Yes, ma'am."

He ran out of rocks to throw and sat down beside her.

Tugging off his ball cap, he lifted his face toward the sky, closed his eyes, and enjoyed the warmth of the afternoon sun upon his skin. Somebody upwind was burning cedar, and he breathed deeply of the tangy fragrance. He loved this place. The FOR SALE sign in the front yard made his chest hurt.

Something brushed against his hair, and he waved it away. A dragonfly swirled and dipped around him, then sailed off across the water.

"Max intends to tell Shannon she has a brother. No matter how you decide to handle your relationship with your father, I expect you to be kind and careful of that little girl's heart."

Ryan's stomach muscles tensed. "Jeez, Mom. What kind of a jerk do you think I am? Just because I accidentally ripped her silly crown . . . I bought her another one, by the way. Had one of the guys get it at home from that store on Harry Hines Boulevard that sells all the purses and jewelry and junk."

Kate did a double take. "You bought her a rhinestone tiara?"

He shrugged. "Girls like shiny stuff."

"She's a lucky little girl to have you for a brother. And Max as a father. We haven't done right by him, Ry. Either one of us."

"Mo-om."

"He loves you. A father's love is a precious thing. It's a crime to waste it."

He gave her a sharp look. Something in her tone, the sad light in her eyes, told him she wasn't just talking about

Max Cooper. "Mom, what's going on? Adele said you and Granddad had a fight."

She shook her head, wouldn't answer. Tears pooled in her eyes and tore at Ryan's heart. "Oh, Mom."

"Give him a chance, Ryan. Please? For me?"

He shrugged, but he didn't tell her no. His mom took it as a victory.

Always one to press an advantage, she stood, brushed dirt and leaves off the seat of her jeans, and added, "About the internship. Could we find a compromise on this? Maybe work part-time at both places if Marvin Groves and your grandfather are amenable?"

"Sure."

"Kate?" Adele called. "Kate, you'd better come here. Something is wrong with your father."

She took off at a run, Ryan right beside her. They rounded the corner of the cabin and saw immediately what had Adele so upset.

"He was talking to the neighbor," Adele said. "They were reminiscing about some party the neighbor had years ago. Next thing I know, I hear the lawn mower fire up, but I don't think anything about it. I thought it was the neighbor. I never guessed that hardheaded old fool would be so stupid as to want to mow his own lawn, even if it is a riding mower. Now look what he's done." She flung out her arm, gesturing toward the neighbor's yard that sloped down to a strip of sandy beach.

Granddad had driven the lawn mower wheel-deep into water. He just sat there, not moving. Ryan thought his own heart stopped.

"Oh, no," Mom breathed. She started running toward the mower. "Dad? Dad? Are you all right?"

Ryan outpaced his mother. *Please be okay. Please be okay.* He reached his grandfather first. "Granddad?"

Jack Harmon turned his head and looked at Ryan. Confusion swam in his eyes. "I don't know what happened. I was mowing and then I . . . I . . ." Tears flooded his eyes, horrifying Ryan.

"Doesn't matter. Let me help you, Granddad. Here." He slipped one arm around his shoulders, the other beneath his knees, and lifted him into his arms. Ryan had carried cheerleaders who were heavier than this. "Let me get you out of the water. Looks like Adele is bringing the car down. We were getting ready to go anyway. Fish aren't biting worth beans."

Ryan toted his grandfather from the water, and out of respect for his pride, set him on his feet as soon as he found a level spot. His mother must have been thinking along the same lines, because she came dashing up with his wheeled walker.

Granddad didn't say anything as he made his way to the car. He sat in the front passenger seat and stared out over the lake.

"Dad?" Kate asked. "Are you all right? What happened, Dad?"

When he still didn't respond, she said, "Ryan, run up to the house and call nine-one-one."

"I don't need a goddamned ambulance. I'm fine. Just take me home. Take me home! I never want to see this cursed lake or this cursed lake house again."

Adele said, "Ryan, help me gather up the picnic things. We can't leave it out for the animals. I wouldn't want to poison a raccoon with those deviled eggs."

He followed Adele toward the picnic table, asking, "What's going on, Adele? What just happened?"

"I think your grandfather is failing."

"Failing? Failing what?"

"People don't live forever, honey."

"You think Granddad is going to . . ."

"Die. Sooner rather than later. I could be wrong, of course. He might up and outlive us all. But I think it's a good bet that this extended visit to Cedar Dell will be your mother's last chance to make things right with her father."

"Nah. I don't believe that." Ryan gazed toward the car. "That sucks."

"Of course," Adele added casually. "Life can always throw you a surprise. Your mom wasn't much older than you are now when her mother died. Goes to show you never know when you might lose a parent, lose the possibility forever of making things right with them."

Ryan knew what she was doing. She was hinting that he should make peace with Max Cooper. "Real subtle there, Auntie Adele."

"Just food for thought, hon. Food for thought."

"All in all, I think I'd rather eat one of those deviled eggs."

Kate knocked at the door of her sister's house Monday morning with coffee cake in her hands and a mixture of anticipation and apprehension in her heart. She'd left her father in Ryan's care, the two of them discussing his duties at the bowling alley. His MRI was scheduled for one o'clock that afternoon.

Sarah's husband opened the door. "Come on in, Kate. Sarah's back in the nursery playing in the baby clothes again."

Kate grinned. She recalled doing something similar in the weeks after Ryan's birth. The social services department of St. John's Episcopal Church had provided her with a crib, a changing table, and a dozen drawstring layette saques. Washing the tiny clothes in Ivory Soap and Downy fabric softener, folding them, tucking them away into the changing table drawers had seemed more like playing with doll clothes than doing a mother's tasks.

Ryan, on the other hand, had never seemed like a doll. He'd been work from day one.

Sarah's one-story, ranch-style house had three bedrooms, two baths, and a landscaped backyard Kate coveted. The room chosen for the nursery boasted a bay window, warm yellow walls trimmed in white, and their mother's golden oak rocker. Standing in the doorway before her sister noticed her, Kate took a moment to gaze at the rocker and remember. To mourn. Linnie Harmon had rocked Ryan only a handful of times in that rocker. Sarah's child would never know the comfort of her grandmother's arms.

"May I rock your baby once she's born?" Kate asked.

Sarah looked up and offered a genuine smile. "When *he's* born."

"It's a boy?"

"We chose not to be told, but I know." She patted her rounded belly. "It's a boy."

"Dad will be happy."

"Yes."

The sisters shared a look of silent communication, and in that moment, some of Kate's apprehension eased. Their father's preference of his son over his daughters had provided a bond between Kate and Sarah all their lives, a bond that apparently survived when others had not.

An offer of food served as an icebreaker, and a short time later, the two women sat at Sarah's kitchen table with slices of coffee cake and glasses of milk.

"Mmm," said Sarah, savoring the taste. "Adele is a treasure. Just don't tell my OB. I'm indulging."

"My lips are sealed." Kate licked her fork, then gave an awkward smile. This was it. A perfect opening. *Do it, Kate. Get it over with.* "Actually, I'm about to break the seal in another respect. I need to talk with you about a couple of things. I thought I should tell you before . . . um . . ."

Sarah arched her brows above her glass of milk and waited.

"Before I tell Cedar Dell that . . . um . . ."

Sarah set down her glass and leaned forward, encouraging Kate with her body language. "Yes?"

"Ryan . . . um . . . um."

"Oh, for crying out loud. Just spit it out. Max Cooper is Ryan's father?"

Kate blew out a heavy breath. "You know?"

"I guessed. They look so much alike."

"Yes."

Sarah took another piece of coffee cake. "I always suspected Ronnie Lewis."

"Ronnie Lewis!" Kate gave a shudder. "Why Ronnie Lewis? He's your age."

"You were the pretty one, and besides, he always had a crush on you. I also considered Charlie Hawkins and Matt Wilson."

Charlie Hawkins, Kate dismissed. Matt Wilson, though . . . hmm. Her mouth twitched in a wicked grin. "I wouldn't have minded Matt Wilson. He was a stud."

" 'Was' being the operative word. Have you seen him since you've returned to town? He dyes his hair and has a paunch, and he wears two gold neck chains and a bracelet." Sarah took a sip of her milk, then added, "Mom told me it was a boy from Fort Worth."

"You're kidding."

"I never questioned it until Max came to town last winter. I saw him in the hardware store one day, and as he reached for a box on a top shelf, I had a flash of Ryan at the lake throwing a fishing line into the water. Just something about it . . ."

Kate didn't know what to say next, and the conversation lagged. However, this was the longest dialogue she'd shared with her sister in years, and she wasn't ready for it to end.

"Did Mom tell you why it happened?"

Sarah dropped her gaze, played with cake crumbs with her fork. She spoke in a quiet voice. "She tried. I'm afraid I wouldn't listen to her. I was . . . angry."

Angry was a mild word for it, to Kate's recollection. Their six-year age difference prevented them from becoming close while growing up. Only during Kate's senior year in high school had she and her sister established tentative, more adult bonds. That ended after one of Sarah's wedding showers where someone commented on the fact that Kate had gained weight. On the ride home, Kate confessed her pregnancy to her mother, who told her father and all hell broke loose.

Sarah had gone glacial. She didn't speak to Kate at all.

"Can we talk plainly, here, Kate?"

"Um . . ."

"I know. It's rare for anyone in this family to speak plainly, and when we do, it always causes more trouble. I'm tired of trouble. I want . . . peace. I want family."

Kate wanted to trade her milk in for something stronger. Scotch, preferably.

"It was my turn for attention," Sarah said. "The first time in my life that I mattered more than Tom. Then in an instant, I became an afterthought."

Her sister spoke the truth. Kate's big announcement had wiped all the joy from the wedding preparations and left the Harmon house simmering with tension.

Sarah sighed, closed her eyes, and shook her head. "I acted like a spoiled brat back then. I'm sorry, Kate."

Kate was taken aback. She'd never expected something like this from Sarah. She opened her mouth, uncertain how to respond, when suddenly, emotions bubbled up from deep inside her and spilled out in a froth of words. "I knew I ruined that time for you, and I felt awful about it. I tried to fix it. I hoped that by telling my friends I was going to summer school at Berkeley, the gossip would die down."

"It did. Mom headed off most of the talk by acting

happy about your 'going off to college.' Still, at home the mood was ugly . . . and then at the wedding . . ."

Tears welled up behind Kate's eyes as she recalled that day, the hard bunk and sterile room at the unwed mothers' home in Fort Worth where she'd spent the past five months. "I shouldn't have called when I went into labor. I knew what day it was. I knew I'd be interrupting. I was scared, and I wanted to talk to Mom. I didn't think she'd skip your rehearsal."

Sarah's mouth twisted. "I was surprised she came back to Cedar Dell for the wedding."

Kate relived the moment her mother left, the loneliness, the pain. The fear. She cleared her throat. "The doctor told her the baby wouldn't come until Sunday."

"And Dad told her to get her butt back to Cedar Dell. I heard him. He said if Mom missed my wedding, folks would find out about your pregnancy. He didn't want the scandal. Said you brought this on yourself, so you should deal with it yourself." Sarah set down her glass. "During my wedding, she wanted to be with you. I could tell, and it hurt me."

Kate rubbed an eye with her index finger, capturing tears before they could fall. She hadn't expected to get into this when she came over here today. Wasn't one crisis from the past enough to deal with in a day? She'd thought to give Sarah a heads up on the news about Max before moving on to the main reason for her visit, her worries about their dad.

"It was a difficult time for all of us," Kate said, putting a note of finality in her voice.

Sarah ignored it.

"I was older. I shouldn't have acted so immature." She swirled the milk in her glass, her gaze fixed on the whirlpool the action created. "When you and Mom had your falling-out, I was glad. Then, when Alan and I couldn't get pregnant and you had Ryan . . . I was insanely jealous. I used to wonder if my jealousy brought on bad karma."

"Oh, Sarah, it doesn't work that way."

Her mouth dipped in a sad smile. "I'm ashamed of how I acted. I'd like a sister in my life. I'd like my baby to have an auntie. I hope you can forgive me, Kate."

Forgive. The word pinged around her head like a pin-ball, bumping against memories, some of them nice, more of them desperate. Kate wished she could smile and reach across the table and hug her sister and say let bygones be bygones . . . but it wasn't that easy. Forgiveness required a strength Kate couldn't find inside herself. Not right now, anyway. Not this soon.

She pushed to her feet, carried her dishes to the sink. From the corner of her eyes she spied her sister's stricken expression, and she winced. "I understand about the wedding. I'd have felt the same way. But what happened at Mom's funeral . . . that's harder to let go. I needed you then, Sarah, but you weren't there for me."

Tears flowed down her sister's pale cheeks. "I was barely there for myself."

Kate washed her plate, lifted a dish towel from a pretty brass rack, and dried it. Kept on drying it. All but wore the finish through until a thought blazed in her brain.

This upset wasn't good for Sarah's baby.

Hanging on to the hurts of the past wasn't good for Sarah and her either. If she couldn't quite feel forgiveness yet, maybe she could act like she felt it and see if real forgiveness grew.

"Let me ask you something, Sarah. Is an 'auntie' different from an 'aunt'?"

Sarah stood. Hope lit her eyes. "Oh, yes. Oh, yes. aunties are special. They're the relatives who matter the most."

"That sounds nice. I think I'd like to be your baby's auntie. Of course, that means we'll have to spend quite a bit of time together, doesn't it? It takes time to build a special relationship."

Sarah wiped away her tears with her napkin and smiled tremulously. "You're right. If you're going to do something, you should take the time to do it right."

"Exactly." Kate held out her plate. "Now, could I have another piece of cake? I want to talk to you about Dad."

Ryan spied Max's truck in the line of mostly mothers lined up in front of Fain Elementary, waiting for their children to be dismissed from school. He took a deep breath and knocked on the driver's side window.

Appearing startled, Max lowered the glass. "Ryan?"

"I'd like to walk Shannon over to the Dairy Queen. Buy her a dip cone."

Max held Ryan's gaze as he puzzled his way through it. "Is your mom with you?"

"No. I'm not inviting you either. This is just me and my sister."

"Sister"? Max's eyes widened at the word. A smile tugged at the corners of his mouth, but Ryan stopped it by shooting him a warning glare. "Um, sure. It's fine with me if she wants to go with you. You'll have to ask her, although I've never known her to turn down ice cream."

"All right, then."

"She'll probably have questions. I told her last night that you were her brother."

"Oh, yeah?"

"She wasn't too impressed. She wants a sister, and besides, you tore her crown."

Ryan wanted to smile, but he stifled the urge. Instead, he nodded once, shoved his hands in his back pockets, and stepped away just as the bell rang. Max climbed out of the truck, walked around the back, then leaned against the passenger-side door. He folded his arms and focused on the school's entrance as children began streaming out. Amidst the shouts and laughter, Ryan thought he heard Max Cooper whistling.

"Daddy, Daddy, Daddy." Shannon ran full throttle into her father's waiting arms. "Guess what happened. Taylor Johnson brought three grass snakes to school in a glass jar and it got knocked over and the snakes got loose and everybody screamed. It was so cool!"

"Did they catch the snakes?"

"Yep. Taylor put them in his lunch box. My teacher told him he can't bring snakes to school ever again, even for show-and-tell."

"That's probably a wise decision."

Max glanced at Ryan, then set the little girl back on her feet. "Honey, Ryan wants to take you for ice cream."

"Are you coming, too?"

"No. Just you and Ryan."

She put her thumb in her mouth and eyed Ryan suspiciously. "What kind?"

"Dairy Queen. We can walk there."

"Can I have a dip cone?"

Ryan cocked his head and worked harder to hold back a grin. "Small or medium?"

She removed her thumb from her mouth. "Large."

Ryan vaguely noted the interest of the minivan moms milling around, but he kept his attention on the kindergartner and made a show of scratching the back of his neck. "Jeez. I don't know. A large is kinda expensive."

Her chin came up. "A sister would buy me a large."

He gave it up and started laughing. "Okay, a large it is."

She handed Max her Dalmatian backpack, told him good-bye, and slipped her hand into Ryan's. "Let's go. I'm hungry. I'm always hungry after school. Are you?"

"Yeah."

"I think it's because our brains work hard thinking, and that makes them hungry."

She continued babbling, and as they waited at the crosswalk for the guard to stop traffic, Ryan reached into his backpack and tugged out his gift. "Here, Shannon. I'm sorry I crushed your other crown."

The rhinestone tiara sparkled in the sun, and the little girl gasped. "Oh, it's so pretty. It's just like Cinderella's. Thank you, Ryan."

Ryan set it gently on her head. "There. Perfect."

She beamed bright as the rhinestones. "I'm a princess."

"Yeah, I think you are."

They crossed the street and strolled through the neighborhood toward the restaurant three blocks away. She told him about Taylor Johnson's snakes and the light-bulb that exploded in the bathroom at the back of her classroom and how she colored all the balloons on her art paper her favorite color, Pig Pink. She stopped once to re-move a pebble from her shoe and veered off onto the grass twice to inspect a flower bed.

It wasn't until the red-and-white Dairy Queen sign came into view a block away that she posed any type of question. "My daddy says you're gonna be my brother."

"That's what they tell me.

"So will I get to be the flower girl?"

"What flower girl?"

"The one at the wedding."

"What wedding?"

She gave him that frustrated, what's-wrong-with-you-stupid look that females gave men all the time. "Where your mommy marries my daddy. When Penny's mom mar-ried Brent's dad, they became brother and sister. Don't you know anything?"

"Hold on a second. Are you saying Mom and Max Cooper are getting married? Is that what he told you?"

Her thumb went back into her mouth. "Yes."

"He said he was marrying my mom?"

Shannon's mouth puckered around her thumb. "Not 'zactly, I guess. He said in a few days you'd be my brother and everyone would know but I'm not supposed to tell any-one even my best friend Patty Lynn Cody because it's a se-cret for just a little while longer and after that I can tell everybody I want. I promised cross my heart and promised on Muffykins's ear. I didn't break it, did I, because I asked you? You're part of the secret so you shouldn't count."

"Honey, I am the secret," Ryan drawled.

"So, do I get to be the flower girl or not?"

"As far as I'm concerned, you can be a flower girl any-time you want. But you're going to have to ask your dad about weddings. I don't know anything about a wedding."

Ryan planned on keeping it that way. While he sus-pected Shannon Cooper had cooked up this wedding non-sense, he wasn't one-hundred percent certain. He didn't think Mom would marry Max after only one date. Of course, it'd only taken them one date to get a kid, so go figure.

They reached the corner of Pecan and Elm, where the residential area merged with the business district. Shannon pushed the walk signal button and waved at every car that passed while waiting for the light to change. About half the drivers rubbernecked at the sight of Max Cooper's daughter standing hand in hand with Kate Harmon's son. Ryan felt a wicked sense of amusement. Kinda fun to be a scandal in a small town.

The light changed to red, and the walk signal flashed. Ryan and Shannon crossed the street to the Dairy Queen. A dozen or so customers waited in line or sat at the tables and booths.

All in all, Ryan found it a good mix of townspeople to accomplish his purpose. Keeping a firm grip on Shannon's hand, he approached the counter and waited for just the right lull in the rumble of conversations taking place around him.

Now. He raised his voice. "I'd like to order some ice cream please? I want a medium chocolate Blizzard, and my sister here wants . . . Shannon? Tell me again? Was that a small or a medium?"

She sighed with exasperation. "A large, Ryan. You promised."

"That's right. I did. Brothers don't break their promises. Let me have a large dip cone for my little sister, would you please?"

In the quiet following his most public announcement, Ryan heard a man's voice speak in a rural country drawl. "Finish up them onion rings, Roy. I gotta git home and tell the wife the news. If she's first on the phone with this, I'll be sittin' in tall cotton."

"And if she's last," his companion offered, "you'll be sleeping on the back porch."

"Exactly. Smart man learns that early on in marriage. Ain't nothin' like a good piece of clothesline talk to put some steam in the sheets."

Shannon bit the top off her ice-cream cone and asked, "Ryan, why would anyone want to have steam in the sheets. Wouldn't that burn your bottom?"

"I think that's a question you need to ask your father, princess. I think Max Cooper deserves to explain."

Kate heard a pounding on her dad's front door, followed immediately by the repeated ringing of the doorbell. "Kate? You home? Kate?"

Max? Why would he . . . oh, God. She shot from her seat and dashed downstairs. Had something happened to Ryan?

She yanked open the door, fear crushing her chest. "What's wrong?"

"Nothing's wrong. It's right. Everything is right. You need to come see this, Kate."

"See what?"

"Ryan and Shan. He showed up at school asking to take

his sister—and that's a quote—for dip cones at the Dairy Queen."

She gasped. "On his own?"

"Yep." Max preened, a proud father. "He took control."

Kate's knees went weak, and she grasped the doorframe to steady herself. "What happened?"

He gave her a quick synopsis of recent events that left her reeling. "He just up and did this? Without discussing it with me?"

"Sounds just like his mama at that age. Decides what he wants and sets out to get it."

Kate shot him a look, uncertain if he meant it as a compliment or criticism.

"Is anyone here who can stay with your dad?"

"Adele."

"Then put your shoes on and let's go," he urged. "I think this play needs an Act III."

Kate grabbed her purse and followed him, wondering what he considered Act I and Act II. It was easier to think about that than going public with her sex life at seventeen.

"How stupid is that," she muttered as she climbed into the passenger seat of Max's truck. "Why should I be nervous because a bunch of busybodies I don't respect are going to launch me to the top of the gossip list today? Why do I care what anyone in this town thinks of me? Did I leave my backbone in Dallas?"

"It's your home."

"No, it's not. It hasn't been my home for years. I'm not certain Cedar Dell was my home when I lived here."

"Sure Cedar Dell is home," Max chastised. "Doesn't matter where else you live, Cedar Dell will always be home, and you're nervous because you want the town's approval."

"I do not."

Max's shrug conveyed his lack of belief, but he said no more about it until he turned his truck into the Dairy Queen parking lot. "Kate, I'm apprehensive, too. This is my home. These people are my neighbors. Shannon's neighbors. I don't want her or Ryan hurt."

"They won't hurt long," Kate reassured herself. "It'll be an F5 gossip tornado, but it'll blow over in a day or so. Our kids are strong enough to weather the storm."

"And so are we. Now, c'mon, Mom. Put your game face on. Let's go make an entrance."

A hum of conversation met them as they stepped into the small restaurant. Seconds later, the sound grew into a definite buzz. Kate remained frozen in front of the door, while Max waved at the kids. He placed a hand against the small of her back and gave her a gentle shove, then guided her toward a table where Ryan and Shannon sat playing a *Sesame Street* guessing game.

Ryan peeled a slab of frozen chocolate fudge off his ice cream and popped it into his mouth. "Mmm. Good."

"That's too easy. You're Cookie Monster. Now it's my turn."

"Hey, guys," Max said.

Shannon beamed a smile. "Hi, Daddy. Hi, Miss . . . um . . . do I call you Mom or Miss Kate now? Daddy, who is she to me?"

"Well." Like a man, Max attempted to avoid the issue. "You know that ice cream sure looks good. What will you have, Kate?"

Kate couldn't tear her gaze from Shannon Cooper's face. "Lemonade, please."

She'd been so busy worrying about a change in Ryan's and Max's relationship that she hadn't given much thought to a shift between her and Shannon. The girl had asked a very good question. What should she call Kate? Not Mom, of course. Not Ms. Harmon. Kate, probably. That felt most appropriate. Miss Kate, in keeping with what good manners required in Cedar Dell, Texas.

"Shannon, why don't you keep calling me Miss Kate."

"Okay." She put her crown back on top of her head. "And after the wedding I call you Mom?"

Kate and Max exchanged a quick glance that conveyed mutual shock, dismay, and uncertainty. Max cleared his throat. "Shanabanana, nobody said anything about a wedding."

"Ryan did."

Now panicked gazes flew to their son. He held up his hands defensively and sat back in his chair.

"He said I needed to ask Daddy if I could wear my new princess crown instead of flowers in my hair when I'm the flower girl at your wedding."

Max rubbed his jaw. "Does Dairy Queen sell beer?"

"This is not what I intended when I suggested a family outing," Kate murmured. By now the restaurant's buzz of conversation had died to near silence as every patron in the place had their ears tuned to the family tableau at table number six.

Once again, Ryan took control. "Look, princess. I think you're getting ahead of yourself talking about weddings. They're not getting married."

"Oh." Shannon frowned and looked at her Dad. "Is that true?"

"Well, honey . . . yes. That's true."

"So Ryan gets a daddy but I don't get a mommy? That's not fair."

Kate gave Max a swift kick beneath the table and mouthed, *What did you tell her?*

Max scowled. *I didn't use the "M" word!* "Look, honey. I um . . . that is, Miss Kate and I . . . um . . ."

To Kate's right, a gray-haired woman Kate didn't recognize lost her balance while leaning over to eavesdrop and fell out of her chair. While Kate helped the woman back into her seat, Max shoved to his feet. "Think I'll get some pictures now."

His action somehow provided a signal for the gossiping hordes to descend.

The PTA moms arrived first. A brunette wearing a denim jumper and white Keds smiled brightly at Kate. "I just wanted to stop by and say hello. I'm Mary Pratt. My son Dakota goes to kindergarten with Shannon. Hi, Shannon." She finger-waved to Max's daughter, then extended her hand toward Ryan. "And you're Ryan, correct? Your grandfather speaks so highly of you. It's nice to finally meet you. I didn't realize you are related to dear little Shannon, too."

Ryan offered up a smile that had Kate wincing in anticipation. "I'm the bastard love child of the family. Pleased to meet you, Mrs. Pratt."

Mary Pratt's green eyes rounded in shock. Then, she gave a sickly smile and backed away. Three more elementary school mothers crowded around the table to offer greetings and gather gossip. Max, the chicken, hid behind his camera.

Once the younger women cleared out, the older crowd descended. Cotton prints, polyester pants, and faux pearls proved the uniform of the day. They asked about Jack, promised more casseroles, commented on the spray of cologne Kate had applied that morning, then stepped back to allow their leader to come in for the kill.

A lady Kate vaguely recognized as having played bunco with her mother years ago walked up to the table, glanced from Kate to Ryan to Max, and burst into tears. Two friends assisted her back to her seat, clucking their tongues, muttering "Jezebel" and "Poor, poor Linnie" just loud enough for everyone in the Dairy Queen to hear.

"We can only hope Max got a good shot of that," Kate muttered beneath her breath. She pasted on a bright, false smile. "Well. This has been lovely. We should probably move along, however. My dad will be wondering about us."

She plucked a napkin from the chrome dispenser in the center of the table and offered it to Shannon, who had managed to transfer a smear of ice cream to her forehead just above her brow. Behind her, she heard the bunco woman let out another wail, while, off to her right, she heard the repeated click of a camera shutter.

It was all she could manage not to give him a one-fingered salute.

Kate's gaze shifted to a man who was coming up behind Max. Something about the smile on his face didn't match the gleam in his eyes. Uneasiness whispered through her, and, instinctively, she reached for Shannon.

"Max Cooper?" the man asked.

Max lowered his camera, turning.

"My name's Eric Lawrence." He stuck out his hand. "I own Do-Right Auto Repair over on Elm Street. Don't believe we've had the opportunity to meet since you moved back to town."

Oblivious, Max accepted the handshake. "Nice to meet you."

Lawrence gestured toward Ryan. "This here your boy?"

Pleasure lit Max's expression as he glanced at Ryan, then proudly, publicly, claimed him for the first time in Cedar Dell, Texas. "My son, Ryan Harmon."

Eric Lawrence drew back a fist and let fly a roundhouse punch to Max's jaw, knocking him to the floor.

"Daddy!" Shannon cried.

"You probably don't remember, but Terri Gantt is my niece. My favorite niece."

The PTA moms battled the blue-hairs in a dash for the Dairy Queen's lone pay phone hanging beside the bathroom wall. Shannon accidentally dumped her ice cream down Kate's shirt in her effort to scramble down from her arms to press get-well kisses against her sputtering father's bruised jaw. Ryan, the bastard love child, hid his laughter behind his hand.

Kate tugged another napkin from the dispenser, tidily wiped her chest, then bent and scooped up Max's camera. She framed a shot of father, daughter, and son, and pressed the shutter button.

As the camera clicked, she announced to the Dairy Queen, "Now, that, folks, is one for the family album."

Chapter Twelve

SUCKER PUNCHED. Dropped like a Hunger-Buster patty on the Dairy Queen grill. Max couldn't recall the last time he'd been this embarrassed.

If Ryan didn't stop snickering, he'd pull the truck over and make the kid walk the rest of the way home.

Of course, that would only make his son happy. Ryan hadn't wanted to get into the truck to begin with, but Kate had insisted for appearance's sake. Personally, Max thought they'd made "appearance" enough, but even under these circumstances, he wasn't ready for their first family outing—such as it was—to come to an end.

After climbing to his feet, scraping the chewing gum off his butt, and grabbing a paper napkin to wipe a hunk of frozen chocolate off his ear courtesy of Shannon's kisses, Max had nodded to Eric Lawrence and said in his best slow Texas drawl, "Reckon you had that one coming to you. One's all you get, though."

After that he'd made as dignified an exit as possible with Shannon whining for another ice cream cone to replace the one she'd smeared across Kate's shirt, Ryan cackling with laughter, and Kate snapping photos of the wide-eyed restaurant patrons.

"Hey, Max?" Ryan asked from the backseat.

Max winced, longing to hear the boy call him Dad, then glanced into the rearview mirror and met his son's amused gaze.

"This took longer than I planned. Would you drop me off at Harmon Lanes?"

Max decided to chance it. "Sure, *son*."

He held his breath in the moment that followed until Ryan simply said, "Thanks."

Taking it as an olive branch, Max decided to count the sucker punch as a lucky punch, and he whistled beneath his breath as he drove the few short blocks to the bowling alley. There, Ryan told his mother and sister good-bye, nodded at Max, and sauntered into work.

Max grinned at Kate. "All in all, I'm as happy as a dog with two tails."

Head cocked, she examined his lower face. "You'd look better with two cheeks the same color and size."

"Wouldn't feel better, though," he admitted, touching the swollen side.

Shannon giggled. The rest of the way home, they discussed how Mutt—*Muffykins, Daddy!*—would enjoy a second tail. Max intended to drive past his house to take Kate to Jack's, but when Shannon expressed an urgent need for the bathroom, Kate told him she'd walk home from his place.

The minute he turned off the engine in his driveway, Shannon unbuckled and raced for the house. "I guess she meant it," Kate observed.

Max spontaneously asked, "You want to come inside?"

She glanced down at her shirt. "I'm a mess. I should probably—"

Max was out of the truck before she could finish her refusal. He didn't want to hear it. He wanted her to stay. Striding around the front of the truck, he opened her door saying, "I'll loan you a shirt. I have some new photos you'll want to see."

"But—"

He took her hand and helped her out of the truck. "Have you had a chance to spend any time at the square since you've been back? They rebuilt the gazebo, you know. Planted lots of flowers. Brought in more benches. Even hung a swing from that big old pecan in the northeast corner. Some of your dad's cronies play checkers there when the weather's nice, and brown-baggers eat lunch there every day."

"I know. Harmon Lanes is only a block away."

"It's a great place, isn't it?" He was chattering like all the widows at once, but Kate was probably too polite to walk away while he was talking to her. "I decided to do a photographic study of the town square, taking the same shots in all four seasons. I actually have pictures of snow on the square, if you can believe that. We had an inch and a half on the fifth of February. They cancelled school for the day. Didn't want the school buses running because the drivers are inexperienced with the white stuff."

Max ushered her into the house, his speech a constant stream, allowing her not a single word in edgewise. "Would you like something to drink? A Coke? A beer? Or just a shirt? You want a dress shirt or a T-shirt? Follow me upstairs. You can change in my room. Take a shower if you want. Since Shannon thinks she has free run of every other room, that and my bathroom are the only safe places in the house to get naked."

Naked. The word floated on the air like a really good idea.

Max's gaze zeroed in on her ice-cream-smeared chest. God help him, he wanted to lick her clean.

Okay, he admitted it. Getting her naked had been on his mind for days.

She watched him warily. Their gazes met and held. She felt the tension, too, hot and pulsing, singeing the air between them. Max saw it in her eyes, and his heart pounded. He took a step forward while she took one, then two, steps back.

Eyes wide, she said, "Maybe I should just head on home."

"Please don't."

The *please* stopped her flight. Manners taught from the cradle were hard to ignore. Max took advantage of the moment by taking the stairs two at a time and disappearing into his bedroom. He reappeared with a maroon Texas A&M T-shirt and a pale blue dress shirt. She chose the tee, and Max appreciated the view as he watched her climb the stairs to his bedroom, where she shut and locked the door.

Shannon emerged from the downstairs powder room. "Hey Daddy, can I take Muffykins for a walk around the block?"

"Not around the block. Not without me. You can take him to the end of the street and back."

"Can we stop at Granny Murphy's for a visit? It's Wednesday night."

Hmm . . . the thought was tempting. Catherine Murphy made beef stew and biscuits for supper on Wednesdays, and invariably, she sent some home with Shannon when she visited. Max tried to reciprocate by grilling an extra couple of steaks on the weekends and sending them over to the Murphys.

"Yeah, you can stop at Granny Murphy's. But don't you go asking her for supper, you hear?"

"I let her send some home with me. Right?"

"Right." While Shannon hunted for the dog's leash, Max opened a bottle of wine. He carried it and two glasses into the living room, stuck a disc into the stereo, then hid a dirty shirt and two Barbie dolls behind a sofa pillow.

A saxophone wept the blues as Kate came downstairs a few moments later. Max dumped a handful of newspapers in the desk drawer and turned to meet her.

His shirt swallowed her, covered her shorts entirely so that it looked like she wore nothing beneath it. Max swallowed hard and cursed the direction of his thoughts. "Wine?"

She hesitated, then nodded. He poured two glasses, handed her one just as Shannon burst into the room, leash in hand. "Miss Kate, can I wear my new princess crown in the wedding?"

"What wedding?"

She rolled her eyes with her whole head, as only five-year-olds can. "That's the same thing Ryan said."

Kate glanced to Max for help, but since he didn't have a clue what turn his daughter's mind had taken, he shrugged. "I'm clueless."

"Your wedding, Daddy. To Miss Kate. So we can be brother and sister."

Kate set down her wine, folded her arms, and gave him a wry look. "That must have been some explanation, Cooper."

Max scratched his jaw. "Shannon, wait a minute. You misunderstood me."

"No, I didn't. You told me Ryan is gonna be my brother."

"He already is your brother."

Now she folded her arms, her expression filled with affront. "You got married without me?"

Now Max rolled his eyes in exasperation, using his entire head. "Kate and I are not getting married. I'm your daddy and I'm Ryan's daddy, and *that* makes you sister and brother. Not a wedding."

She wrinkled up her face in a suspicious frown. "You're Ryan's daddy?"

"Yes, honey."

"When did you get to be Ryan's daddy?"

"When he was in Miss Kate's tummy."

"How did he get there?"

Max shot a panicked look to Kate. Holy hell. Not the sex talk. What do you say to a five-year-old? *I can't do this. I'm not ready for this. I haven't read the books yet.*

This was God getting him back for thinking about having sex with Kate earlier.

The woman's eyes glimmered with amusement. She sipped her wine and left the burden entirely on his shoulders.

"Lot of help you are," he grumbled. He took a deep breath. "Shannon, a man and a woman make a baby by . . . by . . . by . . ." He tossed back half his glass of wine. "You see a daddy has a seed and . . . and . . . and . . ."

His daughter tilted her head and waited expectantly.

Oh, shit. "Magic, Shannon. I'm not sure how it happened. It must be magic."

"O-o-oh." Her gaze shifted from Max, to Kate, then back to Max again. "Did magic make me, too?"

"You betcha."

"Cool. Muffykins and I are going for our walk now, okay?" She went to the base of the stairs and called the dog. Moments later, Mutt came bounding down the stairs. Shannon fixed the leash clip to the dog's collar and opened the front door.

Thinking he had dodged that particular parental bullet well, Max breathed a relieved sigh and topped off his glass. In the portal, the little girl stopped, the dog straining at the leash. "Daddy?"

"Yeah?"

"Ryan is already my brother, right?"

"Right."

"But he has a mommy. He has Miss Kate."

Max glanced at Kate. "Yeah."

"That's not fair. If my brother has a mommy, I should get one, too. Will you get me one?"

"I . . . uh . . ." A quick look showed him Kate still didn't mean to ease his embarrassment.

"And maybe my mommy should be Miss Kate since she's Ryan's. That would be fair."

The dog started yapping. Max started choking. Shannon

beamed a smile at Kate, and said, "I'd like you to be my mommy, and it would be really good if my daddy had more magic and got me a sister. Now that I have a brother, I think I'd like one of those."

Arms crossing over her middle, Kate finally looked as disconcerted as he felt. Served her right for gloating at his discomfort.

Thankfully, Mutt nosed Shannon, and she finally left.

Max stood speechless, staring after his daughter, wondering how he'd managed to get himself in such a mess. At what point had he lost control of the afternoon? Was it when Ryan approached him at the schoolyard? When he'd decided to join his children at the Dairy Queen? When Terri Gantt's uncle decided to have a little payback with his dip cone?

Behind him, the giggles started out soft, then gradually increased in volume. Max straightened his spine, squared his shoulders, and twisted his head to pin her with a look.

Kate's hand covered her mouth. Laughter bubbled behind her fingers like champagne in a crystal flute. Her eyes sparkled as color bloomed on her cheeks. She met his gaze, her eyes dancing. "Magic?"

Ah, to hell with it. He stepped toward her, reached for her. "Damn straight."

He took her mouth in his very best magical kiss.

Kate woke up to the soft *brring* of her telephone the next morning. She glanced at the clock. Eight-thirty-five. Shannon must have been late to school today. Oh, but wait. School was finally out for the summer in Cedar Dell.

Brring. She snuggled under the covers, feeling all soft

and warm and womanly, and reached for the phone. "Good morning."

"Hello, Kate."

Startled awake by the deep, cultured voice, she sat up in bed. "Nicholas."

"I know I'm calling early. I hope I didn't wake you."

"Oh, no. I'm up."

"I've been thinking of you quite a lot, but this is the first time I've had the opportunity to call when time differences didn't make it rude."

"So you're still out of town?"

"Actually, I'm in Moscow."

"I've been to Moscow. I love that part of East Texas." As soon as she said it, she knew she'd drawn the wrong conclusion. East Texas wasn't a different time zone, *dummy*.

He laughed as if she'd made a joke instead of a provincial blunder. "That is a beautiful part of our state. However, I'm afraid I'm a bit farther east than that. I'm in Russia, Kate."

Think a little faster next time, idiot. "Oh, of course."

Static interfered with the reception, and Kate held the receiver away from her ear for a second until it died down.

Nick was saying, ". . . look forward to seeing you Saturday night."

"So you'll be back?" Call waiting beeped in, but she ignored it.

"Definitely. I'm wrapping up business here today and will fly out this evening. I plan to arrive in Cedar Dell in plenty of time for the fish fry. Six-thirty, you said?"

"Yes. Bingo starts at eight." Grimacing, she realized how bingo must sound to a jet-setter in Russia. The call-waiting signal beeped again in her ear. It was Max. She knew it. She felt like a teenager flirting with a boy in the hall after she'd made a date for Homecoming with someone else. Guilt made her turn to business. "I've made a little progress on your chess piece."

"You have?"

She explained that Mrs. Gault identified the drawing at the beauty shop, and spoke of how she'd spent a morning on the Cedar Dell garage sale trail attempting to discover who had bought the piece from Helen Brown.

"You went to garage sales?"

The incredulous tone in his voice made her laugh. "I did. It's a regular pastime here in Cedar Dell. On Wednesday afternoon the serious searchers line up in front of the *Shopper*—that's the local, weekly free newspaper—to get the garage sale ads hot off the press. That evening they'll spend an hour or so planning out their route to hit the most auspicious-sounding sales first."

"Fascinating."

His elegant tone reminded her that she was detailing small-town minutiae at international phone rates.

He continued, "And this Brown woman sold my grandmother's chess piece to one of these serious shoppers?"

"I believe so. Helen Brown identified the drawing and told me she'd owned the figurine for years. She'd bought it from Harold Winslow's widow when she sold her big house and moved into a duplex with her sister."

"Mrs. Brown didn't remember who bought the Aphrodite?"

"I'm afraid not. That's why I plan to attend the flea market on Thursday. It's held at dawn each Thursday morning in a field off the highway toward Loving. If the emerald

Aphrodite has made an appearance at any garage sale since Mrs. Brown's, somebody there will know."

"A sunrise flea market. Kate, my dear, you amaze me. Based on your reputation in town, I expected you to be resourceful. However, flea markets are one resource I never considered. Actually, it sounds like it might be fun. The thrill of the hunt without having to carry a gun and kill. If I didn't have another commitment, I'd come with you. But you say they have one every week? I might work it into my schedule."

James Bond at a flea market? Kate couldn't quite picture that. "Let's see how you make out at Bingo Night, first. I wouldn't want to overwhelm you. Or the vendors."

Static increased, and she couldn't make out his next few sentences. When the line next cleared, they said hasty good-byes and reaffirmed their plans for Saturday night, then signed off. Kate decided to look for martini glasses at the flea market on Thursday, in case she needed to entertain this Bond-type with more than iced tea.

She no sooner replaced the phone in its cradle than it rang again. "Hello."

"Your line's been busy."

That comment always made her feel slightly defensive. "Good morning, Max."

"Are you already at work? Am I interrupting?"

"No. I was visiting with a friend." She resisted providing more information, though the lapse in conversation suggested he wished for it.

After last night, keeping Max Cooper wishing was probably a pretty good idea.

The first kiss had knocked her socks off. The second had

melted her knees. The third . . . well . . . the third took them into territory familiar enough to frighten them both back to their senses.

"I've been thinking about last night," rumbled Max's voice over the phone line. His tone was deeper than Nicholas's, with just a hint of rural Texas in his inflection. Those years when he'd lived overseas and visited Ryan periodically, he'd lost his accent entirely. Life in Cedar Dell was apparently bringing it back. It sounded good on him. It sounded . . . sexy.

"Have you?" She tried to sound noncommittal.

"Haven't you?" His tone carried a challenge.

"I haven't been awake long enough." Although she had dreamed about it. About him. First sex dream she'd had in ages. Her cheeks grew warm at the memory.

As if he read her mind, Max chuckled. "You thought about it."

She snuggled back down into her covers. "Maybe."

"What are you thinking?"

"You first."

"You sure you're ready to hear it?"

"Probably not."

"I think Shanabanana had a pretty good idea."

Kate sat straight up in her bed. "Which idea are we talking about?" Weddings? A sister for Shannon? Babies in tummies?

"The one where she and I come to your house for dinner tonight, so she can chat up 'Mr. Wilson' about being her granddad, too."

Kate relaxed back against her pillow. "I don't remember that conversation."

"It must have happened after you ran away."

"I didn't run away."

"Sure you did. You tucked in my T-shirt, slipped on your sandals, and dashed for the doorway."

"What was I supposed to do? You asked me up to your tree house."

"I don't have a tree house. Although I will admit I'm thinking of making a run to the lumber yard this morning and taking a look at the two-by-fours."

"Been there, done that, Max Cooper. Had the baby."

"Yeah." She could hear the smile in his voice. "Isn't he great, Kate? I was so proud of the way he took control of claiming Shannon as his sister. I feel truly hopeful about the future and our family."

A ribbon of warning fluttered through her. She remembered something about Max Cooper. The man could do a fine imitation of a steamroller upon occasion. What in the world was he thinking? Ryan gets a dad, Shannon gets a mother and a grandfather. Max gets a wife to help raise his little, albeit darling, girl and regular sex. *What's in it for me?*

Regular sex. With Max Cooper. It sounded way too good.

"Slow down," she cautioned, more out of defense than necessity. "You're not out of the woods with Ryan yet. Don't rush him, Max, or you'll blow the whole thing."

He remained silent a moment. She heard the creak of bedsprings in the background and wished she hadn't. The picture that popped into her mind was all too enticing.

"Are we talking about Ryan here? Just Ryan?"

Kate took some time to formulate her response, hoping as she did that he'd understand this was of major importance to her. "For a year or so now, I've realized I'm approaching another stage of life. Staring down the barrel of it. In just over a year, I'll be an empty-nester. For a long time, the thought of it bothered me. Ryan has been the focus of my entire adult life. I married Roger as much for him as for myself. I wanted him to have a father."

"Wait a minute. You married after I started seeing Ryan. He had a father."

"Who lived in Germany. I thought he needed a man around on a daily basis, and Roger loved me. I thought it would be enough."

"You're saying you never loved your husband? No wonder he was jealous of me."

It was true. Old memories washed over her and filled her with regret. Marrying Roger, knowing she was settling for something less than what she'd dreamed of, had proved to be a huge mistake. She'd tried to will herself into loving Roger, but the harder she tried, the worse she failed. He'd sensed it and had grown unhappy, and that eventually led to that awful evening when he used Ryan to strike out at her.

"I've made more than my share of mistakes, Max. I'm trying not to make any more. Not big, life-altering ones, anyway. That's why I'm going to embark on this second half of life of mine in a cautious and deliberate manner. I have dreams that I've buried over time, and I'm just beginning to excavate them. I'm not ready or willing to abandon them again."

"I'm talking one dinner here, Kate," he responded in a disgruntled tone. "Not all-you-can-eat."

But that was the problem, from her viewpoint. A little

overindulgence with Max Cooper sounded really, really good right now. "I don't think it's a good idea. Besides, tonight's not a good night for y'all to come to dinner. I have a date this weekend, and I'd planned to shop for something to wear after work."

The drawn-out silence on the other end of the phone had Kate holding her breath, biting her tongue not to fill it just to make the moment more comfortable.

"All right. Well. You have a nice day, Kate." He hung up so softly, so gently, it made her wince. The man was not happy.

It was always good practice to stand up to a man, she reminded herself, and heaven knew she'd fight that battle this afternoon. Dad would want her to remain in the waiting room when he talked to Dr. Hardesty, but to hell with that. She intended to hear everything the doctor had to say about her father's condition.

Later that morning, Adele poked her head into Kate's makeshift office. "That was the twelfth call this morning— on top of the twenty-two that came in last night. Don't people in small towns have anything better to do than gossip? I like a good story just as much as the next girl, but heavens, some folks seem to work at it full-time. Is there some sort of government program for gossips that I don't know about? Where do I go to sign up?"

In the middle of running a column of numbers on her calculator, Kate didn't look up. "Just keep running interference for me, and I'll buy you that new waffle iron you have your eye on at Williams-Sonoma."

"You already bought it for me. I found the receipt in

your Levi's pocket last time I did laundry. And, now that the secret's out, I don't see why you should wait until my birthday to give it to me."

"That receipt was not in my jeans pocket. You've been snooping in my closet."

"Why, what an awful accusation."

Now Kate looked up. "In my closet, underneath a stack of shoe boxes, inside a box marked CHRISTMAS DECORATIONS."

Adele dusted her knuckles on her shoulder. "You used that box as a hiding place four years ago, honey. You should know better."

"My mistake," Kate said with a sigh.

"Speaking of mistakes," Adele drawled, "has your brother returned your phone call yet?"

Kate glanced at the silent business line and shook her head. "I told him in my voice mail it wasn't an emergency. I guess that was probably a mistake."

"He is the most selfish, self-absorbed human being on God's green earth. The way your father all but worships at his feet makes me want to scream. Why I — "

"Adele, please." Uncomfortable at hearing her guilty feelings toward her brother coming from Adele's mouth, Kate bent over the calculator. "I need to get these figures run."

Adele turned to leave, then stopped in the doorway. "If you want to get out that waffle iron, I'll make—"

"Good-bye, Adele." Kate returned to her work, her fingers flying over calculator keys.

Not five minutes later, Adele was back again. "Honey?"

Aargh! "All right. Take the waffle iron from—"

"The Realtor's downstairs."

Kate's fingers mishit the keypad. Realtor? Oh, jeez. "I'll be right down. Thanks, Adele."

She stretched and pointed her feet, fumbling for her shoes in the crawl space beneath her desk, then remembered she'd come barefoot to the office that morning. Screw it. She descended the stairs barefooted.

The Realtor didn't hear her arrive, which gave Kate a moment to study the woman. Her business suit, sleeked-back hairstyle, and no-nonsense pumps and panty hose relayed the fact she wasn't a local girl. This gal's purse had Wichita Falls written all over it.

Definitely the tight-lipped lady she'd spoken with the other day. "Can I help you?"

The woman spun around. "Hello. I'm here to speak with Jack."

"I assume you have another offer for him to consider?"

"I do. I think he'll be very pleased this time."

"Please, have a seat. My father will be out in a few minutes. He moves rather slowly these days. May I offer you something to drink?"

"Water, please."

Kate returned to the room with a water pitcher, three glasses filled with ice, and a plate of the Widow Mallow's oatmeal cookies—Adele's choice.

Kate sat on the arm of the sofa, swung her bare foot casually back and forth, and sipped her water. With the visitor dressed in city clothes, rather than Cedar Dell wear, Kate felt less inclined to make the usual small-town small talk that she otherwise would.

Using his cane for support, Jack Harmon slowly shuffled

into the room. "Hello, Mr. Harmon," chirped the Realtor. "I think we might have a deal. I believe you'll be very pleased this time."

He glared at Kate. "What are you doing here?"

"I'm listening in on this meeting."

"No you're not. Get along."

"No, Dad. I'm not leaving." She smiled pleasantly at the Realtor. "You brought a sales contract with you?"

She looked from Kate to Jack. He scowled, but he must have seen the determination on Kate's face, because he dismissed her with a snort and took a seat at the dining room table. He gestured for the Realtor to spread out her papers.

Kate took a seat opposite her dad and leaned forward expectantly as the Realtor removed a stack of legal-sized papers and set them in front of Jack. "The buyers have made you a contingency offer for the full asking price. They have a list of items they want repaired or replaced, but I don't believe any request is unreasonable."

Jack tugged his reading glasses from his shirt pocket and slipped them on. He pursed his lips, and his brow furrowed as he carefully read each line on the page. A few minutes into it, he stopped. "What's this about a ninety-day contingency?"

"They want to buy your house contingent on the sale of their own. Once you've agreed to their terms, they'll put their place up for sale and have ninety days to sell it."

"So I won't get my money for ninety days?"

"Well, yes," the Realtor said. "Unless the house sells quickly, and it is a fairly nice property in Wichita Falls."

He set down the contract. "No. That won't do. You have to find somebody with the money now."

"But Mr. Harmon, it takes time for a mortgage to go through. A survey must be done, an inspection, a title search, just to name a few."

"Find a buyer who doesn't need a mortgage. I don't have time for all that."

"No one uses cash these days."

"That's what's wrong with America. Too much credit. When I buy a house, I pay cash for it."

The Realtor grimaced, then pleaded. "Sir, this is a fair offer. They're giving you your total asking price."

"I need the money by the Fourth of July. I told you that when I called the first time. Don't imagine why you think I'd up and change my mind."

"It's a negotiation, Mr. Harmon. It's how the process is done."

With a wry smile, Kate observed, "Not in this household. My father doesn't negotiate. Period."

"We will lose this buyer," the Realtor warned.

"No skin off my nose. Doesn't do me a damned bit of good if the money comes too late."

For what, Dad? Kate was determined to ask her questions and learn the answers today, just as soon as she showed their visitor to the door. To that end, knowing her father had made his point about the offer, she took control of the meeting and shortly ushered the Realtor outside.

She cornered her dad before he could rise from his seat and escape. "All right, Dad. No more putting me off. Why do you need one hundred fifty thousand dollars?"

Scowling, he looked everywhere but at her. "I don't need a hundred and a half. The extra's to pay the real estate fees. Costs a bundle to use a Realtor. Ridiculous waste of money. If I weren't in a hurry, I'd sell the place myself."

Quietly, she reiterated. "What do you need the money for, Dad?"

Face reddening, he shook his head at her. "I don't like nosy kids."

"Too bad, because I'm sticking my nose right in the middle of this. That's a lot of money, Dad, and if you're in trouble we need—"

"I'm not in any goddamn trouble. Maybe I want to take a trip or something. Maybe I want to go to Las Vegas and gamble the money away. It's my lake house, my money, and it's not your concern what I do with it."

She acted like she hadn't heard him. "Have you bought something we don't know about? A new business, maybe? Or do you have doctor bills we don't know about? Or maybe you're helping a friend. Do you need to loan someone money?" She paused. "Tom, perhaps?"

"Tom! Why would I want to give your brother money? He's doing just fine, just fine. Doesn't he have a thriving business? Doesn't he have a good head on his shoulders? Doesn't he have the drive to succeed in whatever he chooses to do?"

Well, hell. Dad's giving Tom money.

Chapter Thirteen

KATE FELT AS IF she'd been slapped across the face with a ten-pound striper right out of Possum Kingdom Lake. Not even a loan. *Give* her brother money, he'd said.

She eyed her father's stubborn, bulldog expression and bitterness rose in her throat. Tom. The Golden Boy. Mr. Perfect Son. What happened? Did he find a new mansion to buy? A new boat? Does he want his inheritance just a little prematurely? Heaven forbid Tom Harmon would go wanting for anything.

Her brother had never wanted for a thing longer than it took to ask for it. "What's going on, Dad? Why does Tom need money?"

"It's none of your business! How many times to I have to say this, girl. It's my property. Mine to do with as I wish."

"True. I can't argue with that." She decided to approach it from a different direction. "I'll be honest with you. I'm concerned that someone might be taking advantage of you."

"What?" Temper snapped in his eyes. "Do you think that because I'm old, I'm stupid?"

"I know you're not stupid, Dad, but I read articles in newspapers every day about scam artists and con men who target the elderly and take advantage of them—not that I'm calling you elderly." Jack might call himself old, but he wouldn't take it kindly from her. "I saw a news story just last week about some men out of Fort Worth who've made themselves rich by going into small towns and offering to resurface driveways. The job looks nice when they leave, but the first rain washes it all away."

His defensive posture softened enough to allow him to lean back in the dining room chair. "I've heard of those boys. They came through town last fall. Offered to resurface the parking lot at Harmon Lanes. I told them to take a hike. They got Tiny Hardy over at the feed store, though."

"See? Tiny Hardy's an intelligent man. He's twenty years younger than you. People of all ages sometimes can use help making decisions. I know if I wanted to spend a hundred twenty-five thousand dollars, I'd discuss my plan with someone in the family I know I can trust."

"Didn't hear you calling me when you bought that fancy house Ryan showed me pictures of. You didn't call Sarah."

She was surprised he knew whether she talked with Sarah, let alone the subjects. "No, but Adele helped me make that decision. She's handled her own sizable investment program for years, and besides, she's my family. Who's helping you make this decision, Dad?"

"Hand me my walking wheels. I've got to go to the bathroom."

Stubborn old coot. She wasn't going to get anywhere this way. Wordlessly, Kate rose and retrieved his walker. She helped him stand, then said, "I'll be here when you come out."

"Damn the bad luck," he grumbled as he shut the bathroom door.

Kate went immediately to the phone beside her father's recliner and dialed her brother's office. This time she told his secretary to put her through due to a family emergency. Almost immediately, Tom came on the line. "Kate? What's wrong? How's Dad?"

Her hand gripped the receiver hard. "Did you ask him for the money, Tom, or did he offer?"

The silence lasted a long, pregnant moment. "He offered."

Kate shut her eyes, sank onto Jack Harmon's chair as a sickening blend of ugly emotions rippled down her spine.

She recalled standing in line for food stamps with infant Ryan in her arms. She remembered waiting for hours and hours at the public health clinic as Ryan whimpered in pain with an ear infection. She'd never forget the longing in her son's face that Christmas morning when the neighborhood kids rode shiny red-and-white scooters up and down the street while he pumped air into his new football, a dollar store bargain that never stayed inflated.

"Why do you need it?" *If the money is for a new house or new boat, I think I'll throw up.*

"Look, Kate. This is really not your concern."

Look Kate, you're really not part of the family.

"I'll buy the lake house." As the words tumbled from her mouth, she knew the thought had simmered for some time. "I'll buy the lake house and get you your money by July 4, but I want to know what I'm helping you buy."

A pause. A long, drawn-out pause. "It's the IRS."

"The IRS!" she repeated. *My God, Tom, what have you done?*

"We had a bookkeeping problem. A mix-up in payroll taxes. We didn't pay them."

"Oh, Tom."

"I'll lose my business."

With that, the dam broke. Words spilled from her brother's mouth with a force and an honesty she'd not heard her entire life. "They're sending us awful letters. I have until the tenth of July to pay, or they'll put liens against everything and lock the door. It's my fault, I know. I shouldn't have asked Sharon to do the books. Should have paid closer attention. This year has been tough, and we started juggling our bills and everything just went south. I made some stupid decisions, but I honestly think we could have recovered. Can recover. Understand it was just a mistake. We weren't out to cheat or anything. Oh, God, this is the worst thing to ever happen to me, to Sharon and the kids. I should never have said anything to Dad, but it just slipped out. Told him I was looking for investors—thought about Bob Simons. You heard they found natural gas out on their ranch. Dad asked why I wanted investors, and I went and spilled my guts."

He drew an audible breath, then asked, "Do you really have the money?"

No, but Adele did, and Kate knew she'd float the note until Kate could secure a mortgage. "I can get you the money, don't worry. But Tom, where was your accountant in all of this?"

"Sharon and I have been doing it ourselves. I . . . uh . . . we haven't paid the accountant, either."

Oh, for crying out loud. She asked him a few pointed questions about dates, amounts, and his contact with the IRS in the Houston office. When he admitted he'd only placed general calls and had not been assigned a case-worker, she took a silent moment to debate the question of family loyalty. "Fax me a power of attorney. I'll call . . . wait . . ."

She checked her watch. Considered a moment. "Better yet, catch Southwest up to Love Field in Dallas and drive home. Bring your books, your files, every scrap of paper you've received regarding this. Bring numbers for every-thing from your bank account to your Social Security card to your Sam's Club card. Be here before four."

He could take Dad to the doctor.

"But Kate. I can't make it to Cedar Dell by four."

"Sure you can. If I'm going to help you with this, you need to go with Dad to see Dr. Hardesty. Leave now. Bring files. I'll see what I can do about getting you a payment schedule you can live with."

"You can do that? How?"

"I'm an accountant, Tom. This is what accountants do."

"Dad won't have to sell the lake house?"

"That depends. I still want to buy the lake house. Dad can do whatever he wants with the money. Now get mov-ing and make sure you bring *everything*."

"Okay. I will." He cleared his throat, then added, "Thanks, Kate."

She hung up, shaking her head, then looked up to see her father standing in the living room doorway. His gray hair appeared mussed, his thick brows dipped over a sour expression. "You can't buy it."

Matter-of-factly, she replied, "Yes, I can. You don't know anything about my job, my salary, or my savings. I've done all right for myself since I left Cedar Dell. In fact, Daddy, it's certain that I'm worth more than your dear, darling Tom. That's why I'll buy the lake house and save his overextended posterior."

Now she saw the shock in his eyes. Was it truly that difficult for her father to believe in her success?

She'd worked hard for it. Earned every penny. She thought of the night classes, of studying late and rising early to work the breakfast shift at the pancake house. She recalled her first day on the job at the firm, and the April 16 she'd received her very first bonus. She thought of the thank-you spa package that had arrived special delivery from a grateful client.

"You want to buy the lake house to help Tom?" His bewilderment brought a crooked smile to her face.

"No. I'm not that nice. I'll buy the lake house for Ryan, of course. I'll do anything for my son." She wasn't big enough to hold back her sarcasm. "Gee, Dad, I guess I'm just like you."

The bowling ball slammed into the pins with a satisfying clatter. Seeing the final pin fall, Ryan pivoted on rubber heels, theatrically dusted his hands, and swaggered back to his seat. "I do believe that does it, Adele. I beat you by seven pins."

"Brat," Adele groused, her dangling, red-and-white bowling-pin earrings swinging back and forth as she studied the scorecard. "A split, a spare, a strike, and a turkey. Sounds like my love life."

Ryan leaned over and kissed his surrogate grandmother on the cheek. "You'll do better next time."

A spark of mischief lit the older woman's eyes. "You might be right about that. I have a date to the fish fry tonight. Bob Simons. He's into natural gas, you know."

"So was the last guy you dated. Mom's living room still needs airing out."

As Adele slapped him on the shoulder, Ryan swiped an onion ring from her basket and ate half of it in one bite. He savored the batter-fried flavor melting through his mouth, then returned the waves of a trio of giggling girls who strolled by. When they called out "Hi, Ryan" come-ons, he winked, flashed them his best get-the-girl grin, and watched them virtually puddle at his feet.

Life simply didn't get much better.

A glance at the clock trimmed in pink neon hanging on the wall revealed less than five minutes remaining in his dinner break. "Well, better get moving. I hear the Lysol can calling me."

"Are you working the rental shoe counter again?"

"For an hour. We had Daisy Day Care in here this afternoon. I have a whole rack of size twos, threes, and fours to spray. I have to tell you, I'm afraid to look inside of some of them."

Adele laughed, then reached for his hand. Her tone grew serious. "You like your job here, honey? People treating you okay?"

"I love it. People are great. I've had a few jerks make cracks about Mom, but nothing I can't handle. It's weird, Adele. This place feels . . . homey. More so than Dallas. It's like I've lived here all my life and have only been visiting there."

"Hi, Ryan," came the calls of yet another group of girls. Four of them, this time.

He waved, grinned. "I'm telling you, Adele, Cedar Dell is a piece of paradise."

Ryan's opinion didn't change after cleaning seventeen pair of preschool-sized shoes. Even the appearance of Max Cooper at the counter had minimal negative effect. He'd done a lot of thinking the last few days, and he realized his resentment was beginning to fade.

"Hi, Ryan."

He liked hearing that from the girls a whole lot better. "Hi."

"How's the job going?"

"Good." He grabbed a new pair of shoelaces from a box beneath the counter and began to change the laces in a pair of ladies' size nines.

"I spoke with Martin Groves at the Rotary Club luncheon this morning. He said the internship is going well."

Ryan nodded. "It's okay. Mr. Groves is cool."

Max smiled, appearing pleased to get more than a single word response from Ryan. He set his camera on the counter, and asked, "Can I help you with those laces?"

Mindful of the stack of shoes awaiting similar attention, he pushed the left shoe toward Max. "Go for it. What are you doing here, anyway? I was told you avoid this place like Mrs. Mallow's potato salad."

Max winced. "That is rough stuff. She'll do the world a favor if she takes the identity of her secret ingredient to the grave with her. I dropped by Harmon Lanes to talk to your grandfather. Your mother told me this morning the rest of his tests came back okay."

"Did you call Mom this morning, about seven-thirty?"

"No. I called at eight. Why?"

"Just wondered." He'd heard her singing in the shower, at breakfast, and in her office, and figured it wasn't the IRS who had called. From his viewpoint, Mom had two men hitting on her, and she liked it. Ryan wasn't all that certain how he felt about it, considering that one of those morning callers was Max, but he liked seeing Mom happy.

Besides, if she had a man in her life, maybe she'd lay off him some.

"Speaking of Granddad's doctor's appointment, something's been bothering me about that."

"What is it?"

"Uncle Tom came in and took him to see Dr. Hardesty. Do you know about that . . . weirdness . . . that happened out at the lake Sunday afternoon?" When Max nodded, he continued, "Uncle Tom said that because the tests came back clear, the doctor told him it's nothing to worry about. They aren't sure what caused his, um, spell, but that it wasn't a stroke or anything."

"That's good news, then."

"But don't you think that's strange? They don't know what happened, but we're not supposed to worry about it?"

Max pulled a small pocketknife from his jeans and sliced away a knot in a shoelace. "Of course you're going to worry. I think, however, that you'll probably not get black-and-white answers in this case. I think with an aging brain, medical science has a lot yet to learn."

Ryan absorbed that. Saw the sense in it. "Adele thinks he's not doing so hot. I think that except for his memory misfires, he's doing great. He comes up here a few hours every day. He sure feels good enough to grouse at Mom."

"She mentioned he's not too happy with her."

"I think it's mutual." Ryan shot a glance toward his grandfather's office, where Jack was visiting with a couple other old guys. "She's buying the lake house from him. Did she tell you that?"

Max nodded. "Guess you're happy about that."

"Totally jazzed. Do you remember that time you took me fishing at Lake Ray Hubbard and I hooked that tennis shoe?"

In the process of feeding a shoelace through the eye on a shoe, Max froze. He waited, cleared his throat, then said, "Yeah. Yeah, I do."

"That was the funniest thing."

"Biggest fish we caught all day was hiding in the toe of that shoe."

"It was a minnow, Dad."

Max's hand trembled, and his voice had the slightest of catches in it when he said, "Not our luckiest day on the lake."

"But one of the most fun."

"Maybe we can do it again sometime."

Ryan recognized what he'd just done. He hadn't planned it. Hadn't set out to make a statement the way he had with Shannon the other day. Max's being here had caught him by surprise and rather than mental everything out, he went with his gut. Called him Dad.

"That would be cool. It doesn't take any time at all to

get out to the lake. I heard the sandies are running at sunset. I get off work at five and maybe we could . . . oh, wait. I have a date tonight. How about next Tuesday? That's my next evening off."

"Tuesday sounds great. Really great. I'll get a baby-sitter for Shannon and . . ."

"Nah. Bring her along. It'll be fun."

If Max's smile got any bigger, his face might crack. "All right," he said. "It's settled then. That's great. Really great. Tuesday it is. Better than tonight. Shannon has a sleepover with a friend. So, where you taking your date?"

"Bingo Night. Weather looks good for an outdoor picnic tonight, and girls really like those. Think they're romantic."

In an instant, joy faded from Max Cooper's face. "Yeah. The lodge has fixed up the site as a real picnic spot. They've hung white lights in the trees along the riverbank. Brought in a bunch of picnic benches and citronella candles."

"A buddy I work with said they even have a stack of quilts for those who want to picnic on the ground, watch the stars. Neck."

"Well, hell."

Ryan drew back. "Hey, I'm not an idiot. I won't let history repeat itself. Just because . . ."

"No. No. Not you. I'm not worried about you in that respect. Do you know your mother has a date to the fish fry tonight, too?"

Oh, that's right. And not with you. "Yeah. Nicholas Sutherland. He's cool. He drives a Porsche 911. Bright red."

"Of course he does," Max said glumly. "What else."

Ryan tried to keep his lips from twitching. "Actually, I think he has a truck like yours, too. Except his is bigger."

"It was a rhetorical question." Max yanked on the shoelace hard. "There. That ought to stay. Look, I'd better go pay your grandfather that visit. Enjoyed talking with you, Ryan."

"See you later." Then, because he'd tormented Max on purpose and enjoyed doing it, he added, "Dad."

Max had a bit of a bounce in his step as he walked away from the shoe counter toward Jack's office door.

Ryan returned his attention to a pair of men's size elevens and thought about his upcoming date. Maybe he should call Stephanie and see if he could pick her up fifteen minutes early. Either that, or ask if she had a quilt she could bring. Forget the benches. He wanted to picnic on the ground. That way, he could pick a good spot.

Somewhere he could keep an eye on his mom.

Jack Harmon flipped through a *Car and Driver* magazine as he listened to a longtime friend, Ted Caudell, talk about his trip to Colorado. Jack paid scant attention to the conversation, his thoughts centered primarily on the conversation he had eavesdropped on that morning—Kate and the IRS.

Damned if she didn't sound like she knew what she was doing. Tom said she'd cut right through some red tape for him. Looked like she might help make that whole situation better.

She'd put him in a damned uncomfortable position. This plan of hers to buy the place at the lake . . . how could he take money from her and give it to Tom? How was it she had the means to buy the place anyway? Did that job of hers really pay that well?

Damned Realtor. If she'd done her job right, Kate never would have learned about his plan to help her brother.

Jack wondered what Sarah thought about all of this. She was probably mad at him, too. He'd never given Sarah money. But she didn't need it. Alan took good care of her.

"We took some great pictures from the top of Pikes Peak," Ted said. "Have a special one of the Royal Gorge."

"Rrrr . . ."

The girls should understand how life worked. Tom was a man with a man's responsibilities. He owned a small business with ten employees whose families depended on him. Jack couldn't sit by and let the business fail. Even if Kate talked the IRS into letting Tom make payments, that would be tough on a small concern like Harmon Construction.

It's not like Kate wouldn't be getting something out of the deal. The lake house was a nice place. A good investment. Shoot, he could have asked more for it if he'd fixed it up a bit. If he wasn't in a hurry to sell.

Kate's making the boy happy, that's for certain. He'll have that place all to himself one day. "Hell, they're the lucky ones in the deal."

"Yeah, that's what I thought, too," said Ted. "Imagine. Having a trout stream in your own front yard. I'd spend half the year up there if I could do it."

Jack heard the knock on the door as if it were a rescue bell. Then he looked up. His stomach sank. "Max Cooper."

"Hello, Jack."

The old man tapped a fist on his desk. "Your face is about as welcome around here as a carbuncle on the ass."

"That's what I figured." Max leaned against the door portal and folded his arms. "Still, thought I should come by and give you a chance to let me have it."

"Appreciate that." Jack slammed his magazine shut. "Ted, you mind giving this boy and me a minute?"

"You gonna make me leave? Blue hell, Jack. This'll be more entertainment than *Antiques Road Show*."

"You still watch that crap?"

"Least I watch something with some class. Not just baseball."

"Good-bye, Ted."

He groused and grumbled, but got up and left.

Max took the vacated seat. "Jack, I want to apologize for taking advantage of your daughter that summer after we graduated high school. I was a sorry son of a bitch to do what I did, and while I will never regret Ryan, I am deeply ashamed of my subsequent actions."

Well. That managed to suck a good part of the venom right out of Jack's fangs. "I thought better of you, boy."

"I know that, sir."

"I thought you should have married the girl."

"In hindsight, maybe I should have. I didn't understand the importance of family back then, never having had one myself."

"Kate had family."

Max hesitated, appeared to debate with himself, then said, "Her family didn't do right by her, Jack. She had dreams that meant the world to her, and her family took them away. It's wrong to destroy another person's dreams."

Jack looked away, into the past. "You don't understand. When a man has children—"

"I do have children. Two. If Ryan comes to me with a dream I don't necessarily understand or agree with, I hope I'll listen to him and give his dreams the respect they deserve. Same with Shannon. Just because we gave our children life doesn't mean we have the right to try and live it for them."

Jack bristled. "Wait one goddamned minute. Don't you be accusing me of that. I let my kids go their own way. Hell, I haven't had a say in Kate's life since the night she spent too much time with you."

"Listen, Jack, I respect your accomplishments and position in town. You've been a true asset to Cedar Dell. You're good a man, but you're stubborn. Your daughter acted against you one time, and you wrote her off for life."

"That's not true."

"Yeah, it is. Your hardheadedness drove Kate away."

"Her hardheadedness, you mean. My other kids aren't like that. Sarah and Tom respect their father."

"Sarah and Tom have spent their lives trying to please you."

"They're good kids."

Max lifted his gaze toward the ceiling, and muttered, "It's hopeless."

Jack opened his *Car and Driver* and flipped to the article he wanted to finish. "You done with your business here? I have work to do."

"Yeah, I guess I am."

As Max turned to go, Jack grumbled after him. "Most half-assed effort at an apology I've ever heard."

"Take it as you want. My apology was appropriate and

sincere. The rest of what I said . . . well . . . you needed to hear it, Jack, whether you listened or not."

Jack snorted. "You have the nerve of a root canal, boy. If you think just because you've finally owned up to your part in Ryan's arrival, you get to have an opinion on the private matters of my family, then you're an empty-headed fool."

"I have the right to an opinion owing to my feelings for Kate. She's a strong, beautiful, exciting woman, and I care about her. I'll be damned if I'll let you walk all over her feelings anymore."

Jack started to laugh, softly at first, then with more vigor. Max shot him a narrow-eyed glare.

"So you're looking to act as her protector, huh?"

"Maybe I am."

"You know what she's doin' tonight?"

Cooper spoke through gritted teeth. "Yes."

"She has a date with a millionaire pretty-boy. Whole town is talking about the special arrangements he made for the fish fry picnic. Tell you what, Cooper, from where I sit, looks like you are a day late and a few million short."

"We'll see. We'll just see. Nicholas Sutherland might have looks, money, and a fancy car, but I have a secret weapon of my own."

"What's that? Ryan?"

"No. I won't use my children. Don't need to."

"What is it?"

"Watch and see, Jack. You just watch and see."

Chapter Fourteen

IN PREPARATION FOR HER DATE with Nicholas Sutherland, Kate purchased three new outfits at a little boutique on the square. Fifteen minutes before the man was due to arrive, the outfits lay strewn across her bedroom floor along with half the contents of her closet and most of the items from her dresser drawers.

Deciding what to wear to dinner at the White House would be easier than settling on clothes for tonight's events. She had yet to achieve what felt like a perfect balance between Cedar Dell Fish Fry and Bingo Night casual and appropriately stylish attire for a date with Dallas's version of 007.

In the end, which was the end only because she heard the man's car pull up out front, Kate chose denim shorts, a three-quarter-sleeve white cotton blouse that tied at the waist, and an obscenely expensive pair of designer sandals that shouldn't make a blip on the Cedar Dell radar, but which Nicholas's sophisticated tastes were sure to notice.

Turning her back on the mess in her bedroom, Kate exhaled a deep, cleansing breath, checked to make sure her lipstick was still in her purse, then made her way downstairs just as the doorbell rang.

Smiling with welcome, she opened the door. "Hello."

"Hello, Kate. You look gorgeous."

"Thank you. You look pretty spiffy yourself."

This was a different Nicholas Sutherland than the one she'd previously met. Perfect, she thought with envy in her heart. He'd found the perfect mix. And she bet he hadn't left clothes scattered all over his room to accomplish it, either.

Nicholas wore brown leather sandals, khaki shorts, and a burnt orange University of Texas T-shirt. Oakley sunglasses hung from a cord around his neck and instead of his Piaget, he wore a leather-banded sports watch. He looked more Mel Gibson than James Bond today. He looked . . . delicious.

"You ready for a picnic?"

Kate waited for a leering *oh, yeah* to float through her brain, but instead she had a flashback. To Max Cooper's kiss.

"Oh, no."

"No?"

Stupidly, she gazed up at him and tried to think. "I forgot insect repellent."

Nicholas's lips twitched. "So you think of me as an insect, now?"

"No. No. Of course not." *Jeez, Kate, can you act any ditzier?*

Apparently so, because she began to babble. "Mosquitoes down by the creek. They eat me alive and I always put on Skin-So-Soft before the fish fry only this time I forgot and it's up in my bathroom and last summer Mr. Norris got West Nile virus so everyone should—"

He leaned down and shut her up with a brief, but powerful kiss that sucked away her breath and left her speechless. His eyes gleamed with an appealing combination of amusement, confidence, and lust when he stepped back. "There. Was that what was making you nervous?"

Kate held up her hand, palm out, then left him standing in the doorway. She walked to the kitchen, poured herself a glass of water, drained it, then went upstairs. She rummaged in a bathroom cabinet drawer until she found her Skin-So-Soft. She tucked the tube into her pocket, then made her way back downstairs.

Nicholas sat on the sofa talking to her father about the University of Texas football program. He stood when she walked into the room but waited for her to speak.

She found escape in small talk. "So you're a UT grad?"

"Undergraduate. Went back East to law school."

"Where?"

"Harvard."

Now that he said it, Kate realized she'd read it in one of the numerous bios printed about him. "Ryan is hoping to attend an Ivy League school. I'm hoping—"

"We have to get to Bingo Night on time!" her dad interjected. "Let's go. I don't want to be late. Lorraine King is bringing her macaroni salad, and if you don't get there early, you'll be too late."

Outside, Jack spent a few minutes admiring Nicholas's car before Kate insisted they use hers since he'd find it too difficult to enter and exit the Porsche. Her dad was appalled when she kept the car keys rather than handing them over to Nicholas. "Let him drive, girl. The man always drives."

"Especially on a date with her father throwing in his two cents from the backseat," she grumbled, making Nicholas laugh.

"Don't worry, Mr. Harmon. I like being chauffeured around town by a beautiful woman. Gives me more opportunity to watch her."

Now Jack was the one who grumbled, something about looking is all he'd better be doing. Kate wanted to pound her head on the steering wheel. Could this be any more like a small-town high school?

Glancing at Nicholas, seeing that James Bond I'm-suave-and-debonair-and-I'm-interested-in-you look back in his eyes, made her think twice. Okay, maybe it wasn't high school.

"So tell me about this fish fry," Nicholas said. "It's a fund-raiser for what group?"

"The Cedar Dell Men's Lodge. Just about every man in town belongs to the lodge. It's a combination service and social club. Sort of a Lions Club meets the coffee shop."

Jack spoke up from the backseat. "We all belong to everything anyway. Cut down on business meetings and made more time for horseshoes."

"Good thinking." As Kate approached Cedar Dell's small business district, Nicholas looked around the town with interest. "A hardware store. Clothing. Bakery. Florist. Connie's Candle Shop. I noticed last time I visited town that Cedar Dell appears to have survived the fate of many small towns. These look like thriving businesses."

"They are," Kate said.

Three blocks off the town square, Kate pulled into Pioneer Park and drove down the narrow road toward the red stone building built by the WPA during the Great Depression. The Cedar Dell Men's Lodge met in the all-purpose facility that housed a kitchen, rest rooms, two small meeting rooms, and a larger room about the size of a basketball gymnasium. Out back, an oak-shaded expanse of green Bermuda grass stretched down toward the sleepy flow of Cedar Creek. As long as the weather cooperated, lodge meetings and events took place outdoors in the shade among the benches and begonias.

The weather cooperated beautifully today. Puffy white clouds rode the blue sky on a weak cool front that took the Texas out of the summer evening. As Nicholas helped Jack from the car and handed him his walker, Kate retrieved her family's contribution to the meal from the trunk.

"It's Adele's specialty," she told Nicholas, as he relieved her arms of the large pan and peeled back the aluminum to peek inside. "Her date received last-minute tickets to a concert at Bass Hall, so she's gone into Fort Worth. This is her Southern Sweet Apple Salad. I think you'll enjoy it."

"That sounds delicious," he replied, smiling warmly.

Delicious. There was that word again.

A pair of Jack's cronies spied his arrival and sauntered over to escort him inside to the spot where dominoes aficionados set up to play moon and forty-two. "I need to deliver this salad, then my duties are done."

She walked through the building with Nicholas at her side, acutely conscious of the buzz of conversation that followed them. Stepping out onto the lawn, two visions immediately struck her. First, off to the right at the edge of her vision in the prime picnic spot at Cedar Dell Men's Lodge, a colorful quilt as fluffy as a mattress lay spread across the grass. A silver champagne bucket and two crystal flutes weighted down one corner. A picnic basket the size of Palo Pinto County and a vase of yellow roses nestled next to the champagne.

To her left, beer in his left hand, metal pinchers in his right, wearing jeans and a Texas A&M Corps of Cadets T-shirt and chewing the end of an unlit cigar, Max Cooper stood at the deep fat fryer and tossed hush puppies in the grease.

Tangibly feeling the heat of his glare, Kate thought, *Good God. My catfish is cooked.*

Ryan stood at the horseshoe pit playing pairs with his date, Stephanie Charlton, and another couple his age, and watched his mother introduce Nicholas Sutherland to the people of Cedar Dell. His dad looked mad enough to chew railroad spikes.

Oh, on the outside Max appeared cool enough. He laughed, he joked, he teased Shannon and her rugrat friends. But the light in his eyes and the set of his jaw gave him away. At least to Ryan. After all, he'd seen the same signals in the mirror often enough over the years.

"Ryan? Hel-lo. Your throw," said his date.

He offered her a quick, apologetic grin, then took aim with the red shoe and let it fly. It hit the dirt with a hard thud and rolled halfway to the creek. His second throw landed even farther from the stick. *I suck at this game.*

As his friends discussed his game in derisive terms, Ryan considered the ramifications of what he'd just witnessed. So, Max had the hots for Mom. Was that weird or what?

He turned the idea over in his brain as his date's

horseshoe clanged a ringer. He smiled and gave her a thumbs-up, before his gaze sought his mother once more. How did she feel about Max? Mom and Max Cooper. A couple. That's the last thing Ryan ever expected.

At least, not since he was eight. When Max first came into his life, he used to dream about that. Fantasize about it. Never mind that Max was happily married to Rose, who had written Ryan nice letters and sent cool European stamps for his collection. Never mind that Mom soon fell dippy in love with Roger.

Maybe the attraction was one-sided. After all, Mom was here with the tycoon and Nicholas Sutherland seemed more her type than his dad. Bet he'd take her places. Hawaii. Tahiti. Exotic beach places. She'd always talked about wanting to go to the South Seas.

A horseshoe clanged, dragging Ryan back to the game. His turn came up again, and this time he actually hit the stick. Stephanie cheered, while their opponents chided. Ryan joked, "Watch out. I'm warmed up now."

His little sister's squeals of laughter caught his attention, and he looked around to see Max chasing her around a big old cottonwood tree nearby. The sight and sound of Max catching Shannon, scooping her up into his arms, and blowing raspberries on her stomach gave Ryan a little pang in the chest. He glanced toward his mother and saw her watching the happy spectacle, too.

Max and his mom. What if . . . ? How would he feel if . . . hell. "Don't go there," he muttered.

"Too late," said the girl standing next to him as his shoe sailed way beyond target and splashed into the creek.

He heaved a sigh, kicked off his tennis shoes, rolled up

his jeans, and waded into the water to the catcalls and laughter of picnic attendees. He realized as he reached into the shallows and retrieved the bright red shoe that he'd never felt more accepted, more at home, anywhere at any time in his life.

He'd have sworn that the letters shoved into his jeans pocket, the ones he'd intercepted from the postman earlier that day, started to burn. If he thought it would help, he'd dunk his ass, but he feared this was one fire that wouldn't be put out so easily.

Back on dry land and restored to socks and shoes, Ryan extended a hand toward his date. "You want to go for a walk?"

"Sure."

They walked the dirt footpath that ran alongside the creek, making small talk and learning more about one another. Considering that this was only their second real date, Ryan attempted to be his normal, charming self. His heart wasn't in it. "Have you ever done something your mom disapproved of in a major way? Something that really made her freak out?"

She stopped abruptly. "Ryan, I'm not having sex with you."

"No. No. That's not where I was headed. Not that I wouldn't if you wanted to go there, mind you. You're really hot, Stephanie."

"Thank you. I think."

"So, have you?"

She thought about it a moment. "I'm afraid I'm your classic good girl."

"Oh."

"Have you?"

"Well, I'm kind of in the middle of it now." He tugged a green leaf off a shrub and tore it into pieces as they walked. "I'm afraid she's gonna blow when she finds out."

She gave him a wary glance, just the sort you'd expect from a good girl. "What have you done?"

He should keep his mouth shut. He didn't know Stephanie all that well, but he was busting a gut to tell someone. "You promise you won't tell anybody?"

"That depends. If you've done something illegal or terribly immoral, I'd just as soon not know because then I think I'd be forced to rat you out, and I don't want to be put in that position."

"No, it's nothing like that."

"Then, okay, I promise I won't tell anyone."

"Not even your best friend?"

"Especially not her. She's terrible at keeping secrets."

Ryan considered it, decided he could trust her. Grimacing, he reached into his pocket, and pulled out the envelopes. "We're having our mail forwarded from Dallas so it takes a while to get to us. This stuff came today."

He handed her the first envelope. She read the return address, then shot him a quick, sympathetic look. "Oh, Ryan. Did you bomb your SATs?"

He sighed with the weight of the world upon his shoulders. "Not exactly. Look at it."

Now her sympathy sharpened to curiosity. She tugged the report from the envelope, opened it, then her mouth gaped and she gasped. "My God, Ryan. It's a sixteen hundred! You made a perfect score."

"It gets worse." He handed her the other envelopes.

"Princeton? Yale?" She opened the letters inside and scanned them. "Oh, wow, Ryan. These are invitations to visit!"

"Yep. My mom's gonna be real happy."

She studied him, then her eyes went round with surprise. "You don't want to visit Princeton or Yale?"

"It'd be a waste of time, Stephanie. A big old waste of time."

Kate sipped champagne as she walked with Nicholas beside Cedar Creek. Having spotted Ryan heading north with his girl, they took the south route. Max was back on duty at the fish cooker, supplying the crowd of picnicgoers who wanted second helpings of catfish.

"I ate too much," Nicholas said, a groan in his voice. "Your dad was right about that macaroni salad. It's worth coming early for."

"I didn't have any," Kate replied. "I stuck to the gourmet offerings you provided. That shrimp salad was wonderful."

"Glad you enjoyed it. Cooking relaxes me."

He cooks, too? Could he be any more perfect?

While they walked, he told her stories of his trip to Russia and asked questions about her days in Cedar Dell. They veered away from the creek at the rose garden and eventually took a seat on a wooden porch swing hung inside a honeysuckle-covered gazebo.

Kate's gaze periodically returned to the spot where they'd left the creek path, halfway expecting to see Max.

His proprietary air annoyed her. He had no claim on her, none at all, and he should have kept those offended glares he'd shot her way to himself. Just because they'd shared a kiss or two didn't mean he had any say in her life. He certainly had no excuse for jealousy. Kate hated jealousy, and Max should, too. Hadn't that destructive emotion created havoc in their family once before?

So why did it give her a little warm feeling of pleasure? How stupid was that?

"Why the scowl?" Nicholas asked.

"Hmm? Oh, I'm sorry. I let my thoughts wander. That was rude of me."

"It means you're comfortable with me, and I like that." Nicholas draped his arm on the swing behind her. "So, who's the fry cook? He looked like he wanted to boil me in his oil."

Kate couldn't argue with his observation. "He's Max Cooper. He's . . . um . . . Ryan's father."

"Your ex?"

"No." She blew out a breath. "It's complicated. Max and I were just out of high school, and it was one of those nights that shouldn't have happened; but Ryan happened so it was a good thing, after all."

"Ahh." Nicholas pushed with his foot to set the swing in motion. "The two of you have remained close, though? That's why he'd like to fry my bacon?"

"No, I think he's probably nervous."

Nicholas sputtered a laugh. "That didn't look like nervous to me."

"Like I said, it's complicated. Max and Ryan have been estranged for a few years, and they're just now beginning to repair their relationship. He doesn't want anything or any-one to interfere with that."

"And having a man in your life could do that?"

It seemed egotistical for Kate to think that one date with Nicholas qualified as having a man in her life. Egotistical or pathetic. She *could* have a man in her life if she wanted. If she made the effort.

If she talked on the phone with one every morning.

"No. I don't know. I don't want to talk about Max Cooper. I don't know why I'm telling you all this."

"Like I said before, you are comfortable with me, and I like that." Nicholas clasped her hand and brought it to his lips for a gallant kiss. "Therefore, my lovely Kate, let's get intimate. What's your dream?"

The combination of the kiss with the words "get intimate" left Kate playing catch-up. "Excuse me? What did you say?"

He laughed. "What is your fondest dream?"

"Do you mean my favorite recurring dream? It's the one where I can fly. I love to have that dream."

"That does sound fun, but it's not what I meant. Not the dream you have when you're asleep, but the one you think about before you go to sleep."

The question made Kate uncomfortable. When this man said intimate, he meant it.

"You see, Kate," he continued, "I don't consider myself a goal-oriented man. I work to achieve dreams. Quirky little difference, I know, but it's who I am. Right now, completing this chess set is my dream."

Oh, she had one of those kind of dreams. "Ryan. I want him to go to a good college."

Nicholas smiled gently. "Family. I should have guessed. How can I help? How are his grades? Does he need tutoring? A scholarship, perhaps?"

Stunned at the turn the conversation had taken, she drew back and stared at him. "No, he's smart. Top of his class. I can pay for college."

It was a point of pride with her. Max had made a standing offer to pay Ryan's college expenses, but Kate wanted to do it herself. That way she could be sure her son had the freedom to choose where he truly wanted to go to school, to study what interested him, not what interested his father. She wanted him to follow his dreams.

Kate wanted better for her son than what she'd had. Not community college night classes, but Harvard. Princeton. MIT. Ryan was smart enough. "Do you have an in with any Ivy League admissions boards?"

Nicholas offered an enigmatic smile. "I could help at a place or two, I think."

"You help Ryan get into a great college, and I'll find that Aphrodite if I have to turn Cedar Dell into an archeological dig."

He laughed. "Kate, you misunderstood me. I like Ryan and I'll be happy to help him achieve *his* dream, but I'm asking about yours. Your personal dream, Kate. Something for you and only you."

Oh. "Why?"

"Our dreams define us."

She considered that a moment. Okay. She'd buy that. What was her dream? Flippantly, she responded, "To be a size four?"

He gave her a slow once-over. "Why ruin perfection, Ms. Harmon?"

"Smooth talker," she drawled back, feigning indifference though she couldn't help but be flattered. The man was good. Handsome, charming, wealthy . . . what would he say if she said her dream was to marry him, or at least his sophisticated lifestyle? To live comfortably in worldly circles instead of small-town constriction? Tempted, she decided she didn't know him well enough to tease that way.

"What is it, Kate? A house? A car? An exotic vacation?"

"No. Nothing like that." Of that much she was certain.

He gave her a considering look, then shook his head. "Not jewelry."

"No." Definitely not.

"Something related to your professional life, perhaps? A partnership at Markhum and Frye?"

She nodded slowly. "That's a goal, not a dream."

"Ah-hah." Wearing a smile of satisfaction, he gave the swing a push with his foot. "So you do understand the difference."

"Yes. I think I do."

"Markhum and Frye has a good reputation in town. They're well established. Solid. Strong." His lips twitched. "Boring."

She shot him a sharp look.

"Are you certain they're the right firm for you long-term?"

"Why wouldn't they be?"

"You tell me. Will a partnership at Markhum and Frye

provide you the means—monetary or otherwise—to achieve your dream?"

"It's a difficult question."

"It shouldn't be. Maybe that's an answer in itself."

"You have a point." Hmm, she mused. What did she want? Happiness. Success. Achievement. Yes, all those, but Nicholas asked for something more tangible. What would be . . .

"A bathroom." The moment she thought of it, she knew it was right. "I want a corner office with a private bathroom and, what the heck, a whirlpool tub. A deep one."

Nicholas pursed his lips. "Window?"

"Two of 'em. One on each wall. Bathroom's fine without."

"Furniture?"

"Hmm . . ." She considered the possibilities. "Functional. Style doesn't matter to me as much. I do want lots of electrical outlets, though. An accountant can never have enough electrical outlets."

"Art?"

"Photographs."

"Color or black-and-white?"

"Color. Lots of color and full of life. And plants. I like plants in my office." Enjoying the exercise, Kate turned to him, a smile on her face. "Tell me about your office. Or wait, let me guess. Corner office, private bath."

"With a huge whirlpool tub."

"Oh, just stab me through the heart."

"And a private workout room. Lifting sometimes helps me think."

Kate absently stretched her legs and rotated her ankles. "You can keep your workout room. Do you have art on your walls?"

His gaze fixed on her feet. "Oils by an Austin-area artist. He's working on a suite of the chess pieces that I intend to hang once the set is complete."

"That will be something to see. And to that end"— Kate stood and extended her hand toward Nicholas— "shouldn't we be getting back so you can talk to Mr. Schroeder before bingo begins?"

Mr. Schroeder was the one lead produced by Kate's predawn trek on Thursday to the Loving Highway flea market. While Adele negotiated a price for a sixties-era aluminum Christmas tree, Kate found a doll seller from Graham who thought he remembered the "figurine" in the possession of a dealer from Cedar Dell.

That dealer, Mr. Schroeder, hadn't made the flea market that week since he'd gone into Fort Worth to hit garage sales and restock his inventory. The doll seller told Kate she'd likely find him at Saturday night's fish fry since Mr. Schroeder never missed a Bingo Night.

Sure enough, Mr. Schroeder had arrived at the Cedar Dell Men's Lodge not long after Kate, Nicholas, and her father. Since he'd immediately struck up a dominoes game, Nicholas suggested they wait until after the picnic to approach him.

"Did you bring the sketch?" she asked, as they retraced their steps down the creek path. "Mine's in my purse if we need it."

"I did better than bring the sketch. I have the ruby Aphrodite. She's with the picnic stuff."

Kate's step slowed. "You left her there? Unprotected?"

His lips twisted wryly. "A meeting of the Cedar Dell Men's Lodge is a hotbed of crime?"

"No, but the Bransons brought their new puppy. He could decide to use it as a chew stick."

"Hmm . . . I didn't consider the canine menace."

"I know it's probably silly to fret about it, but if something happened to it here, I'd feel responsible."

"Why? I'm the one who brought the chess piece."

"Yes, but you're here at my invitation, and Cedar Dell is my home."

He shot her a look. "Is it? That's the first time I've heard you claim it. You've always said Dallas is your home."

The question stopped her, left her with an uneasy feeling in her stomach. Dallas was her home. Strange that she had said otherwise.

She gave her shoulders a shake and dismissed the concern. "Semantics, that's all. Let's go get the Aphrodite and see what Mr. Schroeder has to say."

Nicholas lifted a plastic, puppy-proof box from among the picnic supplies. He opened the box, and the sight of the chess piece pushed everything else from her mind. She'd forgotten how beautiful the Aphrodite was.

"How did something so lovely end up at a flea market?" she wondered aloud.

"I have a contact, an expert on old coins, who has worked for PBS's *Antiques Road Show*. He tells stories about lost and found treasures that would make you cringe."

"I don't even want to even think about it. Let's hope Mr. Schroeder gives us something we can cheer about instead."

They found him seated at a redwood picnic table debating the preseason college football polls with Cedar Dell High's algebra teacher, a Baptist minister, and Max Cooper. Lovely. Just lovely. She'd hoped to avoid a direct meeting between Max and Nicholas. She didn't trust Max not to engage in some male chest beating. "Maybe we could do this after bingo."

Nicholas tilted his head toward the serving table laden with bowls, platters, and plates now covered with plastic wrap. "Chicken, sweetheart?"

"Turkey."

Nicholas laughed while they approached the table, and Max's eyes narrowed to slits. As Kate introduced Nicholas to Mr. Schroeder, the minister, and the teacher, Max slipped on his sunglasses. Kate wanted to kick his shin.

"Nicholas, this is Ryan's father, Max Cooper."

"Welcome to Cedar Dell," Max said, rising and offering his hand for a shake. His smile bordered on feral.

"Thank you." Nicholas answered. He and Max did that white-knuckled, I'm-gonna-crush-your-hand thing, as Nicholas's eyes went cold. "Quite a friendly town you have here."

If testosterone were liquid, Cedar Dell would be engulfed by a flash flood right about now.

"It's a nice place for a *quick* visit," Max drawled. "Folks don't really cotton to big-city strangers hanging around too long, so it can turn unfriendly real fast."

Kate rolled her eyes heavenward, then furtively elbowed Max in the side to shush him. "Mr. Schroeder? Nicholas and I are looking for something Mrs. Brown sold at her garage sale a while back, and a dealer out at the

Loving Highway flea market told me you might be able to help." She gestured for Nicholas to show him the chess piece.

"I heard something about that," the minister piped up as he craned to see the piece. "Said you created a stir at the beauty salon the other day with a picture of a statue."

Nicholas held the ruby Aphrodite up for inspection. "It's a chess piece, a queen that's the image of this one, only trimmed in gold with an emerald broach."

Kate held her breath. Mr. Schroeder pursed his lips and frowned, but when Kate spied the cagey horse-trader light in his eyes, her pulse leapt.

"Hmm." Mr. Schroeder rubbed his jaw. "The item does look familiar. Is that a real ruby?"

Max folded his arms and leaned against the picnic table. He appeared all set to enjoy the show.

A hint of a smile played at Nicholas's lips. Kate wondered if Mr. Schroeder recognized the look of a hunter with prey in his sight. "Yes, and the emerald on the other piece is a real emerald, too."

"I seem to recall more gold in the clouds at the feet of the other statue."

Kate's gaze cut to Nicholas. Maybe, just maybe, his eyes had narrowed a little. "That's certainly possible. Over time and usage, gilding will flake."

"What are you looking to pay?"

"Are you offering to negotiate, Mr. Schroeder?" Nicholas sounded genial, offhanded, but his eyes looked relentless. "Do you have the Aphrodite in your possession?"

Again, Schroeder rubbed his jaw. "So it's part of a chess set, huh?"

Another glance at Nicholas told her he might have the patience for this, but she didn't. "Mr. Schroeder. Please! Do you have the chess piece?"

He shot her a scowl and snapped, "I'm trying to do business here, girl."

Nicholas cleared his throat and shifted his stance menacingly closer. Max stood up straight, and said, "Hold on there, George. Let's not be talking to Kate that way. Answer the damned question. Do you have this chess piece or not?"

Mr. Schroeder snarled, but eventually shook his head, dashing Kate's hopes.

"Do you know where it is?" Nicholas pressed.

"No, but I'm good at finding things. I'll be happy to keep an eye out for it, but I want to know it'll be worth my time and effort."

He knew something. Kate could hear it in his voice. But the old horse trader wasn't giving an inch.

They needed to take another tack. "Mr. Schroeder, are you a veteran?"

The question caught him off guard. "A veteran? You mean a war veteran?"

"Yes."

"I served in Korea."

Kate nodded sagely, aware that both Max and Nicholas watched her with interest. "I imagine you are a patriotic man who appreciates the sacrifices our servicemen have made for their country."

"I do. That's why I think you should be at this shindig with Max here, instead of the city boy." He shot Nicholas a look. "Max flew F-16s over Bosnia."

Nicholas offered Max a deadpan glance. "Thank you for your service, Cooper."

Kate rushed to bring the conversation back on topic. "The primary value of the missing chess piece lies not in the piece itself, but in its history as a war relic."

As she'd expected, that made all the men sit up and listen, and Kate proceeded to offer an expurgated version of the emerald Aphrodite's history, leaving out parts she judged might complicate matters, such as the fact the chess set was stolen from the Palace of Versailles. She ended her tale by saying, "We don't know the Cedar Dell soldier's identity or why he didn't keep the chess piece. Even without that information, the emerald Aphrodite will contribute significantly to what I think is a fascinating World War II tale."

Mr. Schroeder folded his arms and addressed Nicholas. "So you're trying to put this chess set back together?"

"Yes, sir, I am."

"And what do you expect to get out of it? A book deal? Movie, maybe?"

Nicholas shook his head. "No. The quest to recover this chess set was my mother's dream in the final years of her life. In honor of her, I intend to see it accomplished."

Take that, Schroeder, Kate thought. If he tried to make this about money now, he'd look the avaricious fool in front of the minister and, therefore, in front of Cedar Dell.

"That is an admirable goal, Mr. Sutherland," the minister said. "Family is important, and wanting to honor it reflects well upon you. However, I see a potential problem in this endeavor."

His theatrical pause bespoke his pulpit experience,

adding tension and anticipation to the moment. Kate tapped her foot. Neither Max nor Nicholas moved.

Mr. Schroeder snorted with impatience. "What problem?"

"Seems to me that the Cedar Dell Historical Society has a superior claim on the chess piece."

"Does Cedar Dell have a historical society?" Max asked. "I didn't know that."

The minister nodded. "I am co-chairman this year along with Mrs. Dickerson. Back in February, we obtained permission from the town council and the library board to create a permanent display in the William B. Travis Room at the Cedar Dell Public Library. *Cedar Dell: A Living History* is due to open in September. The northeastern corner of the Travis Room is devoted to our men who served their country during wartime. We have displays going back to the War of Northern Aggression. Bert Sperry donated a German bayonet and flag for our dubya-dubya-two section. Alma Peters provided transcripts of letters her husband sent from the Japanese theater—minus the personal stuff, of course. The Harris family sent us some horrifying photographs their father took of Buchenwald concentration camp."

"It sounds like an excellent exhibit," Nicholas said. "I'll be happy to contribute photographs and a detailed history of the emerald Aphrodite once I have it in my possession."

"I appreciate the offer," the minister said with grave reproof, "but I believe the chess piece belongs in a museum, the Cedar Dell museum, not in a private collection. It represents a significant story in our local history."

Kate glanced at Nicholas, wondering if he'd mention

the chess set's history at Versailles now. Could Cedar Dell have a better claim than France? She understood the minister's pride in a local serviceman's effort to help orphans. It wasn't as if the serviceman had stolen the piece; it was a reward for good deeds.

"Miss Kate? Daddy?" Shannon Cooper called out. "Would you please tell my brother to come play tag with us?"

"Leave Ryan alone," Max told her. "He has a date."

"I know. But they've been kissing long enough."

Kate and Max shared a grimace as Stephanie's father rose with a growl from a nearby picnic table and marched off toward the trees. "Something tells me he'll be here in a minute, Shannon," Kate said. "Ask him to play then."

"Okay."

"Seems to me," Max said, turning his attention away from his daughter and back to the conversation at hand, "y'all have the cart before the horse. Find the piece first, then worry what to do with it. Mr. Schroeder, tell us what you've been holding back."

Schroeder sputtered. Max pinned him with a look. "Spill it, Schroeder, or I'll sic the Widow Gault on you."

"Marian Wilcox. I sold it to Marian Wilcox."

Kate and the minister groaned in unison. Max chuckled softly, earning a glare from Kate.

"Who's Marian Wilcox?" Nicholas asked.

"She's the wealthiest woman in Cedar Dell," the minister said. "The most scatterbrained, too."

"She's also the pack rat of Cedar Dell," Max added. "You can't take two steps in her house without bumping into something."

Kate rubbed her temples with her fingertips. "She gives things away. To anybody and everybody. We crossed the street together one time when I was about ten, and she reached into her purse and gave me a bearer bond worth five hundred dollars. Mom marched me up the hill to her house to give it back to her, and she wouldn't take it. She didn't remember giving it to me. She said it probably wasn't hers."

Max's lips twisted as if he were holding back a smile. "She bought a computer earlier this year and went on-line. UPS delivers to her place twice a day."

"EBay!" the minister exclaimed in horror.

"We're sunk." Kate sighed loudly.

"No, we're not." Ignoring Max's threatening glare, Nicholas gave Kate's hand a reassuring squeeze, then lifted it to his mouth for a kiss. "Remember what I said earlier? Our dreams define us."

Just as Ryan emerged from the trees, Stephanie's red-faced father at his heels, Kate's father announced from the doorway to the lodge that bingo would begin in five minutes.

Max's gaze never left Nicholas. "So," he drawled, sarcasm dripping from his tone, "you think you're going to search Marian Wilcox's house? You are dreaming, old man."

"Yes." Nicholas spoke with urban aplomb. "That's the great thing about dreams. Sometimes they take you in unexpected directions. In this instance, I get to spend more time with Kate."

"In this instance, I get to spend more time with Kate," Max murmured in a falsetto tone. He sat at a card table inside the lodge, six bingo cards spread before him. Three of the cards were his, three of them Ryan's. The deserter. Not five minutes ago, Max pocketed twenty dollars off a win on one of his son's cards. He might not give it to him. There oughta be a rule about being present to win. There oughta be a rule that you don't get to keep the cash if you bingo when you're out driving a red Porsche 911.

He sipped a glass of sweet tea and muttered sourly. "Damned city-slicker lawyer."

After Stephanie's father ended her date with Ryan prematurely by carting his daughter home, Ryan had sat at Max's table to play a few rounds of bingo, something he'd never done before. Max had anticipated a nice, father-son discussion about sports. After all, the Rangers had made a big trade for a pitcher today that promised to change the outlook of their season. Ryan had something other than baseball on his mind, however. He yammered on about cars. A red Porsche 911 to be exact. He about wore Max's ears out.

"Damned German car," he murmured, searching the bingo cards for N-17. What's so special about a damned Porsche? He drove one when he was stationed in Germany. Yeah they're powerful. Sexy. A chick magnet.

"Women!" Max marked the two cards showing N-17.

During a break between games, Max had gone outside to transfer Shannon's overnight bag from his truck to the Hardys' minivan. When he kissed his daughter good-bye as she left on her first sleepover, Ryan came barreling out of the lodge building, car keys in his fist. Porsche keys.

"He told me to take it for a spin, Max. It's parked back at Granddad's house. Can I borrow your truck to get there?"

Max. Not Dad. His dependable truck was wanted only to carry his son to a shyster's sex machine.

If the damned car were nearby, Max would find an egg and peg it.

Ryan drove off, and Max went back inside to play bingo and brood. Every time Kate smiled at the son of a bitch lawyer, every time she laughed, his tension level climbed. He watched the time tick by on the wall clock above the men's room door, sipping his tea, grumbling to himself, and winning on two more cards.

Eight minutes and thirty-seven seconds after a beaming Ryan returned the Porsche keys to the damned lawyer, Max saw Sutherland reach into his pocket and pull out a small cell phone. "Right on time," Max murmured, satisfaction seeping through him like good whiskey.

The lawyer spoke into the phone, frowned, said something to Kate, then left the table to continue his call. "Cue the good guy," Max said, draining his sweet tea and pushing to his feet. He sauntered over toward Kate, stopping along the way to speak to a person or two like a glad-handing politician.

It seemed appropriate, under the circumstances.

"G-27," announced the caller, as Max strolled up to Kate's table.

"Where's your boyfriend?"

"Bingo!" called a woman from the crowd.

Kate scowled at Max. "Nicholas had to take a phone call."

"Oh, yeah?" Max pulled an empty chair away from Kate's table and straddled it. "That's rude to do while you're on a date. Does he have young children? That's about the only good reason I can think of for answering a phone call while out with you."

Her mouth set. "He doesn't have children, and you'd have taken the call, too. The call is from the lieutenant governor's office."

Kate appeared impressed at the man's connections. Max could have done without that, but he'd been prepared for the possibility. "He's got a thing going with one of the secretaries there?"

"You are such a . . ." She bit off the insult, then continued, "The call was from the lieutenant governor himself."

"No." Max reared back and let his mouth go slack.

She lifted her chin, looking defensive. "Yes."

"Why would the governor be calling your boyfriend? Did he get arrested or something? Need to make bail?"

"Don't you have bingo cards to see to, Cooper?"

"I gave 'em to the Widow Mallow. She's playing to fund an Alaskan cruise for her vacation in August, and I always like to contribute to good local causes. Besides, Cedar Dell can use a little less hot air around town that time of year."

She stifled a smile and Max gave himself free rein. Bingo Night had suddenly turned fun.

Nicholas Sutherland stepped back inside, and at first view of his expression, Max began to whistle beneath his breath.

"Kate," the damned lawyer said as he approached, "I'm afraid I need to cut our evening short."

"Oh."

The disappointment in her tone had Max swallowing his tune.

"The lieutenant governor is in Dallas at a Police

Association awards banquet, and he wants to meet with me when it is over."

"Tonight?" Kate asked.

"What about?" Max threw in.

The shyster didn't bother to so much as look at Max. "In three hours."

"You'll need to hurry, then," Kate said, standing and reaching for her purse. "I'll take you to get your car."

"The motel is on the way to your father's house, isn't it? I have a suit with me. I can change here, then head straight downtown for our meeting."

Max clucked his tongue and made a disdainful sweep of Sutherland's attire. "Can't go to a meeting with the lieutenant governor wearing a tea-sip T-shirt. I do believe the man's an Aggie."

Kate shot him a glare. "Would you stop with the college rivalry nonsense."

"It's not nonsense," Max called to her retreating back. After all, Max's old college roommate, the current lieutenant governor for the great state of Texas, wouldn't have been near so quick to do him this favor had Nicholas Sutherland not been a UT grad.

"Have a safe trip home" he added. Sutherland flourished a wave of acknowledgment. Had he not watched closely, Max would have missed the fact that in the process, the lawyer flipped him off.

Grinning with self-satisfaction, Max checked the wall clock. He'd stop by the house and grab a quick shower. That should time it about right.

City dudes weren't the only ones with connections.

Chapter Fifteen

KATE WATCHED THE PORSCHE's taillights disappear up the street and sighed. At least now she wouldn't have to worry about what she'd say if he asked her back to the Cedar Dell Motor Lodge.

She liked Nicholas Sutherland. He was interesting and intriguing. She ran her tongue over her lips. Plus, the man could kiss.

She sent a longing glance toward the house. A bath, book, and a glass of wine sure sounded good right now, but she needed to pick up Dad and Ryan at the lodge.

A bullfrog croaked in the flower bed behind her. From next door, the rhythmic *chik chik chik* of a water sprinkler drifted though the night. Kate took two steps toward her car and then, as she heard the long, low *whoo* of a train whistle in the distance, tears suddenly filled her eyes.

The people at the fish fry had treated her so nice. Only once or twice had she heard whispers behind her back or seen the glint of disapproval in people's eyes. No one openly insulted her, not even The Widows. No one embarrassed her in front of Nicholas. They'd made her feel welcome. Made her feel like she belonged.

They made her feel at home.

And Ryan. They'd treated him no different from any other native son. They'd accepted him as part of the Cedar Dell family with little resistance. Once they'd learned who fathered her child, rather than holding it against her, against her son, even against Max, they'd had little else to say in the matter. Once she'd appeased their curiosity, they'd gone on to the next item on the scandal sheet—where the Ramseys got the money to buy that twenty-five-foot Cobalt boat. That's what had been the topic of discussion at the fish fry. Not her. Not Ryan. Well, except for speculation about her relationship with Nicholas, and that was normal, run-of-the-mill gossip to be expected.

Emotion clogged her throat. For eighteen years, she'd denied herself her home. For eighteen years, she'd feared Cedar Dell. Needlessly, it turned out.

She drew a deep breath, attempting to settle herself down. Her gaze focused on the window of her father's house, where a lamp burned in his den. "No, not so needlessly," she murmured.

It wasn't fear of her reception by the townspeople that kept her away all these years. What kept her away liked to sit in the La-Z-Boy and watch baseball. Jack and his attitude.

That hadn't changed.

Kate was beginning to think it never would. No matter what she did, she'd never please him. No matter what she accomplished, he'd never approve of her. Even after she'd used her expertise to bail Golden Boy Tom out of trouble, her father's disapproval only marginally mellowed. He gave her no recognition or credit. No pat on the back for a deed well-done.

But tonight, Cedar Dell had welcomed her. She would take it to heart and enjoy the warmth it sparked to life inside her. She could worry about her dad and his attitude tomorrow.

Kate turned away from the house and took a few steps toward her car. Only then did she notice the truck waiting at the curb. "Max?"

The passenger-side door swung open. "Get in, Kate."

She hurried to the pickup. "What's wrong? Did something happen?"

"Nothing's wrong. Everything's fine." He patted the bench seat. "Just get in, would you?"

"Why? I need to go back and pick up Dad and Ryan."

"They're riding home with neighbors. Get in, and I'll explain."

"But why would—?"

"Please?" He said it more as a demand than a plea, and she folded her arms and studied him. He'd changed into jeans and a blue chambray work shirt. She caught a whiff of aftershave. "C'mon, Kate. Come with me."

Her curiosity piqued, Kate couldn't resist. She climbed into the truck, shut the door, and fastened her seat belt. Max pulled away from the curb, whistling softly, his satisfaction obvious.

"Okay, I'm ready for the explanation. What's this about? Where are you taking me?"

"Out."

"Out?"

"Yeah, out. Thought we'd take a little ride."

"Where? Why?"

Ignoring her questions, he adjusted the fan on the

air conditioner. The velocity of the cold air streaming from the dashboard vents decreased. "Temperature okay for you?"

"It's fine, Max. Does this have something to do with the kids?"

"No." He reached beneath his seat and tossed a sleeve of compact discs into her lap. "Pick out some music, would you?"

Kate sighed. Guess she might as well be patient. Knowing Max, he'd get around to his purpose in his own good time.

Meanwhile, a drive did sound nice. It sounded peaceful. Above them, stars sprinkled the night sky like sugar. The sparse traffic made it feel like they were alone on the road. It was a beautiful evening for a drive. Smiling, relaxing, Kate settled back into her seat and perused the selection of CDs.

His eclectic taste in music didn't surprise her. Classical. Jazz. Country. Rock. She smiled at the sight of a recording popular at Cedar Dell High twenty years earlier, and soon, the mellow twang of Jerry Jeff Walker rose from the speakers. "I haven't seen an armadillo in years."

"Not even on the way to the lake? I'm surprised. They're still the most plentiful roadkill around. On second thought, I take that back. Possums probably outnumber armadillos on the shoulders of Texas highways."

"Thank you for that clarification," Kate said dryly. "I meant a living armadillo."

"Oh. You have to get out at night to see them when they're still waddling, sweetheart. Possums, too. And raccoons. They are all nocturnal animals."

"I know that."

"Keep your eyes peeled, then. There's sure to be something in the road tonight. I'll try not to hit it until you've gotten a good look."

"You're so considerate."

They rode a couple miles in silence before Max spoke again. "So, bet you didn't enjoy this sort of scintillating conversation with Shyster Sutherland."

Dashboard lighting softly illuminated his face. A grin flirted at his lips.

"Scintillating?" Kate shot him a droll look and changed the subject. "Sometimes on the way to the lake, Ryan and I play roadkill bingo."

The truck swerved slightly. "Huh?"

"Five columns. Possums, armadillos, raccoons, rabbits, and UIs."

"UIs?"

"Unidentifiables."

His chuckle grew into a full-blown laugh. Kate sat back and enjoyed the drive. They rode in silence for a time, and Kate hummed along to the music, her thoughts drifting back over the day. She'd barely had any contact with her dad. He was getting around better of late and managed to do more and more for himself. He'd had one more fuzzy spell—that she knew of, anyway—since their day at the lake. It was enough to make her question whether he should ever live alone again.

Something darted across the road in front of them, a pair of golden eyes gleaming. "Watch out," she warned.

"Do believe that's a mountain lion. A good-sized one." Max swerved the truck as the animal bounded off into the bushes. "Heard the ranchers out this way have had trouble with those of late."

Kate dragged her gaze off the countryside. "If you run out of gas or break down, you're walking back to town by yourself."

"You're a cruel woman, Kate." Max turned off the highway onto a smaller farm road. "So. Did you have a good time today?"

Was this the beginning of another dig at Nicholas? Shadows shielded his expression so Kate couldn't tell. "Yes."

"Then why were you sad when I pulled up tonight?"

She turned her head, looked out the passenger-side window toward a cotton field. The intimacy of the darkness, the comfort of the history they shared, allowed her to answer honestly. "They accepted me, Max."

After a moment's pause, he said, "Yep. Did you expect them to give you a hard time?"

Kate sighed. "I expected subtle snubs, to be honest. They surprised me. People were really glad I was there."

"Of course they were glad you were there. You're one of us, Kate."

"Still? After everything?"

He reached across the seat, took her hand, and squeezed it. "Always. That's what is special about this place. It's why I came home."

"I never saw it. Growing up here . . . I couldn't wait to leave. I dreamed about going off to college from the time I was in third grade and the neighbor boy went off to Texas Tech. I never appreciated what small-town life, what Cedar Dell life, had to offer."

"What about now, Kate?" Max asked with an odd intensity in his voice as he turned onto another, smaller road. "Do you see it now?"

A familiar red neon OPEN sign caught her eye, distracting her from his question. "Carson's Bait House and Bar? You brought us to the lake?"

He glanced around. "Yeah, I guess I did. Wasn't really paying attention."

Kate didn't know if she believed that or not. It didn't really matter. It was a beautiful night, and, right now, there was no place in the world she'd rather be. "Go by Dad's place. Actually," she added, her voice brightening, "my place. You do have a trailer hitch on this truck, don't you? We can get the boat out. I love riding on the lake at night."

"You think it's safe?"

"It should be. We haven't had rain lately to wash debris into the water. We both know the lake and the stumpy parts. As long as we stay in the main river channel, we shouldn't have to worry."

"That's not the kind of danger I'm talking about."

Oh.

In that instant, the air in the truck cab changed, became charged with tension. Kate's pulse accelerated. Her mouth grew dry. She almost checked the sky to see if a thunderstorm had blown up out of nowhere.

Kate darted a look at Max. Long and lean and powerful, he made her think of that mountain cat out roaming tonight. Hunting.

Is that what this drive is about? Is Max hunting?

Her mouth went dry as an August rain gauge.

Maybe she should tell him to turn the truck around and take her home. After all, what was she doing here? An hour ago, she'd been on a date with another man, a really nice guy who'd had to end their date because of a call from the lieutenant governor's office. Had Nicholas not had to leave, where would she be now? At the Cedar Dell Motor Lodge with him? Was she that fickle? Any man would do?

No, but I am that lonely.

Max pulled into the lane leading to the lake house. He shifted into park and opened his door.

"Max? Maybe we'd better head back to town."

He ignored her. "Your dad still keeps the gate key in the third fence post pipe, doesn't he?"

It seemed easier to go along with him than argue. At least, that's what she tried to tell herself. "Yes. I should probably move it. Everyone in town knows that's where the key is."

"Ever had any trouble with folks coming in and tearing something up?"

"No, but we often find drinks in the fridge or the lawn mowed or food in the freezer." After a moment's pause, she added, "Guess I'll leave the key where it is."

Max's door shut with a quiet *snick*. Kate sat unmoving but for the nervous tap of her right foot against the floorboard. *Don't be silly,* she told herself. *Nothing's going to happen. So what if he kissed me 'til my toes curled last time we were alone together? So what if the last time we'd spent alone together at the lake we ended up in a hormone hurricane?*

"I'm too old for sex in a tree house," she said softly as rusty hinges creaked and the metal gate scraped over rock. *Nothing's going to happen.*

Not unless you want it to.

"Hush," she muttered, as Max opened the door.

"What?"

"Oh, nothing. Never mind."

The truck dipped and bounced over the rutted road up to the house. When his headlights flashed on the boathouse, he braked. "Were you serious about getting the boat out? Not much moon tonight."

She and Max alone on the lake beneath a starlit sky. The gentle rock of a boat at mooring. The soft lap of water against the hull. When was the last time she'd gone skinny-dipping?

"Better not," she hastened to say.

He nodded once, then put the truck in park and turned off the engine. "Walk with me down to the water?"

"Maybe we shouldn't. Mosquitoes are out this time of night. Wouldn't want to catch West Nile virus."

He shook his head, opened his door, and walked around to the passenger side of the truck. The door swung open, and Max held out a hand to her. "Come on, Kate. Be brave."

Oh gosh. Oh gosh. Oh gosh. She put her hand in his. Thoughts flitting like hummingbirds, she wondered if she had felt this fluttering anticipation the last time the two of them were together at the lake. This same refusal to make a choice about what might happen here between them. She didn't have the excuse of being a young, hurt girl. She was old enough not to need excuses but uncertain enough to feel as confused as she had then.

Life didn't get less complicated after you grew up.

A soft breeze rippled the water lighted by a sickle moon

and a million stars. The scent of honeysuckle hung heavy on the air. They didn't speak as they made their way to shoreline. Kate fixed her gaze on the boat dock, then the rock peninsula off to the north, then the fireflies dancing in the tall grass hugging the split-rail fence. She looked anywhere and everywhere except for the tree house.

She'd never been more aware of a man in her life.

He led her out onto the dock, then kicked off his shoes and sat, dangling his feet in the water. He patted the wood beside him, and, slowly, Kate toed off her sandals.

She sat and dipped her feet. The brisk water made her toes tingle. The man beside her made the rest of her tingle. *Oh, God, Kate. What are you doing?* "Why did you bring me here, Max?"

A security light on a neighboring boat slip combined with starlight and moonlight to provide just enough illumination to allow her to see his expression. He skimmed his toes across the surface of the water, stirring up a froth. "I don't know. I wanted to get you alone where we wouldn't be interrupted. Where you couldn't run off."

"That's not exactly reassuring, Cooper. Why would I want to run off?"

"You ran off last time we kissed."

They'd done more than kiss. "You planning on kissing me again?"

"I've been thinking about it." He kicked at the water and white foam sprayed. "Today was a bitch, Kate. When you told me you had a date, I didn't like it. Seeing you with another man . . . well . . . it was hard. Damned hard."

She didn't know how to respond to that. She gazed around, noted with some surprise the lack of boats on the

rolled off her onto his back. "Leave it to a woman to cloud the issue with emotion."

Kate let out a sound some might have termed a feminine growl. She made to sit up, intending to scramble away from him and repair the damage to her clothing when suddenly, she found herself flat on her back once again. Max loomed atop her, his lower body pinning hers, resting his weight on his hands. "For me, this isn't just about sex. I care about you, Kate. I care a lot. In fact, I think the 'L' word might just be involved."

"What?" she squeaked.

"I know. The idea scares me, too. I think we probably shouldn't go there quite yet."

"Max, I . . ."

"Shouldn't have gone out with Shyster Sutherland. I'm just to the point where I'm realizing what I'm feeling, and you have to go wave an Armani cape in my face."

"He wore a T-shirt."

"A *Texas* shirt. That's even worse than Armani. I couldn't let you leave the fish fry with him, maybe go to bed with him, maybe start a relationship so that our timing sucks again."

Something about what he just said nagged at her like a pebble in a shoe, but she forgot it when he yanked off his shirt. Lean and muscled and tanned—Max Cooper was so fine to look at. She hadn't been with a man in so long.

"I didn't plan this, Kate," he continued. "I want you to know that. I came by your house to spend time with you. After spending the day with half of Cedar Dell, I wanted away from prying eyes and wagging tongues, which is probably why we ended up here at the lake. But now that we're here . . ." He dipped his head, licked the valley between her breasts, swirled his tongue around first one lace-covered nipple, then the other. "Hell, Kate. Let me make love to you."

It's been so long. She swelled toward him, every instinct she owned urging her to give herself. But experience and honesty compelled her to caution. "Max, I think it might be a bad idea for us to jump into this. I care about you, too, but I don't know . . . I'm confused about . . . oh, hell. For me, it might be just sex."

"I could live with that. Tonight."

"But it's not just us, Max. We have to think about Ryan and Shannon."

"I won't get you pregnant tonight, I promise."

"That's not what I mean, although we're not making that mistake—" she broke off abruptly when he began to suckle her left breast. Sighing, she sank into the pleasure. When he stripped away her bra and paid similar attention to her other breast, her resistance slowly drifted away.

Max rolled back on his knees. "I'll make you another promise, honey. No matter what happens between you and me, if I fall madly in love with you and you decide you'd rather run off with that snake oil salesman, I won't let it affect Ryan in any way. I'll suck it up and be a man and be the best father I can. Period. If you decide to give us a chance and we both fall madly in love and end up doing what we didn't do the first time, then I'll still be the best father I can be to our son. Nothing is going to change that, okay?"

End up doing what we didn't do the first time. The words

rotated in her mind like a dust devil. What was he talking about? What didn't they do the first time? Why did he mean by fall madly in love and . . . oh. Oh!

"Are you talking marriage?"

"No."

She exhaled with relief.

"I'm thinking about it."

"Oh, God. I'm not, Max. I'm really, *really* not thinking about marriage." She reached up to push him away, but her hands caressed his chest instead.

"Mmmm . . ." he groaned. "Okay. No talking or thinking or committing to anything tonight. I promise. God, I want you, Kate. You're killing me. Let's just enjoy tonight, okay? Let me have you."

His big hands stroked over her skin, igniting her blood, clouding her thoughts, sweeping away her ability to resist. She grabbed his shoulders and pulled him toward her. "Yes," she whispered as her breasts flattened against the delicious weight of his chest. "Yes."

He groaned and kissed her hard, his tongue thrusting, demanding. They rolled and groped and teased and tasted. Both were down to their underwear, panting and gasping and groaning, when Max suddenly pulled back. "To hell with this. We're adults and I want a bed. I'd just as soon not have splinters in my knees. Let's go up to the house."

Kate let out a sound halfway between a groan and a laugh.

He pulled her to her feet, scooped up their clothes, then gave her a chauvinistic swat on the rear. She glared at him, ruined it with a grin, and slipped into her sandals. She led the way toward the house. Halfway there, he groaned and dropped his armful of clothes. He grabbed her, yanking her into his arms. He cupped her bottom with both hands and pulled her against him. "You have the finest ass in seven counties, Ms. Harmon."

He was hot and hard against her, and Kate couldn't help but rub herself against him. "Never mind the bed," he rasped out. "Grass is good."

"Grass is not good," she corrected. "You might find a bed that you're not looking for. A fire-ant bed."

"No grass. We'll go inside. I'll wait. I can wait."

Feeling ornery, she reached into his boxers and caressed him. "Oh, shit," he breathed. He yanked her hand away from him. "A tease. I should have guessed that about you."

Kate's laughter rang out on the air, and she dashed for the lake house back porch and the door key stashed in the end of the drainpipe. Her blood was heated and humming. She felt aroused and alive and anxious to get back to Max. With a stick kept handy for the purpose, she poked the drainpipe, checking for critters, before reaching for the key. It hung from an oval plastic key ring advertising Alamo Insurance. Grinning, she turned around and dangled it at Max.

He impatiently grabbed it from her hand, unlocked the door, and stepped inside, pulling her in behind him. He shut the door and backed her against it, kissing her thoroughly, his practiced hands seeking, exploring, stimulating her senses. Driving her mad.

"Where's a light?" he murmured against her mouth. "I want to see you."

A lamp sat on a table a short step away and Kate reached for it. As her hand closed over the switch, she knew a moment of insecurity and hesitated. The darkness hid flaws. She wasn't a teenager anymore. She'd had a child. She had a few faded stretch marks.

She'd had a child. She'd had *his* child, dammit. If he didn't like it, he could keep his eyes closed.

His fingers closed over hers and the lamp clicked on. His gaze made a slow, heated journey over her from head to toe. "You are breathtaking, Kate."

Kate shuddered at his husky tone. His hand drifted over her stomach, caressing her, teasing her. Arousal pulsed through her, raw and hot and fresh. She yearned. She needed. She craved. "There's a couch behind you."

"Yeah?" His fingers dipped inside her panties, stroked and explored her. A little moan escaped her. "The bed. We made it this far. Take me to your bed."

His hands never left her body as she headed toward the hallway leading to the guest room where she slept on her visits. The king-size mattress in her father's room would suit his size better, but she couldn't sleep with Max in her father's bed. That's not what tonight was about. That much, she knew.

She heard the thump, followed immediately by Max's shout and whirled around.

"Dammit! Son of a bitch!" He leaned against an easy chair and held his bare foot. "What the hell did I kick?"

She glanced down at the cast-iron dachshund boot scraper that belonged on the front porch. "Who brought that inside? Are you okay, Max?"

"I think I broke my damned toe."

"Oh, no!" she exclaimed. She glared at the boot scraper,

wanted to kick it herself. Wanted to cry. "Let me go get you some ice."

"No. Uh-uh. I don't need ice. I need you, Kate."

"But we can't—"

"Sure we can," he said, his scowl as fierce as his tone. "We have to. If we don't, my balls will be as blue as my foot."

She couldn't help it. She started to giggle. He turned a pained glare in her direction, but the twitch of his lips told her he saw the amusement in the moment, too. "You want me to kiss it and make it better."

"Oh, yeah. Definitely. Most definitely. I better warn you, though." He lowered his injured foot to the ground, and carefully stood. "I hurt everywhere."

"Hobble to my bed, and let Nurse Kate take care of it. I'll have you know I have an excellent bedside manner."

"Thank you, God."

She turned the lights on ahead of him the rest of the way to her room, not wanting to risk another accident. Despite the interruption, her body still felt hot and aroused. A glance at Max's boxers told her he'd regained his . . . focus . . . too.

"Honey?" he asked as she reached to turn down the comforter. "About that promise I made earlier? Do you have any condoms here?"

She froze. Oh, *hell*. She whipped her head around, met his gaze. "No."

"You on the pill?"

"No! Dammit, Max Cooper, if you've taken it this far and you didn't come prepared I think I'll—"

"No. No. Not to worry," he interrupted. "I have some in my truck. I just . . . maybe you can go get them so I don't have to walk?"

Sighing, she reached into her closet for a robe and slipped it on. Splinters. Fire ants. Cast-iron dachshunds. "I'm overwhelmed by the romance of the moment."

He sat on the bed, flashed her a quick, crooked grin that offered that combination of mischief and masculinity that tended to melt a woman. "Just get us the rubbers, darlin'. I'll overwhelm you then. I'll make love to you until you scream."

"I assume the condoms are in your glove box?"

"No. Can't leave them there. Shannon's always digging through the glove compartment. They're in the back, inside the toolbox. It's not locked. They're in my blue tackle box."

In the process of knotting the belt on the robe, Kate froze. "You keep condoms in your tackle box?"

"Yeah."

"Your *fishing* tackle box."

"That's right."

"With worms and crank bait?"

He tried the grin again, this time with less success. "And my Jolly Wigglers. Seemed appropriate." Following her screech, he added, "They're plastic worms, Kate."

"That's disgusting."

"Why?" A frown creased his brow and he sounded annoyed. "It's an unopened box. They're sealed inside foil pouches. What's the big deal?"

"Clueless," Kate said, marching out of the room. "The man is clueless."

"Take a flashlight so you can see inside the box," he called.

Maybe she should gather up their clothes instead of rifling through his tackle box. Maybe this wasn't meant to be. No spontaneity. No romance. Lots and lots of heat.

She hadn't had sex in years.

At the pickup, she opened one side of the large, built-in toolbox behind the truck cab and shined the light inside. The blue plastic toolbox sat between a baseball mitt and a basketball. Out of her reach.

"That man," she grumbled as she walked around to the back of the truck, lowered the gate, then climbed into the bed. Slapping at a mosquito, she dropped her flashlight and it clattered against the metal bed. "Maybe I should just forget this."

But she hadn't had sex in *three* years.

She spied three fishing poles, a football, two Frisbees, and a soccer ball. Heavens, like father, like son. The toolbox in Ryan's truck looked just the same way.

As she reached for the tackle box, she groaned at another possible similarity. Did Ryan keep condoms in his tackle box, too?

"Don't go there," she told herself. "You don't want to know."

She lifted the tackle box out of the toolbox, flipped the latch, then opened the lid.

The odor hit her like a fist.

Eyes watering, gagging, she dropped the box. It banged against the truck bed and its contents spilled out. "Oh, eewwww."

Short minutes later, she stood in the bedroom doorway.

"Just a little tip from a friend." Kate flung Max's jeans at his face. "Next time, find something else to do with your stinkbait."

"I'll never go fishing again."

Sitting in his living room with his foot propped on the coffee table, nursing his third scotch, Max gazed forlornly at his swollen toe.

What a disaster. He wanted to kill Brian Harris for leaving his jar of homemade skinkbait in Max's tackle box. "Not to mention failing to screw the freakin' lid on tight."

He'd be lucky if Kate ever spoke to him again, much less let him near her. Oh, God. He'd gotten so near. Come so close. Didn't get to come, dammit.

"Fuck fishing."

She had driven his truck and didn't speak to him all the way home. After parking in his driveway, she tossed him the keys and left him without even a nasty glance. He'd limped into the house, into the shower, then pulled on a pair of gym shorts and headed for his aged, imported painkiller. The first drink numbed the ache in his toe. Now he was working on the pain in his brain.

This was the saddest day of his sex life.

Not even that first outing after Rose's death when he'd failed to get it up had bothered him this much. Had been this humiliating.

He'd blown it with Kate. Hell, she was probably on the horn to her lawyer-boy laughing about what a loser Max was. The City Shyster probably didn't keep his rubbers in a tackle box. He wouldn't worry about splinters in his ass. Hell, he probably only had sex on silk sheets.

If he had sex with Kate, Max would kill him.

He sipped his drink and relished the fire scorching down his throat. Pitiful. Just pitiful. Maybe tomorrow he'd have the gumption to try and fix this fiasco. Things would look brighter then. He'd think of a way to make it up to her. But now, tonight, with his daughter gone and the dog asleep in the laundry room and nobody around to see the sad sight, he wanted to wallow in self-pity.

At first he thought he imagined the *ding* of the doorbell, so he ignored it. The second time he heard it, he frowned in the direction of the door, then checked the clock. Nearly one o'clock in the morning. What the hell?

The kids. Fear flushed through him at the thought, and he began to rise. Before he'd even lowered his foot to the floor, someone tried the doorknob—he hadn't bothered to lock it, of course—and the door swung open.

Kate.

His mouth went dry. His breath whooshed from his body. She wore a little black dress, man-killer heels, and an enigmatic smile.

The blue box with the familiar Greek soldier profile came sailing through the air and hit him square in the chest. He was primed and straining against his shorts by the time it hit his lap. *There is a God.*

She glided toward him, her hips swaying. Max feared he might start drooling. "Kate," he began.

"Hush." She kicked off a shoe.

He swallowed and shut up.

"Don't move except to touch me." She kicked off the second shoe. "Don't open your mouth unless you're putting it on me."

She reached behind her. A zipper rasped. "And, whatever you do, Max Cooper . . ."

Yes. Yes. I'll do anything you want.

The dress dropped. She stood naked before him. "Don't stop until you've made me scream."

God, I love this woman.

Determined to make up for his less-than-romantic performance out at the lake, Max swept her into his arms and carried her, à la Rhett Butler, up the stairs. This time, finally, they made it to a bed.

"You are so beautiful, Kate," he said, stripping off his shorts. "You take my breath away."

A smile played at her lips. "I changed my mind."

His heart stuttered. Panic took flight. "Huh?"

"You can talk."

After a moment's hesitation, Max slowly shook his head. "Don't tease me like that, woman."

He straddled her hips, placed a hand on either side of her head, and leaned down to whisper in her ear. "I'll. Tease. Back."

"Oh, Max," she breathed, as he used his tongue and teeth to make good his threat. "Max."

He took his time with her, tormenting them both. Each whimper, each moan, he coaxed from her was music to his ears. He talked to her while he touched her. Intimate words. Earthy words. Words that made her shudder and sigh.

His touch made her beg.

Then Kate, being Kate, turned the tables on him and gave as good as she got. Soon she had him shuddering, sighing. Soaring. Two hours later, he rolled onto his back and tried to catch his breath. *That's it. I'm done. Any more and they'll have to bury me.*

Beside him, Kate stretched and purred like a happy little kitten. He summoned enough strength to take her hand and bring it to his mouth for a kiss. "By the way, Kate. That's a great dress."

Chapter Sixteen

JACK TOLD HIS SON good-bye and hung up the telephone. "Well," he murmured to himself. "Who'd-a-thunk-it?"

"Are you finally off the phone?" Adele swept into the room with the newspaper and a pencil in hand. She received her own copy of the daily newspaper out of Graham, and lately she'd taken to doing the crossword in Jack's living room in the morning. It drove him crazy. She did her best to finish it before he did.

"Rrrr," Jack said out of habit more than anything. He couldn't be too accommodating, even if he did enjoy the company on the days he beat her, at least two out of every three. Once or twice he wondered if she might be holding back and letting him win, but he quickly dismissed the notion. The old woman was too mean to do that.

"So that was Tom, hmm?" she said, taking her seat on the sofa. "I suppose he told you that the IRS settled with him after our Kate worked her magic. Saved him thousands of dollars, she did."

"Rrrr."

She sat without speaking for a time, thank God. Jack heard a fairly steady scrape of her pencil against paper, so he concentrated on his own puzzle. Unfortunately, his mind kept wandering back to the phone call. Tom could be a little nicer about having his sister's help. Kate had done him a damn good turn. He should be more appreciative. Instead, he was worried over Jack's decision to redistribute the money from the sale of the lake house.

Since Tom didn't need it all now, he'd decided to keep a little for himself, then divvy up the rest in three equal portions. Sarah asked for her share to be put in a college account for her kid. He'd told Kate to use her third to pay down the mortgage she took out on the lake. Damned if she hadn't leaned over, kissed his cheek, and told him thank you.

She'd been in a strange mood for better than a week. Humming around the house. Smiling all the time. The walls of his home had heard more laughter in the last week than they had in the last ten years.

Jack figured out why a couple days ago. She was seeing Cooper. Sneaking out at night. He hoped to hell the two of them at least acted discreet around that sweet little Shannon.

He was still trying to decide what to do about it. As far as he could tell, they hadn't brought their sinful ways into his house, not yet, anyway. Because of that, he'd decided to hold his tongue. At least for now. On account of those two children. Maybe Kate and Cooper would do it right this time and get married.

Wonder if the boy would change his name in that case. Jack kinda liked the fact young Ryan carried the Harmon name.

He was halfway through the crossword when the sound of footsteps on the front porch and the familiar creak of mailbox hinges signaled the postman's arrival. Nosy old Adele popped up from her seat and hurried toward the front door just as Ryan came dashing down the stairs. "I'll get it," he called.

Something fishy going on there, too, Jack thought. Boy watched for the mailman every day. Made him late to his job at Groves Engineering twice in the past week, from Jack's observation. Probably watching the mail for a speeding ticket receipt or some such incriminating thing.

The screen door banged shut as Ryan returned with the mail. "You have something from an insurance company, Granddad. Looks like a check."

"Give it here."

Jack pulled his Old Timer from his pocket and slit the envelope open. He checked the amount on the check, and said, "It's about damned time."

The check was the insurance settlement on his car. It had taken weeks for them to agree on a figure. The bloodsucking bastards didn't want to pay him a fair price, and he'd had to get serious with them. Hell, even Kate got in on that deal, tracing down paperwork to prove he'd run new tires on the Cougar.

Now, though, he had cash in hand. An extra few thousand dollars his son no longer needed to keep his business afloat. Money Jack could add to part of the lake house money to spend as he wished. He glanced up at his grandson. "You going into Groves this morning?"

"No. They're closed for the next two weeks. Mr. Groves has a business trip, then the family is taking a vacation."

"When are you scheduled to go into work at my place?"

"Four o'clock."

Jack pursed his lips and considered. "We'll probably be back by then. If not, you can call."

"We're going somewhere?" Adele piped up.

"Not you. Me and my grandson, here. I have an errand I want him to help me with."

"What errand?"

"None of your business."

"Fine." She sniffed and threw her paper in Jack's face. Shoving to her feet, she said, "There. Take that. I whipped your butt, you old goat."

"Rrr . . ."

Jack told Kate he wanted Ryan to drive him out to the lake house to pick up an old checkers set, and half an hour later, they were on their way. The boy made good time to the lake, but when Jack told him to run in and get the checkers, then come right back out, he protested. "It's a nice day, Granddad. Wouldn't you like to hang around a bit? Maybe go fishing?"

"No. We don't have time. I want you to take me to Fort Worth."

"Fort Worth? Why are we going to Fort Worth?"

"I gotta go see a man. I have an appointment at the Ford house."

"The Ford house." Ryan frowned. "Is that what that Victorian mansion on Highway 80 is called? That bed-and-breakfast?"

"No." Jack scoffed. "The Ford house. The car dealership. I'm gonna pick up my new car. Had 'em get me one of those new T-Birds. Got a yellow one. Almost got the red, but decided a change might be nice. They had it brought in from Dallas for me."

Ryan about ran off the side of the road. "You bought a new Thunderbird?"

"Yep."

"Does Mom know about this?"

"She isn't my mother; I don't have to tell her my business."

Ryan didn't speak for another five miles. Jack only heard him then because he fiddled with his hearing aid, turning up the volume.

"Mom," his grandson said, "is gonna have a cow."

Ryan left a message for his mom on her business line, but he couldn't get through on her cell phone. The lousy cell service was the worst part of living in Cedar Dell.

He was scared to death. It was bad enough that a man who didn't see well, had trouble hearing, and had a reaction time somewhere in the multiple-minute range intended to drive a car with a 250-horsepower, V8 engine. To make matters worse, he'd had another of those crazy spells as they were coming into town.

It didn't last long, and he didn't do anything dangerous this time. He'd started talking to Ryan as if he were his uncle Tom and they were at the bowling alley waxing the lanes. It freaked Ryan out, and when he saw the blue road sign with an arrow pointing to the hospital, he almost took the turn.

Then Granddad snapped out of it and started talking about the T-Bird again. He didn't act as if anything weird had happened, but Ryan felt helpless and alone. He couldn't let Granddad hurt himself, but the man wouldn't listen to anything he said.

Now he planned to take that car out on the highway. The man could barely walk, took forever to get into the 'Bird, and needed help to get out, and he intended to drive on the interstate.

He tried his mom's office again, and when she didn't answer, he considered a moment, shrugged, and called Max.

No one answered at the Cooper house. A glance at his grandfather and the salesman out on the parking lot beside the fine, sexy yellow Thunderbird told him time was running out. He tried her cell once more and this time, miraculously, got through.

When she didn't pick up, he found himself switched over to voice mail. "Great. Mom, where are you? I need you. I'm in Fort Worth with Granddad. He bought a T-Bird, and he's planning to drive it back to Cedar Dell this afternoon. I can't talk him out of it. He had one of those weird spells on the way into town, so I'm afraid to let him go alone, even if I'm following him. Guess I'll ride with him. I don't know what else to do."

He checked his watch and gave the time. "If you get this message in the next ten minutes, call Jarrell Ford. Otherwise, that's my plan."

He delayed as long as possible, but his grandfather eventually lost his patience. "I'm leaving whether you're ready or not. You can follow me."

"Actually, Granddad, I was hoping I could ride home with you. I've decided to leave my truck here for a tune-up."

"A tune-up at a dealership?" Jack scoffed. "Bad idea, son. They always overcharge at a dealership. Don't you know that?"

Ryan thought quickly. "Yeah, but this one is a freebie.

They're running some sort of contest, and the salesman picked my name on purpose since you put him over his sales quota for the month."

"Oh?" Jack frowned suspiciously. "All right. Get in, boy. I'm ready to take this machine for a spin."

"Just one second, Granddad. I need to get something from my truck." While his grandfather revved the 'Bird's engine, Ryan dashed to his truck and swiped the St. Christopher medal off his visor.

At times like this, every little bit helped.

Max bit Kate's toe.

"Ow. Why did you do that?" She sat on the floor in a spare bedroom in Max's house, paintbrush in hand. The baseboard in front of her gleamed with a new coat of white paint, the bubblegum pink—not as pretty a color as Pig Pink, according to Shannon—now a thing of the past.

" 'Cause it's nekkid and within reach."

She sputtered a laugh. "Nekkid, huh? Is that how top gun jet-jockeys talk?"

"As a rule, we do tend to like *nekkid*. You might have noticed that by now."

"I do believe I have."

"Can I tempt you to discuss the subject at further length?" He trailed a finger along the length of her bare leg up to her thigh as he spoke.

Kate glanced at the clock on the bedside table. "I think you've seen as much nekkid as you're gonna see for a while, Daddy. She'll be home any minute."

Her words proved prophetic. Before Kate took her foot

off his lap, the kitchen door opened with a bang, and Shannon called out, "Daddy! I'm home!"

"Upstairs, Shannon." Max looked at Kate with a pained expression. "I'm a terrible father to react with disappointment at such news."

"Zip your britches, Cooper, and be a man."

"How can you make derisive comments about my manhood considering that thirty minutes ago I had you moaning like—" He broke off with a wicked grin as Shannon came bounding up the stairs and burst into the bedroom.

"Oh!" she exclaimed, clapping her hands together. "This is much better. My brother will love it."

Her brother might not see it anytime soon, Kate thought. The idea to redo the extra bedroom in Max's house for Ryan had come from Shannon. She didn't think it fair at all for her brother not to have a room at his daddy's house. Max fell right in with the plan, and the transformation from one of the Gantt girls' bedrooms to a space fit for a young man had begun. Shannon wanted to keep it a surprise until it was finished. Kate intended to take a little different approach. Though he'd come a long way, Ryan continued to be prickly at times about Max. Before the room was ready, she'd give him a heads up. Once he understood the force behind the action, he'd understand and act appropriately. Ryan wouldn't disappoint Shannon.

Kate handed Max her paintbrush, then stood. "I think Ryan will love it, too. Now, I'd better get home. I have work to do."

"But can't you stay and play with me, Miss Kate? You played with me yesterday, and it was fun. I want to play today, too."

Kate kissed the top of Shannon's head. "I'd love to play today, sweetheart, but I'm behind on my work. I've been playing too much lately, and my boss will be mad at me if I don't get some work done today."

"That stinks."

Yes, Kate realized, it did. The fact that it did left her a little nervous. She took little joy in her job of late, and that wasn't at all like her.

Downstairs, she grabbed her purse from the sofa where she'd left it, said her good-byes, and headed home. Halfway up the alley, her cell phone rang. She noticed she had two messages as she flipped it open and said, "Hello?"

A woman asked, "Kate Harmon?"

"Yes."

"This is Marian Wilcox. I just got off the phone with your young man. He is simply a dear, isn't he? We've been conversing for quite a few days now."

Still in Max's backyard, Kate glanced back toward Max's house. He's been talking to Marian? Funny, he didn't mention it.

"He's trying to talk me into letting him get a peek inside my home. That's all right, don't you think? He told me you'd vouch for him. He gave me this number. You are Kate Harmon, aren't you? Jack's girl?"

"Yes." Muffykins came bounding up, and Kate scratched him behind the ears.

"And Nicholas isn't a serial rapist? I don't want to allow a serial rapist in my home."

Nicholas? Rapist? Kate gave her head a shake, a little slow on the uptake. Nicholas, not Max. Marian Wilcox and the chess piece. Of course.

You'd have known this if you weren't dodging his calls.

"Nicholas is a fine man, Mrs. Wilcox. You don't need to worry one bit about letting him visit your home."

"All right, then. I'll let him come. Tomorrow at 9:00 A.M. You'll be here, too, of course."

"Um . . . sure. I'll be there." She took a seat in a nearby lawn chair and massaged the bridge of her nose.

"Good. You're looking for a ceramic cat, isn't that right?"

Kate considered the question a moment. Would he have lied to Mrs. Wilcox about what he's looking for? No. "It's a chess piece, ma'am."

"Oh, that's right. I'm going to dust. I'll keep an eye out for it. Thanks for calling. I'll see you tomorrow."

Hearing a dial tone in her ear, Kate slowly lowered the phone. She checked the numbers on her log of missed calls and recognized Nicholas's number. Giving Muffykins another pat, she inhaled a deep breath and returned the call. His secretary put her right through.

"Hello, beautiful."

Okay, so the man was good for her ego. She smiled. "Hello, Nicholas."

"I'm glad you called. I was beginning to think you were avoiding me."

Now she winced. "I'm sorry I've missed your calls. It's been rather hectic around here of late."

"That's all right. You've been replaced in my affections. Have you spoken with my new Cedar Dell squeeze?"

She laughed. "Yes, I have."

"Did you vouch for my character?"

"I told her you're a character, all right."

"Good. So what about tomorrow? Do you have time to accompany me on this adventure?"

"I do. It should be interesting."

"How about I pick you up at your dad's a little before nine. I'm scheduled to be in court tomorrow afternoon at three, but hopefully, we'll have time for lunch."

Kate licked her lips. She wanted to be honest with Nicholas and tell him she couldn't date him, not now. Better to do that over lunch than at Marian Wilcox's place. "Lunch would be nice, Nicholas. Thanks. I'll see you in the morning."

The moment she flipped the phone shut, she sensed she wasn't alone. The hair on the back of her neck rose, and she knew who stood behind her. Oh, hell. She closed her eyes and waited for Max to turn into a hairy-knuckled alpha male and tell her she was sleeping with him, and by God, she wasn't going anywhere with that shyster lawyer. Then she'd have to get firm with him, and they'd end up having a fight, and she still had to deal with the IRS today. Sighing, she turned and said, "Max . . ."

He stood with his arms folded over his very fine chest, his brow lowered, his frown solemn. "You'll think of me at lunch tomorrow?"

It was, she thought, an amazing example of faith, and it warmed her. "I will think of you, Max."

He nodded once, whistled for Muffykins, and went back into the house. Kate smiled halfway home.

Then she checked her voice mail.

Kate hit the front door of her dad's house yelling. "Ryan? Dad? Hello?"

Adele hurried from the kitchen, wiping flour-dusted hands on her apron. "Kate? What's wrong?"

"They're not back yet? Ryan and Dad?"

"I don't know. I just walked in myself from the beauty shop."

"They weren't there at Harmon Lanes when you left?"

"No. What is it, honey? What's the matter?"

"Ryan called. Dad bought a new car and he's driving it home from Fort Worth and he had another spell this morning so Ryan decided to ride with him."

"From Fort Worth?"

"On the interstate."

"That stupid old goat." Adele covered her mouth with her hands. "What will you do?"

"Pray. At least until they get home safely. I think I'll call Tom. Sarah, too. We've got to do something about this."

"Pray. Yes. I'll get my rosary."

Rosary? The notion momentarily distracted Kate. Adele had a rosary? Since when? Did she get religion when Kate wasn't looking? And Catholic, at that?

Shaking her head, she turned her attention back to more immediate matters. Picking up the phone, she called her brother and relayed the contents of Ryan's message. "How do you think we should handle this?"

"What do you mean?"

"He can't drive, Tom. It's too dangerous. We need to take away his keys. I think you should come home, Tom. He'll take it better from you."

"Wait a minute. Take away his keys? You're crazy."

"Crazy?" Kate sat down. "Dad can't drive anymore. It's not safe! For him or for anyone else on the road."

A long pause came over the line. "He won't let you take away his car."

"That's why I need you here."

Another long pause, then his voice came crisp and cool. "I can't come to Cedar Dell. I have a business to save, remember? You're there. You can take care of it. Get Sarah to help."

You coward. You yellow-bellied, bird-brained coward.

Yet this was too important not to try again. "Tom, please. You know he values your opinion much more than mine. There's a chance he'll listen to you."

Defensiveness bristled in her brother's tone. "Maybe I don't believe he needs to give up driving. Maybe I think he's an adult, and he should make his own decisions. I gave him a brochure of the YMCA's Senior Transportation Service. He knows other options are available, and if he chooses to ignore them . . . well . . . No, Kate. I'm not coming to Cedar Dell. I'm staying out of this. You feel so strongly about this, you take care of it."

Click.

He had hung up on her. Kate's brows arched as she moved the receiver away from her face and gaped at it. She'd saved him thousands of dollars, saved his stupid business, and he had the nerve to hang up on her. "The jerk!"

She slammed the receiver down on the cradle. "Aargh!" she hollered.

Immediately she dialed Max's number. He should know Ryan was in danger. Maybe he'd get in his truck and head out toward Fort Worth until he saw them. He could call her on his cell and tell her Ryan was safe.

Max's line was busy, so Kate called her sister instead.

Sarah wouldn't bail on her. When her sister answered, Kate gave her a quick summary of all that had happened.

"Oh, no," Sarah said. "I didn't think he'd buy a car."

"You do agree he shouldn't be driving, don't you?"

"Yes," her sister said, sighing. "Especially at night. He doesn't see well at night."

"The man has blackouts!" Kate all but shouted. "He shouldn't be behind the wheel at all. He almost killed himself once already. We're lucky he didn't hurt somebody else. And my son is in the car with him now. If he hurts Ryan . . ."

Sarah sucked in a worried breath. "If he can just get back to Cedar Dell safely, it'll be all right. Everyone in town knows to get out of his way."

Kate thought her eyes might pop right out of her head. "It won't be all right. The man should not be driving. It's not safe for him, and it's not safe for the other people on the street. You think people know to stay out of his way? What about little Shannon Cooper? Do you think she knows? What about your baby once he's born and you're out taking him for a walk and Dad decides to pay you a visit in his brand-new sports car, only while he's driving down your street he suddenly thinks he's somewhere else and decides to take a quick left. A very quick left. Will your baby be able to spring from his stroller and get out of the way?"

When Kate finally quit screeching, she realized Sarah was quietly sobbing on the other end of the phone. That only made her feel worse. "I'm sorry. I shouldn't have shouted. I'm nervous. Shoot, I'm scared. I won't take an easy breath until my son walks in the door."

"I understand, Kate, but this is Dad. He doesn't take

kindly to anyone trying to tell him what to do, especially his own children." She sniffled and her voice cracked. "This could break his spirit. He's told me half a dozen times that the day someone takes away his keys is the day they might as well bury him. It'll destroy him. He's recovered from his accident, but he won't recover from this. A car represents his independence. Why, I think he'd rather leave his home than give up his independence."

"That's ridiculous when lives are at stake," Kate protested, with painful awareness that Sarah was right. "We have to be responsible, if he can't. He can still be independent. He can call Bert's taxi or the Y's transportation service when he wants to go somewhere."

"He won't do it. You know he's too proud to do that. He'll sit in his house and never leave and he'll die. This will kill him."

Against that aching fear, Kate set the searing image of her son on the freeway in a speeding sports car, her muddle-minded father at the wheel. "Better that than him killing a child, Sarah. Better than killing an innocent child."

Jack's hip was killing him.

The last sixty miles or so had damn near done him in. Hell, the first sixty miles or so weren't all that great either. Rheumatism, he told himself. Wasn't the way the seat sat in his new car. Guess he should have taken a couple of aspirin. He hated taking pills. Took too many of them.

Damned pain was making it hard to enjoy one of life's special joys—bringing home a new car. The T-Bird was keen. So much power. He used to have power like that. Had plenty of horsepower under his hood.

"There's the city limits sign, Granddad," said Ryan. "We're almost home."

The kid didn't have to sound relieved. "Good. That truck up ahead is really starting to bother me. Every time I try to speed up or pass him, he gets in my way."

"Guess the driver wants to keep his trip at a safe pace," Ryan observed.

Jack snorted. "Safe, shmafe. Going slow is just as dangerous as going fast sometimes. That's the problem with some older drivers. They get on the road and go too slow and end up causing accidents."

The tires on the Thunderbird squealed as Jack took a curve sharply. Ryan winced and grabbed hold of the dashboard. "I don't think we have to worry about that with you, Granddad."

Kate stood in Ryan's bedroom window gazing up the street, her cell phone and the house phone within close reach. She seldom came into this room, respecting her son's privacy, but this particular room offered the best view of the neighborhood streets. From here, she'd see the car the minute they drove up.

Her dad had bought a Thunderbird. She shouldn't be surprised. She should have seen it coming. This man had always fought his way through life. He didn't know how to live it any other way. Sarah said it was a good thing, that if Dad wasn't such a fighter, he wouldn't have survived his heart attack twenty years ago or losing their mother. Every time he showed his mulishness, they needed to be glad he was stubborn. Otherwise, he wouldn't be alive.

She hoped Ryan was still alive.

"There's a difference between stubborn and stupid," Kate murmured, propping a hip on Ryan's desk.

Her cell phone rang, and she grabbed for it, knocking a book and papers off Ryan's desk as she did so. "Yes?"

Max said, "It's me. They're still safe, and we're coming into town now."

"Thank God." Tension seeped from her body as she sank onto Ryan's bed.

"I was able to stay ahead of them on the highway, but here in town, he's liable to take a less direct route home just to avoid me. I think I've frustrated him. He hasn't done a bad job, honey. For the most part, he ran it between the lines."

"For the most part. Lovely." Kate absently nudged the papers she'd knocked to the floor with her shoe. "Now that they're off the highway, I'll quit worrying so much about Ryan and fret about the neighborhood children instead. Maybe you should try to stop him now, Max."

"No. I think it'll be okay now. I truly do."

Kate wouldn't feel that confident until that stupid new car pulled to a safe stop somewhere in the vicinity of the house. Then, the situation was liable to get ugly. "Max, would you do me another favor? Would you stop by here and take Ryan home with you? I think it would be best for all of us if he's not here when I talk with my dad about this car."

"I'll get him away from there, no problem, but would you like me to stay? I'll be happy to give you my support, and Adele said she'd play with Shannon as long as necessary."

She considered it. It would be nice to have someone

standing with her. Her family certainly wouldn't be beside her. Shoot, Max might actually have a chance with Dad. He was a man, after all. That automatically gave his opinion more validity than hers.

The truth of it stirred her anger. "No, I don't think so. Thank you, but I think I'll do this one myself."

"Okay, baby. You know I'm here if you need me. Look up the street. Here they come."

She stood, picked up the papers and book she'd spilled, then gazed out the window. A Tweety-bird yellow sports car drove into view.

The Thunderbird was a beautiful car, and it pulled to a beautiful stop in her father's driveway. Right in the middle of her father's driveway, in fact. As the passenger door swung open and Ryan climbed out of the car, Kate drank in the sight of him, her pulse slowing for the first time in two hours. "Thank you, God."

Max's truck pulled up to the curb just as Ryan slammed his door shut. He jumped out of the cab and sauntered up to the Thunderbird before her dad managed to open his door. Her gaze locked on the scene out front, Kate set the papers in her hand back on the desk. An envelope slipped from the pile and fluttered to the ground once again.

"He can't get out," she murmured, watching as her father tried again and again to stand on his own. He waved off Max's offered hand, sought his way to the edge of the seat. He gripped the car frame in one hand and his cane in the other and slowly, laboriously, rose from the car. Tears glazing her view, Kate thought he might have collapsed had Max not been there to help.

They shared a moment of conversation before Ryan

darted toward the house. As Kate turned away from the window, ready to go downstairs and engage the battle, she leaned down to scoop the envelope off the floor and put it back where it belonged. The return address stabbed her attention. "Princeton University?"

The envelope was empty, so she shuffled through the stack of papers on the desk. Duke? MIT? Harvard! Then a familiar logo caught her incredulous gaze: College Board SAT Score Report.

Kate's stomach clenched. Her heart pounded. She took a deep breath, then read: Verbal Composite 800. Math Composite 800.

"Oh, my God. He's made a perfect score."

Her hands trembled with excitement. She wanted nothing more than to sit on his bed and read this stack of letters from dream colleges. But the clatter of casters against wood reminded her of the unpleasant task ahead. She believed in tackling the hard jobs first, so she folded the college letters and tucked them into her pocket.

They'd give her something to look forward to following this battle with her dad. Something told her she just might need that support.

Jack figured he had probably made a mistake with the car. He shouldn't have bought such a low-slung vehicle. Maybe he should have gone for a full-sized car, maybe a Caddy. Boring, but at least he could climb in and out of it by himself.

Pain clawed its way up his legs into his hips and throughout his entire body as he shifted slowly forward.

"Can I help you up the stairs, Granddad?" Ryan asked.

Jack swallowed a snarl. Wouldn't be right to sound off on the boy when he only tried to help. Besides, as much as he hated to admit it, no way could he make it up those steps right now. "Yeah."

Handing his grandson his cane, he grasped the handrail with his left hand and put his arm on the boy's right shoulder. He didn't see Max Cooper coming up behind him until the son of a bitch slithered in beside him, signaled to Ryan, and bodily lifted him, carrying him up the steps.

"Rrrr," Jack growled, as Ryan and Max set him gently on his feet.

"You're welcome." Max dusted his hands matter-of-factly.

"What are you doing here, Cooper? Was that you in my way half the trip from Fort Worth? It was, wasn't it? You drove like a goddamned turtle."

"Fort Worth? I haven't been to Fort Worth, today. I stopped by to ask Ryan to help me out with a little problem I have at home. Ryan, would you mind coming with me?"

"Uh . . . I should probably talk to my mom, first."

"I cleared it with her. I caught her on her cell phone as she was checking her messages. She wants you to come with me now."

"Oh. Okay. I get it." Ryan glanced toward the door. "You want help getting inside, Granddad?"

"No, goddammit. Go on. Get out of here. Go teach Cooper how to drive."

How the hell was he going to manage the door by himself?

It swung open before he had to try. "Hello, Dad."

Jack didn't respond to his daughter because he was

gritting his teeth against the pain. Once inside, he headed directly for his recliner. He'd put his feet up for a while, get her to bring him some aspirin. He'd be just fine after that.

A little groan slipped out as he sank gratefully into his chair, and Kate frowned at him. "Dad, are you all right?"

"Bring me a couple aspirin and a glass of water, would you?"

She nodded and disappeared into the kitchen. Jack closed his eyes and did his best to will the ache away. Moments later, she was back. "Here, Dad."

He downed the painkillers and half the glass of water, then waited for her to leave. He couldn't give into the grimace as long as she watched him. But instead of doing the decent thing and leaving him alone, the girl took a seat on the sofa.

"We need to talk, Dad."

Gal looked like she hurt as much as he did. "Go away."

"No, I won't. Not until we've discussed this."

He knew, of course. He'd expected her to give him a hard time about the car, but not quite so soon. How did she learn about it so fast? Hell, it didn't matter. Women always knew.

"Leave me alone, Kate."

She ignored his request. "I understand you bought a new car."

Jack glared at her. "I don't want to hear a word about the money. Doesn't matter where the money came from, it's mine to do with as I wish."

"I know that." She sounded insulted. "I don't care about the money. That's not at all what this is about."

Jack rested his head against the chair back and closed his eyes. *Go away, girl.*

"Dad, I understand your need to be independent. I know you want to have control over your daily life. But there are other ways to do it. You don't need to be driving anymore."

"Go away, girl."

"No, Dad. This problem isn't going away, for any of us. It's time to face this. It's not safe for you to drive anymore."

He shoved the recliner to a sitting position and faced her with fire in his eyes to match his joints. "That's not for you to tell me."

"Somebody has to do it, and since Tom isn't here, and Sarah doesn't need the stress in her condition, that leaves it to me. Dad, we love you and we worry about you. We're united on this. Driving is a risk you need not take."

"I still have a license. I can damn well use it."

"You have a license only because Texas has poor licensing laws. If you had to take a test for renewal, you wouldn't pass, Dad. You don't see well enough, hear well enough. Your reaction times are too slow." She looked about to cry. "And then there are the spells. You could have one while you're driving. What would happen in that case, Dad? If you'd had one on the way home, you could have hurt Ryan."

Something new rumbled through his body along with the aches and pains. Guilt. She spoke the truth about his spells. He realized that's why he'd wrecked the Cougar, though he'd never admitted it to a soul.

Hell, if he hurt Ryan, he'd never forgive himself.

"Fine. I won't let the boy ride with me. I won't let anybody ride with me. I'm happier that way."

Kate shook her head. "What about the other drivers on the road. You could hit a car full of children."

He didn't want to hear it. He didn't want to think about it. He wanted a shot of whiskey and a hot bath, that's what he wanted.

"I've programmed the phone number for the Y's Senior Transportation Service on all the phones. Just dial one. I set up an account for you and they'll send the bill to Harmon Lanes every month and the bookkeeper can take care of it. You won't need to do any more than walk out to the curb and get into the van. Or, I guess here in Cedar Dell, it's a Crown Victoria. Someone donated one because they're easier to get into and out of."

An old fart's car. Be damned if he'd ride in an old fart's car around Cedar Dell. Furious now, and maybe just a little afraid, he shoved to his feet. Pain wrenched through his body, adding more sting to his words as he let loose on his daughter. "What the hell is this? It's not bad enough you took over my house? Now you're trying to manage my money?"

"Dad," she protested, rising to her feet. "That's not what I'm—"

"What's the next step?" He shook his finger in her face. "You gonna try and have me declared incompetent? Are you setting me up to steal everything I've got? You have the lake house already. You going after this place next? Maybe Harmon Lanes?"

She fell back a step, her eyes wide with disbelief.

"Well, I've got something to say to you, girl. I'm not, by

God, dead yet. My body may be slowing down, but my mind is still keen. I'll manage my own damned money and my own damned transportation and you can just deal with it. Not that you ever showed much sense in dealing with your own life."

As the color drained from her face, he added, "You just leave me the hell alone, girl. Leave me the hell alone."

She dipped her head, looked down at her feet. Jack watched her take a deep breath, then she pinned him with a determined gaze. "There will be no more driving, Dad. It's over."

The goddamned woman swiped his keys off the table and tucked them into her pocket. Like he was some witless old fool.

"I've already spoken to the manager at the Ford dealership and made arrangements for them to pick up the car."

"You can't do that!"

"It's done."

Hot rage flowed through him in waves and burned away the pain. For the first time in forever, he stood tall and strong. Deliberately, he said, "I'll just buy another car."

"We won't let you keep it. We'll do this over and over again if need be, Dad. You will not drive again."

He wanted to slap her. He drew back his hand, flexed his fingers. Time hung suspended for a long, ugly moment.

The shock on her face and the fact that he'd never hit a woman in his life stopped him.

Wrath fueled his need to strike out with any weapon left to him. "Go," he spat at her. "Get out of here. Now."

"Dad, please. I—"

Pointing toward the door, he shouted, "Go! You are no

longer welcome in my home. By God, you are no longer my daughter."

A sharp-edged laugh bubbled from her lips. "Like the saying goes, Daddy: Been there, done that." Walking out the door, she added, "Be damned if I'll do it again, though."

Ryan stood at the kitchen window and nervously thumbed his fingers against the sill. He kept his gaze fixed on the alley, watching for any sign of his mother.

"I don't understand why she didn't want me there," he stated with some bitterness. "She might be mixed up on exactly what went on. I only left a couple sentences on her voice mail."

Seated at the kitchen table, Max looked up from the coloring book and the picture of kittens he and Shannon had finished but for the sky. "She knows what she needs to do, Ryan. It'll be difficult for her father, and she thinks he'd be more comfortable keeping this just between the two of them. I wanted to stand beside your mom, too, but she was determined to handle it this way."

"She's really taking away his car?"

Max nodded. Shannon piped up. "Miss Adele says Miss Kate's daddy pretends he's not old when he's driving a car. She says he needs to grow up. That's funny, isn't it? He's the most grown-up man I know 'cause he's eighty-five years old."

Ryan looked away from the window long enough to grin at his sister. Then he returned his attention to the alley and the route his mom would take from her father's house.

Time crawled. He poured himself a glass of milk, then

returned to his vigil at the window. He gulped the milk, then polished off three oatmeal cookies that Adele handed him. An entire hour passed, and his gaze never left the alley.

Then his mom came in through the front door, carrying two bags of groceries. "Hello, everyone. I'm ready to celebrate. How about you?"

Adele's mouth gaped. "Celebrate? It went that well with the old goat?"

Shannon put down the blue crayon she had used to color the ribbon around the kitten's neck. "You have a goat, Miss Kate? Where is it? I want to see it."

"No, sweet pea," Max said. "She's just teasing. There's not really a goat."

"That's right," Adele agreed, then lowered her voice and added, "He's a bigger four-legged animal. He's an ass."

"That's enough, Adele," Max cautioned, casting a significant look toward Shannon.

"That's a pretty bow on that kitty, Shanabanana." Adele smoothed Shannon's hair, then asked Kate, "So what did your father say when you took away his keys?"

Hurt flickered like lightning across Kate's features. "Let's not talk about that now. I don't want to think about it. I want to have a party." She pulled a bottle of champagne from one of the paper sacks. "Here, Max. Pop the cork, would you? Adele, the glasses are in the corner cabinet by the table. Ryan, would you slice some cheese for me? The Cedar Dell Grocery didn't have a lot in the way of gourmet goodies, but I think what I found works for this group. Here, Shannon, you want to pour these into a bowl?"

Ryan studied his mother and worried. Something was weird here.

"Cheetos," Shannon cried. "Hurray! I *love* Cheetos. They're my favorite." She added a screech of surprise when Max popped the champagne cork.

Max smirked as he crossed to the counter, where Adele had placed crystal stems. "Cheetos and champagne. Where else but the Cooper house in Cedar Dell, Texas?"

Kate pulled a second bottle from one of the bags. "Cheetos and sparkling grape juice, for Shannon. She'll like it much better."

Hmm. Mom is going all out. Ryan peered into one of the sacks. "What did you get for me?"

"Your favorite."

He perked up. "Steak?"

"No, not steak. This isn't dinner. We're having a celebration. That calls for party food."

Party food. His favorite. He checked the other bag. "Chips and guacamole? Cool!"

This time, Max grimaced. "Champagne and guacamole? Now I think I'm going to be sick."

"Dr Pepper." Ryan flashed his dad a grin as he tugged a six-pack of soft drinks from the sack. "Dr Pepper and guaco is the best."

The three adults in the house winced, then Adele asked, "So, tell us again. I think I must have missed it. What are we celebrating?"

"The best thing to happen in my life since Ryan was born. The only thing that could salvage a day like this one."

Ryan studied him mother intently. Her eyes glittered with a strange light he couldn't quite place, but the smile on her face was bright and joyous. When she looked at him, the smile widened as she pulled familiar papers out of her pocket and waved them. *Oh, no.*

"Get a glass everyone. I want to make a toast."

Oh, great. Ryan's stomach did a slow flip as he poured Dr Pepper into a glass. This couldn't be about him, could it?

"To Ryan Scott Harmon."

Oh, man. I am so toast.

"Or maybe we should call him Mr. SAT."

"Mr. Sat?" Shannon said. "Why would we call him that?"

"Just the letters, darling. They stand for Scholastic Aptitude Test, the scores for which I happened to discover in your brother's room a little while ago." She paused long enough to shoot him an apologetic look. "I assume you were saving those letters for a surprise, and I'm sorry I accidentally ruined it."

He felt off the hook and yet impaled on it. "Uh. That's okay."

Max lifted his glass toward Ryan. "You must have done well for your mom to get this worked up over it."

"Well?" Kate scoffed with delight. "He didn't do well. He did perfect. Your son, Mr. Cooper, scored sixteen hundred. He made a perfect score. A toast to our perfectly brilliant Ryan. Can anybody here say *Ivy League?*"

"Ivy League!" Shannon shouted.

Adele set down her champagne glass and wrapped him in a hug. "Oh, Ryan. That's so wonderful. What special news. I'm so proud of you."

He smiled weakly, and once Adele let loose of him,

Max clapped him on the back. "Way to go, son. Add my scores and your mom's together and we still didn't do that well."

"Oh, that's not true." Kate scowled playfully at Max over her champagne.

Ryan wanted to crawl into a hole. He felt as brittle as a corn chip and as green as the guacamole in the bowl in front of him.

"I have an idea," his mother said. "Why don't we clear our schedules and go visit colleges. Ryan had a stack of invitations to look over the top schools in the USA, and now is a perfect time to do it."

"Uh . . . what about Granddad?" he asked.

His mother acted as if she hadn't heard him. "I'm thinking week after next. I'd need to work ahead a bit, but that shouldn't be a problem."

Max dragged his hand along his jaw. "I can get away. I've promised to photograph a wedding next weekend, but I can't think of anything else I couldn't shift around. Shannon always likes to travel, don't you?"

She bounced and waved a pair of orange Cheetos like a flag. "Do we get to go on an airplane? I like airplanes. Where will we go?"

Cold crept down Ryan's spine as his mother ticked off states on her fingers. "Massachusetts, New Jersey, Connecticut. Exactly which, I guess, depends on Ryan. What do you say, honey? You have your pick of the best. Where would you like to visit. Where do you think you want to go to college?"

She's gonna kill me.

Shannon stuffed a handful of Cheetos into her mouth.

Adele sipped her champagne. They all watched him expectantly.

She's gonna kill me deader'n dirt.

"Ryan?" his mother asked.

"Pa . . . Pa." He cleared his throat and tried again. "Pal . . ."

"Penn?" Adele supplied. "Or do you mean Princeton?"

"No." He blew out a quick, hard breath. "Palo Pinto."

Max figured it out first, and Ryan heard him mutter an expletive beneath his breath. Then Adele's eyes went round as the bottom of the champagne bottle she promptly lifted to her lips. His mom, though, remained clueless.

"Palo Pinto?" she repeated without taking in the name.

Ryan took a chug of Dr Pepper, then took control of his life. "Palo Pinto Junior College. I don't want to go away to school, Mom. I want to stay here. I want to live in Cedar Dell."

Chapter Seventeen

"YOU WHAT?" KATE CROAKED.

Her son's chin came up and his shoulders squared. "I've just found my family, Mom. All my life, I've wanted family and now I've found it and I don't want to leave. I've talked to folks both at Cedar Dell High and at Palo Pinto Junior College. I can finish my senior year of high school and take college classes concurrently. I'll be able to get the basics out of the way and still have time to spend with Granddad."

He looked away, swallowing. "That day out at the lake when he ran the lawn mower into the water, Adele helped me realize that he wouldn't be around a whole lot longer. I don't want him to die before I get the chance to know him better."

"Dad's not going to die," Kate protested.

Ryan gave her a sad, you're-fooling-yourself-Mom look. He placed a hand on Shannon's head. "Then there's Dad and Shannon. I'm just getting to know them both. That's important to me. We have a lot of time to make up for."

"Palo Pinto Junior College?" Kate's mind moved at the pace of cold molasses. For the second time today, she had to deal with a man who didn't make sense. Her coping abilities were on overload. "You're thinking about turning down an Ivy League education to go to Palo Pinto Junior College?"

"We don't know that I'd get in any of those schools, anyway, Mom. Those letters were just invitations to visit. Test scores are just a minor part of the equation."

A perfect SAT score wasn't minor, Kate was certain. Nor was his current class rank at number two out of over five hundred. Or his success in athletics. And student government. Being an Eagle Scout. Working part-time.

Despair rolled through her in waves. Since the day Ryan was born, she'd put something aside for his college education from every paycheck. Sometimes no more than a dollar, but always something. She had made sure they lived in a school district with excellent schools, even though she could have lived more cheaply, more conveniently, somewhere else. She gave up new clothes to pay for computers and vacations to fund computer camps. She'd all but killed herself to provide him the opportunity he was now rejecting.

He might as well have rejected her.

That argument wouldn't sway him. She groped for factors he hadn't considered. "What about your friends? Your teams? You'd throw away your senior year?"

"Better than 'throwing away' family," he snapped back.

Kate reeled away from him, clasping the back of a chair for support, as Max said, "Now, Ryan. Let's keep this respectful."

"What does he mean throw away family, Daddy?" Shannon asked. "Nobody's going to put me in the trash, are they?"

Adele swooped the little girl into her arms. "Let's go see what Muffykins is up to."

"But I want—"

"Muffykins needs a walk, Shan," Max told her. "Why don't you and Adele get his leash and take him around the block."

Shannon gasped, and as Adele carried her from the room, Kate heard her say, "He didn't say Mutt. Did you hear that, Adele? Daddy called my dog Muffykins."

Adele's voice drifted through the doorway. "I heard that."

Max moved to Kate's side, attempted to wrap a comforting arm around her, but she shook him off. She would deal with Ryan alone as she had Jack. Her voice trembled with emotion. "I didn't throw away my family. The two situations don't compare. My family didn't want what was best for me. My father didn't have my best interests at heart. I do—yours."

"Then you should see that it's in my best interests to stay in Cedar Dell. It's important to me to have family in my life. I've never had that." When she gasped, he hastened to say, "I know you tried. That's what Roger was all about, you trying to give me a father, and Adele is as good a grandmother as they come. But look at the wealth of family Cedar Dell can give me. There's Aunt Sarah and Uncle Alan. Soon they'll have their baby, my new cousin."

Ryan stood tall and proud; he pleaded with his eyes. "Cedar Dell would be good for you, too, Mom. You don't have to go back to the firm, you know. Your job seems to be working out okay as things are now. You could stay here and live with Granddad. I thought about that on the way back here today. If we stayed, he wouldn't need to worry about a car or living alone or any other problems. You or me or Adele would always be around to help."

At least the confrontation with Jack had the useful outcome of closing that door. "Your grandfather doesn't want that."

"Are you sure?"

"Positive."

"All right." Ryan frowned, his brow wrinkled in thought. "Then I guess we could live at the lake house. That's too long a drive to school every day, though, so maybe I could just live with Dad. He's already decorated a bedroom for me." He glanced at Max. "You'd let me live here, wouldn't you."

Max scratched his chin. "Well, sure."

Kate froze. "What?"

"I could live with Dad."

That's three for three, Kate thought, as a band of pain wrapped around her chest and squeezed. Betrayal by three men in one day set a new record for her. Dad, Ryan, Max— not one of them showed the least concern for her feelings or needs. She felt hollow inside. It hurt to breathe. It just hurt. Everything hurt.

You'd let me live here? Well, sure. Why didn't they both take a knife and stab her through the heart? It'd be more merciful.

"Kate, this could work out." Enthusiasm warmed Max's voice, and his eyes gleamed with eagerness. "This house is big. You could all move in here, even your dad, if he can't live alone anymore. I'd like that. We could be a family." Reaching out, he touched her cheek. "You and I could get married."

Married. Now he brought it up, after her years of struggle alone? Now? Under these circumstances? When her dream lay shattered around her?

The man was absolutely clueless.

Anger erupted and she batted his hand away. "Wouldn't that be handy. You'd have a nice, easy, little, ready-made family. One you want, now that it's convenient to have it. Unlike years ago. I'm glad it worked out for you with Ryan, but you'll just have to leave me out of your plans."

He grimaced and rubbed the back of his neck. "Look, I obviously didn't handle this right. I love you, Kate. I want you in my life."

"Well, too bad. You don't get every single thing you want. I learned that a long time ago. You're not getting your way this time. It's my turn now. My turn to finally do what's best for me—not for you, not for my dad, and not for Ryan. Me. I want a corner office and a bathroom, not a small-town life making everybody else's dreams come true. That's my dream, and I'm going to have it and you can all just . . . all just . . . ."

Tears overflowed her eyes, which only intensified her anger. She stalked to the kitchen door and yanked it open. Looking back, she managed to choke a few words past her thick throat. "You can all just stay here in Cedar Dell and fry fish!"

Heat radiated off the concrete parking lot in shimmering waves as Kate returned to her office following a downtown business lunch. The haze of yet another official Ozone Alert day choked the air and made it difficult to breathe as she approached the smoked-glass doors of the thirty-two-story office building in far North Dallas. She dug her security badge from her purse and clipped it to the lapel of her smart summer suit as she walked into the cool, air-conditioned comfort of the lobby and crossed to the bank of elevators.

Exiting on the twenty-fourth floor, she waved to the receptionist at a U-shaped desk, then used her electronic key to gain entry through the discreet associate entrance at Hart and Halford Investment Services. She made her way to the corner office, tossed her briefcase and purse onto the green brocade love seat, and went directly to her private bathroom. There she washed her face in cool water and quickly reapplied her makeup.

Twenty minutes later, she'd slogged her way to the final page of a local marketing firm's financial report when a knock sounded on her door.

"You busy, beautiful?"

She looked up with a smile. "Well, if it isn't Lawyer Sutherland come down from the heights to mingle with the peons."

"Hey, life on the top floor isn't all catered meals and window-gazing. My elevator ride is longer than yours."

"Poor baby." When he plopped down on her sofa and propped his Bruno Maglis on her coffee table, she added, "Make yourself comfortable."

"Thank you. I will." He laced his fingers behind his head, studied her a moment, then said, "Jesus, Kate. You look like hell. If I'd thought this job would turn you into a hag, I wouldn't have recommended you to Joe Halford, who I might mention, told me just this morning how thrilled he is with your work."

Torn between pique at his criticism of her appearance and pleasure at the compliment on her work, she sighed and dropped her pen onto the yellow legal pad filled with notes. "Don't you need to be in court or something?"

"Nah. I'm done for the day."

She glanced at her watch. "It's not even two. On a Tuesday."

"Seems like as good a time as any to end my workday. Actually, I have something special to do this afternoon, and I wanted to ask you to go with me."

She closed her eyes. "Nicholas, please. I thought we'd reached an understanding about this. I'm not ready—"

"To date," he finished. "I remember, to my most sincere regret. However, it is not that kind of something special. I'm off to see my grandmother, and I thought it would be nice—and appropriate—if you came along."

"I'd love to meet your grandmother, Nicholas, but why would you say it's appropriate?"

"Because of the reason I'm going. I received a package today. From Cedar Dell."

Everything inside Kate went stiff. "Ryan found the chess piece?"

"Not exactly."

It was the first time Nicholas had mentioned Cedar Dell to her since she'd phoned him from the interstate as she left it on that awful evening. She had poured out her troubles after canceling her participation in the search of

Marian Wilcox's house the following morning. Adele had filled in for Kate, and by the time she and Nicholas had worked their way through the downstairs parlor—a four-and-a-half-hour task—she had convinced Nicholas to hire Ryan to complete the job.

Widow Wilcox would love the company, she'd said.

Ryan reported for "work" the next day. According to Adele, who at Kate's request had remained behind in Cedar Dell for the summer to watch over Ryan, he'd worked his way up to the second floor. However, as of yesterday, when they'd carried on one of their stilted phone conversations, he'd not found the emerald Aphrodite.

"Not Ryan, then, but someone else? Nicholas, do you have the chess piece?"

Reaching into his pocket, he pulled out the emerald Aphrodite. Almost reverently, he set it on her glossy desktop. "She's a little more banged up than the ruby one. About half of the gilt is gone, but isn't she pretty?"

"She's wonderful." Kate picked up the chess piece and marveled over it. "And to think this set graced the halls of Versailles. I wonder if Marie Antoinette played chess. She or the king might have held this, too. Will you return the set to France once it's completed?"

"That depends. If research proves the chess set was taken from Versailles, then yes." Nicholas assumed his knowing, infuriating smile. "If not, I think we'll donate it to a local museum."

"Oh? Which one?"

Nicholas studied the fingernails on his right hand. "The Cedar Dell Historical Society Museum."

Between the extraordinary chess piece and Nicholas talking nonsense, Kate felt as if she'd fallen down the rabbit hole again. "What?"

Staring up at the ceiling, he declaimed, "Because of the stirring and passionate plea of the owner of the chess piece."

Impatient, she asked, "And that would be who?"

Nicholas rose and sauntered to Kate's office door. He opened it, and a waist-high figure streaked inside. Incredulous, Kate said, "Shannon?"

"Miss Kate!" The girl threw herself into Kate's arms. "I've missed you so much. And Muffykins misses you and Adele misses you and Ryan misses you and my daddy misses you *real* bad."

Yeah, right. "Honey, how did you get here? What are you doing here?"

A familiar voice rumbled from the hallway, freezing her in place. "She had your chess piece all the time."

Max.

He stood slouched against the doorjamb, arms folded, legs casually crossed. He wore khaki shorts, a Cedar Dell Girls T-Ball shirt, and tennis shoes. He looked so out of place in this business-suit setting. He looked so good. The heartache inside her that never quite went away burst into full bloom at the sight of him.

His gaze remained locked on hers as he slowly straightened and walked toward her. "Hello, Kate."

"Hi." She didn't know what to say to him, how to respond, so she focused her attention on the child in her lap. "Shannon, I think you've grown an inch since I saw you last."

Shannon shook her head earnestly. "No I haven't. I've been too sad to grow. I don't like it that you're gone. Have you missed me, Miss Kate?"

"Oh, yes. I've missed you very much. So tell me what you've been doing."

The little girl launched into a tale of T-ball and swimming lessons and her new friend Kristen Bailey, who had one green eye and one brown eye. All the while, Kate tangibly felt the gazes of the two men in the room, not to mention the alpha male animosity singeing the air between them. She halfway expected the sprinkler system to go off from the heat. Then Shannon mentioned the picture Ryan had showed her and Kate tuned in more closely.

"He was looking for Matilda in Miss Marian's house."

"Matilda?" Kate asked.

Shannon leaned toward the desk to point at the emerald-and-gilt chess piece. "That's my Matilda, and Ryan had a picture of her 'cause he was looking for her. I thought about it and thought about it, because I didn't want to give her away because Miss Marian gave her to me as a present, but I wanted to help my brother because I love him." Clasping her hands, she looked soulful. "I love him as much as Muffykins."

Wow. That was a major declaration. Kate wondered if Ryan appreciated his status. "I love Ryan, too. Tell me more about Matilda."

Shannon said with great patience, "I am telling you. Then I couldn't find her because I forgot to look in my school box because I took her for show-and-tell. Only we had a fire drill that day so we didn't have it, and next time I wanted to bring a stopper. I found her because I wanted my

Pig Pink crayon to color my new farm animals coloring book Miss Adele bought me, and I looked in my school box and there was Matilda, and Daddy said he'd been looking for an excuse to come see you anyway, so we came today. The end."

Kate glanced up at Max, who was shaking his head at his daughter. "Is Ryan with you?"

"No," Shannon answered. "He and Granddad went fishing today."

"Oh." Kate swallowed her disappointment.

Max cleared his throat. "He said he'd call you tonight."

"Oh." Hearing the gloom in her tone, she added, "All right. Good."

Shannon tugged open Kate's desk drawer and began to snoop. "Do you have a Pig Pink crayon, Miss Kate? I want to draw you a picture. You can hang it on your wall."

"No, honey. I don't. I have a yellow highlighter, though. Maybe green or orange. Will that do?"

Nicholas pushed to his feet. "I think my secretary has some markers upstairs, even a flamingo pink one that might do. You want to come with me, Shannon, and we'll see?"

"Okay. I need to tinkle first." She squirmed on Kate's lap. "I gotta go bad. Where's the bathroom, Miss Kate?"

"Through there, sweetheart," Kate said, nodding toward the door as she set Shannon on her feet.

When the bathroom door closed behind Max's daughter, Nicholas approached Kate. He placed both hands on the desk and leaned toward her.

"Rrr . . ." said Max, sounding so much like her father that Kate started.

Nicholas looked her straight in the eyes. "I'll stay if you want, but I think you need to talk to him."

Though her stomach did a flip, Kate slowly nodded.

Inside the bathroom, the toilet flushed.

"Before I leave, I have a point I wish to make," Nicholas continued. "Remember our talk about dreams?"

"Yes."

"There are no rules, no time limits. Not to achieve them or to keep them, once attained." He leaned over farther, kissed her cheek, and whispered in her ear. "A dream, like the emerald chess piece, may be right under your pretty nose if you just look." He straightened, shot Max a challenging look over his shoulder, then kissed her again. On the lips. Thoroughly.

"Rrrr . . . dammit!"

The bathroom door opened. "Daddy! Don't say bad words."

Nicholas broke the kiss with a laugh, and murmured, "Give him hell."

Holding out his hand to Shannon, he added, "Come on, sweetheart. I'll bet my secretary can rustle up some ice cream."

Taking the offered hand, Shannon headed out of the office at a fast pace. "Cool."

Silence descended in their wake. Seated at her desk, Kate felt at a disadvantage. "Would you like to sit down, Max?"

"Thanks." He sat in the chair on the other side of her desk and glared around the room. "Congratulations on your new job. Corner office with windows and private bath—pretty fancy."

"Thank you." Kate expected a rush of pride at having her achievement noted, but it didn't happen. She folded her hands and waited for him to speak.

After a full minute of silence, he pushed to his feet and started pacing. *So much for sitting,* she thought. She stood, walked to the window, and gazed out at the baking bustle of city life below her.

"I'm so bad at this," Max said behind her. "I swore I wouldn't screw it up again. I planned what I wanted to say. Rehearsed it. Had it down pat. Then I see that shyster put his hands on you, his mouth on you, and all my common sense flies out the window. I want to state for the record, however, that I needed to throw him through the window, but I restrained myself."

Shielding herself against his ready charm, she glanced over her shoulder. "Give the man a medal."

"I'd say I earned it." He flashed her that crooked, sheepish grin that gave her heart a twist. "That's not why I came here, though."

She turned fully around and waited for him to elaborate.

"I love you, Kate. I miss you. I want you back in my life."

Maybe she should sit down after all.

"I have a history of handling things poorly where you're concerned, so you shouldn't be surprised that I held true to form. I screwed up, Kate. That last evening we were together in Cedar Dell was the wrong time and the wrong place to ask you to marry me. When I propose to you next time, it will be about you and me, period. Not Ryan or Shannon or your father or your job. It'll be about you and me and the love we share. That's the bottom line."

Yes, she should definitely sit down.

Stumbling to the executive chair behind her desk, she picked out his last words about shared love. "And what makes you think I'm in love with you? I've never said that."

"Yes, you have." His warm gaze dared her to deny it. "You told me every time we made love. Maybe not verbally, but you told me, Kate. Have no doubt about it. I don't."

Kate opened her mouth to refute him, but different words emerged. "It's taken you almost six weeks to figure this out?"

"I was angry when you left."

"Angry." Recalling his cluelessness the night she left, she bristled. "Why were you angry? *I'm* the one who was angry."

"You're the one who left us and went running to your cosmopolitan boyfriend. I had to stew about that a bit."

"Nicholas is not my boyfriend." *Not that he wouldn't like to be*, she silently admitted. "He is, however, a friend. A good friend."

"I realize that. I had to stew about that, too. I've decided I can live with it, but really, Kate. The kissing has to stop."

Damned if she didn't want to grin.

He wiped away any sense of amusement when he returned to his seat, leaned forward, propped his elbows on his knees, and spoke earnestly. "Now, it's true we have some logistical issues to work out. Cedar Dell is obviously too far to commute, and I wouldn't ask you to give up your job. Adele has explained to me how much it means to you—not something you bothered to do, by the way, which is a point in my defense."

Shaking her head, she reminded him, "You didn't bother to ask about my dreams."

"I'm sorry, love. I won't make that mistake again." Leaning his elbows on her desk, he laid both hands palm up before her. "One thing we might consider is living here during the week and spending weekends at home. I believe—though I haven't confirmed it—that Ryan might be amenable to such a solution. Speaking of Ryan, I'd like to talk to you about our son."

Alarmed, she demanded, "Is something wrong?"

Max shook his head. "Physically, he's fine. Mentally, he's a wreck. This estrangement between the two of you hurts him, Kate. I know it hurts you, too."

Leaning back in the high-backed chair, she frowned. "We're not estranged. We talk on the phone at least twice a week, and he instant-messages me most every day."

Max didn't look convinced. "Things aren't right between you and Ryan, honey. Don't try to deny it. I see him when he gets off the phone with you. He's torn up."

Kate folded her arms. She wasn't exactly Miss Happy Camper following their phone conversations, either. She simply couldn't get past the idea of her gifted son wasting his abilities at Palo Pinto Junior College. "When I came home from work yesterday, I found a message from Ryan's robotics team sponsor. Someone from MIT wants to talk to Ryan."

Max leaned back too. "He's been fishing with his grandfather six times since you left Cedar Dell."

"He's received recruitment mail from fourteen different colleges just in the past three weeks."

"He takes his sister swimming every day."

"He could go anywhere, do anything he wants."

Max put both hands flat on her desk. "Yes, he could. And he is, Kate. Ryan is exactly where he wants to be, doing exactly what he wants to do. The only problem — and it's a big problem—is that you're not there with him. Why can't you see that?"

Exasperated, she shoved to her feet. "Because he's throwing away his dream, Max."

"No, Kate." Max stood also and slapped the desk between them. "You can't see that he's decided against *your* dream. Not his. A big-name-college education is your dream. His is something different. Just as valid. Just as worthy. Just as important."

He leaned forward, stared deep into her eyes, willing her to listen. "Think about it. By denying Ryan the validity of his dream, you are treating him just like your father treated you. You're acting just like your father."

"No." Kate backed away in horror. "No!"

Grimly, he said, "Yes."

She stood frozen in place for a long moment before the urge to flee overwhelmed her, and she took off. She ran away from Max and his crushing accusation. *Running away from reality*, whispered a voice in her head.

Max called after her, his voice echoing down the marble hallway. "Dammit, Kate. Don't do this again."

The elevator doors opened, thank God, and she hurried inside and pushed the lobby button. Moments later, she burst from the building into the stifling heat of a scorching summer day.

Kate put her head down to avoid seeing anyone or being seen and walked. She had no destination, no direction in mind. She baked on the concrete griddle of the sidewalk, broiled in her business suit, boiled in the turmoil of her thoughts.

Acting like her dad? No. Never.

Exactly.

"No!" She kicked at a cigarette butt. "Dad's cold. I'm warm. He's distant. I make a point to be interested in the lives of friends and family. He's harsh and critical and judgmental. Grumpy."

Okay, so she could be grumpy, too.

She'd been downright grouchy of late, rattling around their house all by herself. She missed Adele, pined for Ryan. Yearned to know what Shannon—okay, and Max— were doing. Alone with the loud silences of her Dallas home at night, she had even missed Cedar Dell's nosy widows. The only time she was happy was when she was at work. And to think this was supposed to be "her time," when she did for herself instead of others. Well, she'd been doing for herself for the past six weeks, and where had that gotten her?

Grouchy. Grumpy. Just like her dad.

She took off her jacket and slung it over one shoulder as she walked across a chain restaurant's parking lot. She eyed the Dumpster in back and briefly considered throwing the jacket away. She didn't like this suit. Didn't like donning business dress in the dog days of a Dallas August. She despised panty hose and heels. She much preferred wearing shorts, T-shirts, and bare feet to work like she had in Cedar Dell.

"You're acting just like your father," he'd accused.

No. Absolutely not.

Well, all right. Maybe a little.

Her dad worked hard all his life. He provided his family a nice home. The two of them shared the same politics, a passion for Mexican food, and a disdain for bowlers who failed to throw away their trash upon leaving the lane at the end of a game.

Kate and Ryan were much more alike than she and her dad. She and Ryan loved to laugh together. They rooted for one another. They commiserated with each other when bad things happened. They both put family first.

Family. Kate let out a semihysterical laugh. Right now, they basically didn't agree on what, on who, constituted family.

"We've gotten along fine, just the three of us, all these years. Ryan and I didn't need fathers in our lives." She spied a beer can lying against a concrete curb, and she veered out of her way to give it a swift kick.

Okay, so maybe that wasn't exactly true. She'd yearned for her dad at times over the years, and Max was good for Ryan. He loved their son, and he provided the male perspective that Kate couldn't give.

You're acting just like your father.

"Rrrr . . ." she muttered.

It wasn't true. She loved Ryan. Deeply. Desperately. She'd do anything for him. Give him everything within her power to give.

Liar. You refuse to give him his dream. You want him to live yours instead.

"So?" she snapped. "So what if it *is* my dream? It's a worthy dream and he should do it because it's the right thing to do and because, by God, he owes me."

He owes me? Where in the world did that come from?

She stumbled over to a strip shopping center's shaded walkway and leaned against a brick support post. "He owes me? Is that what I've been thinking all along?"

The heavy weight of emotion crushed her chest, and she had trouble catching her breath. *He owes me? Why? Because I gave up my dream for him?*

"You selfish witch." Shame coursed through her, bringing chills to her skin. Tears swam in her eyes. She didn't want an Ivy League education for Ryan. She wanted it for herself. She'd turned a deaf ear and a blind eye to his dream because of her own disappointments. By being so intolerant, so unyielding, she had acted just like her father.

The truth of it took her breath away.

The world around her began to swirl. Light-headed, downright dizzy, she vaguely wondered if she suffered dehydration or had become as muddle-minded as Jack. Walking the city streets, talking to herself, didn't look sane.

Moving like an old woman, Kate pushed away from the post and stopped again. Max stood waiting a short distance away. Throughout her dazed wandering, she'd never been alone.

Straightening in the sticky heat, she said, "I'm so ashamed."

"No." He shook his head and frowned. "You shouldn't be. You're human. Humans make mistakes. He won't hold it against you."

"I'll hold it against me. I didn't accept him, Max. That's my duty as a parent—to love him and accept him for the person he really is. Why did I, of all people, with my experience, do that?"

"Maybe," he said, walking toward her, "because you have never accepted yourself for the person you really are."

"Maybe?" It was a startling thought. "Maybe." She paused a moment, then asked, "Who am I?"

"You gotta figure that one out, honey. I know who I think you are, but that's not the question here. Nor, may I point out, does it matter who your father thinks you are or should be."

A deep breath of the ovenlike air hurt her dry throat. "He's never accepted me."

"Nope, he hasn't. He probably never will. You can't change him, so you need to let that one go."

Need pushed her to say, "But he's my father; he's supposed to accept me."

"And you're supposed to accept Ryan." Hands in pockets, he rocked on his Nikes. "Confusing, isn't it? As a child, you want your parent's acceptance of you as you are. As a parent, you want your child's acceptance of what you want for him. You're both parent and child, with warring attitudes."

Kate started to walk again, and Max fell in beside her. "Warring" sounded right for the roiling confusion in her head. Who was she? "My boss would tell you I'm an excellent worker."

"I'm sure."

"Adele would tell you I'm a good friend."

"Yes."

"Sarah would say I'm becoming a decent sister."

"She'd go better than 'decent,' and since you're counting these things off, I want to go on record as saying you're a damn fine lover. The best."

Kate smiled, the first one in a long while. "Up until recently, I've been an excellent mom."

"I disagree with the qualifier."

That earned yet another quick grin. "That brings me to 'daughter.' What kind of a daughter am I?"

"I'm chewing my tongue in two not to butt in on this one. You need to figure this out by yourself."

Kate trudged another block and a half without speaking, turning the question over and over in her mind. How would her mother have described her? "Mom thought I was a good daughter."

Max shoved his hands in his pockets and nodded.

"She wouldn't like what's gone on in our family since her death, but she'd know it wasn't all my fault."

"Do you agree?"

She considered that another half block. "Yes. Yes, I do. I've done the best I can, Max. I've been respectful of Jack even when he didn't respect me. I've lived my life in a manner he should be proud of, whether he is or not. My duty to him isn't any different than it is to Ryan. I owe him my love and my acceptance. I've loved him. I've always loved him. I've not done as well on the acceptance part. I think . . ."

She paused, thought about it a moment. "I think my mistake has been trying to win Dad's approval all my life. I need to stop that. I'm never going to have it, Max. Not the way I want it, anyway. I need to accept my dad for the person he is. Why haven't I seen that before?"

A smile played at the corners of his mouth. "So what kind of daughter are you, Kate Harmon?"

"I'm a good daughter. I'm a good friend, sister, mother, and daughter. Right?"

"Right." He grinned. "Don't forget lover."

"No, I won't forget lover." She went up on her tiptoes and pressed a kiss to his cheek. When he tugged her into his arms and tried to move her lips to his mouth, she frowned and pulled away. "Wait. What about the worker part, Max? The professional part. Am I a small-town girl with big-city dreams? Or a big-city girl with small-town roots?"

He sighed and gently touched her cheek. "Must they be mutually exclusive?"

Kate blinked. Was that her whole life in a sentence? Believing she had to exclude one thing or person in order to have another?

She folded her arms, pursed her lips, and pondered the question. Oh, my. Oh, oh my.

Abruptly, she said, "I don't have my purse. Can I borrow some money?"

"What?"

She rubbed thumb and fingers together in a "gimme" motion. "Fork over five dollars, Cooper."

"O-kay." He reached for his wallet.

"Wait over by that crepe myrtle, would you?" Kate plucked the bill out of his fingers, tossed him her suit jacket, and headed for the convenience store across the street. Five minutes later, she returned carrying two bottled waters and a pair of plastic thongs.

"Thank you," Max said, his expression reserved as she handed him one of the waters. "Why did you buy the flip-flops?"

"Because." Shielded only by the pink flowers and foliage of the crepe myrtle, Kate reached up under her skirt, hooked her thumbs in the waist of her panty hose, and began to peel them down her sweaty legs.

"Jesus, Kate. Put your skirt down. I can see your ass." He paused a second, then added. "I like those black panties."

She laughed, removed the restrictive heels and panty hose, and tossed the shoes and stockings over her shoulder. "And I figured out one important thing. I really, really don't like panty hose."

She slipped into the plastic shoes and turned back toward her office building, holding out her hand. "C'mon, Max. Let's go home."

The view from Kate's bedroom window showed a faint morning breeze rippling the surface of the lake. The puffy white clouds dotting the sky offered little threat of rain and the promise of occasional shade—something always appreciated on a Labor Day weekend. On the dock, life jackets, water skis, wake boards, and kneeboards sat ready to be loaded into one of the half dozen boats awaiting the partygoers. On shore, guests began to take seats in the dozens of folding chairs facing the century-old oak. Dress ranged from coats and ties and church dresses, to Hawaiian shirts and swimsuit cover-ups. The sound of conversation, easy laughter, and waves slapping the boats filled the air.

All in all, Kate thought, *it looks to be a wonderful day for a wedding*.

The door opened behind her, and she turned as Shannon streaked into the room. "Oh, Miss Kate—no, Mama is what I get to call you now. Mama, you look even more beautiful than Matilda or even Muffykins after a bath."

Kneeling in a swirl of barely pink skirt, Kate leaned forward to exchange nose-nuzzles with her new daughter. "You look beautiful yourself in that dress. Where are your flowers?"

"Ryan's got them because I was trying to get Muffykins to hold the basket in his mouth, and Ryan said it was getting sticky so I gave it to him to hold." Twirling, Shannon held out her skirts. "Aren't you sorry that you didn't get a dress the same color as mine? Yours is pretty, but it looks faded instead of bright and warm like my Pig Pink one and we could have matched."

Kate laughed and felt like twirling a little, too. "I feel all Pig Pink on the inside today, so we do match."

A knock sounded on her door, and Adele poked her head inside. "There you are, Shannon. Your daddy's waiting to get a picture of you with Muffykins like you wanted."

As Shannon flew out the door with a shriek of joy, Adele surveyed Kate with a suspicion of moisture to her eyes. "Oh, honey; don't you look beautiful."

"Thank you." She held out the full skirt of her pale pink lace dress and twirled around. "I feel pretty."

"It's a great dress, but then you always choose great dresses. Max will swallow his tongue when he sees you. Of course, he won't like that at all. I imagine he has plans for that tongue this evening."

"Adele!"

She laughed and gave Kate a hug. "I'm so happy for you, honey. Happy for us all. I am so going to enjoy playing grandmother to that little girl on the weekends."

"If you change your mind about joining us in Dallas during the week, all you have to do is say so."

"I know. I'm happy in Cedar Dell, though. I love Max's house, and I have to tell you, Kate, I adore being a thorn under those Widows' saddles. Speaking of which, have you spotted Martha Gault's outfit? Tacky, tacky, tacky. Now, I had a reason for coming in here. Your dad is in the living room. He wants to talk to you, and I chased Max outside so he wouldn't see you."

"Oh." Her mouth went dry. "Okay."

Kate couldn't help but feel a little trepidation as she walked toward the living room. Jack still hadn't forgiven her for taking away his keys. The live-in housekeeper and driver Sarah had found for him had helped thaw him to the point of speaking civilly. Luck put her sister at the beauty shop with Stella Johnson when she finally got fed up with the Widow Mallow and decided to quit. Sarah hired her in less time than it took to roll a perm rod.

Dressed in his good blue suit, Jack Harmon stood at the window in a similar position to hers a few minutes ago, gazing down toward the lake.

"Hello, Dad."

He didn't turn around. "You remember when we built that tree house at the lake?"

"Yes."

"That was a nice time."

"Yes. Yes, it was."

"That's about the only time I remember us being on the same wavelength."

Kate's stomach sank. Why did he have to bring this up today of all days? Annoyance loosened her tongue and allowed a comment from deep within her to escape. "That was the only time I felt you truly loved me."

His grip tightened around his cane. Gruffly, he said, "That's not right. I've always loved you. I just never understood you. It bothered me that you thought Cedar Dell and the life I provided wasn't good enough for you."

Kate gasped a silent breath. He actually said he loved her? "Oh, Dad; it's plenty good for me. I just like other places, too."

"I didn't know why you felt you had to go to college," he continued, as if he hadn't heard her. "Secretarial school should have been enough. It was good enough for Sarah, wasn't it? And she's been happy all these years. You got your fancy college degree, but has that made you happy? Here you are, fixing to marry Max Cooper, and you could have done the same eighteen years ago and avoided all this grief."

Kate's smile was bittersweet. "Maybe it's the grief that helps us learn to be happy with what we have and who we are, Dad. For instance, I'm happy my education and experience allowed me to help Tom and keep this lake house in the family. Maybe I had to go through every pang of my past to become who I am today."

"Rrr . . ."

She thought of Max and Shannon, waiting to become a family with her and Ryan through the ceremony of marriage. Both she and Max had to grow a long way to find this unity. "Good things can come from grief, and today I'd like to celebrate the good things."

"Seems like life could have been easier for all of us if you'd paid more attention to me," Jack grumbled. "But you didn't turn out bad even if you did have to take your own road to do it. Guess you're just too danged much like me."

Clearing his throat, he turned away from the window. "You look pretty."

"Thank you."

"Here." He reached into his pocket and pulled out an embroidered handkerchief trimmed in lace. "Your mother carried this on our wedding day. Thought you should have it today."

It took her a moment to process what he'd said. When she did, she smiled and accepted the gift, her heart warming. Gruff old goat. It might not be everything she needed, but she could use whatever he could offer. "Thank you, Daddy."

He shrugged, then shuffled toward the door. As he pushed the screen door open, he muttered, "Nope, I'll never understand you."

"That's okay, Dad," she whispered after him. "I finally understand myself."

At exactly 9:50 A.M., Ryan knocked on her bedroom door. "Bad news, Mom," Max's best man said as he handed her a bouquet of yellow roses. "Shannon poured some orange juice a few minutes ago and splashed your flowers. The ribbon is kinda gunky in a couple of spots."

He looked so handsome in his tux, it almost made her cry and made her briefly reconsider the action she had planned. But no, this felt right. "In that case I'll make sure to throw it to one of The Widows."

He snickered as she lifted a gift bag from the rocking chair. "I have a present for you, Ry. I'm hoping you'll wear it for the wedding."

"If it's some sort of froufrou pin, I won't be happy about . . ." He held up the T-shirt and started to laugh. "Jeez, Mom. Are you ever gonna give up?"

"Probably not."

Ryan shook his head, then leaned over and kissed her cheek. "I love you, Mom."

"I love you, too, baby."

At exactly ten o'clock, shaded by the thick, leafy boughs of the century oak, Ryan and Max took their places. The best man wore tuxedo pants and a T-shirt that read PRINCETON, BY WAY OF PALO PINTO JUNIOR COLLEGE; the groom, a formal black tux and a joyous grin. The flower girl hummed "Here Comes the Bride" and emptied her basket of rose petals a quarter way down the makeshift aisle. After handing her empty basket to her grandfather, she took her place between her brother and her father, and together, they awaited the bride.

Above them, a new sign hung on the Pig Pink walls of the newly refurbished tree house: OUR FAMILY HIDEOUT. EVERYBODY WELCOME.

Come back home to
Cedar Dell, Texas, in 2004.

Watch for Nicholas Sutherland's story!

Coming from Pocket Books in 2004.